S T O R M C A S T E R

DATE DUE

The Library Store #47-0119

REALMS

FROZEN SEA

Grey Lady

THE VALE

Invaders Bay

Wizard Head

Fellsmarch

Chalk Cliffs

Marisa Pines Camp

Firehole R.

Fortress Rock

Marisa Pines Pass

Way Camp

Hunter's Camp

Queen Court

Alyssa Plateau

The Harlot

Spiritgate

Delphi

KINGDOM of ARDEN

Heartfang Mtns.

Middlesea

Temple Church

North Rd.

Ardenswater

Bittersweet Keep

THE INDIO OCEAN

Ardenscourt

East Rd.

Baston Bay

Ardenswater

Heartfang R.

Bright Stone Keep

Bitter Springs R.

Watergate

Gryphon Pt.

The Claw

The Wastes

WE'ENHAVEN

Hidden Bay

Northern Islands

Demon's Wounds

JARTHIS

Deepwater Court

Salt Sea

The Indio Ocean

Dragonback Mountains

Tarvos River

Guardians Tarvos

Scorched Lands

Endru

CINDA WILLIAMS CHIMA

Shattered Realms #3 (handwritten)

STORMCASTER

A
SHATTERED REALMS
NOVEL

HARPER TEEN
An Imprint of HarperCollinsPublishers

Map illustration © 2009 by Disney Enterprises, Inc.,
from THE SEVEN REALMS SERIES by Cinda Williams Chima.
Reprinted by permission of Disney·Hyperion Books. All rights reserved.
Additional map illustration by Laszlo Kubinyi.

Library of Congress Control Number: 2017962820
ISBN 978-0-06-238101-9

Typography by Erin Fitzsimmons
18 19 20 21 22   PC/LSCH   10 9 8 7 6 5 4 3 2 1
❖
First paperback edition, 2019

Also by Cinda Williams Chima

THE SHATTERED REALMS SERIES
Flamecaster
Shadowcaster

THE HEIR CHRONICLES
The Warrior Heir
The Wizard Heir
The Dragon Heir
The Enchanter Heir
The Sorcerer Heir

THE SEVEN REALMS SERIES
The Demon King
The Exiled Queen
The Gray Wolf Throne
The Crimson Crown

For Jess—thank you for wading into this family, hand in hand,
eyes wide open. We love you.

A MEETING AT SEA

Evan of Tarvos stood at the stern rail, his eyes fixed on the ship that had been following them for the better part of a day. The sleek three-master stayed just at the horizon, neither approaching nor losing ground. Strange. Most ships fled in a hurry when they spotted Captain Latham Strangward's stormlord standard.

People said that all of the Strangwards were true stormcasters—weather mages—though Evan had never seen his captain conjure up so much as a shower. People said a lot of things, so maybe it was just a tale. Or, maybe, as he got older, Strangward's magery was fading.

Evan should have felt lucky to be crewing for a pirate whose reputation kept trouble away. But trouble looked a lot like a chance to make his name, since he'd never had one of his own. *Cloud Spirit*'s hold was already overflowing with stolen goods, but he was still salivating for a fight.

Evan had been sailing before the mast for three years, since he was a ten-year, by his best guess. This year, for the first time, he'd been given a share of the takings. Captain Strangward had watched with a faint smile as Evan pawed through the long strands of Sand Harbor pearls and Tamric gold glitterbits, holding them up so they caught the light, sliding rings onto his narrow fingers, slipping the gold cuffs onto his wrists. Evan favored wearables and coin—portable wealth. He had no use for silver goblets or candlesticks.

When he'd made his choices, he tucked them under his roughspun shirt and jammed them into his breeches pockets. He tried not to think of all the books he could buy with his portion.

You can't spend it all, he thought. You've got to save enough to buy a piece of a venture. And go on from there. Ships were the key to a future in which he could buy all the books he wanted.

"You might want me to hold your share for you," the captain said, frowning, as if now reluctant to let it go. "There's plenty in this crew would be happy to win that lot from you at cards or nicks and bones before we get to port. Or club you over the head and take it outright."

Evan pressed one hand against his shirt, protecting his

stake. "Tully says that a shiplord always wears his wealth. That way, anyone who means to take it has to fight you for it."

"Tully is a man who's always looking for a fight," Strangward said. "A man who's looking for a fight will usually find one."

Strangward was a peace-loving sort. For a pirate.

"*Ev*. Look alive."

Startled out of his reverie, Evan turned, and Brody Baines slapped the spyglass into his hand. "Captain says to lay aloft again and have another look at the ship that's been eating our wake."

"They've kept their distance so far," Evan said, rolling his eyes. "Besides, we're almost home." He nodded shoreward, where the high cliffs of Tarvos smudged the horizon.

Brody was two years older than Evan and more than a foot taller, with broad shoulders, muscled arms, and a growing collection of tattoos. Evan envied Brody's shoulders, his muscles, and his burnished skin, the color of coppers that had passed through many hands. Evan felt pale as mare's milk by comparison.

Maybe it wasn't exactly envy. More and more, Brody stirred feelings in Evan that were hard to ignore on a small ship during long days at sea. Captain Strangward frowned on shipboard romances because they stirred up trouble. That was not to say that they didn't happen—but if the captain got wise to it, the least valuable party would be put ashore. No doubt that would be Evan, the skinny-shanked harbor front foundling.

Which would be a waste, since Brody had made it clear that Evan's feelings were not reciprocated. *Reciprocated*. Evan had come across that word in a book, and now worked it into every conversation. That and *proclivities*.

"*Ev!*" Brody said, poking him. "You ain't paid to daydream. Captain thinks it's the *Siren*, by the way she's rigged. Either that or the wetland navy's got itself a better shipbuilder."

"The *Siren*?" Evan's heartbeat accelerated. He had heard stories about the flagship of the empress of the isles. It was a legend along the Desert Coast, though nobody had seen it for years. But. "What would the empress be doing this far south?"

"That's what the captain wants to know," Brody said, winking at him. Brody knew Evan itched for action. "Now step lively."

Captain Strangward had an agreement with Iona, the Nazari empress of the isles. She sailed out of the Northern Islands and raided wetland traffic from Middlesea and northward, while the stormlord sailed from Tarvos and hunted from Baston Bay and southward. Deepwater Court was a free port, open to all.

Agreements between pirates never lasted very long, and, truth be told, Strangward hadn't always followed theirs to the letter. Especially since Iona was rarely seen these days anywhere along the Desert Coast.

Stuffing the glass into the waist of his breeches, Evan trotted forward to the mizzen and began to climb, his bare feet finding the ratlines as they had a hundred times before. Below, on the quarterdeck, he saw Captain Strangward conferring with Abhayi, the helmsman.

Evan climbed past the topgallant to the royal, straddled the empty yard, put the glass to his eye, and looked astern.

The other ship was a pretty thing, her lines clean and fine as those of their own *Cloud Spirit*. As he watched, he could see her crew scrambling over the decking, working the halyards, shaking out more sail. The mains'ls luffed at first, then swallowed the wind, and she surged forward, splitting the swells like a sword through silk. It *could* be the *Siren*, Evan thought. There weren't many other ships on the Indio that could match their speed. If she kept to her course, she'd be coming up on them before long.

"Still no colors, Captain," Evan called down. "But whoever she is, we'll know soon enough. She's making her move now."

Strangward planted his hands on his hips and scowled. It was not a good day for a hostile meet-up. They'd taken a fat merchant schooner off Baston Bay. Because of that, and their other takings in the wetlands, the *Spirit* sat low in the water—so low that in heavy seas her gunwales were all but awash. Too tight a turn might cause them to founder.

They were thinly crewed as well. The quarrelsome quartermaster, Tully Samara, had chosen out some of their best sailors to take their prize around the Claw to Hidden Bay. There he'd find a willing buyer, no questions asked, and add hard money to the split for the crew. Evan fingered the movables around his neck, wishing he had the coin to get in on the bidding.

One day, he thought, I'll have my own ship, and I'll be giving the orders. He kept his lofty perch, high above the deck, the wind whipping his hair around his face. As he watched the other ship come on, he debated what his orders would be.

"Come about," the captain called to Abhayi. He looked up, searching until he found Evan still clinging to the rigging. "Boy, go down and help Samuel ready the twenty-four-pounders so we can give them a proper welcome if they go foolish on us."

Strangward always called him "boy," and this was beginning to get under Evan's skin. I'm not a boy, Evan thought. I'm nearly grown.

Besides, the gunnery deck wasn't his favorite. He preferred to be above decks. Though Evan was agile and quick, and fair with a curved Carthian blade, Strangward never allowed him to join the boarding parties that followed their grappling hooks onto the enemy decks and fought hand to hand if the crew declined new management.

"If a gale came up, you'd blow away," the captain always

said. "Wait till you muscle up."

Evan was strong and wiry from climbing in the rigging, furling sail and hauling lines and scrubbing all the things on a ship that seemed to need scrubbing. Still, he'd not got his full growth yet, and he had a slender build. Given his years of starving on the streets of Endru, he worried that he would never "muscle up." Why couldn't he at least stay on deck with Brody and the others and get an up-close taste of the fighting? How could he improve if he didn't get to practice?

If he couldn't get in on the hand-to-hand, his second choice was to serve as lookout in a pursuit, calling out to the helmsman from a perch high in the rigging. That always provided an excellent view of the goings-on, even if it made him a target.

For sure, he'd rather play powder monkey than swab decks or repair sails or polish the brightwork. But it was hot work in the thick air belowdecks, where they had to blindly follow orders without really knowing what was going on. His ears rang for days after a watch on the gunnery deck. Plus there was always the danger of a misfire that would leave him a smear of blood and powder on the wall.

Still, orders were orders. Evan scrambled down the shrouds, dropping the last ten feet to the deck. He swung down the ladder to the gunnery deck, where the master gunner Samuel and his crew were already hard at work preparing the guns. Evan joined in, running sacks of powder and wad to each of the cannon. He'd had enough practice that he could do it in his sleep. First the powder, then the wad, then the cannonballs. Then it was down to the magazine, back to the gunnery deck, his thighs complaining about the extra weight of powder and shot.

There were eight twenty-four-pounders. The gunners could prep all eight, but once they touched the match to the lot, it would take time to reload, especially with the guns hot from firing. Speaking of heat, the back of his neck burned as if a bit of match might have fallen in somehow. Evan slid his hand under his collar, groping for the cause. When his hand touched metal, he ripped it away and sucked at his fingers, swearing. It was no wonder his neck was burning. The medallion embedded in the back of his neck was blazing hot. Cautiously, he brushed his fingers over it again.

Captain Strangward called it a "magemark," and it had almost cost Evan this job. "I'll take you on," the pirate had said, after plucking him off the streets in Endru, "but you need to keep that thing hidden. Sailors are a superstitious lot, and I don't want them getting worked up about it. The next thing you know, someone will be pushing you overboard or trying to slice it off you."

Evan hadn't made a fuss. He knew he was damned lucky to be chosen to crew with a master like Strangward, and keeping secrets was a small price to pay.

People said that magemarks were a sign of royal blood and magical power. If so, Evan was still waiting for that promise to be kept. Right now, his biggest worry was that he might start shedding sparks and set the powder off.

"I'm going topside for a minute," he said to Samuel, the gunner's mate, and skinned up the ladder before he could say no.

Cloud Spirit had come about to windward and shortened sail in order to hold her position. Captain Strangward stood on the quarterdeck, his glass trained on the challenger, which by now had come within shouting distance. Even without the glass, Evan could make out the figurehead now—a nude woman with long, webbed fingers, erupting out of a rock. Underneath was emblazoned: *The Siren.*

Evan turned away before he could be spotted, all but running into Brody.

"Aren't you supposed to be below?" Brody said, clapping his big hand on Evan's shoulder and spinning him back toward the stairs.

"Latham Strangward!" a voice called, clear and cold as the snowmelt that ran down off the Dragonback Mountains in spring. "Are you really going to turn your guns on me?"

Evan and Brody swung around in unison, as if they were chained at the hip.

A woman—or maybe a girl—stood in the bow of the

other ship, like a second figurehead in loose breeches and a white linen shirt, a fine gold belt at her waist. She glowed with a brilliant blue-white light that burned so brightly that it hurt Evan's eyes. Still, he couldn't tear his gaze away.

"She's beautiful," Brody whispered, his voice thick with longing. He was gazing at the young captain in a way that he'd never looked at Evan.

Her hair was silver—not the dull color that comes with age, but as bright as a merchant's tea service. It whipped around her head like a halo of snakes. Two locks—two streaks of bright color—had been braided and beaded. Red and blue. Her eyes were a pale purple—the color of sea thistle.

She couldn't be much older than Evan, and she was already a ship's master. She was also a mage, from the shine on her. People claimed you couldn't throw a rock in the north without hitting a mage, but they were rarely seen this far south. Her crew glowed, too, but in a blue-purple color, like a bruise. They lined the decks, blades in hand, as if they'd come looking for a fight. Automatically, he counted. She had double their numbers.

A ship crewed by mages—that had to be bad news.

Apparently, Captain Strangward agreed. He had a good battle face, but right now he looked like he'd opened a hatch and found death waiting below. Instead of answering back, he turned and scanned the open deck, as if looking for someone. Evan slid behind the mizzenmast to avoid being spotted and dismissed. Finally, Strangward turned back to face the girl who'd called to him.

"Celly!" Strangward said. "Bloody hell, girl—is it really you? What's it been—five years?"

"Five very long years," she said, planting her hands on her hips. "Longer for me than for you, I'll wager."

"Let me come around, so we can talk," Strangward said. Evan knew he was buying time. "Abhayi, I'll take the wheel for the moment. You ready the crew."

With Strangward at the helm, Abhayi walked the deck, swinging his big head from side to side, speaking to one crew member, then another, descending the ladder to the gunnery deck.

Brody was still staring at the other ship, looking a little more wary, a little less starstruck. But only a little.

"Who is she?" Evan whispered.

"Celestine Nazari. Firstborn daughter of the empress Iona."

"I didn't know she had a daughter."

Brody snorted. "Why would you know?"

He had a point.

"Celly was on her way to becoming the most powerful pirate mage on the Desert Coast, but she disappeared five years ago—when she was thirteen."

So she was the age I am now when she disappeared, Evan thought. He did the figures in his head. "So she's eighteen now?"

Brody shrugged. "She must be."

"Then she's too old for you," Evan said, sliding a look at Brody.

"Maybe," Brody said, pushing back his shoulders and drawing himself up, but not quite pulling off the display of confidence. "And maybe not."

Evan could understand Brody's fascination. He was drawn to the girl, too, though for different reasons. It was as if, when he looked at her, he saw some version of himself reflected back.

The two ships had been maneuvering so that the captains could converse from a safe distance. The closer the *Siren* came, the more painful the burning on the back of Evan's neck. Yet curiosity kept him on deck.

"Look at that silver hair," Brody said, with a shiver. "She must be a blood mage like Iona."

"Blood mage?" Evan blinked up at Brody. "What do you mean?"

"They make people drink their blood, and turn them into slaves."

"Well, I wouldn't drink it," Evan said.

"Yes, you would. She'd make you. See those streaks in her hair?" Brody pointed. "Magelocks. All of the Nazari have them. Each one represents a kind of magic. The more, the better. In the old days, the Nazari had a hundred colors in their hair."

Evan reached up and fingered his own hair, finding the

smooth, metallic strands by touch. They were silver and blue, barely visible against his white-blond hair. Though he scrubbed at his hair to mingle them in with the rest, they always seemed to slide free.

I'm magemarked in more ways than one, Evan thought, puffing out his chest. In a story, that would mean that he was destined for greatness.

"Captain Strangward knows her?" Evan said.

"He's her uncle, sort of," Brody said. He loved being in the know. "The empress Iona goes through husbands like a dose of salts through a sailor. Harol Strangward was the last of five—the only one that stuck. Harol and Iona agreed to split the Desert Coast between them. Now Harol's dead, and our captain took over."

"What about the purplish people?" Evan asked, pointing at the crew on the *Siren*'s decks. "Are they mages, too?"

Brody looked at him like he was sun-touched. "What purplish people?"

"The ones that—"

"Shhh," Brody said. "I want to hear this."

"And now, here you are, a woman grown," the captain was saying. "If I'd known it was you, I'd have tapped my best barrel and welcomed you properly." The stiffness in the captain's posture, and the tension in his face and shoulders, told a different story.

Celly wasn't fooled. "If you'd known it was me," she said, "you would have found a hole to hide in."

Strangward chose not to respond to that. Instead, he shaded his eyes and scanned the *Siren*'s decks. "Isn't Iona with you?"

"My mother is dead."

This news seemed to knock Captain Strangward back on his heels. Again, he took a quick look over his shoulder, scanning the deck; then he turned back to Celly. "I am so sorry to hear that. When did this happen?"

"A year ago."

Strangward went ashen under his sun weathering. "I wish I'd known. I would have liked to pay my respects and—"

"Telling you was the last thing on my mind," Celestine snapped, "though I'm sure you'd have liked more warning. After Mother died, I found the strength to break out of the prison you built for us, only to find that your gutter-swiving stormcaster brother had surrounded the Sisters with a wall of storms."

Evan knew she must mean the Weeping Sisters, three small islands, in the Northern Islands chain, that spewed steam and flame and hot-spring water the year round. He'd never gone there—nobody did, these days. They were always shrouded in cloud and battered by wind and wave.

"Celly, you can't assume that—"

"I can assume whatever the hell I want! I'm empress now. My mother was too weak to rule the coast, but I am not. Harol stole what belonged to me, and trapped my mother and me on the Sisters with his stormlord magic."

"Your mother wasn't—" Captain Strangward seemed to reconsider finishing that sentence. "It wasn't like that," he said.

"My mother loved me!" Celestine cried, blotting at her eyes with her gauntleted forearms. "But your thrice-damned brother turned her against me after Jak died."

"Your mother loved you," Strangward conceded. "I'll not deny that."

By now, Evan and Brody were getting fidgety, despite the drama going on before their eyes. They'd walked into the middle of it, after all, they didn't know any of the characters, and it seemed to have very little to do with them.

"Five years you've prowled the Indio at will," Celestine said, "naming yourself the lord of the ocean and building an empire at my expense. Now everything changes."

"The only way to make a name is to earn it," Strangward said.

"As I intend to do," she said. She leaned forward, her grip tightening on the rail. "Only a *fool* gets in my way," Celestine said. Reaching into her carry bag, she pulled something out and held it up.

It glittered in the sunlight—a small object dangling from a chain. Evan's heart spasmed, leaving him breathless. It matched the broken pendant he'd worn since a time before memory. He pressed his hand against his shirt, relieved to feel the jagged shape through the linen. More than anything, it resembled the broken innards of a clock, but it had always been his most precious possession. His only possession from a past shrouded in mystery.

Evan's skin prickled, and his magemark burned as he realized that he himself was tangled up in this sailor's knot of secrets. Maybe this girl was the key to untangling it.

Clearly Strangward recognized the pendant, too. "Where did you get that?" he said, as if he didn't really want to hear the answer.

"Claire gave it to me," Celestine said. She gave it a shake, setting it to swinging. "If I'm not mistaken, it's another piece of that medallion Jak used to wear."

Who were Claire and Jak? Missing pieces of the puzzle that had been his life so far? Hope kindled within Evan that he was not just a castaway orphan but a part of something powerful and grand. Someone with a history and a future.

Strangward closed his eyes, swallowed. "Claire," he whispered. "You found Claire."

"Get off your high horse, Uncle," Celestine said, her voice sending shivers up Evan's spine. "They're *mine*. They are a part of the Nazari line. They were created for a purpose, and it's time they served. Harol should have been straight with my mother from the beginning."

"How do you know he wasn't?" Strangward said. "They were in love, Celly."

"Love? Is that what you call it?" Her jaw tightened. "I don't care how charming he was, she would not have traded away my legacy." Celestine rested her forearms on the ship's railing.

"Harol tried to save you, too," Strangward said.

"You call that salvation? It was more like hell, Uncle." Celestine brushed at her clothing. "I will never wash the scent of sulfur and smoke from my skin. No, it was my mother who saved me. She *loved* me."

She already said that, Evan thought, and Captain Strangward said it. Who is she trying to convince?

"If you meant to start a war with me, you should have destroyed them all when you had the chance," Celestine said. "Now. Where are the rest of them?"

"I have my faults, Celly," Strangward said softly, as if confessing in the temple, "but at least I don't make war on children."

That seemed to infuriate the young empress. "A war your brother forced on me! It didn't have to be that way! It has *never* been that way." Raising her hand, she pointed at the mainmast. As Evan watched, wide-eyed, flame jetted from her fingers and engulfed it. A fine white ash settled onto the deck, powdering Evan's hair and clothing. Bits of flaming wood dropped onto the quarterdeck, leaving scorched spots on the planking.

Captain Strangward stared up at the blazing mast as if stunned. All around them, the crew of *Cloud Spirit* muttered mingled oaths and prayers.

Celly laughed. "Behold Claire's other gift to me."

"Whatever you think I've done, I didn't," Strangward said, sounding tired more than anything else. "Whatever you think I know, you're wrong. I told Harol that he was playing with fire, but he wouldn't listen. He was madly in love with Iona, and she with him. Now. I've been at sea for weeks and I'm going home." He went to turn away from the rail.

"Let me save you a trip," Celestine said, her voice like a cutlass. "There's nothing left of Tarvos. I've burned out that nest of vermin and driven your crew of wharf rats into the sea."

Tarvos is gone? Evan's gut clenched as images swam through his head. There was the small room in Strangward's compound where Evan stayed while in port. It held nothing more than a rope bed and a trunk with his belongings, but it was his. It looked out onto the courtyard, so he could hear the splashing fountain from his bed. The deep-blue harbor surrounded by sand-colored cliffs. The weekend markets filled with fish and bright rugs and candies made with piñon. Plenty to eat, every day.

Tarvos had given him a name and a safe harbor when he'd needed one—and now it was gone.

STORMCASTER

Strangward stared at Celestine for a long moment, then said, "You shouldn't have done that."

"*You* should have left well enough alone," the empress said. "Better men, and more powerful mages, have accepted the cards dealt to them with a lot more grace. You call yourself a stormlord, but your dead brother was the one with the talent." She straightened, resting her hands on the rail. "Surrender, Strangward, and I'll let your crew be. They can continue on with *Cloud Spirit*. I'll simply send over a new captain."

With that, someone emerged from the shadow of the wheelhouse and came up to stand next to the empress. Someone with a familiar swagger and stance. And, behind him, the handful of *Cloud Spirit* crew who'd sailed off with him.

"Tully!" Evan and Brody said in unison, as surprise and dismay rumbled through the deck crew.

Celestine ran her fingers down Tully's arm. "I told Captain Samara he could have *Cloud Spirit* if he could arrange this meeting," she said. "He's done his part."

"Lay down your weapons," Tully called. "There's no need for bloodshed. Here's a chance to sign on with the new ruler of the Desert Coast."

Tully had always been ambitious, but this took ambition to a new level. Evan noticed that he didn't glow purple like the rest of the empress's fighters. Like their former shipmates now did.

Brody noticed, too. "So you sold us out for a ship, did you?" he shouted. "Maybe we don't want to be blood slaves."

The crew grumbled agreement. Not one of them laid down his weapon. Tully flushed with embarrassment and slid a look at Celestine. So much for showing off in front of your new boss, Evan thought.

Shaking her head as if disappointment was nothing new, the empress gestured to her crew. Grappling hooks arced through the air, trailing lines, and thudded onto the deck.

Despite the numbers, *Cloud Spirit*'s sailors went at it with a will, manning the rails to drive off the swarms of Celestine's fighters who were attempting to board. They swung their blades and cut the lines that came snaking between the two ships. Blood spattered the deck as they cut down the pirates who made it as far as the railing. Yet the purple-shrouded crew kept coming, even when seemingly mortally wounded, as if they'd lost their fear of dying.

Nobody was paying attention to Evan, so he pulled a watch cap down over his head, lifted a sword from a dead man, and joined in the fighting.

By the time the ship's bell sounded the half hour, there were only a handful of *Cloud Spirit*'s crew left. Strangward still stood exposed on the quarterdeck, chin up, a blade in each hand, cutting down any who came too close. Evan couldn't help wondering why the empress hadn't flamed him and put an end to the standoff.

Then it came to him. *He's protecting the ship by standing in the line of fire. He knows that the empress wants to take him alive, that he has information she wants. That's another reason she hasn't fired on us. She's worried she'll kill him and the information will die with him.*

But that protection didn't extend to everyone, and the empress seemed to be losing patience. Celestine lowered her arm so that she aimed directly at Brody. "I'm weary of this game," she said. "Now, surrender, or I'll incinerate what's left of your crew, one by one, starting with this handsome sailor."

Brody froze like a rabbit under the eye of a snake.

"No!" Evan shouted, leaping forward so he stood next to Brody, even though his neck burned like fury. "Captain Strangward said to shove off. You'd better do it or your fancy ship'll be nothing but splinters on the beach." To his mortification, his voice cracked and trembled.

The empress crowed with laughter. "Who's this, now, Strangward? Your smallest bodyguard? Someone with a harder spine than you?"

With that, Evan drew his throwing knife and sent it flying. It was a good throw, and it would have hit *Siren*'s deck, anyway, had it not slammed into the empress's invisible barrier and gone pinging off into the sea.

Strangward was not amused. "Get below, boy, before I break every bone in your body," he roared, backhanding him across the face. "Abhayi! Get this whelpling out of my sight."

Somehow, Evan was back on his feet again, seized with a cold fury. He could feel blood trickling down his chin, his lip swelling, his magemark ablaze. None of it mattered. Raising his curved Carthian blade, he adopted a fighting stance.

The empress stood, head cocked, like a patron watching a disappointing act at the fair. Then sent flame roaring straight at him. Evan lifted both his hands and desperately pushed out, as if he could shove death away.

As it turned out, he could. The torrent of flames slowed, like a ship sailing into a stiff opposing wind. They piled higher and higher, then crested and flooded back toward the *Siren*, grazing her side and setting her rigging on fire. Her crew stood frozen, gaping, then rushed to quench the flames before they spread.

Celestine stood, eyes wide, seeming more intrigued than frightened. "I'll be gutter-strummed," she said. "There's more to you, boy, than meets the eye." She looked from Evan to Strangward and back again. "Ah," she said. "I see it now. I should have known you'd have at least one of the ratlings with you." She motioned to Evan. "Come here, boy, and let me have a better look at you."

Evan stood, shaking his head, and the medallion on the back of his neck seethed and burned. He raised his blade again. "You come here, and get a taste of this, witch," he said.

She laughed. "Magelings should never throw stones at witches."

The tip of Evan's blade dropped a little. *"Mageling?"*

"Didn't you know? There's magic in you, boy."

Evan was so flummoxed that all he could come back with was, "I'm not a boy. You're not much older than me."

"That's true," she said. "We should be friends, not enemies. What's your name?"

"Don't listen to her," Strangward said. "They don't call her the Siren for nothing."

But Celestine stayed focused on Evan. "What's the matter? Has Captain Strangward been holding out on you?

He hasn't told you his real reasons for bringing you on and keeping you close? He hasn't told you who you really are?"

All of the questions that had been seething deep inside Evan came boiling to the surface. Such as why he'd been chosen over bigger, stronger street-rats. Why his captain always sent him belowdecks when they encountered another ship. Why he'd never been allowed to join in the fighting.

"At least I'll tell you the truth," Celestine said. "You carry Nazari blood—the heartsblood of the empire. You have a magical heritage that goes back centuries. Strangward wants to keep you to himself, but you belong at my side."

"Maybe he carries your blood, Celly," Strangward said, "but he's my blood, too."

Now it was Evan's turn to look between his captain and the empress. No. It wasn't possible. Strangward had plucked him off the streets of Endru, ganging him onto his crew. Evan had gone along, because it was, after all, a bed, and a roof, and food in his belly, with the promise of shares later on.

He'd started out an orphan, and now he had two of his relations fighting over him.

If I'm his blood, why did he never tell me? Did he not want me to make any claim on him? And how, exactly, are we connected?

More importantly, if he had royal blood, and Strangward knew it, why had he kept it secret?

Celly crooked a finger at Evan. "Come here. Let me see how you're marked."

Involuntarily, Evan reached for his neckline. Then forced his hand away. "I don't know what you're talking about."

"Of course you don't. Captain Strangward has lied to you, and betrayed you. Come serve me, and I'll teach you all about how to use your magic."

Evan took a tentative step forward, as if pulled by an invisible tether. Then somebody wrapped a muscled arm around him, pinning his arms to his sides, lifting him so his feet barely touched the deck. He felt the bite of a blade at his throat. It had to be Abhayi, but he couldn't fathom why.

"No!" Celestine said, panic flickering across her face. The empress extended her hands as if she could reach across the water between them.

"Leave off, Celestine," Strangward said, his voice flat, "or the boy dies."

"You wouldn't dare!" Celestine said, licking her lips in a way that suggested she thought he just might. "You wouldn't murder a child."

"I would, to keep him out of your hands," Strangward said.

Evan hung there, frozen, thoughts thrashing around in his head. Was Captain Strangward protecting him from Celestine, or was Celestine rescuing him from Strangward?

Right now, he felt like he needed to be rescued from the both of them.

No. He didn't need rescuing. He needed to rescue himself. He slammed both heels into Abhayi's knees, hearing a crunch when they connected. Howling, the big man fell forward, his grip loosening enough that Evan was able to roll out of the way before he was pinned underneath. Pushing to his feet, he scooped up Abhayi's blade and ran forward and up. He swarmed up the sheets onto the foremast, swinging the blade, recklessly slicing lines along the way, climbing higher and higher until he found a stable perch astride the tops'l yard.

"Hold your fire!" the empress shouted at her crew. "If the mageling gets hurt, you'll answer to me."

Now everyone was shouting at him—Strangward, Abhayi, the empress. The remains of the crew crowded toward him—all people he knew. Zalazar, who'd shown him the ropes. Entebbe, who'd taught him to swim. Akira, who'd covered for him in the early days, when he thought he'd heave his guts out on his first blue-water crossing. Brody, who'd begun climbing the mast toward him, his face set and grim.

Even Brody.

"Stay back," Evan warned, thrusting both hands toward them.

They shrank back, raising their arms in defense. Brody

stopped climbing and clung there, pressing himself against the mast.

They know, Evan thought. They know part of this story, anyway. They've all been keeping secrets. He owed them nothing.

Changing tactics, he took aim at the *Siren*. He extended both hands, palms out, and made a pushing motion, in the hope that flames might shoot out of his palms. Instead, the *Siren* shuddered as her mains'l went taut, the masts creaking and complaining as if under the pressure of a violent squall. With the sudden beam reach wind, the vessel heeled over until seawater slopped over the far rail and the empress had to grab hold of a capstan to keep from sliding across the deck and dropping into the ocean.

Just when Evan thought she might capsize, the crew managed to douse the mains'l and the ship righted herself.

Evan stared at his hands, working the fingers, feeling the texture of the air in his grip.

Celestine pulled herself to a standing position, her lavender eyes wide with surprise, her face a mask of startlement. "Who knew?" she breathed. "We have another stormcaster."

Evan stared down at the crowd of upturned faces, his head a jumble of questions, his heart bruised by lies and betrayal. A stormcaster, was he? He'd give them a storm, then.

Before, Evan had reached for air. This time, he reached for water. He dug a canyon beneath the *Siren*, building a wall of water between them as she sank out of sight. And then he let it go.

He hadn't anticipated the backwash. *Cloud Spirit* bucked and rolled, and he lost his grip on the rigging and fell, screaming, into the sea.

POLITICS IN PORT

Evan leaned against the bollard, watching as the last of the cargo was unloaded from the *New Moon* and transferred to the dockside warehouse.

New Moon was a sturdy, low-slung, single-masted craft built for the coastal trade—one that Evan could pilot with one foot, in his sleep. Each little realm along the coast had its tariffs and fees—costs that could be avoided by a pilot who knew these waters intimately. Evan did.

It had been two years since he'd fallen into the sea off Tarvos. Two years he'd spent schooling himself while crewing for others.

Kadar, the dock boss, strolled over, his thumbs tucked under his purple suspenders. "A good run, Faris," he said, pulling out his pocket watch as if it counted days as well as hours. "You must've had the Breaker on your heels."

"The wind was with us several days running," Evan said. Fair winds and following seas—the life of a stormlord mage.

"Must be why they call you Lucky," Kadar said. His broad smile exposed the gold slides on his teeth.

"Lucky Faris" was the public name Evan had used since he'd left *Cloud Spirit*. It was a kind of personal joke. Not very funny.

Evan had little memory of how he made it to shore after his long fall from *Cloud Spirit*'s foremast. It was lucky he'd hit the water instead of the deck. Lucky that they were close to shore when it happened. Lucky he'd been a strong swimmer for as long as he could remember.

No. Lucky would be if none of this had happened. He wasn't lucky, but he was a survivor, and so somehow he kept swimming, finding a place where the high cliffs gave way to a rocky beach. From there he'd continued south, following the coast back to Endru, where Captain Strangward had plucked him from the streets. He knew that neither Strangward nor the empress was likely to come there. The harbor wasn't deep enough to handle blue-water ships.

Evan had spent a year hiding in Endru, working odd jobs in the port, piloting shallow-draft vessels when he could get that work, struggling between the need to stay dead and the desire to find out his history. Dead was easy. Dead was safe. But it wasn't enough.

The empress had said that he carried Nazari blood. That should make him a princeling. Instead, it seemed to have made him a target. There weren't many bloodsworn this far south, but now and then he'd see them in the taverns on the waterfront. Were they looking for him? Or had the empress moved on, assuming he was dead?

A year ago, he'd risked returning to Tarvos, to find better work and the answers he'd craved. He'd been worried that someone might recognize him, but that wasn't a problem. The compound where he'd lived was gone, replaced by dockside warehouses.

Kadar and his crew had muscled into the port right after the empress destroyed it. He'd bought up all the prime real estate, rebuilt some of it, and gotten his fingers into all the local commerce. No deal was done, no crew was hired, no money came and went through the port without Kadar getting a piece of it.

In Tarvos, people said that Captain Strangward was dead and *Cloud Spirit* sailed for the empress now, with Tully Samara at the helm.

Evan's heart twisted when he heard this. Strangward had been a tough master, but Evan had trusted the bond between them—the unspoken promise of honesty. He'd trusted the crew of *Cloud Spirit*—Brody and the others— and they had betrayed him. He was done with that. He would not give his trust again so readily. The problem was that not even a stormcaster could sail a blue-water ship on his own.

During his year in Tarvos, Evan had been given a few contracts to crew on blue-water ships, but Kadar mainly assigned him to *New Moon*, the one ship the dock boss owned outright. Kadar had learned that with Lucky Faris aboard, cargoes got delivered and goods got smuggled in record time, which put more money in the dock boss's pocket.

Evan still had the share that Strangward had given him. Since arriving in Tarvos, he'd taken all the work he could get, but at this rate, given Kadar's stingy wages, he would be old and gray before he built a stake large enough to buy the kind of ship he wanted.

There was also his addiction to books.

"The packages you brought ashore for me?" Evan said. "Where are they?"

Kadar tipped his head toward the warehouse. "They're just inside the door."

"Thank you." Evan turned back toward the warehouse, but Kadar dropped a hand on his shoulder.

"Look, Faris. I'm having a little gathering at the Windfall later on. I hope you'll join us."

Kadar owned the Windfall—a combined tavern/ clicket-house/company store for sailors. He liked to run a tab for his crews so that he could part them from their pay before they found somewhere else to spend it.

"Lucky Faris" might sound like a name a gambler would use, but Evan had no intention of leaving his earnings on the tables at the Windfall, or getting deep in his cups and deeper in debt and spilling secrets that were better kept close.

Kadar owned everything in Tarvos worth having, but he didn't own Evan—not yet—and that grieved the dock boss.

"Thank you," Evan said, "but I need to get home."

"C'mon," Kadar said. "Be sociable for once. Don't you want a night out after so long at sea?"

It's hardly *at sea*, Evan thought, when I could jump off the boat and swim to shore anywhere along the way.

Evan shook his head. "Not tonight."

"First round's on me."

And that would be watered-down piss. Or the full package—turtled belch, empty pockets, and a knife in the back.

No. Kadar was making too much money off his sweat right now. Plus, Kadar never did anything without an agenda of his own.

"No, thanks. I've got some reading to do."

Kadar cocked his head. "How old *are* you, anyway?"

Evan had to think about it. Had it really been two years

since he'd left Strangward's service? That would make him fifteen. "Seventeen," he said, adding two more years for good measure.

"Seventeen?" Kadar said. "Then you ought to be making the acquaintance of the handsome lads and ladies upstairs. Surely there's somebody to your liking." When Evan shook his head, Kadar's eyes narrowed. "You might as well be a monk. You didn't catch the wetland religion, did you?"

"No," Evan said, an edge to his voice now. "I'm not a monk. I'm just careful with my money." *And my heart.* The last thing he needed was to get entangled with one of Kadar's courtesans. He stuck out his hand. "Speaking of money, if you'll pay off the last of my contract, I'll be on my way."

Kadar scowled. He really, really, really hated parting with money. "Suit yourself," he said, plunking a bag of coin into Evan's waiting hand. His expression grew even darker when Evan proceeded to count it. And count it again. When Evan looked up and opened his mouth to speak, Kadar said, "You might've noticed that it's less than what you're used to."

"It's not that it's less than what I'm used to, it's less than we agreed on," Evan said, looking the boss in the eye.

"Times are hard," Kadar said. "The empress in the north is making life miserable for all of us. A man never knows if his cargo'll get to where it's going these days."

Evan wasn't buying. "So prices of goods are up," he said. "I travel with a full hold and I get it where it's going on time. You should be making more money than before. *I* should be making more money than before."

"I've got more expenses than ever before," Kadar said. "Everyone's taking a pay cut."

"*Every*one?" Evan folded his arms.

"That's what I said, isn't it?"

"If you're going to change the agreement, you should do it before I sign and not after," Evan said. He stuck out his hand again. "Now pay me the rest."

Kadar eyed him for a long moment, as if debating what move to make. Evan knew he was the best pilot sailing out of Tarvos, which was why Kadar routinely put him at the helm of the *New Moon*. Finally, grudgingly, Kadar paid him the balance. Evan counted it again, then put it away. He was turning to go when the dock boss called after him, "Just so you know, I won't have any work for you for a while."

Evan swung back around. "Is that so?" He struggled to control the storm of anger rising inside him. "Why? Are you taking the season off?"

"*New Moon*'s going to be in dry dock for a while," Kadar said. "We're reconfiguring her belowdecks, expanding her hold, making room for more cargo." He clapped Evan on the back. "Don't worry, soon as she's up and running, I'll call on you."

The wind came up, setting *New Moon*'s rigging to flapping, sending a miniature squall line across the water in the harbor. The air thickened, picking up moisture and energy from the sea.

No, Evan thought. *The last thing I need is for people to be talking about a sailor who can make weather.* He breathed in, then released the air slowly, feeling the tingle in his fingers diminish.

"You know I'm happy to crew on any ship, in any role," Evan said. "Rupert Fry said he'd be glad to have me back soon as—"

"If Rupert Fry wants to hire you on permanent, then let him," Kadar said. "I've got men who've been with me for years that I need to go to first. You'll get your turn, just not right away." He waved at Evan's packages by the door. "Cheer up. You can get all those books read."

The dockmaster strutted away like the cock of the yard, which was exactly what he was, here in Tarvos.

Evan knew he was being taught a lesson. It didn't matter to the dock boss if somebody else's cargo took a little longer to get where it was going—it wasn't money out of his pocket. So he'd put Evan back to work when his own ship was back in business. But if Evan spent all his time crewing on *New Moon*, he wouldn't have the chance to show other ship's masters what he could do.

He was damned by his own success.

By now, the sun was low in the sky, burning a bloody path from the harbor mouth to the dockside as it sank into the sea. Evan scooped up his books and shoved them into his carry bag.

The traditional path to ownership by a Desert Coast pirate was to take a ship from someone else. But he couldn't manage that all by himself, and certainly not with *New Moon.*

One thought kept surfacing, like a bloated corpse. *If you want to sail the blue waters, you'll need a crew you can trust.*

Good luck with that.

Shouldering his carry bag, Evan walked away from the waterfront, following a roundabout path to the stable, careful not to be followed.

Djillaba lifted his head and snorted when he heard Evan come in. The stallion was his only other indulgence, beyond books, and this one he kept secret from Kadar and his crew. Celestine might have claimed that Evan had royal blood in his veins, but Djillaba's bloodlines were older and no doubt finer.

"Hello, there," he murmured, stroking the horse's velvety nose. He eyed the bedding in the stall, checked the feed box, and examined Djillaba's hooves and coat to make sure the stable man had kept up with his grooming. Working methodically, he draped the blanket over the stallion's back and followed with the lightweight saddle.

Evan didn't have a ship—not yet—but he could have this, at least.

For a while. But he needed work, and that was going to be hard to find in Tarvos.

AN INFESTATION OF FARMERS

When Evan had arrived in Tarvos a year ago, horse rich and money poor, he'd taken to exploring the countryside whenever he was in port. A short ride south of town, he'd come across an abandoned farm. The cottage was in a pretty spot, next to a river fed by snowmelt from the Dragonback Mountains, and close enough to the sea to suit him. After watching it for several days and seeing no sign of activity, he'd simply moved in. It was dilapidated, falling down in places, but it kept the rain off, saved him paying swiving Kadar palace prices for a room in town, and kept him out of sight when he wasn't crewing somewhere.

It also gave him some space and privacy in which to practice weathermaking. Not that it had helped much. His power came and went, all but impossible to control. He was never sure how much he had on board until he used it, with unpredictable, sometimes disastrous results. He thought of what the empress had said.

Come serve me, and I'll teach you all about how to use your magic.

No doubt there would be a price he was unwilling to pay.

Once he had a stake, he'd inquired into the ownership of the property, but it led to a dead end. After the attack on the port, the few survivors had abandoned homes and businesses and moved to safer places. So he'd stayed, leaving everything pretty much as it was. It allowed him to put his money to other uses. He wasn't a farmer. He was too restless to stay still for long ashore.

Now, as he approached the cottage, he was surprised to see smoke curling from the chimney and light leaking from behind the shutters. Djillaba balked, calling a challenge to unseen horses. Inside the cottage, a dog began barking furiously.

"Scummer!" Evan retreated a few hundred yards down the shore, where a rocky promontory extended nearly all the way to the water. He walked the stallion around to the other side and hid him out of sight. Then he walked back on foot, his knife in his hand, while possibilities slid through his mind. Had the owners returned? Or were the intruders squatters like him? Was it an ambush? Had the empress's bloodsworn somehow found him? If so, why would they advertise their presence by building a fire? Then again, he'd been gone for months. It would be easy to lower your guard after so long a time.

What if Kadar had found out about the farm? What if he had confiscated it in Evan's absence, meaning to force him into renting a room in town? Kadar was accustomed to taking whatever he wanted in and around the port of Tarvos. Was this just one more lesson he had to teach him?

In this situation, the gift of weathermaking seemed a poor weapon unless the newcomers were afraid of a little rain pouring in through the many holes in the roof. Though, given his limited skills, he might just blow the whole place down.

Blessedly, by now the dog had quit barking. Evan circled around the rear of the house, heading for the barn. As he got closer, he stopped in his tracks, gaping. In the months that he'd been gone, the holes in the cottage roof had been repaired, the broken roof tiles replaced, and the mud-brick walls had been replastered. The tumbledown fencing around the paddock had been straightened and lashed to new posts. The ground inside the fence had been beaten down by hooves and was now littered with the leavings of horses. So whoever was living there had been there for a while.

Someone had even diverted part of the river into an ingenious millrace that drove a waterwheel before it drained into a stock pond. It was hard to imagine Kadar going to all this trouble for a tenant. Unless the tenant had done it on his own.

At the barn door, Evan stood, listening, hearing nothing but the sounds sleepy animals make. After one more look back at the house, he slipped inside, to be met by the scents of hay, manure, and fresh-sawn wood. The newcomers had been busy in here, as well. To the left, there were three stalls now, instead of two, and he could see that the tack room wall had been repaired. Djillaba's stall was occupied by a sturdy pony, and another stall by a dun-colored wetland gelding. To the right of the door, the squatters had built a large pen and two smaller ones. From the larger pen, he heard a bleating sound. Goats?

It appeared that he was dealing with an infestation of farmers. Or engineers.

Moving was a job he didn't need, but he'd have to find another bolt-hole. He had no legal claim to the cottage, after all, and spent little time there. These tenants had done more work on the place in a matter of months than he'd done in a year.

He couldn't simply walk away, not yet. His savings, including his shares from his last voyage with Strangward, were hidden in a niche behind the fireplace in the cottage. He'd left his growing collection of books on the shelves to either side.

If Kadar was responsible for this, Evan would find a

way to make him pay. Anger and frustration rose in him like a full-moon tide, and lightning flickered around his fingertips. Not a good thing inside a barn filled with hay.

"If you set this place on fire, I'll kill you," someone behind him said in a cold, flat voice that raised gooseflesh on the back of Evan's neck.

He spun around. The boy was tall—taller than Evan—and, though he was slender, he looked to be all muscle. His sun-streaked brown hair was mussed, like he'd just climbed out of bed. He still wore his linen sleep shirt, but he'd pulled on breeches underneath, and fastened a sword belt over top.

Though he couldn't have been much older than Evan, he carried himself like someone who'd been shaped by a lifetime of discipline—chin up, shoulders back. His left hand gripped a pendant that hung from a chain around his neck, his right rested on the hilt of a wicked-looking sword. Light leaked from between his fingers as the pendant reacted to his touch.

He looked like neither a farmer nor an engineer, nor anyone from Kadar's crew. He was a soldier, and he was gilded with magic—not the purple bruise worn by the empress's crew, but a clear blue-white blaze much like Evan's own. Like the empress's.

"Drop the knife," the glowing soldier said, his voice low and full of the promise of violence.

Evan looked down. He'd all but forgotten the blade still

clutched in his hand. He allowed it to slip through his fingers so that it thudded into the sawdust by his feet. He had a smaller knife in a sheath in his boot, but it was no match for a sword.

Was it possible that this soldier mage had been sent down from the north by the empress? Mages were rare this far south. Evan had seen none in the backwater of Endru, and only a few of the empress's ruddy minions since he'd arrived in Tarvos. But why would Celestine's hired henchman settle down and start up a farm while he waited for his quarry to return?

No. It had to be Kadar. Kadar's tenant, rather.

"*And* your amulet," the soldier said. "Toss it over here."

"Amulet?" Evan shook his head. "I don't know what you're talking about."

The boy's jaw tightened. "That pendant around your neck."

"That's not an amulet," Evan said. "It's . . . a family heirloom."

"Right," the soldier said, drawing the word out like steel against stone. "Whatever it is, toss it here."

Evan broadened his stance. It had been a bad day, and it was getting worse. He was looking for a fight, and this intruder might give him one. "Go to the Breaker."

It was as if he'd handed the soldier the excuse he needed. Releasing his hold on his sword, he thrust his hand at Evan, growling something under his breath. A curse? Whatever it was, it sounded like death but felt like the brush of a feather. Evan felt a tingle run through him, and that was all.

The soldier frowned and looked down at his hand, working the fingers as if they might have malfunctioned.

"What's the matter?" Evan said. "Did you forget to load your finger?"

Before Evan could draw another breath, the soldier had crossed the distance between them, gripped his throat, and slammed him up against the wall. Evan was vaguely aware of the burn on his neck when the stranger ripped the pendant off, the *plink* of it hitting the wall. His attention was riveted on the pressure of fingers against his windpipe, the black spots sliding across his vision, his desperate need for air.

The boy released the pressure a little, and Evan dragged in a breath. His vision cleared, and he saw that he was nearly nose to nose with the mage, all but drowning in his turbulent eyes.

The soldier's fingers slid down to Evan's collarbone, searching, raising gooseflesh all along the way. "What's this—no collar? You mean the general turned you loose without one?"

Evan swallowed, acutely aware of the heat of the soldier's touch. "Who's the general?"

"I'll ask, you answer," the soldier said, now releasing icy tendrils of magic through Evan's skin. "How did you find us?" He spoke Common with a familiar accent that Evan couldn't place right away. His skin was paler than that of most of the tribes along the Desert Coast, though burnished from time in the sun.

"I don't know . . . what you're talking about," Evan gasped. "I wasn't trying to find you. If I'd known you were here, I'd have stayed away."

"Is that why you were creeping through the barn with a dagger in your hand?" Again, the ice poured in. It seemed to run through Evan like rain through a gutter, leaving nothing behind.

Fire and ice, Evan thought. This boy is fire and ice, welded together with pain. He's wounded, though the evidence is hidden under his skin.

The soldier was losing patience. "Say something!" he growled, giving Evan a bone-rattling shake, then slamming his head against the wall.

"Why the goats?" Evan blurted.

The boy blinked at him. "I beg your pardon?" he said, startled into revealing his blueblood roots. So he was a highborn soldier mage.

"Why the goats?" Evan repeated. "Why would you bring goats to an ambush?"

The soldier shook his head, as if to dislodge the words that didn't belong. "I didn't plan on being ambushed," he said.

"*You* ambushed *me*," Evan said.

"If you trespass on someone's property, it's hardly an ambush."

"You're the one that's trespassing," Evan said. "I've been living here for a year."

"Really." The soldier mage raised an eyebrow and took a slow, deliberate look around. "It didn't look lived-in when we arrived."

"I've been away," Evan said, defensive in spite of himself. "I don't spend much time here."

"Obviously."

"You didn't see the books?"

"To hell with your bloody books," the soldier said. "We own this property. We have a deed. Which means that if you've been living here, you owe us rent." Clearly the mage intended to collect in blood.

"Did you buy it from Kadar?" Evan said. "You should know that he's a thief and a liar, with a sideline in forgery."

"Who is Kadar?"

"Who are you?"

"Never mind," the soldier said, slamming shut like a book.

He's got secrets, just like me, Evan thought, remembering what he'd said before. *How did you find us?* The revelation hit him like a runaway cart: *He's being hunted, too.*

He didn't sound like he'd come from the Northern

Islands, either. In fact, he sounded like . . . "You're a wet-lander. Aren't you?"

As soon as he said it, he knew it was a mistake—the last bit of evidence needed to convict. When he looked into the soldier's eyes, he saw the promise of death, and this soldier looked to be good at killing. As if to confirm it, Evan heard the metallic hiss as the soldier drew his dagger.

THE RISK OF MERCY

Evan managed to force a few words past the pressure on his throat. "You're going to kill me for sneaking into your barn?"

"Oh, now it's *my* barn?"

"Whoever's barn it is, it's not worth dying for. If it's that important to you, keep it. You're the one with the goats, after all."

"Mercy is a risk I can't take," the boy said. "It's nothing personal."

"Killing is always personal," Evan said, looking the handsome soldier in the eye. "It's the second-most-intimate thing that can happen between two people."

The mage blinked as he thought that over, which was

the distraction Evan needed. He brought his knee up, hard, into the soldier's groin, folding him over, then followed with a fist to the face.

That combination should have dropped him where he stood, but it didn't. Though he roared with pain, the soldier kept hold of his knife, flung Evan to the barn floor, and leapt to pin him, but Evan rolled to his feet and sprinted for the door. He was nearly there when the mage blocked his path.

Evan turned and charged to the far end of the barn, the soldier at his heels, though he knew there was no way out that way. He vaulted over the fence into the goats' pen and crouched between two shaggy backs, trying to get at the knife in his boot. The goats scattered as the soldier landed in the midst of them. Evan stood, his puny knife in his hand, to find himself facing the business end of the soldier's sword.

"'Let's finish this," the soldier said, his voice clipped, icy. As he came forward, Evan retreated, evading the first thrust of the blade, though it sliced through his shirt. There was limited room to maneuver, though, and he knew his luck couldn't hold forever.

Evan didn't consciously reach for power, but it came unbidden. Small whirlwinds erupted all around his feet, sucked up a mixture of sawdust and straw, and flung it in the soldier's face. He blinked and swiped at his face with his sleeve, while shaking debris from his hair. Evan tried to dodge past him, but he stuck out a foot and tripped him, landing him facedown in the mingled goat dung and bedding. The soldier came down on top of him, pinning him to the floor. Evan could hear his quick breathing, feel him shift his weight. Any second, Evan expected to feel cold steel sliding between his ribs.

A storm surge of magic welled up in him, and electricity crackled across his skin, as if the power that seethed beneath it was leaking out. In desperation, Evan reached for it and called down whatever weather might be at his disposal, figuring he was a dead man anyway.

Momentarily, he couldn't breathe, as if the air in the barn had been confiscated. Then the barn exploded, detonating with a sound like Solstice fireworks. Wood shards, hay, and clay tiles rained down on top of them. Horses were screaming, pigs were squealing, cows were bawling—it was a cacophony of animal sounds.

The soldier swore and rolled off him, dropping his sword and protecting his head with his arms. Evan scrambled to his feet, waist deep in goats. They were at the center of a maelstrom that sucked up loose objects and flung them in all directions. Evan danced sideways to avoid being sliced in half by the soldier's flying sword and covered his eyes with his sleeve.

The wind picked the soldier up like a bit of fluff and flung him into the wall. He went down hard, his leg bent at an impossible angle. With that, the twister died.

It was eerily silent, except for the screaming of the horses and the bleating of terrified goats. Evan retrieved the soldier's dagger and crossed to where he lay crumpled against the wall. His eyes were open, staring up at Evan. Sweat pebbled his forehead and faint freckles stood out against his ashen skin. Given the look of his leg, he must have been in a great deal of pain, but either he was in shock or he'd been taught that screaming was an unacceptable show of weakness.

The soldier licked his lips and said, "But . . . you don't . . . you can't . . ." He gripped his pendant as if to reassure himself it was still there. "Magic doesn't work on you, and you can cast charms without an amulet," he said, as if confirming that Evan had indeed cheated on the rules of magery. He released a long breath and smiled faintly. "Like I said—let's finish this, even if it's not the way I . . . planned." He looked straight into Evan's eyes and waited for death.

He offers no mercy and expects none, Evan thought. *That's fair, I guess.*

The soldier's pendant—amulet?—seemed to be the source of much mischief. Evan pressed the tip of the borrowed dagger into the soldier's throat as a warning and lifted the pendant over his head. Stepping back, he stowed the pendant in his carry bag and slid the dagger into the sheath at his waist.

"Stay there," he said, though it wasn't as if the soldier

was going anywhere on that leg. He crossed to where he thought his own pendant had landed and began rooting through the debris on the barn floor. He could hear the soldier's labored breathing, the heel of his boot scraping on the floor, and the hiss of pain as he tested the leg. Evan found the pendant next to the wall and draped the chain around his neck again.

He returned to the soldier's side. His eyes were closed, but snapped open when Evan approached. Evan wasn't sure what to do. He had no intention of killing him, but it seemed wrong to leave him lying in the ruined barn with a broken leg.

"Destin!"

Evan looked up, startled into drawing his blade again. A woman in a nightgown and boots stood in the doorway, taking in the scene—the missing roof, Evan standing over Destin with a knife in his hand.

What was he supposed to say—*he* started it?

"Mother!" the soldier gasped, raising his hands as if he could push her back through the door. "Run!"

Instead, the woman balled her fists and walked toward them, her jaw set with determination. As she drew closer, Evan could see the resemblance between them. They were both fine-boned thoroughbreds, and they shared the same light-brown hair and hazel eyes. She was not a mage, however.

"Please. Just go, Mother," Destin whispered, without

much conviction, as if he knew it wouldn't do any good. Then he directed a warning glare at Evan that would peel the skin off a Bruinswallow pirate. *Impressive for someone flat on his back, with a broken leg.*

The woman faced off with Evan. "Before you act, you should know that I am not without resources," she said in her clipped, blueblood voice. "I'm willing to more than match whatever you've been offered if you'll agree to leave and say nothing about our presence here."

Another wetlander, Evan thought.

"No, Mother," Destin said. "Don't bargain with him. Don't trust him."

She looked up at the ceiling, at the massive hole above the stalls. She shrugged. "What choice do we have?" she said simply.

Evan was enough of a pirate to be tempted. How much closer would that put him to a ship of his own? Maybe he deserved compensation, for being attacked and nearly killed and for having to find another place to live. He could even ask them to deed the place over to him so that he owned it free and clear.

But in the end, he was not that much of a pirate. Assuming Destin had told the truth, and they did own the property, *he* was the trespasser, and Destin would be laid up at a time that the barn needed immediate repairs.

"It was all a misunderstanding," he said. "I'm a ship's pilot, and so I'm gone most of the time, but I've been staying here when I'm in port. I thought it was abandoned, and I had no idea anyone had moved in here."

"*You're* a ship's pilot?" Destin said, his voice thick with skepticism. "Of what—a jolly boat? A copperhead canoe?"

"Destin!" the mother said, as if her son was poking at a venomous snake.

Evan beat down annoyance. "Maybe we're better sailors on this side of the Indio," he said.

Destin and his mother exchanged glances. The message was clear. *He knows we're wetlanders.*

Destin's mother knelt next to him, seeming oblivious of the mucky ground. Gently, she ran her hands down his injured leg. "Is it just your leg? Is there anything else?"

"That's it," Destin hissed between clenched teeth. And promptly passed out.

Now would be an excellent time for me to get out of here, Evan thought. But his money was still stashed in the house. He needed to retrieve that before he left.

As if she'd overheard the thought, Destin's mother looked up and said, "What's your name?"

"Lucky," he said. "Lucky Faris."

She raised an eyebrow at the name. She and her son had the same eyebrows, the same way of raising them. "My name is Frances," she said. "Wait here."

Frances walked across the barn, rummaged in the corner, and came back with a fence post. Dropping it next to her son, she crossed to Djillaba's old stall and lifted down the blanket hanging there. She returned and spread it out next to Destin. "Please, Mister . . . Faris, I could use some help rolling him onto this blanket and carrying him to the house." She paused, then rushed on. "I'll gladly pay you."

Evan couldn't help thinking that it was risky for her to tell someone like him that she had money around.

It was as if she read his mind. "Captain Faris, we've been on the run for two years now. Running was less risky than staying where we were. Now trusting you is another risk that I have to take."

Well, Evan thought. He *did* want to go up to the house, so it was on his way.

Between the two of them, they managed to ease Destin onto the blanket, though he groaned and struggled as if the maneuver was painful. Evan took the head end of the blanket, and Frances the other end, and they managed to half-drag, half-carry him out of the barn. It took another half hour to get him up the stone pathway to the house.

As soon as they opened the door, a scruffy little dog sprang at Evan, growling, so that he nearly dumped Destin onto the floor.

"Breaker! Stop it!" Frances glowered at the dog, who slunk away.

Breaker, Evan thought. That's a suitable name.

The interior was familiar—only better than before. It was cleaner than it had ever been when Evan lived there, and now there were rugs on the tile floors and curtains at the windows, and a few sticks of furniture, much of which looked homemade.

They carried Destin into the smaller of the two bedrooms and laid him on a mattress on a rope bedstead, even though he was filthy.

"Could you fetch some water and put it on to boil?" Frances said. "There's a pump in the gathering room, and you'll find a pot on the hearth."

There didn't used to be a pump, Evan thought. He did as he was told, one eye on the dog, who kept up a constant rumble of growling from the fireplace corner. When he returned to the small bedroom, Frances was examining the leg, her fingers probing around the site of the swelling.

"It's broken," she said, pressing her lips together as if disappointed by whatever gods she worshipped. She sighed. "Let's do this," she said, looking up at Evan, "while he's still unconscious."

"Let's do what?" Evan said warily.

"Let's straighten out his leg. Hold him down."

Maybe it was because she'd been born to money and was used to ordering people around. Or maybe it was because Evan was curious about this odd pair marooned on the Desert Coast—the angry, wounded soldier mage and his blueblood mother. Whatever the reason, Evan ended up restraining his would-be killer while the boy's mother straightened his leg and bound it to the fence post to keep it in position.

During this operation, Destin woke up and spewed an entire book of wetland curses. This time, Frances scowled at him as if disappointed, but said nothing. Afterward, she brewed up some willow bark tea mingled with turtleweed, and that put her son out like a sailor at Solstice. They returned to the gathering room and she brewed some tay for the two of them.

"You drink tay?" Evan said, surprised. "I didn't think wetlanders went in for that."

"I come from a family of merchants," she said, not specifying where. "They brought back tay from abroad, and I acquired a taste for it. My brother had done business in Endru, so he was the one who arranged the purchase of this property years ago, in case . . . in case I ever needed it." She had a way of seeming like she was confiding in him and yet, at the same time, holding information back.

Evan sipped his tay, wishing it were something stronger. Now he was homeless and jobless both.

"What happened in the barn?"

Evan looked up, startled. "Like I said. A misunderstanding."

"I need more detail than that," she said.

Evan found himself telling her the truth, without trying to pretty it up. By now, he was too tired to lie.

She frowned. "So . . . my son tried to kill you, and you defended yourself by blowing up the barn?"

"You're giving me more credit than I deserve," Evan

said. "I'm sorry about the barn, though."

"So. You're a mage, like he is."

"Well. Not exactly like he is," Evan said, shrugging. "He seems to know what he's doing. I don't—not really. And there seem to be some differences in . . . what we can do, and how."

She thought about this for a long moment. "Would you like to stay here?" she said, pouring more tay.

Evan all but spat out his tay. "Excuse me?"

"We could use some help," she said, "especially until Destin's leg heals." Seeing the expression on his face, she rushed on. "I don't mean it as some kind of penance for breaking his leg. You could continue to stay here, rent free, at least when you're in port, and help with some things."

Playing for time, Evan said, "I'll tell you one thing— you'll find it hard to make a living as a farmer in Carthis."

"You're an expert on farming, are you?"

"No," Evan said. "I want nothing to do with farming. But I'm an expert on living in Carthis. It rains in the mountains here, not on the shore."

"That's why we bought a place on the river," Frances said. "So the water would come to us."

"Aye, it will," Evan said, "along with the dragons."

Frances turned a little pale. "Dragons?"

"There are dragons in the mountains that come down here to hunt. Livestock looks like lunch to them. You may come home one day to find your house in flames and your pastures empty."

"Dragons," Frances murmured, as if she were making a mental note. *Fix the fence. Deal with the dragons.* Then she returned to her topic like a dog to a favorite bone.

"We could pay you," she said, sweetening the deal. "Destin could teach you more about magery," she said. "He's really well schooled in it."

That's what you get for admitting a vulnerability, Evan thought. Why can't somebody teach me about magic with no strings attached?

"Why would he do that?" Evan said. "What's in it for him?"

"I think it would be good for Destin."

"I'm not a nursemaid."

"I'll be the nursemaid," Frances snapped. "As long as he needs one. I was thinking he could use a friend."

Evan rolled his eyes. "We didn't exactly hit it off."

Frances sighed. "He's angry, and he has reason," she said. "It's hard for him to trust anyone."

"Turning it around, why should I trust you? You said you were the run. What's to stop you from creeping in and cutting my throat while I sleep—just to make sure I don't give your secrets away? What if whoever's hunting you shows up? Am I going to be the innocent victim in a vendetta killing?" Evan felt guilty bringing that up, since it seemed more likely that the empress would show up than enemies from across the sea.

"It's possible," Frances said. She smoothed the skirts of her gown. "It's a risk—just like it's a risk for us to take you in. But you could have killed Destin—and me, too, if you'd wanted to. You didn't. You showed mercy. I think you both have lessons to teach each other."

Evan weighed the pros and cons. He needed a place to stay, and he could use a job in the near term. He could stable Djillaba here and save the cost of a stall in town. He wanted to learn about amulets and see if they might help him manage his power.

"All right," Evan said. "We'll try it and see how it goes."

6

SOLDIER

The agreement Evan had made with Frances ushered in months of being ordered around by soldier-mage-engineer Destin Noname. Evan had some experience with carpentry from his time on board ship. Left to his own devices, he could have built something that would have kept the rain out and met his own admittedly loose standards. It was a *barn*, after all, and not a palace.

Destin was a more exacting master. He'd accepted Evan's presence grudgingly, but seemed determined to make sure that he and his mother got value for Evan's maintenance. The wetlander saw the project as more than a chance to repair the barn—it was an opportunity to build the barn of his dreams. His role, as he saw it, was to develop incredibly complex sketches of what should have been simple things—and then hand them off to Evan to execute.

Evan turned one such drawing this way and that, unable to determine how it fit into the overall scheme.

"You've got it upside down," Destin said, in the manner of a man explaining art to the unwashed. He snatched it back and flipped it. "There."

"What is it?" Evan resisted the temptation to turn it upside down again.

"It's the loft."

"That's a loft? I thought it was a chapel in a cathedral church." Evan pointed. "See, that's the choir."

"Upside down, *Pirate*, it's a chapel," Destin said. He'd taken to calling him Pirate when he learned that he'd crewed for the Stormlord of the Indio. "Right side up, it's a loft."

And there it was—a hint that the soldier had a sense of humor, though it was rarely on display—not at first, anyway.

Destin found ways to help with the barn, despite his relative lack of mobility—by sanding down rough tiles, or using mage's flame to cut golden sandstone blocks to size, or packing mud into frames to make bricks, or mixing up plaster for the walls. He stayed in shape by doing pull-ups on the barn beams until sweat dampened his hair and ran down his face. He did this bare-chested, muscles rippling under his skin. Evan had to keep his back turned to avoid getting distracted and mashing his thumb.

Destin continually honed himself like a weapon for a war he knew was coming. He was intense, driven, restless, and very, very private. Their conversations circled a court-yard of unstable ground where secrets bubbled constantly.

When the sun was high in the sky and it was too hot for other chores, they retreated to the cottage for the midday. In late afternoon, as the temperature cooled, they returned to work on the barn until there wasn't enough light to see.

There was always plenty to eat. Frances was the hard-est-working blueblood Evan had ever seen. She'd begun with existing groves of olive and fruit trees. Destin's irri-gation system allowed her to plant a ground garden. She'd brought in beehives, chickens, and, of course, the cows, goats, and pigs. Destin had built a smokehouse to cure bacon and ham and the salmon they netted from the river.

One of Evan's many tasks was to meet ships in port and collect the items they had ordered from the wetlands.

It took a while to persuade Destin to make good on the promise Frances had made—that he would teach Evan about magic. It was like a game of royals and commons where neither wanted to show his hand. Destin was always too tired, or his leg hurt, or he needed to work on draw-ings for the next day, or Breaker needed feeding right then.

He claimed he was waiting for some manuscripts to arrive from a temple in the wetlands—ancient texts that might help Evan better manage and control his abilities as a weather mage.

He doesn't want to give me any more weapons than I already have, Evan thought.

Eventually, the soldier ran out of excuses, and they met for their first lesson at midday in the barn.

Evan was hot and sweaty and dirty from a morning spent hauling sandstone blocks around. Destin lounged back against a bale of hay, legs thrust out in front of him, bad leg propped, shirt open, sleeves rolled, breeches riding low on his hips. He was eating goat cheese, ham, and olives, licking his fingers and washing it down with water from a skin.

Hang on while I jump into the river and cool off, Evan thought. It was a good thing the soldier didn't know what effect he was having on his unwanted guest.

Evan hoped so, at least.

Beside Destin lay a large leather case embossed with symbols, studded with jewels, fastened with a gold-and-silver buckle. Evan eyed it curiously. What could it contain? Guidance from the gods? An extra ration of ale? A second helping?

Breaker sat next to Destin, watching each morsel of food make its way to his mouth.

"So, tell me, Pirate," Destin said, "when did you become aware that you were cursed with magic?"

"Cursed?"

"Back home, magic is considered to be the work of the Breaker," Destin said, scratching his dog behind the ears, "a misfortune that, nonetheless, can be put to use for the greater glory of the crown."

Was that why Evan and his mother were on the run? Was the general who was chasing them an agent of the wetland king? Those were the kinds of clues Destin dropped like a gauntlet in front of him, but Evan knew by now that there was no point in picking it up.

"Pirate?" Evan looked up and Destin was studying him, head cocked, still waiting for an answer.

"I was aboard the stormlord's ship," Evan said, wrenching his mind back to the task at hand and picking through his own secrets. "We were under attack by—we were under attack."

Destin's eyes narrowed, and Evan knew he'd picked up the near slip.

"I was angry—angry and scared, and I stirred up the wind and the sea and nearly capsized both ships." That was like taking a barrel of cider and distilling it down to a tablespoon of brandy.

"And you did this without an amulet?" Destin raised an eyebrow, as if he thought Evan might finally change his story.

"I'd never seen an amulet until we met here in the barn," Evan said. "I don't believe they are known to mages on this side of the Indio. Where do they come from? What do they do?"

"They are made by tribes in the northern mountains in the wetlands," Destin said. "They're used to store and control magical energy, something we call 'flash.' There are other magical tools as well, such as talismans to protect against magical attacks, all made by the upland clans."

"I've never seen them in the markets here," Evan said. Was that the purpose of the magemark? Was it some kind of built-in amulet?

"The tribes control the supply, and so restrict the power of wizards," Destin said, feeding Breaker a bit of ham.

"Wizards?"

"That's what they call mages in the uplands. Amulets are especially hard to come by. . . ." He hesitated, and Evan knew he was choosing how much to share. "They are hard to come by in the Ardenine Empire, since the empire is at war with the uplands. It is said that the wizards in the wetlands originally came from your Northern Islands. That the Northern Islands were a part of a long-ago confederation of realms, ruled by the Gray Wolf queens." He stopped then, as if realizing that this history lesson was more information than Evan wanted or needed.

He lifted the chain from around his neck and cradled the amulet in his hands. It glowed softly, like a Solstice candle, in the dim interior of the barn.

Destin usually kept his amulet hidden under his shirt,

so Evan leaned forward to take a closer look. It was all metal—copper and steel, silver and gold—in an unusual design, like a mechanical device. "What is it?"

"It's an engineer's hammer and tongs," Destin said, sliding his finger along the riveted metal.

"That suits you," Evan said.

He nodded briskly, without looking up. "Of course. My mother had it made for me. She's from the north of Arden, and her family has been trading with the uplanders for years."

"How does it work?"

"Mages produce power constantly, like a kind of magical vapor that dissipates as soon as it appears. Amulets allow us to accumulate enough to work significant charms. Power transfers to it through skin, when you touch it," he said. "Here, you try it." He dropped the pendant into Evan's hands.

It was still warm from Destin's touch. The amulet flared up so brightly when Evan's hands closed around it that it was like holding a star between his hands. Evan could feel the buzz and flow of power both ways. It was oddly intimate, to be holding Destin's amulet, their power—their flash—mingling together. Maybe Destin felt it, too, because when Evan looked up, Destin cleared his throat and looked away.

"It might be that you produce more flash than wetland mages, since we have trouble doing anything significant without our amulets. But you might find you can better control your power by using an amulet. Right now, when you're in danger, it builds up, gushes out, and it's gone"— he looked up at the roof, now mostly replaced—"along with half the barn."

"I hope you'll remember that next time you go to cut my throat," Evan said.

The soldier actually laughed. Then he patted the leather case and said, "These are the manuscripts I mentioned— they finally arrived. They are supposed to be documents about Nazari weather mages and how they worked with the elements of the natural world. It's written in your native language, so hopefully you can read it." He slid the case toward Evan. "Maybe there will be something useful in there."

Evan, oddly touched, stroked the tooled leather. "I'll get these back to you as soon as I—"

Destin put his hand on Evan's arm, setting his heart to flopping like a beached fish. "Keep them. I can't read them, anyway. You can hang them over the mantel when you're done. Right now, let's go outside so you can practice with my amulet. I don't want to blow this barn down again now that it's almost repaired."

The soldier extended his hand. Evan gripped it, set his feet, and pulled him upright. Then, with Destin's arm draped over Evan's shoulders, they hobbled outside.

The weeks flew by, a month, two months. Destin's leg improved enough so that he could put weight on it again, with the help of a crutch. Once the barn was finished, they spent hours on the beach practicing, when they weren't doing chores on the farm.

Evan read the manuscripts through, twice, then studied them page by page. While the dryland mages did not use amulets, they knew how to store energy in the land and the ocean itself, leaving it behind so that it could be retrieved and used later. He sat on the sand, arms wrapped around his knees, staring out at the twin sandstone carvings of dragons that bracketed the mouth of the harbor.

The Guardians, they were called, once used by Nazari mages to protect against enemies that arrived by sea. Evan studied the scripts and vowed to climb to the top of the Guardians one day soon.

Evan experimented with Destin's amulet and found that it enabled him to control the scope and power of wind, waves, and weather using stored flash. He hoped that, with practice, he could learn to use his stormcaster gift more precisely, with or without flashcraft. Especially since there was none to be had in Carthis. And because he suspected, down deep, that this idyll by the sea couldn't last forever.

Where he totally failed, however, was with spoken charms. Destin had an entire menu of nuanced magic he could work using his amulet and specific words spoken in the wetland language. Power including immobilization, persuasion, interrogation, and the like. Also glamours to make him less recognizable. Evan totally failed at all of that.

"So," Destin said, as if summing up data. "You're not able to use spoken charms, nor are you vulnerable to mine."

Well, Evan thought, his cheeks burning, you're wrong about that.

"Unless, for instance, I burn down a building with you in it."

"Good to know," Evan said.

Though Tarvos was beginning to feel like home, Evan still itched to go back to sea. He was not a carpenter, or a farmer—he belonged on a ship. On land, he felt trapped, like an insect pinned to a board. At sea, he could use his gifts to their best advantage. Periodically, he paid his respects at the waterfront. The work on *New Moon* was nearly done, but Kadar still claimed that he had no work for him. Maybe the dock boss meant to wait until that ship was ready to send him out again—no doubt at a lower contract price. But what could Evan do? He couldn't go north—Deepwater Court was too dangerous these days. The harbor at Endru was all but silted up. He was trapped in the middle.

7

PIRATE

From the moment Destin Karn laid eyes on the pirate, he knew he was in trouble. Not because he seriously believed "Lucky Faris" had been sent by the general to do them harm (although it was possible he'd been sent to the Desert Coast as a spy). In his heart, Destin knew that when the general came for them, he would not delegate. He'd come in person.

Still, he'd been ambushed when he saw Faris in the barn, rimed in light, like a vision in the old stories. For one thing, it was a shock to see a mage after so long on the Desert Coast. He'd heard they were more common farther north but rare in this city, which was one reason he and Frances had chosen Tarvos as a sanctuary. Here was someone who would recognize him as a mage. Here was a dangerous connection between his old life and this new one that needed to be broken before the general followed it all the way to them.

He'd learned the cost of mercy, of giving people the benefit of the doubt. He'd shown mercy once, and paid dearly for it. This time, when he and his mother had fled Arden, he'd committed himself to ruthlessness. Take no prisoners, leave no survivors, leave no loose threads that might bring the enemy to their door. The stakes were too high.

So when he'd spotted the intruder in the barn, he'd meant to clip that loose thread before their sanctuary unraveled. If it had gone as planned, the pirate would be dead and buried in an unmarked grave behind the garden. His mother would never have known.

But it had not gone as planned. It was worrisome that he'd been so unmoored by this dryland mage. Unmoored in a dozen ways. Destin was reasonably sure "Lucky Faris" wasn't his real name, based on his repeated hesitation in responding to it. Destin was skilled at reading people, even without the magic of persuasion. It was a survival skill he'd inherited from his mother and honed in the minefield that was the Ardenine court.

Faris moved like quicksilver, his muscles loose and responsive, and his smile came easily and often. His tussah hair was threaded with glittering silver and blue, and the charm and wit in his green eyes was unnerving. He was like a prince of faerie who wielded his rapier-sharp wit to great effect to make Destin's mother laugh, something Destin himself could not do. Faris had bonded with Frances like any orphan looking for a home, and she had begun to treat the pirate like a second son.

Who could blame her? After all she'd been through, his mother deserved a son who wasn't a constant reminder of the past. A son who didn't carry the darkness forward. Monsters beget monsters, after all. Maybe Faris had been wounded, but he'd not been damaged beyond repair. Unlike Destin, he still had a pathway back to the light.

Unlike Destin, Evan wasn't ruthless. At least, he wasn't ruthless *enough*.

When Frances took their goods to market, Faris often went with her so he could speak with the captains and bosses down at the docks; he was always angling for a job. It was odd. Though ships came and went, their new boarder had been in port for months now without a contract. Destin could tell the pirate was frustrated, but his own feelings were mixed. His leg was nearly healed, and the barn was repaired, and so there was no reason Faris needed to stay on.

The problem wasn't jealousy of the affection that grew between his mother and the pirate. The problem was that the feelings Destin had for Faris were something more than brotherly. One minute Destin would be thinking,

When is he going to leave? And the next he'd be thinking, What am I going to do if he leaves? Destin had learned from a young age that connections are vulnerabilities. If he ever forgot it, the general had reminded him, over and over again. He'd learned his lesson well—that love was as risky as mercy. Destin had been a soldier since he was ten years old, and this pirate was the most dangerous adversary he'd ever faced.

Destin took steps to protect himself and his mother. As soon as he was able to get around on his injured leg, he searched through the pirate's meager belongings, finding nothing of value save the broken pendant. No bag of money, no pouch of poison, no correspondence from the general. That could mean nothing more than the fact that the pirate was too smart to keep anything incriminating in the house.

Next, Destin took his investigation to town. At the dock boss's office, he introduced himself as Denis Rocheford, pretending he was looking for a pilot. A sharp-faced man named Kadar suggested several prospects. When Destin inquired about Lucky Faris, saying he'd heard good things about the young captain, Kadar had informed him that Faris was an ungrateful, greedy, unreliable bastard he should steer clear of.

Destin knew that wasn't true—whatever Faris was, he wasn't lazy. But clearly Kadar wasn't sending any work Faris's way.

An investigative trip to Deepwater Court proved more fruitful. There Destin learned that the empress in the north was offering a very large reward for the live delivery of a particular sixteen-year-old boy who might be using the name Evan Strangward. The boy was described as a weather mage and sailor with hair like flax, streaks of silver and blue, and sea-green eyes. Well, not those words exactly, but the message was clear. Destin had noticed that Faris always wore a watch cap when he went to town, even in hot weather. Destin noticed everything.

So the pirate had secrets—a past he was holding close. Secrets could be useful—in particular those you know about somebody else.

Why would the empress be offering such a large reward for a pirate without a ship? Then he answered his own question. Because he's a weather mage—called a "stormcaster" along the Desert Coast. A stormcaster whose skills were improving under Destin's tutelage. Destin credited practice with the amulet more than any instruction he was able to give. He found himself scheming to somehow acquire an amulet for Faris, even though that might leave a trail that could be followed back to Tarvos.

With some questions answered, Destin continued slipping off to town on his own. He was putting together a plan—a legacy of sorts. He discussed it with his mother, but only the part he knew she'd approve of. She'd signed on immediately. One morning, he invited Faris to go with him into town.

"You want *me* . . . to go into town . . . with *you*?" It was no wonder the pirate was surprised. Now that his leg had healed, Destin often spent days away from the cottage, but never invited Faris along.

"That's what I said, isn't it?"

They left the horse and wagon at a livery and walked down to the harbor front. Faris went to meet with whomever he always met with, while Destin searched out his contact at the boatyard and made final plans.

When Faris returned from his meeting, it was clear from his expression that there was no good news.

"Nothing?" Destin said.

"Nothing," Faris said, jaw set, green eyes glittering with anger. "It seems I'm going to have to find another port to sail from."

Faris had not shared any details so far, and Destin hadn't asked, but now seemed to be the time. "What's the problem?" he said.

"I've pissed off the dock boss," Faris said. "Now he won't give me any work."

"What did you do?"

"I refused to be cheated. So he's teaching me a lesson."

"You cheeky bastard," Destin said, with a thin smile. "Here, come with me. I have something to show you that might cheer you up."

Looking mystified, Faris followed Destin to the far end of the harbor. There, in one of the slips, lay a ruin of a ship—an ancient ketch that had seen hard times. It had been there since before Destin and his mother arrived in Tarvos. He'd tracked down the owner, who had owned the slip she occupied since before Kadar came to town. He'd refused to sell his dock space, because then he would have to make a decision about this ship that had belonged to his father and was named after his dead sister Ariya. He couldn't bring himself to beach and break the old ship, but he might consider selling her for the right price.

Destin knew for a fact that her hull was intact. He'd paid off the watch, who'd allowed him to climb inside and inspect her from bow to stern. He didn't know much about ships, but he knew quite a bit about construction. Her deck, however, was a disaster. At some point, the ship had caught fire. Though the blaze had been confined above decks, it had charred the masts, the rigging, and the quarterdeck.

"Captain Faris," Destin said, running his hand along the mooring line with studied nonchalance. "What do you think of this ship?"

Faris stared at it, hands on hips. "That's not a ship," he said finally, "that is a cautionary tale." He looked up at Destin. "Why do you ask?"

"I'm thinking of buying it," Destin said, his confidence

already dwindling. "I've not signed papers yet, and no money has changed hands, so if you—"

"What would you do with a ship?"

"I thought—" Destin cleared his throat. "I thought we could work on it together. You built a barn under my supervision. I could build a ship under yours."

"And then what?" the pirate persisted, staring at him, eyes narrowed, as if trying to peer through his skin to the soul inside.

Pirates don't have plans, Destin thought, exasperated. Soldiers and engineers have plans. "I hoped that once she was seaworthy, you'd sign on as captain and partner." There. He'd said it. He waited, pretending to watch the frigate birds circling the harbor.

Faris turned away from the ship and faced Destin. "Partner?"

"You provide expertise and labor, and I provide the capital. We split the profits."

Something had dawned in Faris's face—hope mingled with a healthy dose of wariness. "But . . . why would you do that for me?"

"It's strictly business, Pirate," Destin said, shrugging, not wanting to seem too hot for the deal. "As you keep saying, this is a hard place to make a living by farming. I want to diversify. And who wouldn't want to partner with a weather mage?"

Faris looked sideways at Destin, unable to hide his

eagerness. "You've inspected her?"

Destin nodded. "I believe the decking is sound, except for a bad patch just behind the mizzen."

Evan put one foot on the gangway. "Do you mind if I have a look?"

"I would like you to have a look, before I put money down. Just watch where you step so you don't fall through."

As he followed Faris down the gangway, Destin thought, Maybe this will actually work.

RUTHLESS

Evan knew from the beginning of this partnership that he was being played by someone adept at identifying vulnerabilities and exploiting them. He was definitely being wooed—he just wasn't sure to what purpose.

Don't trust him, he thought. You trusted Captain Strangward, and look what happened. The empress is still out there, and she may be hunting for you. You can't afford to trust anyone.

Yet, he couldn't say no. What the wetlander offered was impossible to resist. If it was an elaborate trap, the soldier was going to considerable trouble and expense when hitting Evan over the head and delivering him to Deepwater Court would work just as well.

The bottom line was that he *wanted* to trust Destin Karn. He wanted to believe in this ship of dreams they were building.

As partners, they complemented each other like the two halves of a locket. Though both spoke Common, Destin was baffled by Evan's use of maritime terms and directions. Evan knew the basics of ships' carpentry when it came to minor repairs, and he had the barn-building experience behind him, but he was no engineer, and neither had ever built a ship. Fortunately, it was more of a repair job than a scratch build.

Evan made a list of materials and Destin sourced them somehow. Tall, clear pine for masts and spars brought down from the Dragonback Mountains. Iron and wood fittings, lanyards, rope, wire, blocks, and the like from the shipyard at the port. Tools such as prickers, heavers, mallets, and spikes. He ordered sails from the sailmakers, too. Given that it was just the two of them, anything that could be bought ready-made or contracted out, he did. Destin seemed to have a lot of money at his disposal, and he spent it freely.

He was also ingenious at devising ways to reduce the numbers needed to crew the ship. It was sometimes an advantage that he had no crew experience. He wasn't bound by past practice or maritime custom, and so he asked questions about why things were done a certain way and whether they could be done differently. For example, he devised a system of bilge pumps driven by the motion of the ship through water to free up hands for other tasks.

It didn't take long for Kadar to notice the activity around the ketch. First, two of his ruffins came, demanding paperwork proving Destin and Evan had permission to trespass aboard the ship. After Destin proved ownership of the vessel, there came two of Kadar's rent-collectors demanding back payments for the slip space. In response, Destin showed his deed to the dockage. Finally, the big man himself appeared, strolling down the dock to their end. He stood, watching them work, for a few minutes.

"You should be taking this work to the shipyard," he said finally, pointing toward his own establishment across the harbor. "This space ain't meant for shipbuilding."

"We're not shipbuilding," Destin said. "Just doing some dockside repairs."

"You look familiar," Kadar said, scowling. "Haven't we met before?"

"We have," Destin said. "My name's Rocheford. I came to you asking about a pilot."

Rocheford? Evan's head came up, but he realized right away that it wasn't his partner's real name.

Recognition flooded into Kadar's face. "Now I remember. But you never followed up."

"That's because I found one," Destin said, pointing at Evan. During all this, Evan had kept his hands busy, letting Destin handle the heat from the dock boss. Now he waved and smiled, enjoying Kadar's stunned reaction for a few precious seconds before he went back to woolding the mainmast.

"You hired *him*?" Kadar roared. "He works for me!"

Destin shrugged. "He said he needed work, and I needed work done, so we came to terms."

"He's not a shipwright," Kadar said. "If he told you he is, he's lying."

Destin pointed at the rigging rising behind him. "So far, so good. I'm impressed."

"Faris is a pilot, and I have a job for him now."

Destin, raising an eyebrow, looked at Evan.

"I wish I'd known," Evan said, conjuring up a look of regret. "But now I'm under contract. Mister Rocheford offered steady work, so I took it."

"That's fine for now, but what are you going to do when this job is finished?" Kadar tilted his head back, looking at Evan through narrowed eyes. "Don't come crawling to me then. You need to be available when I offer you a contract."

"I anticipate this will be a long-term engagement, if not permanent," Destin said. He made a show of pulling out his pocket watch. "Now. I'm not paying this man to talk. You'll need to continue your conversation later."

"Don't worry," Kadar snarled. "I will."

Evan swung down from the rigging, and they watched, side by side, as Kadar stalked away.

"Well, he's pissed again," Evan said.

"Do you think so?" Destin said, as if unimpressed.

"His thugs will be back tonight," Evan said. "We'll have to sleep on board."

"For one night, maybe."

"He's ruthless."

"I'm ruthless," Destin said.

Evan cleared his throat, avoiding Destin's eyes. "I'd prefer not to use magery," he said. "It might draw attention we don't want." He meant from the empress, though he knew by now that Destin and Frances were on the run as well.

"Never fear," Destin said. "We're not just mages. We are engineers."

In late afternoon, Evan left off working and strolled down to the fish market. After haggling with one of the dragnetters, he came away with an entire basketful of purchases. In the meantime, Destin did his shopping at the city market. Once darkness fell, the two of them met on the pier next to their ship and spent the next hours making ready. Their work finished, they returned to their ship to wait.

Just after the moon had set, a crowd of men gathered at the gate to the pier where the ketch was moored. They were muffled in cloaks and carried axes and clubs. Several were carrying torches, maybe in case something needed to be set on fire. Their leader cut through the lock on the gate and they swarmed through. They hadn't gone more than a few steps farther when there was a snicking sound and the men in the lead began screaming. With that, the entire section of the dock collapsed into the water.

Evan and Destin were sharing a late supper on the quarterdeck, sitting next to the rail, positioned so that they could look down at the pier.

"They found the dragon traps," Destin said, sipping his cider. "And the trip wires."

"Let's see if that stops them."

"I think it's fair to say that the ones that found the dragon traps won't be coming aboard tonight," Destin said, his voice cool and matter-of-fact. "They're already at the bottom of the harbor."

Evan shifted his weight. He suspected he knew some of the men in the water. Most of Kadar's enforcers were mean as badgers, though. "Should we . . . do something to help them?"

Destin shook his head, his lips quirking in amusement. "If our positions were reversed, what do you think they would do?" he said. "Let's see if their colleagues help them out."

Below, men were still thrashing in the water next to the pier. But some had swum to the dock and were climbing up the pilings. Spitting like cats, they hauled themselves up onto the planking on the shore side of the gap. One man lay groaning on the dock, gushing blood, his left leg gone below the knee.

Evan's stomach flipped. He'd seen his share of bloodshed while crewing for Strangward, but always at a distance. Now he'd been two years away from it, and it seemed that his thick skin had been sandpapered away.

Destin surveyed the scene, eyes narrowed, as if tallying up the score in a game of nicks and bones. When he looked up and saw Evan's stricken expression, he grunted. "This is what it takes to survive, Pirate. These are the stakes in the game we're playing."

By the time everyone who hadn't drowned was out of the water, there were only six men milling about, soaked and unhappy, from the swearing that was going on. None of them went back into the water to look for the missing. Nobody seemed particularly eager to continue the mission, either.

Finally, one of them raised his club and shouted, "Come on, boys. Let's break her up."

They split up, each man claiming one of the hawsers. The first man gripped the line and began to climb; but, halfway up, he shrieked and let go, flailing, and dropping back onto the dock with a bloodcurdling *crunch*. Two more ended up back in the water, screaming in pain.

"What's that called again?" Destin peered through the railing, surveying the chaos below.

"Sea nettle," Evan said. "It's a kind of jellyfish. The

tentacles deliver a really nasty sting, even days after they are detached. Some of the healers use them, but personally, I'd rather die."

The dockside raiders had seen enough. Collecting their wounded, they stampeded back up the pier and disappeared into the twisty streets surrounding the harbor.

"Ruthless," Destin said, raising his glass.

"Ruthless," Evan said, and drank deeply, his mind in turmoil. He'd been on his own since he was a ten-year, and nobody would describe his life on the harbor front as sheltered. But he felt like a temple novice next to Destin Karn. Evan didn't know his story—not yet, anyway—but clearly the wetland soldier had lessons to teach him about survival in a brutal world.

Was that what made the soldier so attractive—the sense that nothing was off the table?

There was one more attempt on the ketch, which they repelled once again. That same night, the newly refurbished *New Moon* caught fire and burned to the waterline. The next morning, Evan and Destin walked down the quay to where Kadar stood glaring at the smoking hull.

"Too bad," Evan said. "She was a fine ship." He shook his head sadly. "What's the world coming to?"

"What the hell do you mean?" Kadar said, looking him up and down.

"Last night, for the second time, somebody attacked our ship, too," Evan said. "And now this." He gestured toward the *New Moon*. "Do you think it's the same people?"

Kadar was momentarily speechless, which was a fine thing.

"Look," Destin said. "I might own the mooring, but it seems to me that, as dock boss, you should provide better security."

"Go suck the Breaker's balls," Kadar said, regaining his voice and demonstrating his usual eloquence.

"It's to your advantage to make sure there are no more incidents," Destin said. His gaze swept over the ruins of the *New Moon*, and across the array of ships in the harbor and buildings at dockside. "This whole harbor could go up if it were to catch fire."

"Is that a threat?"

"Not at all," Destin said, looking him in the eye. "I'm the one that's asking you to make sure there will be no more problems."

Kadar, a muscle working in his jaw, stood with his eyes locked on Evan for a long moment. Was it a threat, a promise, or an acknowledgment of defeat? It was impossible to tell. The dock boss turned on his heel and walked away.

Kadar hadn't said yes, and he hadn't said no, but there were no more incidents at the pier.

9

DESTINY

When the day arrived for freeing the ship, Frances, Evan, and Destin took a wagon laden with provisions down to the waterfront. Breaker rode along, curled up in Destin's lap as if he knew they were going somewhere and didn't want to be left behind.

We're only going to be gone three days, Evan thought, shouldering a bag of lentils and carrying it up the gangway while Destin rolled casks of water and wine on board. Evan was used to a shipboard diet of hardtack and salt pork.

When the provisions kept coming, he spoke up. "With just the two of us, we're going to have to focus on sailing, not cooking," he said. *Especially when one of us is as green as grass.* "You've packed enough to take us to Baston Bay and back."

With that, Frances stopped in her tracks and swung round to face her son, who all but ran into her. "You're not planning to do something reckless, are you? Is that what this is all about?"

For what seemed like a long time, they looked at each other, silent messages rippling through the space between them. Obviously, this was a follow-up to conversations Evan had not been privy to.

"Of course not, Mother," Destin said. "As least nothing more reckless than setting sail in a ship built by a pirate and a sword-dangler."

As if unconvinced, she turned to Evan. "Promise me you'll stay on this side of the Indio," she said, gripping both his hands. "Don't let him talk you into going farther. Promise me you'll be back in three days."

Evan, uneasy at being put in the middle, looked from Frances to Destin. "*I'm* planning on three days," he said. "This ship needs a larger crew for a crossing, even with the changes Destin's made."

"Listen to him, Destin," Frances said. "He's the expert."

"Of course he is," Destin said, in the soothing voice of the practiced deceiver.

Frances lowered her voice. "I've lost so much. I don't want to lose you, too."

"Trust me, I have no intention of risking my life, my investment, and six months of hard work by sailing an untried vessel across the ocean. Especially with me as crew."

Frances kept gazing at him until he said, with a flicker of irritation, "Mother, please. Let's get this ship properly launched before she grows a crop of barnacles sitting here at the dock."

Destin had asked Evan to name their new ship.

"It's your ship," Evan had protested. "You should name it."

Destin shook his head. "No. It's your ship. You're the master. Frances and I are just the money."

"We could name it 'The Frances,'" Evan suggested.

"If we're going to have a fleet," Destin said. "We need names that will connect them together."

We're going to have a fleet? And then, *we're* going to have a fleet? That sounded like a promise of sorts.

Evan thought a moment. "Destiny," he said.

"Destiny?" Destin scowled. "You cannot name it after me."

"I didn't," Evan said. "That's a good name for a ship, and it opens up lots of possibilities for other ships. Alacrity. Temerity. Mutiny." When Destin kept scowling, he said, "You were the one who wanted me to name it."

Evan set out the tools for the ceremony—a curved Carthian blade, a small cask of wine, and a large silver cup, provided by Frances, emblazoned with an elaborate *C*. He ran his thumb over the engraving. Was that their initial? Destin C.? That was as far as he could go. Evan wasn't all that familiar with wetland names.

"Are you sure about the cup?" Evan asked, for the third or fourth time.

Frances shrugged. "I have no need of silver cups these days," she said. Then, eyeing the blade, she said, "I hope you don't plan to sacrifice a goat and make us drink the blood. The goats, I need."

"No goats," Evan said. "That whole blood-sacrifice thing went away five or ten years ago."

Strictly speaking, this wasn't a new ship, so the ceremony wasn't necessary. But it was a new venture, and a new name, and they were in the mood to celebrate. Not to mention that they needed the gods on their side.

Evan spiked the cask and let wine flow into the cup until it was full. A bit self-consciously, he raised the cup. "We, the builders of this ship, offer her up to the gods of ocean, sea, and storm and ask for safe passage beyond the shoals and to safe harbor wherever our journey may end." He drank from the cup and passed it to Frances, who drank, and then to Destin, who drank and returned it to him. "I—" Evan stopped, collected himself, but couldn't bring himself to seek the protection and guidance of the gods under a false name. He began again. "I, Evan Strangward, pilot, humbly ask for the skill and courage to chart a true course in fair weather and foul while this ship is under my command." Evan drank. Looking over the rim of the cup, he saw Frances stiffen at the last-minute swap of names. But Destin seemed unperturbed.

He already knew, Evan thought. Once again, suspicion flickered through him. Was it possible that Destin had been working for the empress all along? Was this just a ruse to deliver him to her new capital in Celesgarde?

No. Why would Destin spend six months building a ship that he didn't know how to sail? Besides, only a fool would set sail for the Northern Islands with a weather mage like Evan at the helm. And Destin was no fool.

"Pirate!" Evan looked up, startled, to find Destin checking the time on an imaginary pocket watch. "Quit sailing off inside your head and let's get this done."

"I name this ship 'Destiny,' and commend her to the care of the gods of ocean, sea, and storm, and ask that they welcome her when she sets forth, and give her up when she returns to shore." Evan splashed the wine over the gleaming varnish, newly emblazoned with the name. He raised the empty cup. "To the gods of ocean, sea, and storm, I commit this silver cup, in compensation for their rightful claim to sailors and their ships." With that, he cocked back his arm, and then sent the cup sailing out into the harbor, where it splashed down in the distance.

Now he nodded to Frances, who descended the gangway to the shore. Breaker found a perch on the quarterdeck.

Evan and Destin raised the gangway and slid it into its rack. Evan took his position, where he could manipulate the sheets and get enough canvas to ease away from the pier. Destin raised the curved blade and sliced through the hawser. "I set you free, *Destiny*," he said, and then took his place at the helm.

And so they were under way. Once away from the pier and the other moorings, Evan loosed more canvas and their little ship leapt forward, as if eager to claim her freedom after so long mired at the dock. They threaded their way through the mouth of the harbor, passing in and out of the cool shadow cast by the pillars on either side—the sun dragons glittering in the sun.

Destin stood on the quarterdeck like a figurehead, gloved hands on the wheel, his long weather coat rippling around him. He tipped his head back, gazing up at the sculptures as they passed between them. "Have you learned how to use the dragons?"

"Maybe," Evan said.

Destin looked amused. Then swung around, bracing himself against the sudden force of the winds as they passed into the open sea.

"Thirty degrees to larboard, Helmsman," Evan called.

Destin shot a panicked look back at him, clearly searching through the nautical phrases and orders they'd practiced. Then he collected himself and said, "Aye, aye, Captain." He turned forward, checked the compass, and adjusted their course southwest. Evan had charted a course far enough offshore to be forgiving, but close enough that they could seek an anchorage when they desired one.

Despite Evan's limited ability to manage the sails on his own, and Destin's lack of experience at the helm, *Destiny* turned out to be a nimble and responsive vessel, even with her novice crew. Through the day, they traded places, each playing multiple roles in navigation, piloting, and trimming the sails. They sang sea chanteys as they worked, which grew filthier and filthier as the day wore on.

That first night, they sailed through, each taking three-hour watches. On the second day, with Destin more comfortable trimming the sails and handling the steering, Evan experimented with manipulating the wind and currents. He found that by using weather magic and Destin's amulet, he could more than compensate for their skeleton crew. Soon they were flying, whooping with joy, sails taut and spray needling their faces.

I could sail on like this forever, Evan thought, and never touch shore again.

The second night, having made good time, they anchored in a small cove. Evan cooked fish and lentils in the tiny galley while Destin fussed with a self-steering device he'd devised. He mounted it to the stern of the boat and then squirmed through the cabin, hauling lines to the tiller.

When he was finished, Evan eyed it with deep skepticism. "How does it work?"

Destin ran his fingers lovingly over a flat wooden blade that stuck up in the air. "This senses a change in the wind, which moves the tiller, which changes the direction of the ship to the most favorable point of wind."

"What if that puts us off course?"

Destin shrugged. "It's not for navigating in tight places. It's more for what you call 'blue-water sailing'—crossing large bodies of water where you're not likely to run into anything. It allows for more flexibility with a small crew." He laughed at Evan's expression. "Don't worry, Captain," he said. "It won't put you out of a job."

"Hmm. We'll try it when we're both awake and watching," Evan said. "Let's eat."

They spiked a cask of cider and ate on the deck, side by side, their backs against the cabin wall, hips touching. Wavelets lapped against the hull, and seabirds dove at them, scolding, hoping for a handout.

Destin poured more cider for both of them. When he passed Evan the cup, their fingers touched briefly. He said, "I'll give you fair warning, Pirate, I'm plying you with cider because persuasion doesn't work. If we're going to work together, I'll need some answers."

"What if cider doesn't work?" Evan said, stretching out his legs and wiggling his toes.

"Then I'll have to find something that does," Destin said, pinning him to the wall with those smoke-and-whiskey eyes.

Evan straightened, his heart beginning to hammer. What the hell did that mean? With this boy, there were so many possibilities. The soldier clearly wanted something from him. Was it something Evan would be willing to give?

To distract himself, he tossed a bit of fish to the gulls. That turned out to be a huge mistake. Flocks descended on them, in waves of black beaks and gray and white, so that he had to drive them off with a gust of wind. Breaker charged back and forth across the quarterdeck but came away with nothing more than feathers.

"So 'Lucky Faris' is not your real name," Destin said, with an air of getting down to business.

"No," Evan said, leaving off bird-herding.

"I'm so relieved. I have a hard time saying 'Lucky Faris' with a straight face."

Evan laughed.

"Why did you change it?"

"Right now, certain people think I'm dead, and I'd like to keep it that way," Evan said. He paused, debating whether to go on. Joining up with Destin had given him the leverage he needed to stand up to Kadar. Without Destin, he'd be begging for crumbs at the harbormaster's table, waiting for someone to betray him to Celestine.

After more than six months, Destin was still keeping secrets. Yet Evan had to find a way to trust somebody. He couldn't go it alone forever. He couldn't help hoping that he would find a new life and a livelihood with Destin by his side.

Ship of dreams.

And so, taking a deep breath, Evan went all in. He told Destin about his life on the streets of Endru, his recruitment by Strangward, the encounter with the empress off Tarvos, and his escape from the ship and the empress's bloodsworn crew.

Destin raised an eyebrow. "So, do you think you're the long-lost heir to the Nazari throne?"

"If I were, I hardly think Celestine would want to take me alive. She'd want to eliminate the competition."

"Is that why you declined the honor?"

"I don't trust Celestine. Right now, I don't trust anyone."

"Always a good policy," Destin murmured, sliding him a look, as if questioning Evan's decision to trust present company. "This magemark you're talking about. May I see it?"

Evan shrugged. "Why not? Maybe you'll have some insights." He bowed his head, pushing his hair out of the way. "Captain Strangward said that I needed to keep it hidden or it would stir up the crew."

"What the hell?" Destin's breath warmed the back of Evan's neck, and his fingers whispered over his skin. "Can you feel that?"

"Yes." Gods, yes, he could feel it.

"There's definitely magic in it, though maybe it's just drawing it out of you. Have you heard any stories about the Nazari mages carrying any sort of badge or marking?"

"No." Evan shivered, acutely conscious of Destin's fingers on his skin. "What do you see?" Despite repeated gymnastics with a mirror, Evan had never been able to get a good look at it.

"It's abstract, but it resembles wavelets, clouds piled in a pyramid like a storm is coming, lightning bolts. Weather, basically." He tapped it. "Is this what the empress wants?"

"I don't know, but she definitely knows about it. It—it seemed to . . . It began to burn when she got close enough."

"Was it a warning or a greeting?" Destin murmured, as if to himself. "Have you tried to pry it off?"

"No!" Evan turned abruptly, and they were all but nose to nose. "It doesn't come off."

"Don't worry," Destin said, his hands still loosely circling Evan's neck, his eyes fixed on his lips. "I don't want to hurt you," he said, his voice thick and wistful. All at once, as if coming to his senses, he jerked back his hands and dropped them into his lap, as if he'd been caught reaching for a forbidden treat.

Evan sat back, cheeks burning, heart racing, disappoint-ment mingling with relief. *You are in deep water, Pirate, and you've forgotten how to swim. Do not fall for this dangerous, moody, mercurial boy. It will lead to heartbreak or worse.*

Destin scowled, lips pressed tightly together, as if weighing the pros and cons of opening them again. But what came next was not a confession of love, but a major change in subject.

"Not everyone is convinced by your recent death, Pirate. The empress Celestine is still looking for you."

"What?" This came as a shout that sent the gulls spiral-ing away. "How do you know?"

"I took a trip up the coast. Some of the bloodsworn mages you describe were stationed on the quay in every port, watching comings and goings. Most of the taverns have posted placards offering a reward for your capture and delivery to Celesgarde. It's probably a blessing that Kadar hasn't given you any contracts lately."

"So . . . you've known this all along?" Anger rose up inside Evan, mingled with mortification. So much for his heartfelt confession. So much for his fragile hope of sanctuary.

"Easy, Pirate," Destin said. "I haven't known it all along, but I've known it for a while."

"But you didn't see fit to share it with me."

Destin shrugged.

"So you've been spying on me."

"I have been gathering information, yes," Destin said, without a trace of remorse. "I need to know who I'm partnering with."

Partnering? Evan's mouth went dust dry. "Could you . . . be more specific?"

"I have a business proposal for you, Pirate," Destin said abruptly, as if signaling that the time for moonstruck yearning was over. "I'd like to set you up here in Tarvos. You have one ship now, and eventually you'll have more. You hire a crew, security, all of that."

"You'd like to . . . set . . . me . . . up?" That was an unfortunate use of language.

"Exactly," Destin said, rushing ahead. "With my money, and your talent, you should have no trouble making a go of it."

Clearly this soldier was not used to charming his way to a yes.

"This is all very generous," Evan said warily, "but what's in it for you?"

"I want you to look after my mother," Destin said. "She's very fond of you, and I believe it's mutual. My share of the profits will go to her, for her support. I would ask that you stay at the cottage with her when you're not at sea, and hire staff to make sure she gets the help and protection she needs. She's a strong woman, but she's no soldier, and she'll need help for some of the heavy work."

"Ah," Evan said, hope ebbing. "And where will you be?"

Destin's face closed like the steel door to a vault. "I have business elsewhere."

"Where?"

Destin returned his gaze impassively.

"Are you coming back?"

"I hope so," Destin said, making no promises. "If I don't, the business will be all yours, with a split to Frances. So. What do you say? Can we be partners?"

It was an astonishingly generous offer. A suspiciously generous offer. And Evan was tired of being blindsided and trampled by this wetland soldier mage.

He shook his head. "It's your turn," he said.

"My turn?"

"I need to know who I'm partnering with," he said, taking great pleasure in mimicking Destin's phrase. "I don't even know your real name, or where you came from, exactly, or the source of your money, or who might show up at my door hunting you and find me instead."

Destin stared at him for a long moment. "My real name *is* Destin," he said finally.

"That's a start," Evan said. "Go on." He settled back, gesturing, as if anticipating a long story.

"What's *wrong* with you?" Destin said, furiously. "You're refusing the most generous—"

"That's just it," Evan said. "It's too good to be true, just like Strangward taking me on as crew, and Celestine wanting to take me home and spoil me. I'm learning that whenever this happens, I should run the other way. If you can trust me to look after your mother, you can trust me with your story, too."

Destin sat looking at him—fists clenched, frustration churning in his hazel eyes.

"A partnership implies an equal footing," Evan said softly. "Take or leave."

OLD STORIES AND NEW BEGINNINGS

Destin leaned his head back against the pilothouse, seething, fighting down the urge to throttle Evan Strangward. This was oddly mingled with the desire to kiss him until their lips bled.

You are your father's son, he thought. There is no love without pain.

This was not in the plan he'd crafted so carefully. He'd been blinded by a pretty face. He'd underestimated the pirate, and that was all.

By now, the sun had plunged below the horizon, leaving a bloody wake on the Indio. The first stars had emerged overhead, glittering diamonds in the vault of the sky. At long last, the gulls had gone to roost, leaving it blessedly quiet, except for the lapping of the waves in the cove and the rattle of the rigging in the freshening breeze.

"Well," Evan said, with a sigh, "it seems that we are done here. I'm sure there are some sails that need hemming, and bilges that need pumping." He made as if to get to his feet.

"No," Destin growled. "We're not finished."

Evan settled in again, wrapping his arms around his knees. The wind stirred his hair, and the dying sun glittered on the silver and blue amid the gold.

"Is there anything in particular you'd like to know?" Destin said, chewing each word thoroughly to keep the wrong thing from spilling out.

"Who's the general?" Like any good marksman, Evan had zeroed in on the critical target.

"General Marin Karn, Commander of the Army of Arden and counselor to the king," Destin said. "My father."

All traces of triumph faded from the pirate's face. "Your *father*? Your own father is hunting you?"

Destin nodded. "He's not the kind you can live with. Neither is he the kind you can leave. I was not the son he'd hoped for." He held up a hand. "I don't know if anyone would have suited him, but I was definitely the songbird in the eagle's nest. Or, should I say, the hawk's. He kept pounding on my mother—trying to get her to admit to cheating on him. He didn't want to believe I was really his." He paused for a beat. "That's one thing we agreed on.

I didn't want to believe it, either."

But Evan had seemingly tripped over something he'd said midway through. "What do you mean, he *pounded* on her?"

"He beat her all the time," Destin said, matter-of-fact. "Half to death, once or twice. Sometimes at court, but mostly at his keep on the Bittersweet. He kept a full-time mage healer to patch her up again."

"But, that—why would he *do* that?" Evan growled. "And why would she put up with it? In Carthis, any man who treated a woman like that would never dare close his eyes."

"Things are different in Arden," Destin said. "Everyone puts up with something, women most of all. The fact that my father is a mage made it even more difficult to fight back."

"If he didn't love her, then why couldn't he just set her aside and marry someone else?"

"Love?" Destin shook his head. "For a pirate, you're a romantic sort."

"Yes," Evan said, a shadow crossing his face. "I guess I am."

"A mage is a precarious thing to be in the wetland empire, because of the church," Destin said. "The king finds us useful, but he is as changeable as spring weather when it comes to the tension between magic and religion. My mother is the daughter of a powerful thane. That marriage gave the general a route to power he wouldn't have had otherwise, and so, of course, he resented her. Plus, he wanted her to have a litter of boys, so he could choose out the most promising one and drown the rest of us. But there was only me. He accused her of using maidenweed to keep from having more children. He was always accusing her of something. . . ." He trailed off.

"He sounds like a monster," Evan said.

"Oh, he is. He started beating me, too, once I was too big to ignore and still too small to defend myself. My mother and I—we kept hoping he'd be killed in the war. But once a man gets to be a general, he sees less of the actual fighting, you know?"

Evan nodded, his green eyes fixed on Destin's face, as if afraid to look away.

"He was getting worse and worse, especially when he came home at the end of the marching season." Now that Destin had started talking about it, it was as if a dam had burst and his words flooded out without the usual editing.

Maybe it was more like lancing a boil.

"The war wasn't going well, and the king and the Thane Council were putting pressure on my father. Whenever the general was under pressure, he would take it out on us." Destin brushed his fingers over his cheekbone, which still ached in damp weather. "So, this one day, he hit me and I gut-stabbed him."

He'd ambushed the pirate again. "You *what*?"

"I gut-stabbed him." Destin flexed his hand, as if gripping the hilt of a knife. "I wanted him to die slowly. I'd been practicing, and it should have killed him. Eventually."

"But it didn't kill him," Evan said.

"No, it didn't. If I had it to do over again, I'd have opened his throat and stabbed him through the heart with a poisoned blade and cut off his head and hung it over my door." Destin's voice shook, just a little, before he could get it back under control. "Suffering is all well and good, but I wanted him gone."

Evan stared at him with a stricken expression.

See, Pirate? You wanted to know who you were partnering with. Happy now?

"All that, and no magery?" Evan said finally, as if trying to lighten the mood.

"He wears a talisman," Destin said. When Evan looked puzzled, he added, "Protection against magery, remember? Anyway, the use of magery would have pointed a finger at me."

"So your father survived, and you ran."

"So we ran."

"Is there a price on your head? Will the king hang you if you're caught?"

"The king?" Destin laughed. "He's the least of my worries. My father probably didn't even see fit to mention it to him." He paused, waiting for a question that didn't come. So, he continued. "The general wouldn't want the king to know that a thirteen-year-old stripling could get to him."

"Thirteen?" Evan said.

Destin nodded. "Fifteen, now. We've been on the run for two years, sometimes one step ahead of the general. He wouldn't want to admit that my mother had left him—that would get her family asking questions. If he involved the king, it would tie his hands. No. He'll handle it himself."

"Do you really think he's looking for you after two years? I mean, with the war and the king, he's got—"

"As long as the bastard's alive, he'll be looking for us," Destin said. "Like I told you, he's not the kind you can leave. Tarvos is our last option."

"I'm sorry," Evan said.

"I don't want your sympathy," Destin said. "I want your help." *Why can't you just say yes, like any reasonable person? When someone offers you a ship, and a home, and a bag of money, you say yes.*

"If you want my help, you need to be straight with me, and not try to gammon me like an easy mark. I may be a waterfront rat, but I'm not stupid."

"I deserve that, I suppose."

Evan rolled his eyes. "Yes. You do. So, now—if you plan to leave me with your mother, then where do you plan to be?"

None of your business, Destin wanted to say, but he knew that wouldn't get him where he wanted to go.

"I plan to go back home and finish the job I started,"

Destin said. "That is the only way to end this."

"You mean to kill the general."

"Yes."

Understanding kindled in the pirate's green eyes. "Frances knows. That's what the fight on the quay was all about."

"What she doesn't understand is that it's *my* fault he's still alive." Destin's voice rose. "I should have killed the bastard a long time ago. Every person he kills, every life he ruins, every mage he collars—it's on me." He wiped his hands on his clothes, but he still felt as if they were covered in blood.

"Maybe your mother is right," Evan said. "Maybe you're worth more alive than the general is dead."

With that, the darkness inside Destin came boiling up like the molten rock that spewed from fissures in the north. Before he knew what was happening, he'd gripped Evan's shirtfront and slammed him down on his back on the deck. "You're wrong!" he roared, glaring down at him. "I'm a monster like my father, and the only thing I'm good for is hunting other monsters!"

"No," Evan said. "You are not a monster. Whoever told you that was wrong."

"You don't know me. You don't know what I've done." *You don't know how many I've killed, to survive to this point.*

"I don't care what you've done. I'm more interested in what you're going to do." The pirate gripped Destin's coat, arced his body up, and kissed him firmly on the lips.

It was sweet and potent as Southern Islands rum. And like a name day drunk, Destin lost his head. He answered the kiss hungrily, pressing the pirate all the way to the deck. Then he launched himself backward, landing on his ass on the planking, heart pounding, breathing hard.

The pirate was actually laughing at him. "Ah, Soldier," he said, sitting up. "I have found your vulnerability. Love is the weapon you cannot counter. It leaves you helpless."

Destin glared at him. "It's not love," he said. "It's lust, and desire, and—"

"Are you trying to convince me or yourself?" Evan cocked his head, waiting.

Destin said nothing. His cheeks were flaming, he could tell.

Evan came up on his knees, hands resting on his thighs, like a faerie prince asking him a riddle. "Say it with me now, Destin: *I am not a monster.*"

"No," Destin said. But the fortress of his anger was crumbling, allowing the humor of the situation to seep in.

"Say it," Evan said, in a low, seductive voice, "and I promise, I'll whisper *monster* in your ear whenever you want."

Destin couldn't help it. He began to laugh.

"Now say it."

Destin rolled his eyes. "I am not a monster," he said, though he knew it was a lie.

"Again."

"I am not a monster." He raised his hand to forestall further demands. "That's all you're getting, so leave off."

"Acceptable," Evan said, with grudging approval. "But you're going to need some more practice." He took Destin's hands in his own strong, callused ones. "I would like to be your friend as well as your business partner," he said. "I would like to be somebody you can trust. I would like you to be someone I can trust. Do you think that's possible?"

Destin stared at the pirate, his mind swarming with questions he couldn't ask. How had this pirate survived a violent, brutal childhood and emerged with this generosity of spirit, this willingness to take a chance on someone like him? *What is your secret? What are you made of?*

Destin wanted to say no. He wanted to tell Evan Strangward that the last thing he should do is trust Destin Karn. *It will get you killed, Pirate. It will break your heart.*

But, in the end, he found that he couldn't say no to hope.

"I hope so," he said. "I really hope so."

Evan smiled. "Now. If you insist on going back to the wetlands, you're going to need a pilot. You can't sail this ship on your own. So. We'll sail there together. With me at the helm, it will be a quick journey there, and back again."

THE HANDYMAN

All the way back north, Evan refused to argue when Destin offered one reason after another as to why it was a bad idea for Evan to come along to the wetlands. Evan was busy grappling with the problem of finding a reliable crew. After three days on the water, he'd determined that it would require at least five hands for a blue-water crossing; at least three times that to crew *Destiny* as a privateer.

The challenge would be to find a crew that couldn't be bought off. The knowledge that the empress was still actively hunting him changed everything. He did not relish the notion of being delivered to Celesgarde in his own ship. He wasn't so concerned about the crossing to Baston Bay. It would be there and back, with little opportunity for harborside gossip. But when he began sailing the Desert Coast, and raiding in the wetlands, it would be only a matter of time before he came to the empress's attention, especially if he became known as a stormcaster.

He still hoped that Destin might return to Carthis with him after accomplishing his mission in Arden. Destin's nuanced magery might offer a way to ensure a loyal crew. Together, he and Destin could meet any challenge, stand against any enemy.

He tried not to think of the possibility that their mission might fail. If they couldn't defeat a wetland general, what chance would they have against the empress?

More importantly, the cottage in Tarvos had been closer to a home than anything Evan had experienced before, and Destin and Frances had become a surrogate family. An ember of hope still burned inside him—the hope that they could look forward to a future together.

When *Destiny* sailed back into the harbor at Tarvos, the sun was setting on their third day. On the way in, they passed an unfamiliar three-masted schooner, moored far out in the harbor, where the water was deepest. She flew no colors, but carried a full complement of guns.

Destin rested his forearms on the stern railing, squinting against the sunlight gilding the tops of the Guardians. "Do you recognize that ship?"

"No," Evan said, "but she looks like a wetlander."

Not many wetland ships came and went at Tarvos these

days, since Carthian pirates made the journey perilous. This ship, however, looked like she could fend off most any challenge.

The harbor area was oddly deserted when they tied up at their mooring. Usually, the arrival of any ship brought a handful of people down to the wharf, some intent on commerce, others merely curious. Several jolly boats were tied up at Kadar's public docks.

They quickly unloaded their few personal belongings, meaning to come back with the wagon for the rest. As they walked up the hill, away from the harbor, Evan looked back. He saw sailors swarming over the schooner's decks, as if they were preparing to get under way.

When they rounded the point, the cottage came into view. It was dark—no lights in the windows.

"Frances should be home by now," Evan said. "Right?"

"*Before* now," Destin said, frowning. "Maybe she left a note inside."

They walked to the porch, between the beds of flowers that Frances had planted, and found the door slightly ajar.

Breaker growled, hackles raised, but that was nothing unusual.

"Wait," Destin said, raising his hand. He stood listening for a long moment, then shrugged, pushed the door open, and walked in, with Evan right behind him.

Before Evan's eyes had adjusted to the dim interior, he heard the door slam shut behind them. All around the main room, lanterns were unhooded, flooding the room with light, practically blinding him.

"Where have you been, Corporal?" somebody said in a low, raspy voice. "Weren't you afraid that your mother would be worried?"

Destin must have recognized the voice, because he turned deathly pale. He spun round, scanning the room. Frances wasn't there, but red-brown stains that hadn't been there before were spattered across the tile floor.

"Don't waste your time, Corporal. The bitch is waiting for us aboard ship. I think she'll live."

The man speaking was thickset and barrel-chested, a wetland mage with a flattened nose and a bristle of hair. He was dressed in a brown uniform that carried no emblem of rank. His arms were so muscular that they hung out from his sides like thick branches on a spreading tree.

It was—it had to be—Destin's father, General Karn. But it wasn't just him. A dozen men lined the room's perimeter, similarly dressed, their hands on their weapons, as if looking for a chance to use them.

Grabbing up the fire poker, Destin charged toward his father. But before he'd gone three steps, he was surrounded by soldiers, who pinioned his arms. The poker hit the wood floor with a thud.

Evan thrust out his hand, reaching for lightning, though unsure how that demand would be answered. Something smashed down on the back of his head and he ended up sprawled on his face on the floor, stunned. Karn gestured to his men, and two of them hauled Evan to his feet.

The general looked the pair of them up and down. "Too bad," he said. "Two mages, and we only brought one collar." He gestured toward Destin. While two soldiers fastened a wide silver collar around Destin's neck, the general reached into Evan's neckline, apparently searching for an amulet. He came up with the pendant. He ripped it away, breaking the chain, and tossed it into the corner.

If this keeps happening, Evan thought, I'll need to find a stronger chain.

The general turned back to his collared, pinioned son. "You haven't learned a thing while you've been gone, have you, boy?" Karn drew back and slammed his fist, hard, into Destin's middle, folding him in half. Evan could hear ribs cracking. Then he punched him in the face, snapping Destin's head back.

Breaker sprang forward, moving faster than he'd ever moved before. He sank his teeth into the general's calf and hung on.

Karn swore, trying to shake off the growling dog. Finally, he drew his belt dagger and slashed, practically decapitating the dog. Breaker managed to yelp once, then landed in a heap on the floor. The general kicked him aside with his booted foot.

"Stupid butt-fart of a dog," Karn said. He looked at Destin, who stood, collared, arms pinned, eye purpling, blood streaming down his face. Evan knew Destin had loved that dog, knew he must be in considerable pain, but he displayed no sign of it, no hint of emotion. It was as if he'd retreated to some long-standing shell of survival, where the general couldn't get at him.

As if seeking easier prey, the general turned to Evan. "So," he said. "Who are you, mageling?"

Evan said nothing.

Karn drew his knife. "Speak, boy, or I'll cut out your tongue."

"Mother hired him to do odd jobs around the place," Destin said, in a bored voice. "He claimed to be a handyman, but I haven't seen any sign of it."

"Is that so?" Karn barked a laugh. "What sort of *odd jobs* do you do, boy?" The way he said it, it sounded filthy.

"He spends most of his time sleeping and eating and sneaking off to town." Destin's face was blank, his jaw tense, his glittering eyes sending a message to Evan. *Play along.*

"That's a dirty lie," Evan said. He turned to Karn. "I'm a hard worker, sir. I do whatever needs doing—farming, kitchen work, chopping wood."

"You are a pretty boy," Karn said. "You're not his little sweetheart, are you?" He nodded at Destin.

Evan adopted a puzzled expression. "I don't know what you mean, sir."

Karn waved the knife beneath his nose. "If I cut off

your nose and your ears, you wouldn't be near so pretty, would you?" He shot a look at Destin, as if to see his reaction, but Destin displayed none.

"Or maybe we could just gut-stab you and leave you to die." Again, he shot a look at his son.

"Why don't you just kill *me* and be done with it?" Destin said.

Stop baiting him, Evan thought desperately, unable to watch. It was as if he felt every blow the general landed.

"I never said anything about killing *you*," Karn said to Destin. "That would be too easy. Your mother has done her best to ruin you, but I'm going to make you a man if it's the last thing I do."

"Maybe it will be," Destin said. "Is that why you brought half an army? Because you were worried you couldn't handle it on your own?" That earned him another punch to the gut.

He *wants* his father to kill him, Evan realized. He'd prefer that to what's in store for him. I've got to figure out some way to help him. The best way to do that is to convince Karn there's nothing between us.

"I don't want to be killed, either," Evan whined. "I'm more useful alive than dead."

"Is that so?" Karn said, rubbing his chin, eyeing him speculatively. "We always need mages in the Ardenine army. If you really are a mage. Have you ever thought about a military career?"

"No, sir," Evan said, feigning eagerness. "But I would like to learn more about magery. That's why I took *this* job."

"You seem like a likely lad. Let's see what you're made of. Let him loose," he said to the soldiers pinning his arms.

They released him and stepped back.

Karn pointed at Destin. "Hit him."

Evan, his stomach sinking into his toes, looked from Karn to Destin. "You want me to hit him?"

"That's what I said, didn't I?" Karn pushed him toward Destin. "Don't hold back," he said. "Smash his face in."

"General." It was the only man there not dressed in soldier garb. "It's already late. We're going to have to leave soon if we're going to catch the tide. We can't risk spending another night here."

"We're nearly done here," Karn said.

"Come on, handyman," Destin taunted. "Give it all you've got."

Evan looked into his eyes and saw the pleading there. *He wants me to hit him. He's trying to save my life.*

Evan took a breath, made a fist, and aimed for Destin's middle.

"Hit him in the face," Karn ordered. "It doesn't count if you don't draw blood."

Evan licked his lips, thinking, I can't do this. Destin's eyes said, *Yes, you can.*

Evan pulled back his fist and aimed for Destin's

already-bleeding nose. Blood is blood, he thought.

When he connected, Destin somehow wrenched free of his captors, lurched forward, wrapped his hands around Evan's neck, and began to squeeze. As he did so, Evan felt him drop something into the neck of his shirt. It slid down his chest and landed in the waist of his breeches. It buzzed against his skin, and he knew it was Destin's amulet.

"Stay here," he hissed into Evan's ear. "Don't follow. Remember. Ruthless."

It took three men to peel Destin off Evan.

"What was that—a last kiss?" Karn laughed. "That was quite a show. I wish we had more time." He turned away, and his voice became hard and brisk. "Sublette and Howard. Take the handyman out in the woods and kill him. Meet us at the ship."

Sublette and Howard looked unhappy at this assignment, but not unhappy enough to risk complaining.

"But . . . you said I had a future in the military," Evan protested.

"You think we'd want a preening cock robin like you in the army?" Karn snorted. "You wouldn't last a day."

As his assigned executioners dragged him to the door, Evan caught one last glimpse of Destin. His eye was blackened, his face bloody, his nose probably broken.

But his lips were curved in a shadow of a smile.

All the way into the woods, Sublette and Howard complained about their assignment and Carthis in general. They were speaking Ardenine, so maybe they thought Evan couldn't understand it. Or maybe they didn't care.

"Saints and martyrs," Howard said. "This is the only patch of green I've seen in this whole godforsaken country. Why anyone would come here willingly is beyond me."

"This an't the worst of it," Sublette said. "There's dragons and watergators."

"There couldn't be watergators," Howard countered, "'cause there's no water."

"There's a river," Sublette pointed out.

While they were talking, Evan managed to slide Destin's amulet out of his breeches and loop the chain around his neck. The amulet, warm and primed with flash, rested against his chest. Maybe he didn't know any killing charms, but he'd find a way just the same.

"Let's get this thing done," Sublette muttered. "I'm not getting left here, that's for sure."

Actually, you are, Evan thought.

By now he guessed they were far enough away from the cabin that they wouldn't be seen or heard.

Sublette drew his sword. "Kneel, boy," he said. "If you hold still, I'll cut off your head and you won't feel a thing."

"How do you know?" Evan said. "Have you ever been beheaded?"

"Stop wasting time and kneel!" Howard put his hand on Evan's shoulder to push him down to his knees. Evan turned, pressed his finger into the soldier's chest, and sent lightning rocketing in. Howard dropped like a rock.

"Howard?" Sublette stared at the dead man for a scant few seconds, which was all Evan needed. Reaching from behind, he pressed his fingers into Sublette's throat and did for him, too.

Sometimes simple is best, he thought.

He wrestled Sublette out of his uniform jacket and pulled it on over his shirt. Working feverishly, he strapped on the soldier's belt and shoved his sword back into the scabbard. The disguise wouldn't fool anyone for long, but it might buy him a few seconds, and that might make the difference. There was nothing he could do about his hair, but it was nighttime, after all.

He sprinted back to the cottage, the unfamiliar sword banging against his hip, organizing his story as he ran.

He banged through the door, shouting, "General Karn! The handyman! He pushed Howard in the river and ran off!"

But the interior of the cottage was empty as a tomb. It appeared that Sublette and Howard were right to worry. The rest of the party had already gone.

They'd be on their way to the harbor. No doubt the wetland gunship he and Destin had seen belonged to them. Evan raced back down the path they'd traversed earlier, nearly flying head over heels twice before he discarded the sword that kept tangling in his legs. It wasn't as if a sword would make that much difference—not in *his* hands, anyway. By now it was full dark, with the moon not yet risen above the Dragonbacks.

He skidded to a stop at the quayside. The jolly boats were gone from their mooring at the public dock, so he looked out over the harbor.

He was too late.

Against the western horizon, still bright from the setting sun, he saw the three-masted schooner passing between the twin pillars of the Guardians on its way to the open sea.

Desperately, he reached out with his hands and attempted to take hold of the air and pull it toward him, to create a change in the wind that might bring Destin back. But he hadn't enough practice to gauge the scale and distance, and the ship was already within the protection of the straits. A massive wave of wind and water swept ashore, knocking him flat and drenching him. He could hear trees snapping off behind him.

Somehow, he had to let Destin know that he'd survived, that his gambit had been successful. Evan didn't know whether that would be enough to give his friend the will to live, but it was all he had to offer.

Broadening his stance on the sand, Evan gripped Destin's amulet with both hands and breathed in all the magic he could hold. Letting go of the amulet, he raised both hands and sent bolts of lightning arcing over the sea, colliding high over the Ardenine ship, turning midnight to noon and gilding the waves with silver and gold.

That's a promise, Destin, Evan thought. *Stay alive and we'll see each other again.*

He stood watching as Destin's ship grew smaller and smaller until it winked out over the horizon like a dying star.

BLOOD MAGIC

Evan had no desire to return to the cottage and wallow in his many losses, but he knew he might find clues there that would tell him where the general might have taken Destin. They'd had one conversation about Destin's life in the wetlands, and that had mostly focused on General Karn. Evan had sailed the waters along the wetland coast, but he'd never gone ashore, and he knew no one who lived there. He spoke Common, and Ardenine, now, passably. He had a ship, but no crew.

Still, a general shouldn't be hard to find, once he made that crossing.

Captain Strangward always said that luck visits a man when he's prepared a place for it. If Evan was going looking for Destin, he'd need maps and charts and books. He needed to practice magic so he'd have a chance going up against the Ardenines if it came to that.

The cottage stood rooted in its spot next to the river, but it already seemed to be fading into memory, like a place in a child's storybook, or a dream he'd had once.

Inside, he circled around the spot where Frances had fallen, where her blood had dried on the tiles. He searched the place—it didn't take long. His pendant lay on the floor in the corner. He slipped it into his pocket, meaning to repair the chain later. In the chest beside Frances's bed, he found a locket with a picture of Destin on one side and that of a small family grouping on the other—her parents, brothers, and sisters, maybe. The general wasn't there. In the strongbox under the floor, she'd stowed a small pouch of money—proceeds from sales at the market, no doubt—and a heavy gold ring with a signet in the shape of a bear.

Evan took those things as reminders and talismans, hoping to return them to Destin one day. He also took a map of the Seven Realms he found in a box of papers. Finding the loose stone at the rear of the fireplace, he withdrew the valuables he'd hidden there before Destin Karn arrived in Tarvos.

He was about to continue searching in the sleeping loft when he heard a whimper behind him. He whipped around and saw that Breaker had his eyes open and was looking at him plaintively. The dagger the general had used lay in a pool of blood next to him.

It seemed impossible that the dog could still be alive, with the wound he'd suffered. If he was, he wouldn't be for long. Evan knelt next to him, meaning to put him out of his misery. He picked up the general's dagger and reached for the dog's chin, to tilt his head back. Breaker promptly bit him on the forearm, spattering blood everywhere.

"Blood and bones!" Evan swore, sitting back on his heels, pressing his arm to his side, trying to stanch the bleeding. "I'm trying to help, you ungrateful demon of a dog."

Evan tried to remember how to treat a dog bite. Let it bleed to clean it out? It was doing that all right, soaking his white linen shirt in blood.

Evan let Breaker lie and went into the sleeping room to find Frances's medical supplies. He sat on the bed and dug through the bag, pulling out the torn cloth she used for bandages. He used the general's dagger to cut it into strips. The hilt and crosspiece were fancywork, which seemed odd for Karn to be carrying.

Something nudged Evan's leg, and he practically died of fright. He looked down, and it was Breaker, standing beside the bed, head cocked, staring at him as if waiting for orders. Evan stared back, his heart accelerating into a gallop. There was no way that dog with that wound could be up and walking around.

Evan reached out his hand tentatively, then drew it

back. "If you bite me again, I swear I'll boil you in oil," he said. This time, when he examined the dog's wound, it was nearly closed.

As Evan probed with his fingers, Breaker reached up and licked the blood from his arm. Then he leapt onto the bed and settled in next to Evan like he was his best friend in the world. He kept twisting around, trying to get at Evan's arm.

To tell the truth, Breaker looked better than he had in a long time. It was like he had a glow about him. A familiar glow.

A shudder ran through Evan. Now he knew what it reminded him of—the way the crew on the empress's ship had glowed. Only Celestine's crew looked almost . . . purplish, and Breaker had a reddish glow.

A thought kept surfacing in his mind, despite his efforts to keep it buried. Brody had said that the empress was a blood mage, that she forced people to drink her blood and they became her slaves. What did that mean? It was like Breaker had come back to life after he bit Evan on the arm. Was it possible that the dog had swallowed some blood? Was it possible that there was something about Evan's blood that . . . had a healing quality? Or even . . . raised the dead? Or the nearly dead?

No. That was revolting. That was just . . . wrong.

Maybe it only works on the dying or newly dead, he

thought. Maybe it only works on dogs. *Maybe you've lost your mind.*

Maybe this whole thing is a nightmare, Evan thought, with a flicker of hope. Maybe I'll wake up and have my life back. It didn't help that he was getting a little woozy from loss of blood. He wanted nothing more than to lie back down on the bed and sleep.

No. He needed to leave this place, and soon. He didn't want to be found here, in this blood-spattered place, with a glowing dead dog.

It took just a few minutes more to finish wrapping his arm and pack up the rest of his belongings. Breaker watched him, following him from room to room, looking alert and well and years younger. In a way, it was horrible, but in another way, it was reassuring. At least he'd managed to save somebody. When he finally walked out the door, Breaker went with him.

One day, Evan swore, he would return Destin's dog to his rightful owner.

A CHANGE IN THE WEATHER

It seemed that Omari Kadar, streetlord of the Tarvos water-front, had been abandoned by the gods. First, an unusually fierce storm roared ashore at Tarvos, lashing the shoreline with wind and waves and tides higher and stronger than ever before. By the time it was over, the narrow passage between the Guardians was completely blocked with silt and sand, so that no ship could pass in or out. At great personal expense, Kadar sent a flotilla of small boats and barges out to open the passage. But right after they'd finished, another storm blew in and filled it again. Again, he cleared it, and again, it filled.

Ship's masters began to avoid putting in at Tarvos, since they never knew when they might get out again. Kadar's warehouses sat empty, his longshoremen idling away the time in his harborside taverns until they ran out of money. Then the taverns sat empty, too. The once-thriving harbor withered on the vine. Sailing ships peppered the bay like skeletons, their sails stowed, their masts clawing at the sky.

Maybe it was time to cut his losses. There seemed to have been a change in the weather, and the tides, and the currents that had rendered Tarvos useless as a port. Kadar could not afford to dredge the passage with every new moon. It would destroy his margin completely.

Finally, he heard some good news. An agent for a company called Blue Water Trading had been buying up buildings, dockage, and ships from the few, other than Kadar, who owned property at the port. If this company was foolish enough to throw good money after bad, Kadar would accommodate it. He sent word to the trader, requesting a meeting.

The meeting was set for after dark at one of Blue Water's newly acquired warehouses—the one closest to the dock owned by the late Denis Rocheford. At least, Kadar assumed that Rocheford was dead. Neither he nor the pilot Lucky Faris had been seen since the wetlanders carried them off. Their fancy ketch remained moored at Rocheford's pier, and he'd seen no sign of activity around the cottage they'd occupied.

He'd rid himself of a potential rival and claimed Rocheford's dockage and ship at the same time. He'd made himself a tidy reward—enough money to rebuild the charred *New Moon*. If there had been a way to retain the talents of Lucky Faris, it would have been perfect.

Now, the recent storms had made his holdings nearly valueless. He'd have to salvage what he could and move on.

The guards at the warehouse door insisted that Kadar leave his personal guard outside. Kadar told himself that it didn't matter. They were men of business, after all, and Kadar was the sole predator in the port of Tarvos.

The trader sat at a desk in a dark corner of the warehouse, the light behind him so that his face was obscured in shadow. He wore a loose, hooded garment similar to those worn by desert horselords. On his forefinger, he wore a heavy gold ring.

"I'm Omari Kadar," Kadar said.

"I know." The trader didn't offer tay, didn't adhere to any of the usual niceties, didn't even offer his name.

"What shall I call you?" Kadar said, shifting his weight.

"My crew calls me the Stormcaster," the trader said.

"Stormcaster?" Kadar tilted his head, unsuccessfully trying to get a glimpse of the trader's face. "That's a pirate name," he said, fishing for more information.

"Trader, smuggler, pirate, dock boss—what's the difference?" The trader motioned Kadar to the single visitor chair. The voice seemed younger than it should have been for the business that Kadar hoped to do, and the claim of the stormcaster title was pretentious. He hoped that he wasn't wasting his time.

"What can I do for you?" The voice was familiar, but Kadar couldn't place where he'd heard it before.

"You should be asking what I can do for you," Kadar said, meaning to seize control of the negotiation.

"It's your meeting," the trader said, shrugging, as if not particularly interested in what Kadar had to say.

"I understand that you're buying up property here at the waterfront," Kadar said. "Clearly you're a man who sees what others overlook—an opportunity."

"What I see is cheap property to be had on favorable terms," the trader said. "Given current conditions here at the harbor, it's a risk, but one that I am in a position to take."

Who had taught this stripling the language of commerce? Something about his manner of speech reminded Kadar of the scurrilous Denis Rocheford.

"You are fortunate, then, because I happen to have some waterfront property I'm willing to offer up at the right price," Kadar said. "I . . . ah . . . mean to diversify my portfolio."

"Ah," the trader said. "Unfortunately, you are late to the table. I have as much exposure here as I can afford."

Kadar licked his lips. This wasn't going as planned. "I believe that when you see what I have to offer, you will realize that it represents an opportunity rather than a risk."

"The only way that it would be an opportunity is if

it were available at a rock-bottom price," the trader said, throwing down the gauntlet. "This port is dying. These warehouses, the pier, the shops and taverns—they all rely on shipping, and there is no shipping."

"It may be slow right now," Kadar said, "but no doubt—"

"It is not *slow,* it is *stopped,*" the trader said. "Not only that, the empress continues to expand southward along the coast. Why should I invest in a place that might be overrun next year?"

Why, indeed?

"So," Kadar said, his anger rising, "it seems that we cannot—"

"Show me what you have," the trader said, "and I'll determine whether I can make an offer or not."

At the end of an hour, Kadar had sold off all of his holdings in Tarvos, including the berth owned by Denis Rocheford, for pennies on the dollar. Whenever Kadar tried to negotiate, the trader glanced up at a clock on the shelf on the wall, drummed his fingers on the table, and looked toward the door.

At least I'll come away with something, Kadar kept telling himself. Something is better than nothing, and at least the trader has money in hand. The deal was sweetened by the thought that this arrogant boy stood to lose every penny in the end.

When everything was signed off on, and the money

stowed away in Kadar's money belt, the trader sat back in his chair, templing his fingers together. "I'm curious about the last mooring, the one occupied by the two-masted ketch. According to the records I have, that berth is owned by someone named . . . Rocheford?"

Kadar cursed silently. How could he have known that this trader had researched these waterfront titles? And if he had, why then had he proceeded with the purchase?

Because he got it for next to nothing, that's why. And a disputed title is worth more than no title at all.

"That's right, it did belong to a merchant named Rocheford," Kadar said smoothly, "but he's gone. Some wetlanders came looking for him. Some kind of family trouble."

"You spoke to them?" There was an edge to the trader's voice that hadn't been there before.

"Yes," Kadar said. "The wetlanders were offering a reward for information about a man matching Rocheford's description."

The trader went very still, his expression invisible within the shadow of the hood. "Then what happened?"

Why so much interest in a story that was over?

"He agreed to go back with them for good. Before he left, he sold the wharf and the ship to me." He paused. "Don't worry—he won't be coming back."

"I see," the trader said. "What are your plans?"

"I own a coastal trader, the *New Moon*," Kadar said.

"Once you've dredged out the passage, I intend to travel north, buying up property elsewhere."

"Why would you assume that I'll open the passage?" the trader said.

"You own this port now," Kadar said, with a smug smile, figuring it was safe to show his hand now that the deals were done. "If you can't figure out a way to keep the straits open, you'll lose everything."

"That's true," the trader admitted. He stood. "We're finished here, I think."

The man's calm unnerved Kadar. Was there something he'd overlooked?

No. Couldn't be. He'd made the best deal possible given the circumstances. He was lucky to get out now.

Two days later, another storm blew in. This one drove high seas through the straits, then ended in a riptide that cleared the harbor mouth of the silt and sand that had made it impassable. One by one, the ships still trapped in the harbor set sail for the open sea. Before they left, the man who called himself "the Stormcaster" met with each of the ship's masters, informing them that he was the new harbormaster and guaranteeing them a deep, clear channel, reasonable dockage fees, and a willing dockside crew.

He also met with the idled longshoremen who had not yet departed for more prosperous ports. He persuaded them to stay with promises of future work and a small retainer in the meantime.

Omari Kadar watched all this with dismay, and the growing conviction that he'd been had.

But that was impossible. How could the trader have known that the blockage would clear?

Unless he'd had a hand in it. Could it be that "stormcaster" was more than a brag and a pirate title? Should Kadar have seen this coming?

In the past, the Carthian stormlords had ruled the seas along the Desert Coast. Literally. But the last stormlord had been ineffective, to say the least, the proof being that the empress had killed him and taken his ship.

Kadar resolved to ask questions as he traveled from harbor to harbor. Maybe someone had heard of this stormcaster before.

He'd hoped to confront the owner of Blue Water Trading before he sailed, but men who'd until recently worked for him now guarded the stormcaster's holdings and the stormcaster's time.

On the day of sailing, Kadar stowed his belongings and strongboxes in the hold of the *New Moon*. The waterfront seethed with activity. Two more ships were moored in the harbor and another at the dock. Longshoremen were unloading cargo and stowing it in the warehouses that had once belonged to him. With deep bitterness, Kadar cast off and threaded his little smuggler through the near-shore moorings. When he'd emerged from the crowd, he raised the jib and made for the straits.

As he neared the Guardians, he could see someone standing atop one of them, high above the water, arms folded, the wind ripping at his cloak. Kadar recognized him as the stormcaster. Was he up there gloating as the *New Moon* sailed by? Or was he using some kind of magery to keep the passage open?

As the *New Moon* entered the straits, the stormlord's hood fell back and sunlight glinted on his fair hair. Kadar blinked, looked again, squinting against the sunlight reflecting from stone.

It was Lucky Faris, very much alive, looking down at him. As their eyes met, Faris waved farewell. He wasn't smiling. In fact, his expression could have been described as *ruthless*.

New Moon bucked, quivering under Kadar's feet, forcing his attention forward. Ahead, the air rippled and swam as energy crackled between the Guardians. The sea churned as if some giant beast circled just beneath the surface. Kadar gripped the rail to keep from being pitched into the sea. *New Moon* was spinning, spinning as the water rose all around, pouring over the gunwales, sucking the ship down. Kadar spat out salt water and cursed the gods of sea and storm as he and his ship plunged beneath the surface.

14

BASTON BAY

It had been two years since Evan lost Destin Karn, gained his first ship, and won control of the port of Tarvos. Two years during which he'd been in constant motion, building his fleet and his Stormborn crew in the ports along the Desert Coast and taking them across the Indio to the hunting grounds in the wetlands.

He couldn't afford to dawdle. As soon as Celestine realized who the new stormlord was, she'd hounded him mercilessly at sea until the loss of three ships forced her to respect his growing power. After that, she came at him mostly through trickery, bribery, and subterfuge.

Most of his crew members came from among the empress's bloodsworn. He'd taken *Cloud Spirit* back from

Celestine a year ago, when he'd spotted her off Gryphon Point with a full hold and a light crew, including his former shipmates Brody Baines, Abhayi Arya, and Teza Von. Evan had hoped to find Tully aboard, but his luck didn't extend that far.

It wasn't difficult to persuade them to drink the brew of allegiance. The empress, it seemed, was not an easy mistress, and they'd not gone willingly into her service.

Evan was glad to be back among familiar faces, though it was difficult sometimes to navigate the change in their relationship. In the space of four years he'd gone from being a kind of shipboard mascot to being "Lord Strangward," the central deity of a Stormborn cult. All around him, he felt the constant pressure of avid eyes. It was exhausting.

Despite frequent visits to ports in the wetlands, it had taken Evan the better part of a year to track Destin down in the capital at Ardenscourt. But when he'd reached out to him, there had been no response. When he persisted, Destin had sent a brief, curt note telling Evan to let go and move on, that any continuing correspondence would put them both in danger.

No matter what kind of shine Evan wanted to put on it, the message was clear—they had no future, as far as Destin was concerned. A romance on the beach—was that all it had been? It came down to one kiss and a lot of longing—on his part, anyway. It seemed that Destin had been seeking a business partner and nothing more.

And so Evan had done his best to move on. There were other, less complicated lovers in the ports on both sides of the Indio, boys who offered sweet kisses and warm embraces. Still, none could surprise and delight and challenge him like the soldier. Unfortunately, it seemed that Evan preferred complicated and dangerous to simple and sweet.

And then, out of the blue, a note from Destin, this urgent request for a meeting.

Evan knew that it could be a trap. The empress might have discovered the connection between them and used it against him. Back home, he'd already turned away one would-be lover who'd been sent to lure him into Celestine's arms.

Then again, the empress might have nothing to do with it. Evan's growing fleet had hammered shipping along the wetland coast, sometimes attacking the ports themselves. The price on his head increased with every taking under his stormcaster flag, whether he was personally involved or not. The capture of the stormlord might be the win that Destin needed to get ahead at the wetland court.

There was no way to justify taking this risk, and yet Evan couldn't stay away. His crew couldn't understand it, and made it clear they disapproved.

And so he found himself in the Ardenine port of Baston Bay in the shrinking days just before Solstice.

The city rose from the ocean's edge like a fine lady

whose skirts drag in the muck at the hem. Up above were the mansions of merchants and sea captains, with their towers and widow's walks. Farther down, a mingle of modest houses and shops. And finally, down at the waterfront, the clicket-houses and taverns and gritty maritime businesses that served the shipping trade.

As the major deepwater port serving the Ardenine capital and the down-realms, the Bay seethed with commerce of all kinds, licit and illicit. Evan had been in the city a number of times over the past two years—though, more often, he'd lain offshore, waiting for some of that commerce to come his way. The richest cargoes and the prime ships came and went through Baston Bay.

This time, though, Evan wasn't thinking about cargo. He was thinking of a boy who liked to build things. A boy with a wellspring of pain hidden behind his stony face, his eyes the only window into a dark history.

The meeting was to take place at the Barrister's Inn, one of those places where the name promises more than the establishment delivers. Evan couldn't imagine that any self-respecting barrister would be seen in this hangdog little dive on the Heartfang River, just west of the harbor itself. Maybe that was why Destin had suggested it.

And now, here Evan was, dressed in his best leathers and linen, Destin's amulet resting against his chest, Destin's dog sprawled like a warm rug over his feet. Evan, as nervous as any untouched groom on his wedding day, was surrounded by an unlikely crew of pierced and tattooed chaperones. The only other people in the taproom were the bartender and a table of seamen deep in their cups.

Evan had been watching all the comings and goings through the front door, so he was surprised when one of the seamen heaved himself out of his chair and strolled over to their table. "Lieutenant Rocheford has asked you to join him in the back room," he said in Common.

"Lieutenant . . . Rocheford?"

"Aye," the suddenly sober seaman said. "He says the two of you used to go salmon fishing together when you were young. He'd like to buy you a drink."

Only Destin would know that, which meant either the meeting was on the level, or Destin had betrayed him in great detail.

He kept secrets when you were together. There's every reason to think that he's still at it.

Across the table, Brody Baines scowled and shook his head. The message was clear: *Don't fall for it.*

"Ah," Evan said. "Now I remember." He stood, and the others pushed back their chairs, too.

"He wants to meet with you alone," the seaman said, stepping into their path. "He says you'll understand once you hear what he has to say."

"No, Captain," Teza Von said quickly, putting his bulk in the way of the seaman. He made an impressive wall. "If he wants to talk to you, he can do it out here." The rest of the crew muttered agreement.

That was when Breaker burst out from under the table, charged across the room, and began flinging himself at the back door, bouncing off, and doing it all over again.

Evan's heart all but stopped, and then it seemed like he couldn't get his breath. It was true. Destin was—he must be—just on the other side of that door. Evan had to take this chance. He had to.

"Wait here," he said to his crew. "I'll call you in if it goes wrong."

"But what if we're too late?" Jorani cried. She was the newest addition to the crew, and the youngest.

"Make sure you're not," Evan said. He crossed to the door, nudged Breaker to the side with his foot, and opened the door. As soon as it opened wide enough, the dog shot past him and into the back room.

And, there, in a chair by the fire, was Destin Karn, fending off Breaker the demon dog, who was doing his best to lick him in the face. When Destin looked up at Evan, Breaker finally made contact and then, apparently satisfied, curled up in Destin's lap.

Evan turned, nodded reassurance to his crew, then stepped across the threshold, pulling the door shut behind him. "I brought your dog back," he said, leaning against the door.

"So I see," Destin said, stroking Breaker's head. His face was concealed, then revealed by the light from the flickering flames. He was dressed entirely in black—the colors of the Ardenine King's Guard. Evan wondered if that was intentional—meant to maintain a distance between them. "It seems that you have acquired the ability to raise the dead."

"Some of the dead, some of the time," Evan said. He paused. "Are you with the King's Guard now?" He gestured toward the uniform.

Destin nodded. "I'm in a . . . particular division of the King's Guard. Outside of the normal chain of command."

"Does the fact you came in costume indicate that you're here in an official capacity?"

Destin laughed. "If I were here in an official capacity, you would be in chains. You've become quite notorious, here in the wetlands. I'm proud of you, Pirate." He pushed a chair out with his booted foot. "Would you like to sit down?"

Feeling a little foolish, Evan crossed the room and sat down in the chair nearest the hearth. Still country to this city boy. If Evan was deadly, Destin was always deadlier.

Evan had grown, but Destin had grown, too, so that the soldier still had a good three inches on him. He was thinner, too, though maybe the proper word was *honed*. Honed by whatever had happened since they'd been apart. Honed into a sleek and deadly weapon for the wetland king.

The silence between them grew until it was awkward.

For two years Evan had dreamed of this meeting, and now he had nothing to say.

"I believe this is your meeting," he said finally.

Destin lifted a decanter of amber liquid, poured for himself, and then extended it toward Evan. "Would you like any—?"

"No, thank you," Evan said. He needed a clear head to pick his way through this minefield of a meeting. "I'm—I just had something."

Destin's smile was hard-edged, bitter, almost a grimace. "A wise move, Pirate. Never accept a drink from me. I am the midwife who delivers the king's enemies into hell." Destin swirled the liquid in his glass and drank it down, his throat jumping. The message seemed clear. *I am not for you, and you are not for me.*

"Am I one of the king's enemies, Des?" Evan asked softly.

"Well, there *is* a heavy price on your head," Destin said, studying his empty glass, as if deciding whether to refill it. "However, as an official of the king, I'm not allowed to collect."

"Too bad," Evan said. He lifted the hammer-and-tongs amulet from around his neck, wadded the chain in his hand, and extended it toward Destin. "Thank you for the loan of your amulet."

"Keep it," Destin said, waving it away. "I replaced it a long time ago."

Evan slipped the chain over his head, pleased to feel the familiar weight of the flash against his skin. He fished a small velvet bag from inside his coat and slid it across the table, feeling like a suitor offering a series of unworthy gifts. "I saved your mother's ring and locket for you." He pulled a leather-wrapped bundle from his carry bag and set it next to the rest. "And . . . your father's dagger. In case you wanted that, too."

Surprise cleared the bitterness from Destin's face. "You . . ." He stopped, swallowed hard, and brushed his long fingers across the leather, then met Evan's gaze for the first time. "Thank you. It's my mother's dagger, actually," he said, a bit of color staining his pale cheeks. "My father took it away from her the first time she tried to defend herself." He paused, as if steeling himself to go on. "She's alive, you know. My mother, I mean. If you can call it that."

Evan sat forward, a spark of hope kindling in his middle. "Frances is alive?"

Destin nodded. "She lives with her family in Tamron."

Memories flooded in. Frances asking Evan to stay on and be a friend to her son. *I think you both have lessons to teach each other.* Frances saying to Dustin, *I've lost so much. I don't want to lose you, too.*

"Can I—? I would love to see her again."

"No," Destin said, with a bleak finality. "You wouldn't. Leave well enough alone." That seemed to be the theme of the entire conversation.

Then why have a meeting at all?

"What about your father?"

"Still living," Destin said.

"Why?" Evan met Destin's eyes directly. *If you're such a dangerous, despicable, ruthless person.*

"He's not the king's enemy," Destin said. "Not yet." He shifted his eyes away and methodically refilled his glass. "Why do you think he brought my mother back alive? The general has made it clear that if anything happens to him, Frances and her family will pay a dear price. But he knows it's a card he can play only once, so right now, it's a standoff. He'd better get down on his knees every night and pray for their good health."

"I'll kill him for you, if you want," Evan said. "Though, admittedly, it would be easier if you could lure him to the coast. Even better, suggest a father-son fishing trip."

Destin laughed, low in his throat. "Thank you, Pirate," he said, "but killing is something I'm actually quite good at. The general is mine. I can wait." He fingered Breaker's ears, ruffling up his fur. "Is it my imagination, or has my dog joined the bloodsworn? I couldn't help noticing that he and your crew share a certain reddish glow."

"It's not your imagination," Evan said, "though I prefer the term 'Stormborn.'" He explained what had happened at the cottage and after.

"So, how does it work, this blood magic?"

Evan hesitated. He hadn't shared this with anyone else.

It wasn't something he was particularly proud of.

"It is a magic I share with the empress. My blood has the power to raise the recent dead and nearly dead. Once raised, the Stormborn are fearless, exceedingly strong, impervious to pain, and unflinchingly loyal."

"The perfect soldier," Destin murmured.

"There is a price to be paid," Evan said. "They lose some of their mental edge, creativity, decision-making ability, and the like. And the desire for more blood never leaves them."

"I'm surprised at you," Destin said, his face mingling grudging respect and a trace of surprise. "You used to be annoyingly ethical."

"I'm a pirate, not a priest," Evan snapped. "Most of my crews are converts from the empress's bloodsworn that I bind with my blood. That takes them out of Celestine's hands and delivers to me the most experienced sailors and fighters. They also know her weaknesses and strengths."

"Is that how you justify it?" Destin raised an eyebrow. Same eyebrow, same way. Joltingly familiar.

"They are all given a choice—stay with the empress and die, or serve me and live. Most don't find it a difficult decision." Evan took a breath, forcing his muscles to relax. There was no reason to be defensive. It was just Destin, pulling whatever chain he could get hold of. "I do what's necessary to stay alive, and make a living. Tarvos is thriving. I've made it into a sanctuary and fortress that the empress can't breach. The Guardians stand watch when I am not there."

"So you've figured out how to use them?" Destin said, brightening. "Did that manuscript I found—?"

"That manuscript you found was a lifesaver," Evan said. "Thank you."

"What about Celestine? Any meet-ups with the empress in the north?" Destin toyed with his mother's dagger, as if half-listening, but something in the way he said it suggested he was striking close to the bone.

"She used to stalk me continually, every time I put to sea," Evan said. "After losing several ships, she learned to keep her distance, for fear of being swamped. However, I believe the price on my head in Carthis is higher than the one your king is offering. Which is why I need a crew I can trust."

Destin studied Evan's face, the heat of his scrutiny bringing the blood up under his skin. "It seems what I've been hearing about you is true."

"That depends," Evan said. "What have you been hearing?"

"I am the spymaster for the king now, Pirate. I have eyes and ears across the Indio. They call you the Stormcaster of the Desert Coast and the Scourge of the Wetlands. They say you're the only one who still defies the empress in the east. They say you are ruthless."

Evan half-shrugged, oddly touched that Destin had

been keeping track of him. "I suppose you could still call me the lord of the ocean, but Celestine has gobbled up nearly all the land. Sooner or later I have to put in to a port, and the only stronghold I have along the Desert Coast is Tarvos. Even that's becoming more and more dangerous." He paused, then forged ahead. "When you called me here, I thought maybe you intended to cash in."

"No," Destin said, "but it does have to do with the empress." He released a long breath. "You see, a few months ago, my king sent me to Delphi to hunt down a girl with a magemark."

Evan listened with growing alarm as Destin told his story. He'd always known this would happen—sooner or later the empress would run down her quarry and add another weapon to her armory. But to know it was actually happening was like a bolt to the heart.

"Her name is Jenna?" Evan found himself wishing that he'd accepted Destin's offer of a drink.

"That's the name she goes by now. Jenna Bandelow."

"Bandelow," Evan repeated, as if that would deliver some insight. That was not a name that Celestine had mentioned the day they'd first met, but then again, she'd only named the ones she'd already found. "You've seen her magemark?"

Destin nodded. He pulled out a folded paper and handed it over. "This is the sketch the king gave me."

Evan studied it. "The jewel in the center—?"

"It appears to be a ruby. And there's this." Destin reached under the table and retrieved a black leather case. Setting it between them, he opened it, revealing a curved Carthian blade like the ones carried by Celestine's horselords. "It was left to Jenna, supposedly by her mother. She killed one of the King's Guard in Delphi with this blade."

When Evan reached for it, Destin gripped his wrist, hard. Evan looked up, startled, all but undone by the pressure of Destin's fingers against his pulse point. For a long moment, they stared at each other.

"Careful you don't cut yourself," Destin said. "It's magicked. Jenna stabbed herself with it and nearly died." One heartbeat. Two heartbeats. Then he let go.

But it was too late. Destin had shown his hand. It had been a huge risk to contact Evan, to hold this meeting, to commit treason against the king he served. It proved that, despite his claims to the contrary, the connection between them remained. Destin hadn't moved on, either.

Evan swallowed hard, undone by the gratitude that welled up inside him. He wrenched his mind back to the conversation. "Jenna nearly died—but she *is* alive?"

Destin nodded. "She's recovering. The king has sent word to the empress, but I took steps to make sure it would take a long time to get there. Still, at best we have a few weeks before Celestine comes to collect. Maybe less."

Evan was ambushed by a mixture of hope and dread. A few weeks. They had a few weeks. He had to find a way to . . . "You've questioned this . . . Jenna?"

Destin nodded. "I used persuasion on her, but it doesn't seem to work. As you'll recall, it doesn't work on you, either. Still, I've interrogated a lot of people, and I think she was telling the truth when she said she had no idea what the magemark means."

Hope diminished, just a bit. "What are her gifts?"

Destin frowned, as if trying to remember every detail. "As I said, she's resistant to magery. She claims to be clairvoyant—that she sometimes sees images of the future, sees people as they really are, or can tell when someone is lying. She claims that her senses are sharper than most— vision, hearing, sense of smell. She heals quickly, and is resistant to flame. In fact, she develops a kind of armor for protection."

Evan shook his head, bewildered. He couldn't put those details together into any kind of theory that made sense. But, maybe, together they could—

Destin rolled his glass between his hands. "If worse comes to worst, I could kill her before the empress arrives, but—"

"No!" Evan all but shouted.

The door banged open, and Brody, Jorani, and Teza crowded into the doorway. "My lord?" Teza said. "Is everything all right?"

"Everything is fine," Evan said. "I'm sorry. We were just having a . . . political discussion."

Jorani gave Destin the evil eye, and then they withdrew.

"Back to Jenna," Evan said. "I don't want to kill her! I want to save her if I can. I have to talk to her. I've never met anyone else like me. I just—"

Destin raised both hands. "Calm down, Pirate. I guessed that you would. So. I do have another plan. It's a terrible, foolhardy, hastily made plan that will probably get us both killed. It involves the weapon I asked you to bring with you." He paused. "You did bring a weapon, didn't you?"

Evan nodded. "I brought a sun dragon."

Destin stared at him. "A sun dragon?"

Evan nodded. "It's still rather small, but it's growing fast. We need to act before it outgrows the hold."

"You weren't worried that it would set fire to your ship?"

"It came with a flashcraft collar that blocks magic," Evan said. He paused, then continued, eagerly, "Would you like to see it?"

Destin laughed, his first deep, genuine laugh of the day. And suddenly, they were back in Tarvos, two boys laying plans and building their ship of dreams.

"Gods, Pirate, I have missed you," Destin said, shaking his head. "Let's go see this dragon and I'll go over the plan."

15

DEBRIEFING

Hal Matelon crawled forward on his belly until he could look over the edge of the cliff. The wind off the Indio drove a freezing rain inland in sheets, plastering his hair to his head, running under his collar and down his neck, and dripping off the tip of his nose.

Below and to the south lay the city and harbor of Chalk Cliffs. His heart sank when he saw that the same siren flag flew over the battlements as had flown over the ships that attacked the city a scant few days ago. It was what he had expected, but still . . . disappointing.

The harbor was packed with ships, and the waterfront seethed with activity despite the rain, like an anthill that's been overturned. The invaders were wasting no time off-loading soldiers, horses, and supplies.

Horsemen rode up and down the beach in their thickly padded coats, head wraps, and knee-length breeches. They carried the curved swords they'd used so effectively on the city battlements. Some wore bits and pieces of Highlander uniforms along with traditional garb.

Corporal Sasha Talbot eased up beside him. She stared down at the scene for a long moment, swore softly, then blotted at her eyes with her sleeve. She cleared her throat. "That answers that," she said. "It looks like they mean to stay awhile."

Hal nodded, watching her out of the corner of his eye. The statuesque bluejacket had been subdued and gloomy since the city fell and the empress Celestine sailed off with the heir to the Gray Wolf throne. At least she no longer talked about drawing her sword and charging down into the midst of the horselord pirates, taking out as many as she could before she went down herself.

She blames herself, he thought. And I blame myself. He guessed there was more than enough blame to go around.

"Do you see any of ours?" he said, focusing on the scene below.

Talbot slowly turned her head and stared at him.

"Yours, I mean," he amended quickly. He and Talbot got on fairly well, except for the fact that she still considered him to be a prisoner of the crown. At least she'd allowed him to keep the weapons he'd collected off a dead soldier.

Talbot looked again, then murmured, "I think they've got some of ours repairing the fortifications."

Hal saw it now, teams of workers hauling rock under the supervision of the riders. It seemed that one of them wasn't moving fast enough, because his horselord guard unslung his blade and cut him down.

Talbot swore again. "I wish we could help them." She fingered the hilt of her sword.

"Come back with an army," Hal said quickly. "Then you can help them."

Talbot grunted. "I don't know if we can field an army that can stand against them," she said, her expression bleak.

"Buck up, Talbot," Hal said, punching her lightly on the shoulder. "It's not like you to surrender before the battle begins."

"I've never fought soldiers like these," she said.

Hal knew she was second-guessing every move she'd made, all the choices that resulted in the loss of her captain. Her princess. Her friend. Hal was doing a lot of that himself.

"We'll be ready for them, next time," Hal said. "They may be fierce and fearless, but they'll bleed like any other soldier."

"I'm not so sure," Talbot said. She shot Hal a defiant

look, as if daring him to contradict her.

Hal fully intended to bring that same story to his father, but he knew better than to go before the thane unprepared. He needed more information.

"Stay here," Hal said. "I'll be right back."

When he began scrambling back, away from the cliff, Talbot gripped his arm. "Where do you think you're going?"

"I'm going to go down and see if I can find out a little more about who we're up against."

"What if you don't come back?"

Hal struggled not to lose his temper. "If I don't come back, I'll be dead, but you'll be alive, so you can go tell *your* Captain Byrne and *your* queen what's going on."

Talbot scowled, but released her hold. Hal crept south along the cliff until he found an icy streambed where he could descend to the beach. Once on the sand, he threaded his way forward between huge chalk slabs until he could get a clear view.

The horses were being ferried ashore in small boats south of the high cliffs and kept in temporary paddocks until they could be moved into the city. They were not the dun-colored Ardenine military mounts Hal was used to, nor the sturdy, shaggy ponies used in the highlands. These horses had chiseled heads, arched necks, and long legs, and they carried their tails high.

A sentry leaned on the paddock fence, watching the

progress of a longboat back to the ship anchored offshore. Unlike most of the others, he was bareheaded. He wore his hair in a long plait that extended nearly to his waist, though the top of his head was shaved clean. His beard was also braided and decorated. He wore light armor over loose-fitting clothing. More than anything, he resembled the horselords from the desert realms across the Indio.

Hal was still debating whether to kill him outright or to try to take him alive and risk giving himself away when the rattle of pebbles on stone behind him alerted him to danger. He dove sideways in time to avoid being beheaded by the curved blade of the horselord who'd crept up on him. Hal rolled to his feet, his sword in one hand, a fistful of sand in the other. He managed to block his attacker's next swing, but the force of the blow all but rattled the teeth from his head.

Hal was no slouch, but it didn't take long for him to realize that he was outmatched. The horselord was strong as an ox, and yet so quick on his feet that Hal could scarcely do more than dodge and feint, rarely getting in a blow of his own. The horselord's next swing all but disarmed Hal, but the curved blade caught against his own, and Hal took that opportunity to come in close enough to fling the sand in the horselord's eyes. When his blade dropped away, Hal drove his sword beneath his rib cage, all the way to the hilt.

The horselord smashed his gauntleted arm across Hal's

face, pitching him backward onto the sand. Then the other sentry was there, his blade at Hal's throat, pinning him to the beach. Hal watched in horror as the man he'd skewered yanked the blade free and tossed it aside on the sand.

No, Hal thought, spitting out blood. That wound is not survivable, let alone ignorable. Not by any mortal man. I need to apologize to Talbot for questioning her description of the invading army.

The way things were going, he might never get the chance.

The two enemy soldiers were arguing now, in a language akin enough to Common that Hal realized that they were arguing over whether to kill him now or deliver him to the empress alive.

If they took him to the empress, would Lyssa Gray be there? Could he devise a way to rescue her and the busker?

"You know the empress will want this one alive," one of the horselords said, pointing at Hal, and then toward the ship. "He is young and strong, and a good fighter."

The skewered man fingered the hilt of his sword and scowled at Hal; the man's jaw was set stubbornly, as if he took being skewered rather personally. "Celestine has many new recruits to choose from, Hoshua," he said. "She can spare this one."

"She will need many more bloodsworn in the coming days," Hoshua said. "These wetlands have plenty of seasoned soldiers. They have been at war for years."

Wetlands, Hal thought. That must mean that they are from the drylands across the sea. And what did that mean—*bloodsworn*? Was it simply the name used for the horselord fighters, or did it have something to do with their superhuman strength and stamina?

"I don't want to have to keep watch on him all the way to Celesgarde," the wounded man said.

Where is Celesgarde? Is that where they would have carried Lyssa Gray?

"Don't worry, Enebish. We can chain him belowdecks. He won't be any trouble."

After a heated discussion, his captors finally agreed that maybe the empress *could* spare this one particular soldier.

"Take me to Celestine," Hal said in Common, startling the two horselords, who looked down at him as if a rock on the beach had begun speaking. These bloodsworn might be relentless, but they were not particularly quick-witted.

Enebish, the skewered man, drew back his foot and kicked him. The movement caused the horselord to stagger a bit, as if his body was catching up to the fact that it was in serious trouble. That's when Hal heard a familiar *thwack*. Now an arrow shaft was centered in Hoshua's chest.

Hal rolled onto his side, gripped Enebish's boot, and gave it a hard twist. Bone cracked and the horselord went down. Focus on breaking bones, Hal thought. That makes them less mobile.

Hal scrambled over the sand to where Enebish had

dropped his sword, scooped it up, and turned to see Hoshua bearing down on him, as unconcerned about his arrow as Enebish had been about being run through. The bow sounded again, and the horselord stumbled as a second arrow hit him in the back. Hal took advantage of the distraction to behead his opponent with a two-handed swing. The head splashed into the water, but the body continued to stagger around, spraying blood from its severed neck until it tripped over a rock slab and went down.

"Matelon! Look out!" Hal turned, and Talbot was sprinting toward him, nocking an arrow as she ran. Between them, Enebish was crawling across the sand toward Hal, pulling with his arms, pushing with one leg and dragging the broken one, his dagger in his teeth. In desperation, Hal threw his shoulder against a slab of rock, toppling it over so Enebish was pinned underneath.

Breathing hard, Hal bent down, resting his hands on his knees, and tried not to spew sick all over the sand.

Talbot knelt next to Enebish's head. She swore softly. "He's dead," she said, glaring at Hal. "I wanted to interrogate him."

"Sorry," Hal muttered. "But I . . . ah . . . questioned him before he died."

Talbot eyed him suspiciously. "What do you mean? What did you find out?"

It was the first time he'd interrogated someone from

the wrong end of a sword, but he knew more now than he had before.

"They're Empress Celestine's army," Hal said. "They sail out of her capital at Celesgarde, wherever that is. That's where they likely took the busker and Captain Gray."

Hal and Talbot chose new mounts from among the long-legged desert horses in the temporary paddocks on the beach. They stole weapons and other gear from the dead horselords. Hal wasn't in love with the curved blades the pirates carried, but now he knew from experience that they were good at removing heads with a single swipe, which seemed to be one of the few ways to put these demon soldiers down for good. Their bows were strange, also—lightweight, with limbs that curved back toward the archer. Hal was good with a crossbow, and fair with a longbow, but it would take practice to learn how to use one of these.

They rode west toward Fortress Rocks, continuing until their horses were exhausted. When they didn't dare push them any further, they found lodging at an inn along the road. To say they found lodging was being generous. The inn was already packed with refugees heading inland. Hal and Talbot slept in the barn, in a stall with three other people. Talbot had a small amount of money, but all Hal had were a handful of unfamiliar coins he'd taken from Enebish.

To say they slept was being generous.

Hal rose at first light and saddled his horse. He'd named the stallion Bosley because he was balky, full of himself, and obsessed with getting at the mares. Hal filled the panniers with food for several days, his quiver with arrows, and lashed a blanket roll behind his saddle. He was swinging open the barn doors when Talbot appeared, her hair in a tangle, wiping sleep from her eyes.

"Where do you think you're going?" she demanded, her hand on the hilt of her sword.

"This is where we say good-bye." Hal led his mount out into the stable yard, with Talbot hard on his heels.

"What do you mean, good-bye?" Talbot planted herself in his path. "You're coming with me to Fortress Rocks, and then on to Fellsmarch. The queen will want to question you along with me."

"I have business in Arden," Hal said. "I need to go home."

"You are a prisoner of the queen," Talbot said, "and it's not my place to decide to set you free."

"I won't tell if you don't," Hal said, but she didn't crack a smile. He sighed. It was unfair for her to keep playing by the book when he'd already strayed so far from it. "After what we faced together in Chalk Cliffs, do you really want to shed blood between us?" He knew Talbot well enough by now not to suggest whose. He swung up into the saddle, and Talbot gripped the stallion's cheek piece. Never a good idea where Bosley was concerned. He showed his teeth, jerking his head to one side so that she lost her hold. Hal reined in, forcing the stallion back a few steps.

Talbot drew her sword. "I like you, Matelon," she said, "but I can't just let you ride back home when you are a prisoner of war."

"We're all prisoners of war, aren't we?" Hal said, but that gained him no ground. He leaned down toward her, using all the persuasion at his command, which, admittedly, wasn't much. "Look, I know you don't want to go back to your queen and report that you lost your commanding officer, your post, *and* your prisoner. If I had my way, I would go after that ship even if I had to row all the way to Celesgarde."

By now, Talbot was nodding her agreement.

"But," he said, which stopped her nodding. "I'm tactician enough to know that the only thing I'd likely achieve by doing that is an early grave. We need more information. We need more firepower. And the only connections I have are in Arden. Holding me hostage and hoping my father responds for the first time in his life is a waste of time. I can do your queen and your queendom a lot more good by going home and making a case in person than by cooling my heels in a dungeon in Fellsmarch."

"How, exactly, could you do us good?" Talbot asked, scowling. "And *why* would you, once you're home?"

Hal had lots of possible answers.

Because I've fallen for your Captain Gray. Because, when it comes to choosing between her and the despicable Montaignes, it's no choice at all. Because I've never seen a people so devoted to their line of queens. Because, after swimming for so long in the political swill of Ardenscourt, I've gotten used to breathing clean air here in the north.

Because I'm a fool for lost causes.

"Captain Gray and I had an argument about the war," Hal said. "I told her flat-out you were going to lose. I told her we had better weapons, a bigger army, deeper pockets, and an entire empire to draw upon. It's a total mismatch. Only a fool would bet on you."

Talbot's face was getting redder and redder. "And she said . . . ?"

He laughed. "She disagreed."

"What's your point, Matelon?"

"The point is, now I'm not so sure. Winning a war depends on more than armament and numbers. An army can't fight on heart alone, but it can't fight without it, either. That said, the empress Celestine and her army of bloodsworn scare the hell out of me. I've never seen soldiers like them. From what Enebish said, she has an endless supply. After Chalk Cliffs, I am sure of one thing: if the Realms cannot unite against the threat from the east, we will all lose."

Talbot nodded grudgingly. "Maybe so, but if you think that after twenty-five years of war, Queen Raisa is going to bend the knee to the empire, you're wrong."

"I didn't say the empire. I said the Realms. Give your queen my regards." With that, Hal set his knees to the stallion's sides. As he rode away, he was reasonably sure that Talbot wouldn't put an arrow in his back. Mostly because she didn't have a bow in her hands. Still, the tension didn't leave his back and shoulders until he rounded a turn and was out of sight.

16

PRODIGAL SON

Hal rode south over the Alyssa Plateau, taking the path he'd traveled after his escape from the debacle at Queen Court. He crossed into Arden west of Spiritgate, but he didn't feel any safer on the southern side of the border. For all he knew, the empress was attacking ports up and down the coast. For all he knew, he was a hunted man in Arden.

Once he was well into Arden, he began asking questions about the state of the dispute between the king and the Thane Council. But when your sources are tavern gossip, you get creative and conflicting stories.

Some said King Jarat had freed all political prisoners and was negotiating with the thanes in a new spirit of collaboration. Some said that the full power of the army of Arden would take the field against the thanes any day now.

Another common line was that Queen Marina had seized power and was running the kingdom in the name of her son. Still others expected that Jarat's betrothal would be announced any day, bringing one of the powerful thane families to his side. If not Jarat's, then his sister's.

In short, the information was as reliable as tavern gossip usually is. Nobody recalled hearing anything about Lady Matelon or her daughter, but almost everyone had heard that Thane Matelon and his surviving son were gathering troops in the countryside.

Hal wondered if word had reached his father that he was alive, and held captive by the Gray Wolf queen. Or if the messages the wolf queen had promised to send had been intercepted by his family's enemies. Or if she'd sent any messages at all.

He considered taking ship from Spiritgate to Middle-sea, but, given what he'd seen at Chalk Cliffs, he decided to stay as far away from the coast as possible. He traveled overland, hoping that the passes through the Heartfangs would be open by now. Anyone keeping watch for him wouldn't expect him to come that way.

After a series of frustrating delays due to the dregs of an especially hard winter, he made it through the mountains in time to meet spring as it climbed the western slopes.

Hal methodically stripped off layers of clothing as the snows thinned, then disappeared from all but the shadiest spots. After a year in Delphi, and his winter travels through the frozen north, the scent of earth and flowers went to his head like the ten-year brandy his father reserved for special occasions.

His desert horse Bosley seemed as pleased as Hal to be leaving the cold mountains behind.

Now Hal looked down over the valley that he'd called home from birth. Though he hadn't spent much time here since he'd left for the army at the age of eleven, it was still the center of his personal compass. He scanned the scene below, looking for signs of disorder.

The river was out of its banks, but that wasn't unusual this time of year, when the melting snows in the mountains sent waterfalls roaring down the lower slopes of the Heartfangs. The runoff fed the northern branch of the Ardenswater that joined her southern sister on the way to the sea.

From the looks of things, the tenants had already been working the close-in shares. New crops greened the better allotments near the river. But other, less fertile fields lay fallow, suggesting that some who normally worked the fields might have been turned to bloodier work.

At least the keep wasn't ringed by armies flying the red hawk, and the manor house still stood intact amid his lady mother's gardens. The dying sun colored the low hills to the west and smoke curled from the kitchens that would be preparing the evening meal. The joy of homecoming was tempered by the knowledge that his mother and sister weren't there.

Nudging his horse into motion, Hal began his descent. He'd only just reached the flatlands at the bottom when he saw horsemen riding hard toward him. Hal rested his hand on his curved sword until the riders were close enough that he could see that they wore the spreading oak signia pinned to their clothes. Militia, then, not his father's regulars. Hal didn't see any familiar faces.

Nobody seemed to recognize Hal, either. And why would they? He was a scruffy stranger on a stolen horse carrying an exotic blade.

The horses were motley, and the riders were, too, so Hal guessed they were farmers and farmers' sons, called into service. All except for their officer, a corporal who rode a fine horse with elaborate trappings and looked to be about twelve years old. He wore a different signia than the others—the shield and cross. Hal racked his brain, trying to recall what house that was.

"State your name and business," the baby officer said. "You've crossed into Lord Matelon's holdings."

Before Delphi, Hal would have freely volunteered his name and business at the border of his father's lands to people wearing his signia. But he did not know for sure who these people were and he'd developed some skills at staying alive off the battlefield as well as on it.

"I'm here to see Lord Matelon," Hal said, holding on to

his own name for the moment.

"Is that so?" The corporal looked him up and down, taking in Hal's stubble of beard and his travel-stained clothing. "Why would he want to meet with *you*?"

"That's between me and Matelon," Hal said.

"Then you should know that he's not here."

Then where is he? Hal was tempted to say. Instead, he said, "Of course he's not here. He's going to meet me here in two days' time."

"Then come back in two days," the boy said.

"What's your name, Corporal?" Hal barked it with enough authority that the boy replied before he thought it through.

"It's Rolande DeLacroix," he said.

"Son of Pascal?"

The boy blinked at Hal, as if surprised he would know the name. "Yes, he's my father."

That was it, the shield and cross belonged to the DeLacroix, though a bunch of grapes and a cask would be more accurate. They were a family of wine merchants, originally from Tamron, highly skilled at avoiding any actual service in the war, which was why Hal hadn't recognized their signia at first.

There was something else, though. Hal tightened his grip on the hilt of his sword. "Brother to Estelle, then?"

Estelle DeLacroix was mistress to King Gerard, and her family had prospered when she became his favorite.

Hal usually didn't follow court gossip, but he knew all this courtesy of his mother's and sister's newsy letters while he was in exile in Delphi.

The letters had stopped, of course, when Delphi fell and the Matelon women were taken hostage, so he was no longer up to date.

Rolande flushed scarlet. "Estelle *was* my sister, yes, until swiving King Gerard executed her for treason. Like she would try to kill him by putting an adder in her own bed. How stupid would that be?" Rolande clapped his mouth shut then, as if realizing how much he was revealing to this scruffy stranger and a dozen onlooking farmers.

"I'm sorry to hear about your sister," Hal said, and meant it. "So, what are you doing here? Has your family allied with White Oaks?"

"White Oaks has allied with *us*," Rolande said loftily. "I've been charged with organizing local forces to protect the keeps in the area while my father and his allies march on the capital."

Your father's with them, then? Hal wanted to say. That would be a first. Has anyone explained which end of the sword to stick them with?

Instead, he said, "Have you heard any news about Lady Matelon and the other hostages?"

Rolande shook his head. "If you want my opinion, they're all dead," he said. "How foolish was that, to gather in the capital like that, with their families? They were sitting ducks. As soon as things went sour with Estelle, we withdrew to our holdings in the east to await developments."

Rolande focused in on Hal's face, and it seemed he saw something dangerous there, because he paled and pulled back on his horse's reins, retreating a few steps.

"So," he went on. "Now that I've been so frank with you, you can see that we've naught to feed nameless travelers."

"What about one with a name, then?" Hal said. "They call me Halston Matelon, son of Arschel and Lady Marjorie Scoville, and brother to Robert and Harper."

"Matelon!" Rolande stared at him, his mouth dropping open. Once alerted, even Rolande couldn't fail to see the resemblance between Hal and his father. "But . . . you're the dead one."

"Not yet," Hal said. "Hopefully not for a while."

TWO PIRATES WALK INTO A BAR

The *icelands* would be a better name for this country than the *wetlands*, Evan thought, especially in this cold season. He and his crew had traveled south to Spiritgate, hoping to avoid the snow-stuffed high passes by taking a more southerly road west, into the interior. Their chosen route led through the borderlands, skirting the southern flank of a massive peak that was hidden in cloud most of the time. The southerners called it the Harlot; the northerners, Mount Alyssa.

Alyssa. The name of a queen.

His Stormborn were all capable riders, at least. Carthis was a land of horselords and pirates, where people routinely climbed off a horse and stepped directly onto a ship.

They'd bought cold-weather clothes and ponies in the markets on the coast before setting out for the capital city, Fellsmarch.

Still, the northern winds seemed to drive right through wool and leather. Snow and sleet stung their exposed skin like a sandstorm at home. Evan considered using his magic to improve the weather, but decided against it. It was one thing to stir up a favorable wind at sea. He did not understand this weather—or this terrain—and he worried that tampering with it might have unexpected consequences, like the dangerous snow slides they called "avalanches." But, with every frustrating delay, Evan worried that the empress was launching her invasion of the wetland realms.

The seas had once seemed boundless, a place where a gifted pilot with a good ship could lose himself. Now all of his horizons seemed to be shrinking. Eventually, he'd be cornered.

Celestine's words came back to him, from the day they'd first met, when she and Captain Strangward were arguing about the magemarked.

They're mine. They are a part of the Nazari line. They were created for a purpose, and it's time they served.

That was the most honesty he'd ever had from her. Usually, her words were as sweet as prickly pear jelly. The empress always looked at Evan with a mixture of greed, lust, envy, and desire. The only thing missing was love.

The sea had always offered him the illusion of freedom,

but now it was dissipating like a wetland mist.

Some nights, despite his exhaustion, he played the game of *Where is she now?* Other nights, it was memories of Destin that kept him awake.

Evan had left Destin behind in Ardenscourt. The soldier had claimed that he could be of more use to Evan in the capital than at his side. How was he faring in that nest of vipers to the south? Had he made any headway in persuading the boy king that the empress in the east was a greater danger than the queen in the north?

I don't want you to be of use to me, Evan thought, for the hundredth time. *I want you to forget about me. I want you to kill that monster of a father, leave Arden, and find another house by the sea. I want you to be happy.*

Yet he couldn't help wishing they were facing these challenges together. It would be worth it, even for a short while.

It seemed that the fates had decreed that he go through life alone.

The heavily fortified border town of Delphi seethed with activity. Word had come that the northern passes had finally opened, and the traders, brokers, and travelers who had been bottled up there all winter prepared to journey on. The coal mines and foundries of the queendom had been producing all winter, and now wagon after wagon took the road north. Evan and his party joined a band of travelers on horseback with a weatherbeaten upland trader to serve as guide.

It was a good military road, when it wasn't chin deep in snow, with stone and steel bridges where it crossed and recrossed the rivers and streams roaring with snowmelt. Every night, travelers packed into bare-bones lodges situated a day's ride apart. First arrivals claimed the bunks that lined the walls. The less fortunate slept shoulder to shoulder on the floor. One night, a blinding snowstorm gave notice that winter wasn't quite finished in these mountains. The next day, teams of ponies dragged huge blades over the road, scraping the deep snow away. The tracks of wolves were everywhere, and their howling sometimes woke Evan in the night. Even with so much company on the road, he couldn't shake the feeling that he and his crew were being watched, every step of the way, by malevolent eyes.

As their journey neared its end, they encountered small bands of uplanders, men and women, hair done up in braids, and armed to the teeth. This, apparently, was how the north welcomed newcomers. After a long conversation with their guide, and a hostile look-over, they were allowed to move on.

At long last, one afternoon they rounded a shoulder of a massive peak to see the Vale spread out before them. The clouds they'd seen earlier had cleared somewhat as the day warmed, though steam rose from several large fissures in the near distance. Here, the air was noticeably warmer, and moist, with a faint scent of sulfur. The valley was amazingly green, for late winter. A river cut through the Vale, tumbling out of the mountains in a series of waterfalls. At the north end of the Vale, snuggled against the mountains, was the city of Fellsmarch. Their destination.

They descended into the Vale, striking north across the relatively flat terrain. As they drew closer to Fellsmarch, Evan could see that the builders had made good use of the materials all around them. It was a city built of stone—but a very different stone from what Evan was used to. At home, buildings were built of buff-colored sandstone and stucco. Here, there was more variety—sandstone, yes, but also granites and limestone. The town itself was a warren of steep, twisting cobbled streets, with scarcely a level place big enough to pitch a tent unless it was in the middle of the Way. The skyline boasted a number of pretty spires—temples, probably.

Evan had half-expected to see mages everywhere, but there were few abroad on the streets of the capital. On the positive side of the ledger, he saw no sign that the bloodsworn had infiltrated this far inland. As other travelers peeled off to individual destinations, Evan spurred ahead so that he could converse with their guide, a man of few words and fewer smiles.

"Where are all the mages?" Evan said as they turned onto a cobbled street that ran next to the river.

"They tend to stay on Gray Lady," the trader said, motioning toward a peak to the north with its head in the clouds. "They only descend into the Vale for business and politics."

Ahead, the graceful stone towers of a palace rose from high banks next to the river. Evan took a deep breath, releasing it slowly. The wolf queen within represented what might be his last hope for alliance and sanctuary.

Their guide directed them to an inn he knew, just outside the castle close, then took his leave.

Now that they were in the capital, Evan considered the best way to connect with the Fellsian authorities. He'd told everyone along the road that they were emissaries from Carthis, representing shipbuilders, merchants, and smugglers who hoped to do business with the queendom. But he worried whether that device would be enough to earn him a face-to-face with a queen grappling with the demands of an endless war. He needed to speak with her directly. It wouldn't do to be handed off to a quartermaster or castle steward.

That evening, he was sitting in the common room of the inn with Teza and Brody, debating his next move, when a young woman entered, bringing with her a blast of snow and cold and the unmistakable blue-white glow of magery. She drew his attention for other reasons, too. She looked more like a pirate than anyone he'd seen in the wetlands. Her hair was dyed black streaked with blue, and her exposed skin was layered in tattoos and piercings. Her skin might have been fair underneath, but it was burnt by sun and wind.

She also looked beaten down, exhausted, and sad, like the only survivor of a catastrophe.

She looked around the taproom, her gaze lighting briefly on Evan and his two companions. Dropping her hat and gloves on the table next to theirs, she elbowed her way through the crowd at the bar.

"You're still here, Captain?" the barkeep said, turning toward the kegs lining the wall without waiting for an order. "I thought you'd left yesterday."

"The queen asked me to stay a little longer," the woman said. "She's still—she needed—" She stopped, cleared her throat. "She still had some questions she wanted answered before I go."

Evan came instantly alert. This chance encounter might be a stroke of luck. This captain, whoever she was, could be his connection to the queen.

The barkeep plunked two brimming cups down in front of her. "Too bad," he said. "I know you're anxious to get back to your ship."

Even better, she *was* a mariner, maybe even a privateer working for the queen.

"At least maybe the weather'll be better when I head to

the coast," she said, pulling out her purse.

The barkeep shook his head. "On the house," he said. "We all appreciate what you're doing, ma'am."

Evan watched her carry the cups to her table and settle heavily into her seat. He raised his cup. "Fair winds, following seas, and a safe harbor at journey's end," he said in Common. It was the traditional sailor's blessing.

She turned and studied him, her eyes narrowed. Then took in Teza and Brody as well. "And the same to you." She turned back to her ale.

"We are merchants from Carthis," Evan said. "We are on our way to meet with your queen to discuss the possibility of trade between our countries."

"Merchants, are you?" The captain raised an eyebrow.

"Sort of," Evan said, turning his cup between his hands.

"You look like a wizard to me," she said, using the northern term.

"Sort of," Evan said again.

"And a pirate."

"Sort of." He laughed. "Since you brought it up, you look a bit like a pirate yourself."

This time, he managed to break through her brusque resistance. "I'm not a pirate," she said, "but I am a ship's captain." She extended her hand. "I'm Hadley DeVilliers."

Her name was vaguely familiar, but he couldn't place where he'd heard it. He gripped her hand, and the sting of magic flowed between them. "Lucky Faris."

"Faris?" Her grip tightened before she let go. "I was thinking of a different name."

"You must be thinking of a different pirate," Evan said, meeting her gaze.

"Really?" she said. "I could have sworn that you were Evan Strangward, known as the Stormcaster of the Indio."

Brody and Teza shifted in their seats, their hands sliding toward their weapons. DeVilliers noticed—he knew she did—but pretended not to.

Evan ran his finger around the rim of his glass, playing for time. Of course she would figure it out, being a mage, and a ship's captain. There weren't that many pirates with auras.

"Congratulations, Captain, you've found me out." Evan swallowed down his ale and signaled the bartender for another. "I hope that doesn't ruin our nascent friendship."

She raised an eyebrow. "You don't talk like any pirate I've ever met," she said.

"That's because you've never met a pirate like me," Evan said.

"You're a long way from the ocean, Stormcaster," De-Villiers said. "Where's your ship?" She looked around the room, as if he might have hung it on a hook by the door.

"Actually, I seem to be without a ship at the moment," Evan said.

"Ah," she said, shaking her head. "A shipless pirate? There's nothing sadder—or more dangerous—than that."

"What about you? What's your ship?"

"The *Sea Wolf*. She sails out of Chalk Cliffs. Have you heard of her?"

Evan nearly choked on his cider. Then checked their surroundings to see if she'd brought any crew with her. She had not. It was just the four of them, so he had the numbers.

"I take it you have," she said, her eyes crinkling in amusement.

The *Sea Wolf* was the sleek, three-masted flagship of the Fellsian navy. It was the bane of pirates and Ardenine warships alike. Its captain was known as one of the savviest masters afloat.

It was just his luck that he'd run into the chief officer of the Fellsian navy in a mountain town. A naval officer who looked like a pirate. One of the few wetlanders who would recognize him.

She tilted her chin up. "Now that we've been introduced, I have a question. I've heard rumors about your Stormborn crew—that they are fierce fighters with reddish auras." She pointed at Teza and Brody. "Here is living proof. What does it mean, and how do they get that way?"

Evan shrugged, downplaying it. "It simply indicates that they are sworn to me."

"I'm sworn to the Gray Wolf queen, but I've not grown furry ears," DeVilliers said, running a hand through her hair as if to verify. "So these Stormborn—they are not wizards?"

Evan thought of describing them as *made mages*, but that would naturally spawn questions as to exactly how they were made, which was territory he didn't want to get into. Blood magery was not a topic he wanted to raise on a first meeting.

"Not exactly. I suppose you could say that they are mages with specialized gifts."

DeVilliers cocked her head, as if still puzzled. "Such as?"

"They are fierce fighters," Evan said. "Very difficult to kill."

He deflected three more questions before the Fellsian captain realized that he'd said all he was going to say on that topic. That didn't mean that she was out of questions.

"So you're from Carthis," she mused. "Tell me, have you ever heard of a musical instrument called a 'jafasa'?"

Evan could not fathom why this captain would be asking this particular question at this particular time. He nodded. "They are traditional instruments used by the horselords of Carthis, because they are light and portable. They are rare these days, because they are so difficult to play."

DeVilliers toyed with a small dagger, flipping it and catching it in a way that might cost anyone else a finger. "Are they . . . magical at all?"

"Only in that they are good for making the time pass

more quickly," Evan said.

"You've explained these red mages. Tell me, have you ever seen a mage with an amulet embedded in his skin?"

This time, at least, Evan was somewhat prepared for the verbal cannonball. Still, it was all he could do to maintain his relaxed stance, to resist taking hold of his amulet and fighting his way out of the room. Evan sensed Teza and Brody shifting their weight, leaning forward, preparing to fight or flee.

He conjured up a puzzled frown. "Are you speaking of someone in particular? Someone you have seen or heard of?" *Was someone asking about magemarks recently?*

"I . . . I've heard about it and wondered if it was true," DeVilliers said.

As a liar, she had a long way to go.

Sticking with bewilderment, he said, "Is it supposed to be something that was done intentionally, or was it the result of a horrible accident?"

She laughed. "I just wondered if you'd seen that before, is all." After a pause, she fortunately changed the subject. "Is my queen expecting you?"

Evan considered lying, but decided that might lead to trouble later on. "No," he said.

"Why would she want to meet with you? What kind of trade are you proposing?"

Maybe it was because Evan knew that she didn't believe his cover story. Maybe it was because she seemed like a kindred spirit. But he found himself telling the truth.

Sort of.

"Actually, the most important thing I have to offer is information and a possible alliance," Evan said.

"An alliance with a notorious pirate without a ship?" DeVilliers laughed. "That seems like a good way to end with your throat cut and your purse stolen."

"I have ships at home," Evan said, growing testy in spite of himself. "We sail both the Desert Coast and the wetland coast from the Southern Islands to Invaders Bay. Your navy is small, and stretched thin. There's no reason we cannot travel with a full hold both ways."

"So you'll sell us goods and then steal from us?"

"Frankly, the takings are better farther south," Evan said. "Everything we steal from Arden helps you. Plus, we can alert you to dangers that you might not anticipate." Evan stopped with that.

DeVilliers was giving him a close look-over, too. Finally, she seemed to have come to a decision.

"I will see the queen tomorrow, and will let her know about your desire for a meeting."

"Thank you, Captain," Evan said. "I hope you'll let her know how much I—"

"I'll make no promises. This is a bad time to request an audience. I'll send a message to you here at the inn if I'm able to arrange something."

Evan wanted to go on, to tell this navy captain about the

danger bearing down on Chalk Cliffs, especially because she was bent on returning there. But he couldn't risk it. She did, after all, look like a pirate. There was no telling who she really sailed for.

After all, Tully Samara sailed for Latham Strangward. Until he didn't.

BACK FROM THE DEAD

Adrian sul'Han and Lila Byrne took the North Road from Ardenscourt to the border at Marisa Pines Pass, finally traveling the way they'd planned, back in the fall, before their long and eventful winter in the Ardenine capital.

Ash had accomplished his mission. The king of Arden was dead, and an alliance between Arden and the mysterious empress in the east had been averted, but this small triumph still tasted like ashes in his mouth. Given a choice, would he have traded Jenna's death for King Gerard's?

He'd not been offered a choice, and what was done was done. He recalled an argument he'd had with his teacher, Taliesin Beaugarde, back at Oden's Ford, what seemed like a lifetime ago.

"The day will come that you'll wish you were a better healer," the Voyageur had said.

"Teach me how to raise the dead," he'd said, "and then we'll talk."

He still believed that. Even the most skilled healer can only delay the inevitable. Eventually, they lose. Killers and healers both work the borderlands between life and death. The difference is that, at best, healing is a temporary victory. The dead stay dead.

Their chosen road took them through Delphi, now ruled by a coalition of Delphian patriots. The town was swarming with travelers, so that it wasn't easy to find a place to stay. The snows had been deep and relentless in late winter, and many travelers had stayed longer than they'd planned on, waiting for better weather. The city was in a bit of a hangover from its recent victory celebration, now grappling with the hard work of self-rule. There was still at least a salvo of Highlanders working with the fledgling Delphian army, but no one they knew.

So, in the interest of speed and safety, Ash and Lila did not announce themselves. He preferred not to have his return to the queendom heralded by a bird from Delphi. His father had given him a message for his mother when he lay dying on the streets of Ragmarket. Ash felt like he owed it to his mother to deliver it in person. Lila, too, seemed eager to move on, so they pushed on north after spending just one night in the gritty mining town.

The road north was crowded, too, in both directions. Families separated by the long occupation were taking advantage of the open border to visit relatives they hadn't seen in decades.

Security was still tight at the border crossing between Delphi and the queendom. The border officer seemed to know Lila, though, and so accepted her companion, Ash Hanson, a farrier from Tamron. Ash kept expecting to see someone he knew, worrying that he might be recognized, but it didn't happen. He guessed he was scarcely recognizable as the bookish, solitary thirteen-year-old who'd disappeared after his father's murder.

As they climbed toward the pass, the air carried the sweet promise that spring would come. At lower altitudes, he saw maiden's kiss and trout lily, buttercups and foamflowers and trillium. The names came back to him readily, as if he'd never been away. Who knew that the memory of flowers went so deep? Whenever they stopped to rest the horses, even Lila picked a few sprigs from the roadside. Who knew that Lila was fond of flowers?

At higher altitudes, flowers became scarce, and eventually the trail changed from mud to beaten-down snow. The high pass was a tunnel of weeping ice that would freeze again with nightfall. Now, the wind blew down from Hanalea, carrying with it the lonely sound of howling wolves. Gooseflesh rose on Ash's neck and arms.

When the wolves walk, the queendom is in danger. That's what the clan elders said.

The wolves are always walking in this queendom, Ash thought.

For once, Lila did more thinking than talking. Just past the top of the pass, she reined in and dismounted, then walked along the trailside, as if searching for something.

"What are you looking for?" Ash looked down at her from atop his pony.

"Here it is." Lila dropped to her knees beside a half-buried stone marker. Using her gloved hands, she brushed snow away from it, then laid a small bunch of flowers on top.

"What is that?"

"My grandfather died here, defending your mother," Lila said, coming to her feet and scrubbing snow off the knees of her breeches. "Your father found his body."

"That was *here*?" After Hanalea's death, the queen had kept her other children close, so Ash had spent little time exploring the borderlands.

She nodded. "I usually stop, whenever I come through here. I consider it a monument to foolish self-sacrifice." Fitting her boot into the stirrup, she remounted her pony. "Let's go."

As Ash and Lila descended into the Vale, the trail widened until it was more of a road. Ash was shocked by how much had changed. Many small farms had been abandoned, their buildings falling into disrepair. Though Gray Wolf banners still flew celebrating the Delphian victory at Solstice, some homes stood dark and empty, their windows as opaque as the eyes of the dead.

"Too many houses, not enough people these days," Lila said, following his gaze. "It's hard to work the land with so many off fighting in the summers."

The Dyrnnewater was running high, fed by the melting snow, roaring down out of the mountains on her way to the sea. They crossed the river several times on arched stone bridges, freezing spray needling their faces.

"Lila," Ash said, "could I ask a favor?"

"Depends."

"Just hear me out. When my father was murdered, it was like I turned into a different person. I did some things I'm not proud of."

"Look," Lila said, "if you want absolution, go to a speaker or a priest. I'm hardly in a position to give you advice."

"I'm not asking for advice *or* absolution," Ash growled. "I'm asking you to keep quiet about my being at Ardenscourt—all of that. I'd really like to go back to being Adrian sul'Han, aspiring healer. Just give me this, and I'll owe you."

"You think you can shed your past like a set of scummery smallclothes?" Lila raised an eyebrow. "If I were you, I'd want to take credit. I won't say a word, if that's what you want, but you'd better come up with your own story about where you've been all this time."

Dirt turned to brick and cobblestones as they followed the Way of the Queens through the market districts of Southbridge and Ragmarket. Ash saw little on offer there—bags of barley, mostly, and rice from the Shivering Fens. Even the pawnshops and secondhand shops had little to display—most likely everything of value had been sold off long ago. Food was dear, though clan-made goods were less expensive than he remembered, reflecting the law of supply and demand.

Ash was no longer the boy who had fled the Vale four years ago, driven by grief and guilt. He knew he shouldn't expect to find the city that he remembered on his return. He had changed, and it made sense that the city would, too. His head told him that, but his heart wasn't listening. The Vale he was returning to seemed smaller, shabbier, and sadder—the visible cost of five years of brutal war.

They stowed their ponies at a livery outside of the castle close. Maybe he should find a place to stay, so he could bathe and get a good night's sleep before he presented himself at court.

You're just stalling. The queen's reaction to his return would have little to do with his appearance or state of hygiene. According to Lila, his mother had known he was alive, and at Oden's Ford, all along. Yet she'd never reached out and tried to persuade him to come home.

He'd prefer that Lila wasn't there to see the reunion. He knew she would have something to say, now or later.

"You don't have to come with me right now," Ash said as they approached the castle close. "If you want to get settled, or if you have other things to take care of, you—"

"Oh, I wouldn't miss it," Lila said, rolling her eyes. "If the queen is in her castle, no doubt my father will be there, too. Besides, I've always wanted to see what it looks like inside."

Ash stopped so quickly that Lila all but ran into him. "You've never been to the palace?"

"Well, I've been *around* the palace," Lila said. "I've been in the stable yard and the gatehouse and the army barracks. I've been in quite a few inns and taverns and alleys." She laughed at his expression. "Look, it's not like my father wants to meet with his black sheep, smuggler, spy daughter in the palace or have me call on the queen. There are too many enemy eyes and ears there. It might have put the prince of the realm at risk, and we wouldn't want that."

Ash, momentarily speechless, stared at her. I left of my own accord, he thought. But she's been shut out by her own father because of the job she'd been assigned to do— nannying me.

"I'm sorry, Lila," he said simply. "I didn't know."

"No worries," she said. "I only have to see it once. My home is on the coast, with my aunts, uncles, and cousins.

Besides, things have changed around here. You won't get through the gates without me."

Lila had a writ from the Queen's Guard that was enough to get them inside the walls of the close and across the drawbridge into the inner bailey. At the palace gate, they ran into a stone wall in the form of Ruby Greenholt.

Ruby was a war orphan who'd been adopted by two of the queen's most trusted Wolves—Pearlie Greenholt and Talia Abbott. Ruby and Ash had played together as children, since her parents often escorted the royal family when they traveled within the queendom.

Ruby was as tall as Ash, but was still totally recognizable with her auburn hair pulled back onto the nape of her neck, her face nearly freckled over from the sun. When he'd left, she'd just been accepted into the elite Gray Wolves. Now a lieutenant's scarf was knotted around her neck, so she must've done well. He stood there mutely, hands clenched, heart pounding in his throat, waiting to be recognized.

But he wasn't, at least not at first. Ruby was all business.

"I know these are the queen's public hours, but she's not receiving anyone today," Ruby said. "I don't know whether she'll be granting audiences anytime this week." Looking them up and down, taking in their travel-worn appearance, she softened a bit. "It looks like you've been a long time on the road. I'm sorry if you've wasted a trip."

Lila hesitated, shooting a look at Ash as if to see if he

wanted to speak up. When he didn't, she said, "Tell her it's Lila Barrowhill. I think she'll remember my name."

Ruby shook her head. "Her Majesty said she was not to be disturbed, and so it doesn't matter who you are."

"What about Captain Byrne?" Lila persisted. "Is he available? Tell him Lila is here and needs to see him."

She shook her head. "He's in with the queen and some others, meeting with—they're having a meeting," she finished lamely. "If I disturb him, I'll be disturbing the queen."

"Ruby," Ash said softly. "Don't you know me?"

Their eyes met, with Ruby's as hard and blank as an ice field. Then doubt crept into her face, followed by disbelief and a trace of fear. "By the Martyred Queens," she whispered. "It can't be—is it really . . . Adrian?"

"Yes," he said, clearing his throat. "It's me. I am so glad to see you alive and well."

"Me? You're glad to see *me* alive?" Ruby's voice was rising. She gripped the front of his coat and fingered the rough fabric, patted him on the cheek with her rough palm. "Blood and bones! You feel real enough. You're so tall, and thin, and—that head of hair! Are you risen from the dead in our hour of need or what?"

Adrian shook his head, his cheeks heating with embarrassment. "Not exactly. I am alive, and it's a long story, but right now I would very much like to see my mother."

"Follow me," Ruby said, turning and striding off down

the hallway so that Ash had to trot to keep up. As they twisted and turned down the corridors, it was like revisiting the time-blurred setting of a childhood dream, the spaces narrower and smaller and plainer than he remembered.

Lila trailed along behind them, shifting her eyes from ceiling to floor, peering down cross corridors.

"It's not as fancy as I thought it would be," she murmured. "I guess I've gotten used to the palace at Ardenscourt."

Really? Ash thought. I never got used to that place.

When they reached the familiar door that led to the queen's audience chamber, Ruby pounded on it. And then, as if she couldn't wait for a response, she wrenched it open, to be met by a snarling brace of the queen's Gray Wolf guards.

They quit snarling when they saw it was Ruby, but they didn't step out of the way. "Greenholt!" one of them said. "You heard the morning orders. What the hell are you doing?"

"Just . . . fetch Captain Byrne," Ruby said.

But the captain was already on his way. The commander of the Queen's Guard was leaner and grayer than before, though his eyes were as sharp as they ever were.

"I told you we were not to be disturbed, Lieutenant," he growled. "For *any* reason."

"Sir," Ruby said, then looked beyond him, into the room. "Your Majesty. It—it—it—"

"Captain Byrne," Lila said, oddly formal to be speaking

to her father. "We're back."

They stared mutely at each other for what seemed like a long time. Then Byrne pulled Lila into a hard embrace. "Sweet Lady of Grace," he whispered. "I thought I'd lost you, too."

Without waiting for an introduction, Ash stepped around Ruby and fully into the room, where two guards seized hold of him.

He spotted his mother immediately, sitting by the fire, a glass of wine cradled between her hands. Like nearly everything else, she looked smaller than he remembered. Her face was drawn and sad, and she was dressed all in a sooty black that absorbed the light. Was it possible she'd never left off mourning colors? He recognized Aunt Mellony, dressed all in black as well, and Micah Bayar, looking grim and grave, but then that was his default. And, next to him, that must be Cousin Julianna. He took another look around, to make sure. No. Lyss wasn't there.

Hearing the commotion at the door, his mother stood and craned her neck, peering at them.

"Hello, Mother," Ash said, his voice echoing through the suddenly silent hall. "I'm back, and I am so very sorry."

19

ONE-ON-ONE

The blood left his mother's face as if she were, in fact, seeing a ghost. She lost hold of the glass in her hand and it fell, scattering shards of glass and droplets of blood-red wine all around her feet. Planting her hands on the arms of her chair, she stood. She took one step toward him, then another, her boots crunching on the glass, her arms outstretched, palms up. "Hanalea's blood and bones," she whispered. "It can't be—is it really you?" Her expression mingled hope and dread, as if she didn't dare believe the evidence of her eyes. All around her, the faces of the council members were like spots of suspicion and doubt.

Strange. From what Lila had said, his mother and Captain Byrne had known all along that he was alive and hiding out in Oden's Ford. But this reaction was more like . . . like she'd actually thought he was dead.

Aunt Mellony stood, also, her face even paler than usual, pointing a shaking hand at Ash. "It's a trick, Raisa," she said. "A despicable Ardenine trick. There's a resemblance, I'll admit, but—"

His mother shook her head, raising a hand to hush her sister, her eyes still fixed on his face.

He wanted to rush forward, to embrace her, so that she could feel that he was living flesh and blood, but the guards still had hold of him, waiting for some signal from their queen. Anyway, that was her move to make. He couldn't blame her if she ordered him out of the queendom he'd abandoned for so long.

All at once, it was as if the wall of doubt came down. His mother leapt forward, closing the distance between them, and flung her arms around him as the two guards hastily released him and stepped back.

"They said you were dead," she murmured, her forehead pressed against his chest. Her entire body was trembling, trembling, and so thin that she seemed fragile, even though he knew she was all muscle and bone. "When I—when I thought I'd lost you, too, I was closer to despair than I've ever been."

"I'm sorry," Adrian said, over and over. And, sometimes, "I'm so sorry." Wishing he could put more power into the words.

Finally, she took a step back. Coming up on her toes, she put her hands on either side of his face, exploring the bone structure with her fingers. "When did you get so tall—and so sad?"

"I . . . need to explain . . . where I've been and what I've been doing . . . all this time," he said awkwardly.

"And you will," his mother said, pulling him close again. "Right now, I just want to hold on to you."

In the background, he could hear Captain Byrne barking orders. One of them must have been to clear the room, because everyone disappeared, except for a handful of Wolves, including Ruby. They stayed close, keeping a close eye on Ash until Captain Byrne ushered the two of them into the small reception room attached to the queen's private suite.

Byrne hesitated in the doorway. "It's good to have you home again, Prince Adrian."

"Prince Adrian" hit Ash's ear wrong. It had been a long time since anyone had called him that. Besides, he'd never really thought of himself as a prince—just the son of a queen, and the brother of the heir to the throne. He'd used so many names since he left home that none of them seemed quite right.

Byrne turned to the queen. "I'll give the two of you some privacy. Is there anything else you need?"

In a way, Adrian dreaded the idea of privacy, terrified as he was of a heart-to-heart. He had no defense to offer, no excuse for what he'd done, and now he was getting ready to lie about it again.

"What about Lyss?" he said, asking what seemed an obvious question. "She should be here. I need to apologize to her. I made her a promise, and I've really let her down."

"Lyss is at Chalk Cliffs," his mother said, and bit her lip. She turned back to Byrne. "Tell the others that we'll have a small reception after the council meeting tomorrow."

Byrne cocked his head. "Will there be a council meeting tomorrow? I thought all meetings were cancelled this week."

"That was before I began to believe in miracles again," the queen said. "I'm sure we'll have lots to discuss tomorrow."

After Byrne saluted and left, Ash used flash to rekindle the fire on the hearth, spending considerably more time on it than the task required.

"Is that your father's amulet?" she said finally, to his back.

Ash swung around to face her, his cheeks burning. "You've probably been wondering what happened to it. Da gave it to me that day in Ragmarket. I'll understand if you want it back."

The queen shook her head. "If he gave it to you, keep it. It suits you." She motioned to two chairs under the window. "That will *do*, Adrian. Let's sit."

Ash sat. His mother sat across from him. He had too

much to say, and no clue as to how to begin. He'd hoped she might begin spitting out questions, but she just kept looking at him as if memorizing every new detail.

Finally, she breathed deeply and said, "You smell of the road—sweat and horses and leather, meadowsweet and pine." She put up a hand when he tried to apologize. "No. I like it. My father was a clan trader, and he always came home smelling like faraway places. It reminds me of something your father said once." She closed her eyes, remembering. "He said, 'I want to breathe you in for the rest of my life.'"

Ash swallowed hard, guilt rising in him. "Mother, I—"

"We are wolves, Adrian. For us, scent is the seat of memory. It is how wolves recognize family, friends, and enemies." She paused. "I miss the road. Wolves run free. Do you know that I have not been out of the queendom since the war began?" She smiled wistfully. "My children have gone much farther afield."

Right, Ash thought. Your daughter Hanalea went into the borderlands, and was murdered. Your son went south, and became a murderer. And Lyss—

"Speaking of traveling, what's Lyss doing in Chalk Cliffs?" The Chalk Cliffs he remembered was little more than a gritty port with a military barracks, bars and clicket-houses, and a stone keep. What business would his sister have in such a place?

That question must have shown on his face, because his

mother said, "Alyssa has changed since you last saw her. And I'm afraid that she's angry with me right now."

Ash was mystified. "Angry? I can understand if she's angry with *me*, but why would she—?"

"Soon after you . . . disappeared . . . I found out you were alive, and I didn't tell her."

"So you did know," he said. "Lila told me that you did."

His mother nodded. "I knew. I decided—I decided that after Hanalea's and Han's murders, maybe you were safer there, under an assumed name, than here at court. I didn't tell Alyssa, though."

She fingered the wolf ring that always hung from a chain around her neck. "We'd already had your funeral, and she was just beginning to recover from that. I thought it was too dangerous a secret to tell an eleven-year-old. Knowing your sister, she would have insisted on going to Oden's Ford and bringing you back. If agents from Arden had found out where you were, they would have murdered you."

"Well," he said. "They tried."

"As I found out, a few days ago, when the team I sent to Oden's Ford to fetch you home returned with the news of the attack on your dormitory and your apparent death." Tears welled up, and spilled over once again. "I blamed myself."

"I'm the one who ran away," Ash said. It hadn't occurred to him that his mother would hear about the attack, because, for all intents and purposes, he was already dead. He hadn't known that Taliesin had ratted him out.

"Why did you decide to bring me home now, after four years?"

"There was an assassination attempt on your sister."

That punch to the gut nearly folded him in two. "Wait—what? The bastards went after *Lyss*? They're targeting children now? Is she . . . what did she—"

His mother raised an eyebrow. "She's not a child. She's just two years younger than you, and she's grown up fast," she said. "That's what happens when you go away. You think time stops at home while you grow and change." She paused, in case he wanted to argue, but he didn't.

"So. She overheard me talking about bringing you home from the academy. She was furious on the one hand, but so very happy that you were alive. She went to Chalk Cliffs to meet your ship when it arrived. And then, when Captain DeVilliers and the others told her you were dead after all—"

Ash sighed. "No wonder she's angry."

"Right. You could have been together, these past four years, but I left you there, unprotected, to be murdered. That's how she sees it. So, when she . . . when she heard the news, she refused to come back here. She said she was afraid she would say something unforgivable. I've not seen her since I visited her in Delphi soon after Solstice."

Another unexpected consequence of what he'd done.

He'd never considered that it might drive a wedge between his mother and sister.

"Will she come home now, do you think?"

"I think the news that you've survived will bring her home," the queen said, with a wry smile. "Especially if you send her a message and ask her to come."

"I'd like to go to Chalk Cliffs and bring her home myself," Ash said.

"No!" She said it with such force that he flinched back. "I'm sorry," she said, "but you've just come back and I'll not have you leaving again right away. I've come to feel like each time I say good-bye to my children it may be the last time I see them."

"Right," he said, chastened. "How do you want to handle it, then?"

"Here's what we'll do. The weather has been so bad that we've received no communication from Chalk Cliffs in weeks. I think that's easing now. General Dunedain's in Delphi right now, getting ready for the spring campaign. We'll ask her to send a salvo to Chalk Cliffs to relieve Lyss, and send her back to Delphi. We'll meet her there."

To relieve Lyss? Relieve her of what? Ash felt like he'd walked into the third act of a play.

His mother rose, crossed to the fireplace, and brought back a framed portrait. "This was done at Solstice." She handed it to him.

His mother was right. Lyss was no longer a child. What

had seemed like scrappiness in childhood had become confidence and resolve. She was all golds and coppers—deep golden hair, coppery skin, steady brown eyes. Her chin was tilted up a bit, as if to say, *Try me.*

Most surprising of all, she was wearing a spattercloth uniform with an officer's scarf.

Ash looked up at the queen. "Lyss is wearing a uniform. Does that mean she's in the *army*?"

His mother nodded. "She's a captain in the Highlanders now, and she has made quite a reputation for herself."

"But . . . what happened to music, and drawing, and stories? She has so much talent, and—"

"I believe she's decided that those skills are not well suited for the world she lives in. But, happily, she seems to excel at warfare, too. They call her the Gray Wolf in the field."

Jenna's words came back to him. *I will try and think of you as a wolf called Adam.* She'd seen the wolf in him, too.

Is that what war does? It turns us into wolves? Or does the wolf have to be there to begin with?

"Adrian?" His mother touched his arm and he realized he'd gone silent for too long.

"I'm sorry. I just hope that she'll return to the arts someday."

"I do, too. I hope the time will come when we don't need her martial talents so much, anymore. We've had so many losses. Most of us have had to develop new skills.

Your cousin Julianna, for instance. She's directing the intelligence service now."

"Julianna?" Ash shook his head. "I never would have predicted that."

"She's very different from Mellony. Very different," she repeated, for emphasis. "That's becoming clearer every day."

That had raised another question, one that Ash was afraid to ask. "If Julianna is heading up the intelligence service, then what about Cat Tyburn? What's she doing?"

"She's dead. Murdered. Nearly three years ago now."

"Cat, too?" Ash took in that news like a punch to the gut. "I can't imagine anyone taking her by surprise."

"None of us can. No one is safe, apparently."

"So maybe Lyss is safer in the army than here in the city. At least there, you know you have a fight on your hands."

"Maybe. Anyway, it's part of her role as a wartime queen."

Ash handed the painting of his sister back. "I can understand why soldiers are willing to follow her. She looks . . . formidable."

"She is. It's not easy to get her to sit for a portrait. I tried to persuade her to wear a gown suitable for her name day, but she said she'd rather look like herself. I think she wants to put any possible suitors on notice."

"Suitors?" Ash said, feeling pummeled. "Isn't she a little young to be thinking about that?"

His mother smiled at his expression. "Her name day is this June, and that's when that kind of talk begins. Not by her choice. She's about as eager to get married as I was at that age."

"That's just a few months away." It wasn't easy to get his mind around that. It was as if he was going to lose his sister all over again.

"It doesn't mean that she'll be getting married anytime soon. Though I wasn't that much older than she is when I married your father." She sighed and twisted her wedding ring. "I'm glad, now, that I married young, so that Han and I had more time together. It was twenty-five years, but it just flew by." She stood, extending her hand. "Speaking of your father, let's go see him."

IN THE CITY
OF THE DEAD

His mother led the way through narrow passageways and up back staircases, taking routes he'd probably once known but had since forgotten. Fellsmarch Castle was a labyrinth of hidden ways, some of them built by his many-greats grandfather Alger Waterlow, and many added since. Growing up, Ash and his friends, including Finn sul'Mander, Ty Gryphon, and Ruby Greenholt, had burrowed into all the dark places, seeking routes that would enable them to go wherever they wanted, while avoiding parents and schoolmasters and nurses.

His mother had always had the uncanny ability to find him when she really wanted to. "Don't fool yourself, Adrian. Though I don't pretend to know all the secrets of this palace, there is no one living who knows them better than me."

Eventually, Ash and his mother crossed the bridge into the cathedral temple. Ash had spent hours in the libraries there, studying old histories and books about healing plants and poisons and magic.

He'd spent less time in the sanctuary, preferring the small temple in his mother's garden or Southbridge Temple, which seemed cozier to a small boy.

The Gray Wolf queens were not buried here. Their ashes were interred on the flank of a mountain that would forever after carry their names. Wolves run free.

But the cathedral was the final resting place for generations of royal relations, temple speakers, court officials, and friends of the Line. Most High Wizards preferred to be buried with their own kind on Gray Lady, where the Wizard Council met and many wizards had estates. But some had chosen to be buried here at the cathedral, close to the center of power.

The crypt was reserved for the most important of the dead—royal princes and princesses, consorts, and those bound captains who did not choose to be buried with their queens.

At first, Ash thought the sanctuary was unchanged from the last time he'd seen it, at his sister Hanalea's funeral. But now he saw that there was a new side chapel, flooded with light from an adjacent courtyard.

Instead of leading him down the stairs into the crypt, his mother led him into the light.

Like most older temples, this chapel had apertures oriented to admit the rising and setting sun. Other than that, it was more of a library, with shelves lined with books about botanicals and horticulture. A plaque on the wall was inscribed Alister Reading Room.

"This began as your father's project," his mother said. "It was going to be a surprise for me, to honor your sister Hanalea. Hana didn't live long enough to be crowned, so she wasn't buried in the Spirits like the rest of us. Han didn't want to send her to the crypt—he couldn't imagine that a young woman would want to go down there with all the old people. Plus, she wouldn't want to hear speakers droning on every day. As you know, some are better than others.

"I wanted her close, though. I wanted to be able to come see her whenever I wished. So he created a churchyard." She threw open a set of wrought-iron doors in a design featuring the Waterlow ravens, the royal wolves, Hanalea's winged torch, and the briar rose.

The courtyard reminded Ash of a churchyard in a small mountain town, or a private family cemetery on an estate. Trees had been planted, but they were still small, though the courtyard would be shaded for a good part of the day by the surrounding temple. It was slightly overgrown with meadowgrass, as a country churchyard should be.

Their family plot contained three stones. The largest was for Princess Hanalea, as befitted her status.

Hanalea ana'Raisa, Princess Heir
34th in the New Line of Gray Wolf Queens
Naemed Running Wolf in the Uplands
Killed in the Borderlands
With her Bound Captain
Simon Byrne
Wolves Run Free

On the other side of Hana's plot, his father's stone.

Hanson Alister (Han sul'Alger)
High Wizard
Consort to Queen Raisa ana'Marianna
33rd in the New Line of Gray Wolf Queens
Naemed Hunts Alone in the Uplands
"You don't get what you don't go after."

The third stone was his own.

Adrian sul'Han (Ash)
Prince of the Realms
Wizard and Healer
Son of Queen Raisa ana'Marianna
And Han sul'Alger, Consort

Streetlord of the Borderlands
Between Life and Death

It was more than peculiar, standing here, reading his own gravestone inscription, feeling unworthy of it.

"You really went to a lot of trouble," he said, embarrassed. "You could have just built a cairn or something. Especially once you knew I was really alive."

"Your sister insisted. At first, she wanted nothing to do with holding a funeral for you. She never lost hope that you were still alive. When we went ahead anyway, she refused to attend. Finally, I was able to persuade her to take charge of your epitaph. That's what she chose."

Ash was beginning to realize what a force his sister had become. She occupied space, even when she wasn't here.

His mother knelt and began pulling out some weeds that had crept into one of the flower beds around the plot. "Remember when we used to work in the garden together?" she said.

Ash stared down at the flower bed. The flowers were familiar—foxflowers, and trueheart, and maiden's kiss. Red, white, and blue. The same as the ones his father had bought his mother on the day he died.

"Those flowers," he said hoarsely, pointing. "That was—that was—"

"I know," the queen said, without looking up. "Your father knew these were my favorite flowers. They still are.

I refuse to let an assassin take that enjoyment away from me."

Ash knelt beside his mother, awash in memories from when they gardened together when he was a boy. At the time, he'd mainly noticed her many absences, their many differences. Now he remembered how much they'd shared.

He cleared his throat. "Speaking of Da, I have a message for you. From him."

This time, she looked up at him. "A message?"

He took his mother's hands and looked into her eyes. It was a job to force the words out, though they were engraved on his soul. "Something he said to me that day in Ragmarket. When he knew he was dying, he said . . . he said to tell you . . . that having you . . . that being with you . . . that loving you—it was worth it." He swallowed hard, then repeated it softly. "He said it was *worth* it."

His father's amulet buzzed against Ash's skin, startling him. It was as if it were underlining the message, or reacting to it. But he kept his focus on his mother's face.

She sat for a long moment, eyes closed, until tears leaked out from under her lashes. She swallowed hard, and then said in a husky voice, "I might have to add that to both our stones."

"So it was worth it for you?"

"How can you ask that question?" she said. "Falling in love in wartime is chancy, just like having children. We've had a lot of pain, but a lot of joy, all the same. Of course it's been worth it for me, too."

"How much time does it take?" Ash blurted.

His mother frowned, as if puzzled. She let go of his hands and sat back on her heels. "How much time does it take for what?"

"How much time does it take to stop feeling guilty for surviving? How much time do you have to have together to make it worth the pain of saying good-bye?"

"There's not a rule for that," she said, searching his face. "You've met someone—haven't you." It was a statement, not really a question.

He nodded. "I met a girl," he said.

"Is she a student at the Ford?"

Memories rushed in at him from all sides—the acrid scent of the torches, the dance of the light on the walls of the dungeon, Jenna in her filthy finery, saying, "For a healer, you have a very dark soul."

He shook his head. "It's a long story—one maybe I'll tell later." *Once I figure out what to say.* "Anyway. Her name was Jenna. We weren't even together that long, so I don't know whether to call it love." He looked up at her. "How do you even know?"

"Love is not measured by the amount of time you spend together," his mother said. "It's how that time is spent." She smiled wryly. "Love moves fast in wartime—it has to. And it's not particularly useful to try to put a label on it."

"It doesn't matter, anyway," he said. "She's dead."

"Dead?" His mother sighed and squeezed his shoulder. "I'm so sorry, sweetling."

An hour with his mother, and he was already handing off sorrows. It wasn't fair.

"I feel stupid bringing this up," he said. "There's no comparison with what you had with Da, with what you lost, and yet—does it ever get easier? Do you ever wake up and it doesn't run you over, when you remember?"

She frowned, thinking. Ash liked that she didn't answer right away with a platitude or dismiss his pain as trivial.

"It does get easier," she said finally. "There will come a time when your memories will bring you more joy than pain. It's taken me four years to get to that point."

"I see." He took a quick breath. "I know I have no right to ask this, but—"

"But have I thought of remarrying?" She snorted. "Everyone else asks it, so why shouldn't you? The answer is yes, of course I've thought of it, but that's as far as it goes. I see no reason to marry right now. Sometimes it seems that I would only be putting one more person at risk."

"What do you mean?"

"Our family has suffered more than our share of loss, and yet the losses keep coming. The wolves keep running."

The queens of the Gray Wolf line saw wolves in times of danger and change. "Are you . . . are you seeing wolves now? Still?"

"The wolves are always with me, these days," his mother said, gripping the wolf ring that hung from a chain around her neck. "I can't help wondering if we are reaching the end of the Gray Wolf line."

Ash had never heard his mother sound so despondent. But then, so much had happened these past four years that he hadn't been around to see.

"No!" he practically shouted. And then, more quietly, "Mother, I—I can't believe that this—that this is all for nothing. I can't believe that we live in a world that rewards evil and punishes the good."

"Some speakers say that we must wait to be rewarded in the next life." She shook her head. "Forgive me for being maudlin. We should be celebrating your return from the dead, and looking forward to your reunion with Alyssa."

Clearly that was all she meant to say on the topic, because she stood, and said briskly, "Enough. I've asked Magret to open up your old room, and by now it should have had time to air out."

He looked up, startled. "Magret? She's still . . . in service?" He was going to say *alive*, but thought better of it.

"Don't be so surprised," the queen said, smiling. "Four years is a longer time in the life of a thirteen-year-old than in that of one who's nearing eighty. And she intends to serve until death calls her away."

Hanalea's Maidens were an order of warriors bound to

the service and protection of the Gray Wolf line. Magret had served as nurse, teacher, and protector to his mother and Aunt Mellony, and then to Hanalea, Adrian, and Lyss. She had brought an array of skills to the job. More than once, she'd drawn her sword to protect the royal family.

She had a tongue like a sword as well, when she believed that her young charges required correction. Ash didn't look forward to feeling the bite of it now.

A MIXED RECEPTION

Ash had been struggling to come up with a story to tell when his mother and her council began asking hard questions. They must know that he and Lila had been missing from school since Solstice. The next morning, at a private breakfast in her chambers, he asked about plans for a debriefing. But the queen seemed in no hurry to move on to that phase of this reunion.

"I had cleared my calendar so that I could spend this week at temple, mourning for you," she said wryly. "Since that's no longer necessary, we will lay plans for your resurrection. Rumors are flying already. I've scheduled one meeting with the council for this afternoon. Tonight, we'll hold a small reception for family, close friends, and high officials only. When people ask questions, tell them you'll need to speak with me first.

"Tomorrow, we'll announce your miraculous return with a service in the cathedral temple, a parade through the city, and a street party. Beginning the day after that, you'll have more than your fill of meetings. So enjoy these two days before the ordeal begins."

He had two days, then, to settle on a plan. He spent the rest of the morning being bathed, shaved, and shorn to make him as presentable as possible. To his surprise, he found four fine coats hanging in his closet, along with three pairs of breeches and a pair of clan-made boots.

"Where did these come from?" he asked Magret, who was filling drawers with smallclothes and shirts and tidying what didn't really need to be tidied.

"Most of those clothes belonged to your da, may he rest in peace," Magret said. She looked him up and down. "It might be that now you're big enough to fill them. Your sister the princess Alyssa had them cleaned and hung them in the closet so they'd be here when you returned."

Startled, Ash looked up at Magret. "She did? When?"

"Right after your father was killed and you were carried off. She never gave up hope that you were alive. She used to come in here now and then and brush the dust off so they'd be ready. On the day of your funeral she locked herself in her room and refused to come out." The eye she fixed on him was disapproving.

"I'm sorry I put her through that," Adrian said. He could spend the rest of his life apologizing and it still wouldn't be enough. There was no way to atone for this, no penance great enough to even the scales.

"Her Majesty had new stoles made for you with your father's ravens. They're in the drawer. Will you be needing anything else, Your Highness?"

Not if it comes with a lecture. "No, thank you."

"Don't forget, Her Majesty the Queen's reception begins at six, and it's quarter past five now. You'll hear the bells in the cathedral temple—"

"I remember," he said. "I'll be there." *She probably thinks I'll run out on that, too.* He waited until he was sure Magret was gone before he fingered the nearest coat, an emerald silk. He leaned down to sniff it, hoping it might still carry a trace of his father's scent, but, whether due to cleaning or the passage of time, it did not.

What would it have been like had he stayed? If he and Lyss had worked through their grief together instead of each on his or her own? He wouldn't have met Jenna, and Gerard Montaigne might still be alive. He might be married now. Or he might be dead.

There was no fair way to compare what had been with what might have been. He just had to find a way forward.

Here was a coat he recognized, one that sent his stomach plummeting into his boots. It was his father's clan mourning coat, stitched with his sister Hanalea's gray wolves.

On the back, the Waterlow ravens, and the High Wizard flame and sword down the sleeves. His father had worn it to Hana's funeral.

Ash sank onto the bed, cradling the coat in his arms, his tears falling on the leather and wool, his fingers tracing the intricate stitching. He shivered, the hairs on the back of his neck standing on end. It was almost as if his father had prepared this coat for him, blazoned with the signia of those Ash had loved and lost.

Should he wear it in honor of his father? Or would it be seen as arrogant, as if he'd wandered back home and made an immediate claim on his father's legacy, down to his serpent amulet?

He decided he didn't care.

It had been a long time since he'd worn anything but the drab brown healer's garb at Ardenscourt and the non-descript breeches and coats that had served him well on the road from Ardenscourt to Fellsmarch.

He was just fumbling with the tiny buttons on his shirt when someone banged on the door.

"Come," Ash said, guessing he was far enough along in dressing to entertain company.

It was Lila Barrowhill Byrne, unfamiliar in the blue uniform of the Queen's Guard. She ran her eyes up and down the length of him and snorted.

"Back for a day, and already tricked out like a proper princeling," she said, flopping into a chair. Something about the scene reverberated in Ash's memory, recalling his last day at Oden's Ford, when Lila barged into his room and invited him to a party at Wien House.

"You should talk," Ash said. "Looks like you're planning to join the family business."

She shook her head. "Nah," she said. "I'm in disguise."

"That's a disguise?" Ash raised an eyebrow.

"I'm disguised as someone who could fit in here," she said, thrusting her fingers into her collar and yanking at it until a button popped off. "That's better," she said. "This comes off as soon as I cross the border. By the way, you can forget Lila Byrne. I'm still Barrowhill."

"Barrowhill? I was just getting used to Byrne."

"As someone who has more names than a clicket-house rusher, you'll get no sympathy from me."

"But . . ."

"I'm a spy," Lila said. "And a smuggler and a fixer. If I want to keep working that line, I can't show up here at court and be Captain Amazing Byrne's daughter. If you think this place isn't full of spies, you're wrong. There's too great a chance I'll be seen by unfriendly eyes and heard by unfriendly ears." She gave him a measuring sort of look. "Somebody gave you up to Arden, and that somebody wasn't me. It wasn't widely known here at court, either— I hear that the queen didn't even tell your little sister. So who would it've been?"

Ash couldn't help thinking of Micah Bayar, his father's

default when it came to villains. "You'd probably know better than me," he said.

"Anyway. I need to get back to Ardenscourt before everyone forgets how very helpful I can be. Out of sight, out of mind, you know."

"You're going back there?" Ash stared at her.

"I'm leaving within the hour."

"I thought maybe you'd stay here permanently now that you don't have to watch over me at Oden's Ford." Though keeping Lila here had its risks, Ash was suddenly eager to have someone around who didn't remember him as a thirteen-year-old runaway. "I'm sure Captain Byrne could use your help to—"

"No!" Lila said. When Ash stared at her, she added, "I hate it here. Isn't that enough of a reason? This is just a job to me. The family I care about is at Wolf's Head, on the coast."

"Wolf's Head?"

"You wouldn't know it," Lila said. "You're not supposed to. Anyway, they're the ones who raised me. I'm traveling south by way of Spiritgate so I can visit with them."

"Oh," Ash said. "All right then."

But Lila seemed compelled to make her case. "You don't think the queendom needs eyes and ears in Arden with a new king and a civil war in the offing? Anyway, the food is better down there. I've never been much for barley, and I do love me some Tamric wine."

"Don't you think that with King Gerard dead and the thanes in rebellion, King Jarat will have enough on his hands without turning his eyes to the north? Especially since my mother didn't spurn *his* offer of marriage."

"Maybe," Lila said. "I wouldn't count on it. Besides, if this war ever ends, I'll be out of a job."

"Maybe," Ash said. "I wouldn't count on it."

After a brief silence, during which Lila showed no inclination to leave, Ash said, "Is there something you want, or are you just trying to fill the empty hour until you go?"

"Who will be at this reception tonight?" Lila was staring up at the ceiling, but Ash couldn't help thinking she was focused closely on his answer.

"I don't know," he said. "My mother said that it would be family, close friends, and high-ups. The general announcement of my resurrection isn't until tomorrow, so I can't imagine it would be a big crowd tonight."

"What about Shadow Dancer? Will he be there?" Lila cut her eyes toward Ash, then away again.

"If he's in town, I expect he will be," Ash said. "I haven't seen either Shadow or his father in years, and they were practically family, growing up." He paused. "Why?"

"Oh, I worked with Shadow quite a bit on various . . . projects . . . having to do with Arden," Lila said, nibbling on a fingernail. "The last time I saw him was at Chalk Cliffs. It was right after his fiancée was killed in an Ardenine attack. He was in pretty bad shape."

Ash was embarrassed to know so little about what had been happening in his homeland. Lila had never lived here; in fact, she said she hated it here, yet she was much more up on the latest news than he was.

"Bones," he said. "I didn't even know he was engaged. Who was she?"

"Her name was Aspen Silverleaf," Lila said. "A clan leatherworker. I suppose that's what he . . ." Her voice trailed off. "Anyway. I thought I'd better mention it."

"I didn't know about that. Thank you for letting me know, so I can avoid saying anything stupid."

"I'm mainly looking out for *him*," Lila said. "Don't worry, there's plenty of room for you to be stupid on lots of other topics." She said this with an echo of her usual snarkiness, but Ash could tell that her heart wasn't in it.

Just then, the cathedral temple bells sounded the quarter hour.

Ash draped his wizard stoles over his coat. They weighed on him, more than silk and stitchery ever had before. "I suppose I'd better go. Are you going to stop in for a little while?"

Lila came to her feet and shook her head. "Nah. I've seen the people I need to see. If I stay any longer, I'll see the people I'd just as soon avoid."

"Well, be careful," Ash said.

"I'm not the one with a target on his back." She hesitated

a moment, then grudgingly embraced him. "Take care of yourself, healer."

As soon as he was ushered into the queen's reception chamber, Ash all but ran into Micah Bayar. The wizard took a quick step back, nimbly avoiding the collision.

"Welcome home, Your Highness," Bayar said, inclining his head in a polite bow. "Your sudden resurrection has brought joy into your mother's heart after an unusually dark season, and for that I am glad."

Ash's heart-to-heart with Lila had kindled old suspicions. *Did Bayar know I was alive all along? Did my mother tell him or not? Did she trust him to know? Was he the one who betrayed me?* He tried not to stare at Bayar's High Wizard stoles—the colors he'd last seen draped over his father's shoulders.

Bayar made no attempt to hide his own slow study of Ash. "I see your father in you more clearly now than before," he said. It was impossible to tell from the wizard's tone and expression whether he thought that was a good thing or a bad thing.

"If you see any element of my father in me, I consider that a compliment," Ash said.

Bayar turned and motioned to a tall young wizard with white-blond hair, who stood just behind him and to one side. "I believe you know my nephew, Finn."

"Finn!" Ash said, with real warmth this time. "It's good to see that you—that you—"

"That I'm still alive?" Finn smiled a crooked smile. "That's *my* line, I believe."

They embraced.

"Finn has been attending the academy at Oden's Ford," Bayar continued. "Now I hear that you've been studying there as well." He paused long enough to give that sentence a little extra bite. Did that mean that he hadn't known Ash was alive, that his mother *hadn't* confided in him? "Interesting that the two of you never crossed paths."

Does he think I'm lying about being at Oden's Ford? Why would I do that? So I could bask on a beach somewhere?

"Maybe we did, Uncle Micah," Finn said, rolling his eyes. "It's been four years. We've both changed. I'm not sure I could have picked Adrian out of a crowd—especially since I wasn't looking for him, because we all thought he was dead."

Really? Ash thought. Finn *had* changed—he appeared gaunt, a bit hollow-eyed, the bones in his face standing out more than before. But four years wasn't all that long, and the wizard academy was smaller than in the past. Ash couldn't help thinking that if he had seen him, he would have recognized him.

"Every marching season, Finn's been fighting for the queendom," Bayar said. "He's played a pivotal role in keeping the southerners at bay." Maybe Bayar was just proud of his nephew, but Ash wondered if that was intended as a dig at the runaway prince.

By now, Finn's pale cheeks were stained with color. "Uncle," he said, "I'd like to hear more about what Adrian has been doing."

"Hasn't the spring term already started?" Ash said.

Finn nodded. "It has, but I'm not going back. I have a new calling. I'm apprenticed to Lord Vega in the healing halls."

Ash stared at him. "In the *healing* halls? You . . . you mean to be a healer?" Ash couldn't ever remember Finn expressing an interest in that field.

Finn nodded, laughing. "Is that so hard to believe? As I said, we've both changed over the past four years."

"Finn suffered a serious wound on the battlefield last summer," Bayar said. "He spent a great deal of time under Lord Vega's care. Now he's got it into his head that he wants to be a healer. Hopefully a season emptying bedpans and treating Tamric boils will—"

"This is not some kind of whim, Uncle Micah," Finn said. "I know you think I should have returned to the academy, but this is the path I've chosen. My parents are supportive, and that should be enough for you."

"They're more supportive of your betrothal than of your chosen vocation," Bayar retorted. "Anything that keeps you here until the deed is accomplished is—"

"You're out of line, Uncle," Finn snapped. "If you want

to run somebody's life, then you should have had a son of your own."

Bayar gazed at him for a long moment. "Perhaps so," he said. He delivered another brief bow to Ash. "Your Highness." And he walked away, his robes swirling around him.

"He had such high hopes for me," Finn said in a flat voice, looking after the High Wizard. "He doesn't understand that I've changed. He thinks I don't know what I'm doing, but I do."

"Don't let it bother you," Ash said, instantly on Finn's side. Anyone in opposition to Bayar was an ally. "What's this about a betrothal? Who's the bride-to-be?"

Finn brightened, looking over Ash's shoulder. "Here she comes now."

Ash turned to see his cousin Julianna striding toward them, lit up like Solstice. She'd changed as well. In contrast to the frilly clothes Aunt Mellony used to dress her in, she wore a long wool skirt and a tailored jacket. Her hair was wound into a twist on the back of her head.

He'd always thought of her as something of a lightweight, but now she looked like someone who could get things done.

"Cousin!" she said, embracing him. "I see you've found my fiancé."

Ash stood like a stump, rooted to the floor, but Julianna had enough enthusiasm for both of them. After a moment, she held him out at arm's length, laughing.

"You look like you've been run over by a cart," she said. "I hope you approve?"

"Of course I approve," Ash said. "I just . . . I never realized . . . you and Finn?" He remembered what his mother had said. *You think time stops at home while you grow and change.*

"It's very recent news," Julianna said, splaying her hand in front of Ash's face, showing off her emerald ring. "So you're not too far behind everyone else. I've asked Alyssa to stand up with us, and I hope . . ." She glanced at Finn, then back at Ash. "It might not be my place to ask, but I hope you will, too. Now that you're back from the dead."

"From dead to living," Finn said. "I think you've changed more than anyone. And of course I would be honored to have you as part of our celebration, if you are still here."

Another dig?

No, Ash thought. Not from Finn. You've got to grow a thicker skin, sul'Han, if you're going to see subtext in every remark.

"My mother's made it clear that she's not letting me out of her sight for a good while," Ash said, grimacing.

"Can you blame her?" This was a new voice, a clan voice, coming from behind. Ash turned to see Fire Dancer, possibly his father's oldest friend. He was a little more weathered than before, but blessedly familiar.

"Dancer!" he said. "I—I heard about Cat. I am so sorry."

"Catfire went down fighting, which is the way she would have wanted it," Dancer said, using her upland name. "The time for your Naeming has come and gone. Are you still Speaks to Horses? Or have you taken a new name since you went away?"

"I've taken many new names," Ash said, "but I've not let go of that one yet."

"Then perhaps we can do that at midsummer," Dancer said. "When you've decided what your name should be."

Runs Away? Ash thought. Flees the Field?

"I heard about Shadow's fiancée," Ash said in a low voice. "Is he here?"

With that, a heavy hand fell on his shoulder. Adrian spun, his hand automatically finding his amulet, until he saw that it was Shadow Dancer, a cup in his hand.

"I am here, Speaks to Horses," Shadow said. "It does my heart good to see that you are quicker than you used to be." His words were thick, and Ash caught the scent of blue ruin on his breath.

"And you are slower than you should be," Fire Dancer said, taking the cup from his son's hand and setting it on a nearby table. He nodded at both of them before he walked away.

"Better slow than dead," Shadow said, gazing after his father.

"I heard about your betrothed," Ash said, not wanting to dance around the topic. "I'm so sorry."

"Everyone is," Shadow said. "And, now, even my revenge has been stolen from me."

"What do you mean?"

"Somebody got to the king of Arden before I did," Shadow said, retrieving his cup and draining it. "Killing him was the only thing I had to look forward to." He thumped his cup down on the table. When he turned back to Ash, he frowned. "What?"

"N-nothing," Ash said. "Let's just celebrate the fact that he's dead. Maybe this will be an opportunity for peace."

"Southerners killed my mother and my fiancée," Shadow said. "There is a huge blood debt that has not yet been paid."

"Collecting on a blood debt is never as satisfying as you think it will be," Ash said, feeling like the worst kind of hypocrite.

"How do you know?" Shadow growled. "Flatlanders murdered your father and sister, and they tried to murder you. Haven't you ever wanted to take revenge?"

"Of course," Ash said, wishing he could extricate himself from this awkward conversation. "But if the war goes on, there's a cost. We've already spent a fortune in blood and treasure. We'll always have reasons to keep fighting, but maybe there are reasons to stop."

"I'm not ready to stop," Shadow said, "until they pay for what they've done. Then I will be ready to talk about peace." He refilled his cup. "We had a visitor this afternoon who wants us to get in bed with Arden for mutual defense. If I have my way, that will never happen."

"A visitor?" Ash said, grateful for this partial change of subject. "An emissary from Arden?"

Shadow shook his head. "A pirate from Carthis. I don't think he was going to admit it, but Hadley DeVilliers recognized him. Remember her? She's commander of the navy now. Anyway, she says he surfaced two or three years ago, and has been working the entire east coast, down to the Southern Islands and beyond. She wasn't sure how many ships he controls, but shipping has taken a huge hit."

A pirate from Carthis? Ash's mouth had gone dry, and yet it was as if he tasted blood, metallic on his tongue. "Why would a pirate from Carthis involve himself in our war?"

Shadow laughed. "He wants to involve us in *his* war. He came to warn us that an empress from Carthis was planning to invade with a huge army. He claims that he just came from Ardenscourt, where he managed to prevent an agreement between Arden and the empress."

"He just came . . . from Ardenscourt?"

Shadow nodded. "We think that he and this empress must be rivals, and he wants to poison us against her."

Ash cleared his throat. "What was his name, this visitor?"

"His name is Evan Strangward," Shadow said. "He's known as the Stormcaster." He paused, frowning. "What is it? Do you know him?"

"Where is he now?" Adrian demanded, his heart thumping painfully. "He hasn't left the city, has he?"

"I don't believe so," Shadow said. He looked over Ash's shoulder. "In fact, he just walked in with your mother."

QUEENS AND
KNAVES

"You should get dressed now," Evan said to Brody. "We don't want to be late."

His first mate was stripped down to his smallclothes, sprawled across a delicate velvet chair that looked like it might collapse under his weight at any moment. He was distracting, as always, but in a distant way, like a platter of sweetmeats after a feast.

"We should *go home* now, Captain," Brody said. "You've had your meeting with the queen and her crew. She'll decide what she decides. The longer we stay, the more likely it is that we'll get into trouble. I don't like being so far from the sea."

Brody was right—they'd had their meeting with the

queen and her small council that afternoon. Hadley DeVilliers introduced them without a hint of endorsement. There were several other mages present, including the High Wizard, Micah Bayar, and a healer, Lord Vega. The wetlanders had been polite enough, but they'd questioned and debated him on every detail. When he told them he'd seen Celestine's ships off their coast, they shrugged and said that pirates had been a problem for years. When he warned them that the empress in the east had all but conquered the Desert Coast and was preparing to invade the wetland realms, they said they'd been fighting off invaders for decades. Besides, pirates knew better than to venture too far from the sea. Fierce, fearless, unstoppable desert horselords? They'll freeze to death in the mountains.

One uplander in particular, Shadow Dancer, seemed convinced that Evan was trying to persuade the Fells to get involved in his personal feud.

They saved their deepest skepticism for his suggestion that the Fells seek peace with Arden so that they could join forces against Celestine.

"Captain Strangward," Queen Raisa said finally, "we must direct our resources to the war we have. If another war comes to us, we'll fight that one, too. As for suing for peace, you should be speaking with the young king in the south. We did not start this war, but we intend to finish it. We do not intend to bend the knee, and we do not intend to lose—to anyone."

The meeting had been disappointing, to say the least. And then, hours later, this invitation to a reception. It had rekindled Evan's hope that something had changed, that somehow he could come away with an agreement.

"The queen invited us to this reception," Evan said. "It would be rude to refuse. It is in honor of the queen's son, who has come home after a long absence, so it will be a chance to meet him. Maybe we can win him over. Anyway, parties are often where important business gets done at court."

"What do you know about how queens do business?"

"It's in books," Evan said. "I've read about it."

"You're always reading," Brody said, like it was an accusation. "I don't trust the wolf queen."

"That's fair, because she doesn't trust us."

"If she intended to do business with us, she would have shown you more respect in the meeting."

"You are the one who needs to show some respect, youngling," Teza said. "Your job is to follow orders, not to argue with the captain."

"It's not that the queen doesn't respect us," Evan said. "I think it's exhaustion, more than anything. They've been fighting this war for more than twenty-five years. The queendom is surrounded by enemies. They really don't need more bad news. Their resources are stretched to the limit."

"That's not our fault," Brody pointed out.

"No, it's not, but that doesn't make them eager to take on one more complication. The thing is, I don't want to leave without a commitment from her. It's not like we have an ambassador here who will follow up after we're gone."

"And if she won't commit?" Brody said.

"She has to." This was their best option, because it was their only option.

"She doesn't *have* to do anything," Brody said. "We'll freeze to death while we wait."

"If you'd put on some clothes, you'd be warmer," Evan said.

"I don't like wearing so many clothes," Brody protested. But he levered himself out of the chair, retrieved his shirt from where he'd dropped it on the floor, and slipped it on.

"*I'd* like to go to a party," Jorani said wistfully, smoothing the skirts of her silk dress. She'd been closemouthed and wide-eyed ever since they arrived at the palace.

"You can come to the next one," Evan said. "Especially if Brody keeps complaining."

They were met at the palace gate by a handful of the queen's blue-coated guards, who escorted them to a small reception hall.

As soon as they were ushered through the doorway, Evan recognized several people from the meeting earlier in the day. As the queen had promised, this was an intimate, informal gathering. The queen herself was welcoming newcomers and directing them to food and drink.

"Captain Strangward," she said graciously. "I'm glad that you and Brody were able to come and celebrate with us." She stood on tiptoe, scanning the crowd. "I know Adrian is here somewhere, no doubt catching up with old friends. Ah. There he is. Come with me." The queen led him toward the back of the room, to where the uplander, Shadow Dancer, waited with a tall, broad-shouldered young mage wearing an elaborately stitched coat and a scowl.

"Adrian, this is Evan Strangward, from Carthis. Lord Strangward, this is my son, Adrian sul'Han."

But no, it wasn't. It couldn't be. Evan found himself looking into the icy blue-green eyes of the king of Arden's gifted healer, Adam Freeman.

"We've met, Mother," Freeman said through his teeth. He gripped his amulet. "Step away from the queen, you murderous bastard."

Evan saw no point in denying who he was, or forcing the hand of the Queen's Guard by refusing. He'd have to talk fast if he wanted to survive the night.

"Healer," he said, taking two steps away from the wolf queen and keeping his hands at his sides. "I'm glad to see that you survived that unpleasantness at Ardenscourt."

"What unpleasantness?" the queen said, looking from Evan to the healer and back again. "What's this about Ardenscourt?"

"*I* survived," Freeman said, still fixed on Evan. "And,

unfortunately, you survived. But not everyone did."

"Surely you don't regret killing the king of Arden," Evan said, taking a blind shot, hoping it hit home. "I can't imagine that anyone is mourning him on this side of the border."

"*You* killed King Gerard?" It was Shadow Dancer, his body rigid, his eyes wide with surprise.

"One thing confuses me, though," Evan said. "In Ardenscourt, I knew you as Adam Freeman."

"In Ardenscourt," the queen said, as if she couldn't believe her ears. She turned to the healer. "What is he talking about, Adrian?"

"I told you about Jenna," the healer said. He pointed at Evan. "This is the man who murdered her."

"You said that you met a girl," the queen said, her back stiff with disapproval. "You didn't mention that you met this girl in Ardenscourt."

"As I told you, it's a long story."

A story that he hasn't told, up to now, Evan thought. And that gave him an opportunity.

"The good news is that Jenna is very much alive," he said. "In fact, I just saw her on the coast, near Chalk Cliffs."

"Chalk Cliffs," the healer repeated. Hope flickered in his eyes for a moment. "Why would she be in Chalk Cliffs, and how would she get there?"

"Apparently, Chalk Cliffs is the place to be," Evan said. "We did not have a long conversation, because she was accompanied by a large and surly dragon. They flew off together."

The hope in the healer's eyes was crowded off by disbelief and hostility. He shook his head, dismissing Evan, and turned to the queen. "So. What story is this pirate telling *you?*"

The wolf queen folded her arms, as if to fend off lies from pirates and errant sons. "He *says* he came to warn us about an empress from across the Indio who may be planning to attack the Realms. He claimed that the entire east coast was at risk."

"Interesting," the healer said. "Just a few weeks ago, he was in Ardenscourt, negotiating with the king, and claiming to be the empress's representative."

The look in the wolf queen's eyes was a familiar one—one Evan had seen on the healer too many times. He resisted the impulse to protect his throat.

Just then, Shadow Dancer gripped the healer's arm. "Speaks to Horses," he said. "What does this Jenna look like?"

Speaks to Horses? Evan thought. How many names can one person have? I'm a slacker next to him.

It took the healer a moment or two to tear himself away from the argument. He turned to the uplander and said, "Her hair was wavy, metallic-looking, streaked with copper, and she had golden eyes."

Evan noticed that he used the past tense. *He doesn't believe me,* he thought.

"A girl approached me in Middlesea," Shadow said. "She wanted some leatherwork done. She said her name was Riley, but, from your description, it sounds like the same person."

Now the healer's full attention was on Shadow. *"Riley? That was Jenna's friend when she was little. She sometimes used that name herself."* He looked from Shadow to Evan and back to the uplander. "What kind of leatherwork?"

"She had drawn a pattern for it, but it was like nothing I'd seen before. It was a harness, but it was huge, and oddly shaped. She claimed she rode the gryphons and elyphants in the circus and needed new gear for a growing gryphon. Sparrow made it, and Riley picked it up in Fortress Rocks."

"When was that?"

"A few weeks ago. I was on my way back from Arden."

Evan was beginning to feel a bit superfluous, which was fine with him. The reception was apparently over, and the room had emptied out during their conversation. He began to edge away, but the queen noticed, and raised her hand to stop him.

"Captain Strangward," she said. "We need to continue this conversation in a more private place, after I have spoken to my son, and to Shadow Dancer, and collected more

247

information. I hope you will understand that we'll need to confine you and your crew to your quarters under guard until we can sort out truth from lies." Her jaw tightened, her eyes as hard and brilliant as emeralds. "Do know that if you came here intending to lead us into some sort of trap, I will deal with you with a hard hand."

Evan could sense Brody stiffening behind him. Evan knew that his crewman wanted them to try to fight their way out before the healer shared his story and the upland queen ordered their execution. What Brody didn't understand was that there was nowhere to run. Evan and his handful of Stormborn couldn't keep on sailing while Celestine conquered the rest of the world. Even a pirate needs a port, eventually.

He needed to make a stand and somehow convince the wolf queen that they shared a common enemy. If she ordered him beheaded or incinerated (if he had to choose, he hoped for the former), it would likely be better than whatever Celestine had planned for him. It was some small consolation that, from the looks of things, the wolf queen intended to deal with her son with a hard hand as well.

So he stood, forcing his muscles to relax, meeting the gaze of anyone who chose to look at him. "I understand, Your Majesty," he said. "But I beg you to move quickly. Once Celestine gains a foothold in the Realms . . ." He trailed off, because he could see that the queen was being distracted by a commotion at the door—raised voices, and a small crowd of bluejackets milling about.

"See what that's about, Captain Byrne," the queen snapped. Turning to another one of her guards, she said, "Clear everyone else out of the room. I think this party is over, anyway, and we don't need a lot of tongues wagging before we get this sorted out."

Captain Byrne wavered, as if unsure whether to leave the queen in Evan's company to investigate. Finally, he crossed the room to the door as the room emptied.

Moments later, he returned, accompanied by a travel-worn soldier, who was still muddied from the road. She was a woman, but she dwarfed nearly everyone else in the room.

"Corporal Talbot!" the queen said. "What are you doing here?" A look of hope dawned in her eyes. "Did—did Captain Gray come back with you?" She looked past the newcomer as if she expected this Captain Gray to be right behind.

"Your Majesty," the soldier said, saluting, her expression haggard and grim. "I bring bad news from Chalk Cliffs. After a fierce battle, the city has fallen."

Queen Raisa went pale, her green eyes wide. "Chalk Cliffs . . . has *fallen*? But . . . how did this happen?"

"We were caught between an army from the west and warships from seaward. And clearly there were traitors within the walls that opened the gates to them."

The queen glanced at Evan, then back to the distraught

soldier. "An army? Was it Arden or—?"

Talbot shook her head. "They sailed for someone called Empress Celestine, and they fought like—like demons. Even if we hadn't been massively outnumbered, they were all but impossible to kill."

Evan's heart sank like a stone. This was exactly the disaster he'd hoped to prevent. It was little solace that the empress's arrival lent credence to his warning.

Queen Raisa straightened, clenched her fists, and lifted her chin. "What about survivors?"

Talbot hung her head, as if ashamed to be among them. "A small group of us took a boat out of the water gate, and we managed to get out of the bay and down the shoreline a bit. But one of the enemy ships gave chase and ran us down."

"Captain Gray?" the queen said, her voice flat.

Talbot looked around, as if to see who was within earshot. "We need to speak privately, Your Majesty."

KINGS AND PAWNS

Hal's few days at home were less than satisfying. None of the people he wanted to see were there, and the familiar surroundings only brought back memories of what he stood to lose. His mother had always taken great pride in her gardens. Now the borders were blurred, overrun by thistle, the flowers blown and gone to seed.

At the center stood the massive spreading white oak, symbol of their house. Legend said that it predated the Breaking and the Montaigne line of kings. His little sister Harper used to lurk within its branches to avoid her scripture tutor and to intercept her brothers on their way to adventures outside the walls. Eventually, she talked the blacksmith's boy into setting iron bars into the wall of the back garden so that she could engineer her own escapes.

No doubt, even now, she was scheming to escape her current predicament.

Wait for me, Harper, Hal thought. He would not rest until he'd got them back.

The prospect of seeing the empress's hordes come riding down the western slopes of the Heartfangs lent a special urgency to his mission. It was fortunate that the empress's obsession with finding the magemarked busker had sent her north instead of south. But he was under no illusion that she would be satisfied with the Fells.

His father had been in the field for months, so Hal was swarmed with petitioners and requests to settle disputes or make decisions on matters that had been deferred for too long. He'd spent so much time away that he was of little help in directing the household or answering questions from the farm managers and rent collectors. He was, however, a convenient target for complaints about shortages of, well, nearly everything, from wine to salt to fodder to men to work in the fields.

This even though the larders were overflowing compared to what he'd seen in the queendom of the Fells.

Rolande was a nuisance as well. Since Hal was the highest-ranking person he could get at, the thaneling was constantly at his heels, offering silly advice on all topics.

At least Rolande had birds on hand to communicate with the rebel forces. Hal sent a message to his father in the code they'd used since he was a boy.

It's Halston. I'm at White Oaks. Orders?

A message came back the next day, in his father's usual effusive style.

Glad to hear it. You're needed. Report to Temple Church as soon as able.

As soon as Hal could extract himself, he was riding hard toward Temple Church, where the rebellious thanes had gathered. Rolande was, of course, eager to come along, but Hal ordered him to stay behind on pain of court-martial.

Temple Church was a good strategic position—astride the North Road so that they had a good road straight to the enemy should they choose to use it. The same could be said for the king's forces, of course. Prior to the fall of Delphi, such a position would also have blocked access to the weapons factories and mines in the north.

Now, with Delphi at their backs, hills to the east, and Tamron Forest to their west, it wouldn't be easy to come at the thanes from any direction other than the south.

Ordinarily, Hal might have actually looked forward to fighting in the flatlands for the first time in a long time. But this time, he'd be pushing for diplomacy and negotiation, tasks he had no skills for.

There had always been a small garrison house and other military facilities at Temple Church. Hal arrived after sunset, and it seemed that campfires and tents spread across the plains as far as he could see. That was good news—up to a point. Armies are not good at waiting around with nothing to do and nowhere to go.

Hal guessed that the command post would be in the garrison house; if not, those posted there would be able to tell him where to find his father.

As it happened, he didn't have to do any fast talking to get in to see his father. The first person he encountered after handing off his horse was Jan Rives, who was walking the paddocks, a list in his hand. Rives had been one of the first officers Hal served under when he joined the army, before he'd got his growth.

"Why, it's Little Hal, I believe," Rives said, a smile breaking across his face. "Lord Matelon told me that you'd survived that hellhole in Delphi after all."

After Rives had lost an arm during an uprising in Bruinswallow, Lord Matelon had taken him on as quartermaster for White Oaks. Hal still called him Sergeant, and Rives still called him Little Hal, though Hal towered over him now.

Rives was the only one allowed to call him that, as Hal had made clear to some of his fellow soldiers who'd tried to follow suit.

"Sergeant Rives," Hal said, grinning and clapping him on the back. "Can you tell me where to find my father?"

"He's in with some of the other lords, fighting toe to toe as usual," Rives said. "It'll do him good to see you."

"I hope so," Hal said, wishing he could meet privately

with his father and win him over before springing his news on the other thanes.

He heard voices before he reached the door of the meeting room.

"My men need to get home and into the fields or we'll have no harvest at all this year," someone was saying. It was a voice Hal didn't recognize. "The buds are already breaking, and with the vines not properly trellised, the quality of the—"

"Blood of the Martyr, DeLacroix, can you give it a rest?" That was his father's unmistakable bass rumble. So the first speaker was Pascal DeLacroix, Rolande's father, until recently a firm ally of the king. "If we don't strike now, when we have the advantage, you won't have to worry about your swiving harvest this fall. Someone else will be drinking your wine."

"All I'm asking for is a few weeks to get the estates in order," DeLacroix said, his tone suggesting that he was trying to reason with the unreasonable. "I don't understand why you say we have the advantage when the king still holds our families hostage. We should attempt to negotiate their release before we—"

"Jarat is stalling," Matelon growled. "We both know that. He wants to put us off until the marching season is over in the north so he can commit his full army to dealing with us. Better to go now, when his forces are divided."

Bloody hell, Hal thought. I'm coming in on the wrong

side already. Taking a deep breath, he pushed open the door.

There were a half dozen thanes in the room, and all heads turned as he entered. He recognized DeLacroix, young Lord Heresford, Lord Henri Tourant, and his father, huddled around a battered wooden table. Dirty cups and plates around them suggested they had been at it for a while.

Hal brought his fist to his chest in a salute. "Captain Halston Matelon, reporting as ordered, sir," he said.

Wood scraped on wood as his father shoved his chair back and stood. He crossed the room and roughly embraced Hal, murmuring in his ear, "Good to have you home, Son." Holding him out at arm's length, he looked him up and down. "You need a shave," he said.

"I know, sir," Hal said. "But you said to come as soon as I was able."

Sliding his arm around Hal, Matelon turned him to face the other thanes. "I believe you all know my son Captain Matelon," he said. "He was taken prisoner in the fall of Delphi. By the grace of the Maker, he's escaped and come back to us."

They all stared at him. From the look on their faces, none of the others had been alerted to his recent resurrection. Which meant that his father didn't trust any of them to know.

Finally, DeLacroix said, "I was told that you and everyone

under your command were killed at Delphi."

"A few of us were taken prisoner, sir," Hal said.

"My son Armond was with you at Delphi," Tourant said eagerly. "Was he captured as well?"

"I don't know, sir," Hal said. "I didn't see him among the prisoners, but that doesn't mean that he didn't survive. There were thirty men being held in Delphi, but there may have been some prisoners held separately from me."

"You didn't even ask about the soldiers in your own command?" DeLacroix raised an eyebrow. DeLacroix, who'd managed to avoid any military service up to now.

Wrestling with his temper, Hal gritted his teeth. "I did ask, and I was told that there were few survivors," he said. "I didn't know whether to believe them or not. Then I was moved to Chalk Cliffs, where I was the only Ardenine prisoner."

"And you've been a captive in the north for *three months*?" It was as if DeLacroix was suggesting that any soldier worth his salt would have escaped before now. As if Hal had taken advantage of the situation to enjoy a three-month vacation. "And now you're the only one to escape." The thane tapped his fingers together as if this was significant.

"Quit interrogating him," Heresford said. "We should be welcoming him home, not grilling him about how he came to survive. We're going to need him if it comes to a fight with Jarat."

"It will come to a fight, Heresford, you know it will," Matelon said. "I've seen nothing in the son that makes me think otherwise."

"Half the boy king's army will come over to us when they find out Captain Matelon is with us," Heresford said, grinning.

Hal cleared his throat. "I have some news about events in the north that might have bearing on a decision about whether this is the right time to take the fight to King Jarat."

Hal's father raised both hands, giving Hal a warning look. "Gentlemen, we've been at it since early this morning," he said. "This is a good time to break for the day, so we can all take a piss and have a bite and I can debrief my son about events in the north. We'll reconvene tomorrow morning."

24

KILLING THE MESSENGER

Hal knew going in that persuading his father to make peace with King Jarat in order to unite against a common enemy would be a hard sell. He hadn't expected it to be impossible.

He booked a room at the inn where his father and Robert were staying. It seemed like his little brother had aged a year and grown an inch in three months. He kept staring at Hal as if he might disappear. Apparently, he'd blamed himself for being elsewhere when the city fell.

Over dinner, Hal relayed what had happened since the fall of Delphi. Well, not everything. Traitorous or not, he did not choose to share Captain Gray's true identity, or dwell on the bond that had grown between them during his time in the north. That would make his motivations even more suspect than they already were.

His father asked few questions until Hal described his meeting with the wolf queen, and her hope that the death of King Gerard might signal a new opportunity to end the war between the Realms.

"If she wants peace, she should be sending word to the fledgling hawk in Ardenscourt," his father said. "That's how this whole thing started. After the fall of Delphi, I informed Gerard that I would not be spending more men and money to further his grudge match with the witch in the north. That's when he took our families hostage."

"Queen Raisa is not just asking for a truce, Father," Hal said. "She wants an alliance against an enemy who threatens us both."

"Who? Jarat?" His father snorted. "Isn't it enough that we're no longer supporting the war? She cannot expect us to turn traitor against our homeland." His eyes narrowed. "Why are we even talking about this? Are you here as her emissary or what?"

"I'm not her emissary, and I'm not talking about Jarat. I'm talking about the empress in the east. Celestine."

His father frowned. "Celestine. Isn't she the Carthian pirate that promised Gerard an army of mages? I was never sure she really existed except in the king's imagination. I haven't heard another word about her since he died."

"She's real," Hal said. "She's taken Chalk Cliffs. It looks

like she's here to stay."

His father stared at him. "Where did you hear that? It's news to me."

"I was there," Hal said. "Being held prisoner in the keep there. I saw it happen."

"Did she bring an army of mages, as promised?"

"If her soldiers are mages, they're not the kind we're used to."

"What do you mean?" Robert stuffed an end of bread in his mouth and chased it with a swallow of ale. "What are they like?"

"They're nearly impossible to kill. They don't have amulets, and I don't think they use magic in the way our mages do."

"Really," his father said. "Do you know that from personal experience? Were you in on the fighting?"

"Yes," Hal said. Then thought a moment. "Well, actually, no. One of them . . . ah . . . dropped out of the sky when I was up on the battlements."

"Dropped out of the sky?" Matelon reared back in his chair, as if Hal might have something catching. "They can fly?"

Hal realized how implausible that sounded. "Well, no, I don't think so. There was a beast, or a bird, that dropped him."

"A beast or bird. Dropped a soldier on you." From the skepticism in his father's face, Hal knew he was losing ground. There wasn't even a question there.

Robert was instantly on board, of course. "What did it look like? Did it have scales or feathers? Was it a gryphon or a dragon or—?"

"Robert." Their father shook his head as if saying, *Don't encourage him.* "So you didn't actually see the battle," he said to Hal.

Hal shook his head. "I was locked in the keep during the fighting, but I could hear it well enough."

"How did you escape?"

"We . . . we left through the water gate during the battle."

"We?" His father raised an eyebrow.

"Me and another prisoner," Hal said. He saw no reason to get into the details and thereby raise more questions than he already had.

Matelon sighed heavily. He drummed his fingers on the table, looking at him from under his bushy brows. "I'm sorry, Son. It sounds to me like the witch queen fed you a story and let you go."

"She didn't let me go," Hal said.

Or had she?

I'm no good at this, he thought. Words are not my weapons of choice. Nobody in her right mind would choose me as an emissary.

"If this was staged for my benefit, the queen went to a lot of trouble," Hal said. "After the battle, the entire harbor was crowded with ships flying the empress's siren banner. They were offloading soldiers and weapons and supplies. A huge army. I saw that with my own eyes."

"Could it have been conjury of some kind?"

"It was not conjury. I spoke afterwards to some who were in the battle, and interrogated one of the Carthian fighters."

"How did you come to interrogate—?"

"I took a mount from the Carthian horse-line," Hal said. "I questioned one of their sentries before I killed him."

"So they are killable?"

Hal nodded. "They are. But it's not easy. I ran one of them through and he kept right on fighting. The only thing that brought him down was cutting off his head."

His father studied him. "You're a good soldier, Son, and a savvy officer, possibly the best in the empire, but you are no politician. Apparently I did not pass on the gene for connivery and subterfuge. Always look for the simplest explanation. If what you're saying is true, that the Fells is under attack by a Carthian army—"

"Why would Hal lie about that?" Robert put in, then subsided under his father's withering gaze.

"—the most likely explanation is that either Gerard or Jarat struck a deal with this Celestine," Matelon went on. "While she sends her armies into the north, it frees Jarat to come after us. Even if there is no collusion between them, he will move against us when word reaches him that the wolf queen is otherwise occupied. So. It behooves us to march on the capital sooner rather than later."

"That's just what we shouldn't do," Hal said. "While we're fighting among ourselves, Celestine will be winning territory in the north. Sooner or later she will turn south."

"And by the time she does, we'll have united the empire and can contend with her." He sighed and rubbed the back of his neck, looked at Hal, then away. "Has it occurred to you that the witch in the north has—" He paused, as if reluctant to speak the words. "—has bewitched you?"

"No!" Hal said, his cheeks heating with embarrassment. "I am not bewitched. I know what I saw."

"Look, I don't know what was done to you while you were held captive in the north," his father said. "I have no knowledge or understanding of sorcery. I leave those matters to the church." He brightened. "It might do you good to speak with the chaplain. Father Menard is with us, and he might have some insights as to—"

"No," Hal said. "I don't want to talk to Menard. I don't need an exorcism. I need an army." He tried to quash the doubt that welled up from deep inside him. Could it have been an elaborate ruse, put on for his benefit? Had he been played?

If it had been a ruse, it was a drama worthy of any stage in Tamron, complete with a cast of thousands.

"I can't give you an army, Hal," his father said. "I will need every sword I have."

"Are you really going to march on the capital when the king is holding your wife and daughter hostage?" Without meaning to, Hal had raised his voice.

"Is that what this is about?" Matelon drained his cup and slammed it down. "You know I do not negotiate with hostage-takers. We did send a message to Ardenscourt after Gerard died, demanding that Jarat release the hostages straightaway as a gesture of good faith. He countered with a demand that we surrender to the king's justice."

If he offered justice, that would be a first in that family, Hal thought. "Has there been any word about the whereabouts of those he's holding?"

"They are somewhere in the capital, I presume," his father said sourly. "The king would want to keep them close. He assumes that we won't attack as long as he holds that card. And that means he has no incentive to make concessions." Matelon gave Hal a long, measured look. "Frankly, we are not interested in a peace that maintains the status quo. Why should we reward the son for his father's bad behavior? There is not a thane in the empire who hasn't suffered massive losses of land, men, and money under Gerard. If we submit to Jarat, he comes away with everything Gerard has stolen from us, and we'll go to the block. The thanes don't agree on much, but we are in agreement on this point—we must negotiate from strength, not as supplicants. So. As things stand, there is no avoiding a fight. If we are going to make our move, this is the time to do it, when he is at his weakest. Why wait until he's found his footing? As for our families, any harm that comes to them will be repaid in kind."

"But . . . that won't bring Harper or Mother back," Robert said.

Their father squeezed Robert's shoulder. "We are men, Robert," he said. "Sometimes men have to make hard decisions."

Robert twisted away from Matelon's hand. "If the hostages were freed, wouldn't King Jarat be more likely to negotiate?"

"No doubt," their father said, with a hoarse laugh. "Jarat has an army, but armies need feeding whether they are fighting or not. He has no money and no territory north of the capital. If the savages in Bruinswallow and We'enhaven sense weakness on his part, they'll be pressing in at the borders. Right now, I'd rather be us than him."

"Well, I don't want to be us!" Robert shouted. "I don't want to be us at all. If the king won't let our families go, we need to free them ourselves." And he stomped up the stairs, leaving Hal and his father staring at each other across the table.

"It's hard to be young," Matelon said, shaking his head.

"It's hard, period," Hal said, pushing his last bite of meat around on his plate. He considered asking for permission to go to the capital to see if he could find out where the hostages were being kept. He still had friends in the Ardenine army that he would trust with his life. But he suspected that Matelon would be reluctant to approve any enterprise that might result in putting one more hostage in Jarat's keep.

If he asked permission and his father said no, then he definitely couldn't go.

Better to ask forgiveness than to ask permission, Hal thought.

Matelon cocked his head. "Robert has always been headstrong, but you've always been the steady one," he said. "Enchanted or not, your time in the north has changed you."

Hal nodded. That, at least, was something they could agree on.

"I know that you're disappointed that we can't open another front right now, but we have to choose our battles. As you've seen, it's hard enough to persuade the thanes to finish the war we're in. I'll tell you right now, there will be no support for coming to the aid of the witch queen."

Hal pushed his plate away and drained his cup, knowing there was no point in continuing to argue. "I understand, sir."

In the past, that would have ended it, but his father continued to study Hal, as if seeing something he hadn't seen before. "I have agents in the north. I promise I'll get in touch with them and see what we can find out. In the meantime, we need to take advantage of this opportunity to end the civil war. That will make us strong enough to resist outside forces."

Lord Matelon paused, and when Hal said nothing, continued. "We've been able to persuade a number of soldiers from the regular army to come over to our side. Once word gets out that you're with us, more will come. I would like to consolidate all of our soldiers under your command. I'll make that case when we meet with the others tomorrow."

Hal nodded. "What about mages? Have any of them come over?"

Matelon rubbed his chin. "Not many, and most of those are collared, so it's hard to predict what they might do in a battle situation. It's hard to argue with a collar."

"How are we doing for ordnance?"

"I've been building a stockpile, but our allies have not been particularly forthcoming." Matelon grimaced. "Each man wants to hold on to what's his. It's not just the war with Jarat that they're concerned about, it's after. But there's someone I want you to meet. She's been sourcing weapons for the crown for a year or two, and she thinks she can help us with magical ordnance."

"She's been working for the crown?" Hal raised an

eyebrow. "Do you trust her?"

His father laughed hoarsely. "She's a practical sort," he said. "Our money spends as well as any, and right now we're the ones who are buying." He looked toward the door. "There she is now."

The girl who'd just entered shook rainwater from her dark curls and looked around the room. When she spotted them at their corner table, she shed her cloak and draped it over her arm, signaled to the barkeep, then crossed the room to them. "Lord Matelon," she said. "Good to see you."

"Barrowhill," Hal's father said. "We were just talking about you. Please join us."

Years of his mother's training kicked in. Hal stood, bowed, and pulled out a chair for her. Barrowhill slowly turned her head and looked him up and down as if he were a creature she'd not seen before. Then plucked at her skirts as if they were the fanciest of ball gowns and lowered herself into the chair, ruining the effect by squirming a bit to get settled. The server plunked a pint of bingo down in front of her.

A pint? Hal thought. That would put any teamster on his back in short order.

She raised her glass in a toast. "I see that the rumors are true, Captain. Welcome back from the dead. Tell me what it's like on the other side."

Hours later, when Hal went upstairs, he knocked at

Robert's door, hoping to settle him a little. There was no answer. He knocked again. His brother was usually a light sleeper. Finally, he pushed the door open.

The bed was empty. Robert was gone.

POINT AND COUNTERPOINT

Corporal Talbot's timely arrival was both a blessing and a curse, as far as Evan was concerned. The news about the attack on Chalk Cliffs supported parts of the story that Evan was telling, but it also meant that his warning had come too late. The fact that Celestine already had a foothold in the east made him feel crowded. It made him want to keep traveling west until he reached the edge of the world. And maybe jump off.

It also meant that his movements were limited now. It didn't help that he and his crew were locked up together in a suite of rooms. It was like being penned in with a pack of nervous cats. Not even the ritual of tay would settle their nerves.

He wondered if Destin knew about the attack on Chalk Cliffs. If he didn't, he would hear about it before long. Would that make Evan's job easier or harder?

Evan was almost grateful when the wetlanders called him into the queen's small hall for questioning. His crew, not so much.

"What if you never come back?" Brody said, shifting from foot to foot in his agitation. "What will become of us?"

"We should fight our way out," Jorani said, producing a dagger from some hidden place. Evan half-expected her to come up with a bow and a quiver of arrows and a trebuchet as well.

"If we try to fight our way out, I will be killed, and you won't," Evan said. He brushed at his fine breeches, which by now were looking less fine. "How is that helpful?"

She seemed stumped by that question. After a moment's pause, she stowed the blade away.

The bloodsworn turned Stormborn were the fiercest, most loyal crew he'd ever known, but they were like children in some ways. They could be led, but they weren't skilled at making decisions on their own.

Celestine probably likes it that way, he thought, *but I don't. I could use a little help.*

When Evan arrived at the small hall, his interrogators were waiting for him. All the faces were at least marginally familiar. The wolf queen. Captain Byrne. The queen's niece, Lady Barrett. The queen's sister, the princess Mellony. Lord Bayar, the High Wizard. Hadley DeVilliers. The upland mage, Shadow Dancer. Corporal Talbot, who'd brought the news of the fall of Chalk Cliffs. And, of course, the healer—Prince Adrian sul'Han, who sat in the corner nearest the hearth, his face in and out of shadow.

In Ardenscourt, sul'Han had always worn drab healer's colors, so it was a bit of a shock to see him dressed in velvets and satin. The prince had his mother's eyes, with a bit more blue in them, and a hint of her coppery complexion below his coppery hair.

Evan was beginning to realize that there was no way to win over the queen if he didn't win over the healer. Sul'Han was the son of the queen, after all, and blood trumps everything else. Even if she believed what Evan had to say, when it came to a choice, she would choose her own blood. That was the way the world worked.

But winning over the healer was going to be like climbing a mountain from deep underground. It would help considerably if Evan could convince him that Jenna was still alive.

Talbot opened the session with a brisk overview of what had happened in Chalk Cliffs. It was all too familiar.

"This is what the empress does," Evan said. "For the past five years, she has been systematically winning the free cities of the Desert Coast. First, infiltration by her bloodsworn. Then, the taking of the port, the off-loading of her armies, and an invasion that extends her control as far as the Dragonbacks. Here, let me show you." He'd brought his maps along, and he laid them out on the table and traced the backbone of Carthis from north to south.

"Where is her stronghold?" Captain Byrne leaned over the map.

"Here." Evan unfurled another map, an older one, of the Northern Islands at the time that they were conquered by the Nazari family. "I found this in your temple library," he said. "I assume this was brought here by some of those who fled Nazari rule eons ago. It's out of date, but the geography should be the same."

He turned the map so that Byrne could get a better look. "For years, the Northern Islands have been battered by storms that made it difficult even to approach the shoreline," he said. "In recent years, the weather has seemingly improved. Celestine has been rebuilding the ancient Nazari capital of Celesgarde on one of the Weeping Sisters—I'm not sure which one."

"The Weeping Sisters?" The queen cocked her head. "I'm not familiar with those."

"They are three islands in the Northern Islands that are known for volcanic activity—like many of the mountains in the Fells. I've not been there, but I would expect that the defenses would be formidable."

The healer watched silently throughout the geography lesson, taking notes, the scratch of his quill audible now and then when the conversation died.

"The empress's ships carried off dozens of prisoners," Barrett said, "including one of our best officers. Based on past practice, where would she take them and what—what does she intend to do with them?"

Evan looked from face to face, seeking clues. The atmosphere in the room was fraught, full of tension, unstable, seething with secrets. It reminded Evan of when a storm was about to break, the clouds piling up, the air so thick with electricity that it was difficult to breathe.

"Would this officer be Captain Gray?" he said.

The whole room flinched—all except the healer, who went very, very still.

"What do you know about Captain Gray?" Barrett said.

"Just a guess," Evan said disarmingly. "At the reception, Queen Raisa mentioned that a Captain Gray was at Chalk Cliffs, and expressed concerns about his safety. And now, it seems, all your worst fears have come true."

From the looks on their faces, he'd struck a vein.

Who is this Captain Gray, and why is he so important?

"So," Byrne said, breaking the silence, "going back to Lady Barrett's earlier question . . . ?"

"She might very well take prisoners to Celesgarde," Evan said. "On the other hand, she controls most of the Desert Coast, now, so it's difficult to say. It would depend on how she intends to . . . use them. Most of her prisoners go directly into her bloodsworn army."

"What does that mean, *bloodsworn*?" Talbot wore an expression of sick dread.

"They are bound to the empress in a blood ritual," Evan said.

This was met with a collective shudder. Sul'Han ran a finger over his forearm, as if tracing a memory. He exchanged glances with the queen.

"Have you heard of an order of bloodthirsty priests called the Darian Brothers?" Queen Raisa asked abruptly. "Is there a connection?"

"Not to my knowledge, no," Evan said. "I've not heard of them."

That, at least, seemed to be the right answer.

"Your crewman Brody says that he was bloodsworn, and you 'freed' him," Bayar said, speaking up for the first time. "Does that mean there is a way to undo the blood-magic charm once it's cast?"

Evan struggled to come up with an answer. "I don't know that you can undo it. Celestine doesn't let go of anything easily. But it seems that you can replace it with something else. That's what I did with the Stormborn. That is why their auras are red instead of purple."

"So you are a blood mage also," Bayar said, tapping his fingers on the arm of his chair.

"Apparently, yes."

They all looked at one another. After a moment, Barrett cleared her throat and made a show of consulting her notes. "Why is the empress interested in the magemarked, as you call them?"

The questioning continued, covering much of the same ground as in his earlier meeting with them. Didn't anyone take notes? He supposed that now they had more reason to be interested in what he had to say. Or maybe this repeat was for Talbot's and the healer's benefit. Talbot asked a few questions, but the healer remained silent. Evan kept looking at him, waiting for him to weigh in, make a face, dispute something he said, or provide additional information, but he didn't.

That's when Evan realized—the queen must have told sul'Han to keep quiet. Was it because she was angry with her son? Or was the intent to—what was the expression?—give Evan enough rope to hang himself?

"How is it that you are the only holdout along the Desert Coast?"

Evan wrenched himself back to the interrogation, realizing that Barrett had just asked him a question.

"I have built a fortified stronghold," Evan said. "And I am one of only a few gifted ship's masters that are left. That gives me an advantage. But I am under no illusion that we can hold out forever. I have to go to sea in order to make a living."

"By attacking our ships and stealing our goods," the queen said.

"It's nothing personal," Evan said. "We steal from

everyone, northerner and southerner, Desert Coast and wetland coast. We are equal opportunity brigands in that regard."

This was met with stony silence, finally broken by the queen.

"For the next series of questions, I've asked Lord Bayar to take over the questioning, and use persuasion. Are you familiar with that?"

Evan sat up straighter. Persuasion? Was that the wetland word for torture? "I am not," he admitted, his mouth dry. "Could you, perhaps, explain?"

"I'll use magic to ensure that your answers are true," Bayar said. "Don't worry," he added. "It's not painful, but I would ask you not to do anything to interfere with it."

"I wouldn't know how," Evan said, busily sorting through the secrets he wanted to keep. He should be all right, assuming a partial truth would be enough.

He and the High Wizard sat on either side of a small table and Bayar gripped his hands. Magic flowed from the wizard's hands to his own. Evan had expected that it might be similar to the sensation of rum or blue ruin running down his throat. Or that it might be painful, despite the high wizard's assurances. But no. It was more like a cold river running through Evan's veins that eventually disappeared as it mingled with his blood, leaving no trace behind.

Bayar frowned, looking down at their joined hands.

Then said, "Prince Adrian has told us that he met you in Ardenscourt this winter. Why did you go there?"

Evan glanced at the healer, who sat in shadow, fingers laced, his chin resting on his hands. He offered no clues.

"I went there to prevent the empress Celestine from making a deal with the king of Arden."

"How did you know that such a deal was on the table?"

Evan hesitated. "I had a source in Ardenscourt who sent word to me."

"So this plan was common knowledge in the Ardenine capital?" Barrett raised an eyebrow. "None of my eyes and ears reported that."

"It was not well known," Evan said. "My source is close to the king, and was involved in the negotiations." He was watching the healer when he said that. Sul'Han straightened, as if he'd finally heard something he didn't already know. He waited for Bayar to ask who his source was, and the High Wizard didn't disappoint.

"Who was this source who was close to the king?"

Evan had no intention of giving Destin away. "I would rather not say. It would put this person in grave danger."

"Don't worry," Bayar said. "What is said here stays here. You can speak freely."

Evan could continue to object, but that would be the same as saying "I don't trust you," and that wouldn't advance his diplomatic agenda. So he found himself lying, and then waiting to be struck dead. Or at least called on it. "It was Queen Marina," he said. "We met once, when I boarded her ship in the Southern Islands. I must have made a good impression."

They all looked at each other, faces full of doubt.

"Well," the queen said, glancing at the healer. "I suppose it's possible. She is a Tomlin, after all."

Bayar still looked puzzled. With a faint shake of his head, he tightened his grip so that the pressure was almost painful. "Why didn't you want this deal to go forward?"

"I did not want the empress's influence to spread farther than it already has," Evan said. "Trust me—you don't want Celestine for a neighbor."

Bayar abruptly let go of Evan's hands. "Something's wrong," he said flatly.

Barrett leaned forward. "With—? Do you mean that he's not telling the truth?"

"I have no idea if he's telling the truth," Bayar said. "I don't think it's working." He turned back to Evan. "Are you blocking me? Because if you are—"

"I'm not blocking you," Evan said. "How could I? You took my amulet. Besides, as I already said, I wouldn't know how."

"It's in your best interest to cooperate," the queen said to Evan.

"I am not trying to interfere with the High Wizard's magic. The truth serves me as well as you."

The High Wizard rubbed the back of his neck, his expression making it clear that he didn't believe him.

"Doesn't persuasion work on you?" Queen Raisa said.

Evan shrugged. "I don't know. I've never . . . submitted to this kind of magic before."

Sul'Han was staring at Evan now, eyes narrowed, as if he'd had some kind of epiphany. He leaned over and whispered something to Shadow Dancer, who nodded.

"Well," the queen said briskly, "we've been at this a good while already. Perhaps we should—"

"Let me try," Prince Adrian said.

Suddenly, the healer was the center of attention.

Queen Raisa shook her head. "I was about to say that perhaps we should recess for now and review what—"

"I promise I won't hurt him, Mother," the healer said, those remarkable blue-green eyes fixed on Evan. "But I believe I can get at the truth."

"Lord Bayar is as capable as any wizard in the realm when it comes to interrogation," the queen said, her voice low and furious.

Now the healer looked at Evan. "Do you object?" he said.

Sweat trickled between Evan's shoulder blades, but he shrugged and said, "Why not?"

The prince swapped places with the High Wizard. Sul'Han sat across the table from Evan, shook back the sleeves of his jacket, reached across, and gripped his hands. The prince's hands were strong, callused, buzzing with energy. There came that same cold current as before, though perhaps a bit more . . . intuitive. Then the prince said, "What's that on the back of your neck?"

Evan's heart plummeted to his toes, and his palms grew slippery with sweat. They stared into each other's eyes for what felt like a lifetime.

Outed, Evan thought. But how? He'd made sure to keep his neck under cover. He said nothing aloud.

"Lord Bayar," Prince Adrian said, his grip tightening on Evan's hands, pinning them in place. "Could you examine the back of Strangward's neck and tell us what you see?"

Evan heard the wizard's robes rustle as he crossed to where he could stand behind him. He could feel Bayar's fingers brushing his skin, raising gooseflesh as the wizard swept his hair aside. It reminded him of that day in Montaigne's palace at Ardenscourt, when he'd done the same to Jenna Bandelow in front of an audience of gawkers.

What goes around comes around, he thought. What you cast into the waves often washes up on your own private beach.

He heard Bayar's dry, amused voice. "It would appear to be a metal-and-stone badge, like an embedded amulet," he said, his breath warming the back of Evan's neck. "I assume that it is what we have been calling a magemark."

Evan heard chairs scraping, the sound of feet padding across the floor as they all had their look. He kept his eyes on the healer, who wore a trace of a smile.

"I think now would be a good time to have a recess," the healer said.

A COMMON CAUSE

When Evan returned to the suite of rooms he shared with his crew, they were boiling with curiosity about the interrogation. Evan kept them in suspense while he retrieved his burner and kettle from the corner, put water on to heat, and set out the tiny cups for the tay ceremony. He knew they would need fortification against this news. Those reborn in blood never lost their desire for it.

When the water was steaming, they watched in avid silence as Evan added the smoky leaves to the brew. While they steeped, he stripped back his sleeve, found a spot on his scarred forearm, and sliced it open, dripping his blood into the common pot.

Evan served each crew member himself. It was the least

he could do for people cursed with a thirst that would never be quenched.

When all had been served, Evan slumped into a chair, stirred the fire with a stick, and said, "They know."

They all looked at one another, as if each hoped that somebody else would ask a question.

"They know . . . what?" Brody said finally.

"They know about the magemark," Evan said. This was met with a collective groan. Secrets like that didn't keep. There was no stronghold, no prison strong enough to keep them safe, once Celestine knew where he was. It was all Evan could do to stay in his seat and not stand and begin pacing, which would not help the mood in the room.

"What are we going to do?" Teza said.

"I'm not sure it much matters what we do," Evan said.

"Do you think they will sell you to the empress?" Brody said. "Or trade you to get their port back?" That was Brody—always the cheerful one.

"I don't really have control of this story going forward," Evan said. "A lot depends on the healer."

"The healer?" Jorani scowled. "He hates you, doesn't he?"

"Maybe," Evan said. "I think I'm beginning to win him over, though. If I can stay alive another year or two, we might be friends."

"Let's go find the healer and *make* him be your friend," Jorani said.

Right, Evan thought. That could go wrong in oh, so many ways.

This pessimistic thought was interrupted by voices outside the door, as if the guards outside were arguing with someone. Finally, the door banged open, revealing the surly healer prince, Adrian sul'Han.

The bluejackets guarding the door admitted him, then pulled the door shut behind him. Instantly, Teza, Jorani, Brody, and the others fanned out, forming a wall in front of Evan.

Evan pushed his way to the front of his crew, waving them off. "Don't worry," he said. "I'm sure this is a friendly visit." Turning to the healer, he said, "Good evening. To what do I owe this unexpected—"

"We need to talk," sul'Han said, displaying his usual charm.

"I agree," Evan said. "But what's it been, two hours, since we last spoke? Do you have those notes with you? It might save some time."

"I'd rather start fresh, and speak frankly. There's too much at stake to waste time sparring with you." The healer was as serious as death.

Evan folded his arms and broadened his stance. "Will *you* speak frankly as well?"

"Of course," the healer said, as if *that* point was never in question. He ran his eyes over the hovering Stormborn. "I'd prefer to meet privately."

This brought protests from Evan's crew.

"The healer doesn't mean me any harm," Evan said. "Else he wouldn't have come alone."

This spawned another chorus of objections.

Evan lifted the pot from the burner and handed it off to Teza. "Go. And take this with you."

They were still grumbling when they went out the door. With the tay.

"Your crew seems . . . unusually loyal," the wolf prince said, staring after them in a way that suggested that he really meant "fanatical," "obsessive," or "paranoid."

"The empress has put a sizable price on my head, and there are always those who would like to cash in. The only way I've been able to keep a crew that won't betray me is through a blood bond. There's a price to be paid for that." Evan gathered pillows from the furniture and tossed them down, onto the rug. "Let's sit, shall we, and have a civilized conversation. I've not much to offer in the way of refreshments, but I could brew up a fresh pot of tay. It's a beverage popular in Carthis for bringing people—"

"No," the healer said. Then added, "Thank you."

Evan shrugged and sat down on one of the pillows. After a moment's hesitation, the healer sat, his hands resting on his knees, the lamps behind him sending his long shadow across the floor.

"Now, then," Evan said, figuring that he would get a

question in first if he could. "I'm curious. What tipped you off to the magemark?"

"Your resistance to direct magic," sul'Han said. "I had the same kind of sensation when I questioned Jenna." He paused. "So, what can you tell me about magemarks?"

"Disappointingly little, I'm afraid," Evan said. "For five years now, I've been looking for someone who can explain it to me. Someone besides the empress, I mean, who no doubt would be happy to fill me in."

"So. Is she hunting you, too? Or are you working for her?" Sul'Han rolled his eyes. "I'm so confused."

Evan laughed, a little amazed to find out that the healer had a sense of humor.

"One thing I've learned in the past five years is to trust no one with the truth. Lying about nearly everything has become a habit—it's how I stay alive."

"If you plan to keep lying, tell me now, and that will save us both some time," the healer said, all traces of humor gone.

"I have no plans to lie to you," Evan said, which was true enough. Then again, plans change.

"So. About magemarks," the healer said.

"I've been marked for as long as I can remember," Evan said. "My first memories date from when I was four or five, running the streets of Endru in Carthis, doing whatever I needed to do to stay alive." Evan relayed the rest of the story—how he'd been plucked from the streets by

Latham Strangward and added to his crew.

"Captain Strangward told me to keep the magemark hidden, that it would rile up the crew. It wasn't until I met Celestine Nazari for the first time that I found out she was hunting the magemarked. So. When the empress learned that I was aboard Strangward's ship, she demanded that he give me up. Strangward refused. In fact, he threatened to kill me rather than turn me over to her." Evan paused, the old pain, the questions elbowing forward. "I'm still not sure who he was protecting—me, or everyone else. What-ever his motive, it didn't work out well for him. He lost his ship, his crew, and his life. I escaped."

The prince, head cocked, was studying him. He didn't seem to be coiled quite as tightly as he had been. "We may have more in common than I thought," he said.

Evan nodded, thinking it was ironic that he was having this heart-to-heart with sul'Han, of all people.

"So," the healer said, with an air of getting down to the real business of the evening, "you say the empress is your enemy. Why, then, did you go to Ardenscourt pretending to be representing her?"

"As I told the council, I went to try to prevent the king of Arden from making an alliance with Celestine, and so acquiring a person with a magemark. That person turned out to be Jenna Bandelow."

"Did you know Jenna before then?"

Evan shook his head. "I had not known there was

another one of us hiding in the wetlands until I got the message that a deal was in the offing. I couldn't offer an army, but there is a huge population of dragons in the mountains at home. I hoped that if I could persuade King Gerard to trade Jenna for the dragon, I could kill the deal. King Gerard wouldn't have an army, and Celestine wouldn't have Jenna." *Plus, the dragon might burn the capital to the ground.*

"So Montaigne's refusal to make a trade for the dragon ruined that plan," the healer said.

Evan nodded, wishing he could leave it at that. But if Jenna told the healer about his visit to the tower room, the truce between them would be over.

"Then, I made a mistake," Evan said, looking down at his hands.

"What do you mean?"

"After King Gerard declined my proposal, I went to Jenna's room to find out what she knew. I thought—I hoped she would be able to tell me something that would reassure me."

"Reassure you?"

"Something that would convince me that even if Montaigne sent her to the empress it would not end in disaster."

"Was Jenna able to reassure you?"

Evan shook his head. "No. It turned out that she knows less than I do. So. Teza and I were—were talking about what to do when she took matters into her own hands. She smashed one of the lamps on the floor and set the room on fire."

"Why would she do that?"

"Isn't it obvious? She was trying to escape."

"By setting fire to herself?" The healer snorted. "That makes sense. Did she blow a hole in the tower, too?"

"That happened after I left," Evan said. "I have a theory, though."

Sul'Han tilted his head back, his hands resting on his thighs. "I can't wait to hear it."

"Someone unchained the dragon in the hold of my ship," Evan said, looking straight into the healer's eyes. "Someone who left his wizard collar behind."

Sul'Han's eyes narrowed, and he shifted on his cushion. Message received. "Really?"

"Really. The dragon escaped, flew straight to the tower, and rescued Jenna."

The healer's wary interest dissolved into skepticism. "The dragon again. *That's* your theory? That after spending weeks confined belowdecks, this Carthian dragon's first instinct was to fly across town and smash a hole in a castle to rescue a girl he'd never met?" Sul'Han shook his head. "How long did it take you to come up with that?"

"I think Jenna is a shape-shifter, or at least someone with a special affinity for dragons."

"Convince me," the healer said, looking obstinate as a rock.

"When Jenna's in danger, have you noticed that she develops scales?"

The healer, frowning, stared at him, then nodded. "I did see something like that," he said. "When I was treating Jenna in Ardenscourt, and her wound was healing up, there was, at first, something that looked like scales. I didn't know what to make of it."

"Exactly. I couldn't imagine how anyone would have survived that fire in the tower. But she did. I think that she is resistant to flame."

"Something you hadn't counted on," the healer said.

"You're wrong. Nobody is happier than I am that Jenna survived and escaped," Evan said. Looking into the healer's face, he thought, Well, maybe somebody is.

He pressed on, building his case. "Did you notice her eyes?"

"What about them?" From the healer's expression, it seemed he didn't like Evan noticing anything about Jenna.

"Beautiful, golden, almost reptilian, wouldn't you say?"

"I suppose," sul'Han said grudgingly. "Though I never really thought of them that way."

"Something smashes a hole in the tower. Jenna and the sun dragon disappear. The next thing we know, Jenna is in the mountains, ordering an extra-large harness from the upland trader. A harness for a dragon, perhaps?"

The healer grunted, still uncommitted, but wavering, as if weighing the evidence.

"Finally, the dragon was with Jenna when I saw her on the coast. It was wearing a harness. After incinerating my ship, she mounted up, and they flew off together."

"Jenna. Was riding on the dragon."

Evan nodded. "Exactly. Legend has it that the ancient Nazari rulers fielded squadrons of dragon fighters. There are images of them in the ancient texts."

The healer scrubbed his hands through his hair. "All right. Leaving the topic of dragons for the moment—let's say you'd succeeded, and your deal had gone forward. What did you plan to do with Jenna after the trade was made?"

Evan looked down at his hands and considered what to say. "Being the target of someone like Celestine is a lonely business," he said finally. "There's nobody I can really trust, and no source of information that I can access without risking my life. I hoped that Jenna was ahead of me, that she knew more about this magic than I do. I hoped that we could share information and find a way to fight back."

"Did you tell her that?"

Evan nodded. "Eventually. But not until we met again, on the coast near Chalk Cliffs. I couldn't risk telling her while we were in Ardenscourt."

"How did she respond?"

Evan laughed. "Not well. I'm the last person she wants for a partner. The way she sees it, I ruined her life."

"I don't think it's a matter of perspective," the healer

said. "You did ruin her life."

"Her life would have been ruined with or without my involvement. You may not believe me, but I was trying to help. I told her the truth—about the magemark, all of it. I tried to persuade Jenna that we are natural allies, that we share the same blood."

"What do you mean, you share the same blood?" sul'Han said, leaping on that like a trout on a fly.

"Celestine claims that the magemarked are related to her, that we have Nazari blood, which is why we belong together. Remember, it was Jenna who drew Celestine to the wetlands."

"Jenna and the busker," sul'Han said, half to himself.

Evan's mind was racing along, and now it skidded to a stop. "Busker? What do you mean?"

The healer sighed. "Back at Solstice, when I was still in Arden, a street performer—a musician—led my sister into an ambush."

"Oh!" Evan said, unsure where this was going. "Did it—? Was she—?"

"She was unhurt, but one of her personal guards was killed. The Queen's Guard tracked the busker down in Chalk Cliffs, and he turned out to have a magemark, too."

Evan was stunned. He'd been living alone with this secret for most of his life, but now the magemarked seemed to be surfacing at every turn, flushed out of hiding by Celestine.

"Did you ask him about the mark?" Evan leaned forward. "What did he tell you?"

The healer shook his head. "He claimed he didn't know much about it, either. He'd been working with a gang out of Baston Bay when he was recruited to do a street concert, supposedly to try to woo my sister on behalf of a suitor."

"So . . . this person . . . used his gift to try to murder the heir to the throne?" Evan felt as if he were standing on a sandbar that was being washed out from under him.

Sul'Han nodded. "Now, bear in mind, most of this is secondhand, because I just arrived home after . . . after a long time away."

"In Ardenscourt."

"In the south, yes."

"So . . . the busker . . . What is his name?"

"Breon d'Tarvos, he calls himself." The healer was watching Evan closely.

Evan made no attempt to hide his surprise. "Tarvos! But that's where—"

"That's where your stronghold is," sul'Han said, nodding.

Evan was beginning to see why the wetlanders might be wary of him. How could he possibly win their trust with that history on the books?

"The busker has the gift of . . . ensnarement? Enticement?"

"Something like that. My sister—she wouldn't—
anyway." The healer fumbled his way to the end of that
sentence as if changing his mind several times on the way.
"So you can see why we're trying to jam all these pieces
into the same puzzle. One theory is that Arden's behind
it, because we've been enemies for so long. That assumes
that Carthis is here as a proxy for the Montaignes, hired as
mercenaries to fight their battle for them, since the thanes
are in rebellion."

"Celestine is nobody's proxy," Evan said. "If the young
king thinks she's biddable, he will learn to his sorrow that
she is not."

The healer nodded. "I agree. Given what happened in
Ardenscourt, and the fact that the busker was in Chalk
Cliffs when it came under attack, I'm inclined to think
that the empress came north on her own, and she was after
the busker."

Evan didn't want to ask, but he had to know. "You
mentioned that the busker was in Chalk Cliffs. Where is
he now?"

"We don't know," sul'Han said. "He was in the city
when it fell. We believe that he might be among the prisoners the empress took back to her capital." Again, it
seemed like he had more to say, but didn't.

Evan tried not to surrender to despair. Despite everything he'd done, all the plans he'd laid with Destin, another
of the magemarked was in the empress's hands.

So, now what? Maybe Brody was right. These wetland-ers might decide to trade him to the empress in an effort to make her go away. They might believe they had no other skin in the game. Evan had to convince them otherwise.

"Once Celestine realizes that Jenna is still alive, she will conquer the wetlands, realm by realm, until she finds her. If you want to defeat the empress, you are going to have to join together. If you don't, she will win. Ask the survivors of Chalk Cliffs." He paused. "Do you think there's any chance of that—joining together?"

"It won't be easy," the healer said. "There's too much blood on the ground already."

"And there will be more—you can count on that," Evan said. "What about you? Why are we having this meeting? What are you hoping for?"

The healer held his gaze for a long moment. And then, somehow, chose to trust him. "You've heard people speak of a Captain Gray," he said.

Evan nodded. "He was at Chalk Cliffs," he said. "Every-one seemed to be worried about him."

"*She* was at Chalk Cliffs," the healer corrected him. "Captain Gray is my sister Alyssa, the heir to the Gray Wolf throne. We believe that the empress took her captive, and that she is now somewhere in Carthis. I intend to go after her, and I'm going to need your help."

SETTING THE TRAP

When it came to political intrigue, Hal Matelon had one thing going for him: by now he had a network of men he could trust with his life—men he'd fought alongside on multiple battlegrounds in this never-ending war. He was counting on that now to help him find his brother.

On the downside, his was a well-known face in Ardens-court, even after a year away, since he'd spent most of his winters at court. So he sat in the corner of the tavern, collar turned up, face turned away from the lamp, hoping that he wouldn't be recognized. The last thing they needed was another Matelon held hostage by the boy king.

He was all but positive that Robert would have come

here to Ardenscourt to hunt for their mother and sister before the thanes marched on the capital.

Hal heard the door bang open and shut as someone new came into the tavern. The newcomer, dressed in military garb, stopped at the bar to make inquiries. Now he walked purposefully toward Hal's table, bringing with him the scent of the spring evening. Hal tensed momentarily, then relaxed when he recognized him.

It was Eric Bellamy, the son of the master of horse at Ardenscourt. Though Bellamy was a year or two older than Hal, he'd served under him for several years in the field. Only now, Hal noted, he wore a captain's braid on his shoulders.

"Sir? I'm told you have a message for— Saints and martyrs!" Bellamy stared at Hal as if he'd been raised from the dead, then made the sign of Malthus.

"Shhh. Sit down," Hal said, waving him to a seat.

Bellamy sat, nearly stumbling over the table leg. He seemed to be afraid to take his eyes off Hal, as if he might lunge at him and suck out his soul if he did.

"But . . . Captain . . . I heard you were dead—that you died at Delphi!" Bellamy hissed.

"No, not dead yet," Hal said.

Bellamy looked around, to see if anyone was close enough to have heard. "You shouldn't be here," he whispered. "What if someone sees you?"

"I'm hoping it will help that nobody will be looking for a dead man," Hal said. He signaled for the server. "What'll you have?"

"Small beer," Bellamy said. "I'm on duty in a little while." He paused. "On second thought, I'll have bingo. A double."

Hal put in the order and turned back to Bellamy, who was studying him with narrowed eyes. "You look like you've put on some hard miles since I saw you last, sir," he said. "When's the last time you had a good meal?"

"I just ate an entire lamb pie," Hal said, pushing his empty plate back, "and I'm seriously considering having another. I've been in a northern prison, where food is hard to come by."

"How'd you get away?"

"The guards got tired of losing to me at nicks and bones," Hal said. "So they let me go."

"Right," Bellamy said skeptically. He paused, as if groping for something to say. "I've never seen you with a beard before."

Hal fingered his chin, still thickly forested with a black stubble. "Enjoy it while you can. What are you up to these days?"

Bellamy rolled his eyes. "I've been working with my da over the winter, trying to teach new recruits from the down-realms which end of a horse is the front. When I'm not doing that, my mother is trotting me around to parties, hoping I'll meet some rich widow. There's a shortage of dance partners at court, since so many of the thanes have taken the field against the king. Those that haven't are staying away, for fear of being here when the thanes sack the city."

"Could be your golden ticket," Hal said drily.

"Ha," Bellamy said. "The widows I fall for are always penniless."

"To penniless widows," Hal said, raising his glass in a toast.

Bellamy laughed, but quickly sobered. "If fortune finds me, it'll be because I've been a good soldier."

Hal nodded toward Bellamy's new signia. "You've done well, Captain."

"I'm up for colonel now," Bellamy said, then colored. "You're the one who's earned it. I just don't get why—"

Hal raised his hand. "Congratulations, Colonel. Guess I'll have to get used to calling you 'sir.'"

"I may have reason to regret this promotion," Bellamy said. "Now that it's looking to be a two-front war, they're in need of more sacrificial officers. Rumor has it that I may lead our forces in the north while General Karn deals with the thanes." He stopped, then, as if realizing that he might be giving away tactics to the enemy. "Everybody says the rebels are going to march on the city any day now. But maybe they won't, since you're here." He looked sideways at Hal, as if hoping he'd confirm or deny.

"I haven't seen my father since I came back," Hal lied. "I leave the politics to him."

Bellamy sighed. "I hate this, sir. I'm glad to go north, so I don't have to take the field against my friends."

"We're soldiers, Bellamy," Hal said, shrugging. "We follow orders. Listen, the reason I asked to meet with you is that I'm looking for my brother, Robert. We were together at Delphi, but he left for Temple Church before the city fell. I'm hoping he's all right. Have you seen him? Do you know where he's posted?"

"Robert? Haven't seen him," Bellamy said, shifting his eyes away, staring down into his glass. "You sure he's not with your father?"

"He's not at White Oaks," Hal said. "I know that for a fact." He waited one heartbeat, then two, for Bellamy to speak up; then he planted his hands on the table. "Now—be straight with me. What have you heard?"

Bellamy began picking at a scab on his wrist. "I told the truth when I said I haven't seen him. But I've heard he's been in and out of taverns and barracks houses for the past few days, asking a lot of questions about where the king might be holding prisoners. I went looking for him—I was going to sit him down and tell him to quit that foolishness and go home. But it always seems like I'm a few steps behind. One thing I'll say for him, he moves quick and he doesn't lay his head down in the same place twice."

Hal swore. Robert was as subtle and stealthy as any

charging bull. It wouldn't take long for the blackbirds to catch wind of this. But if Robert found out Hal was here looking for him, he'd go deeper underground than ever. The city was too big and the situation too dangerous to be playing hounds and hares.

But he had to try.

"Tell me he's using a fake name, at least?"

Bellamy laughed. "He's calling himself Cordray."

That was the name of their old tutor.

"Could I ask for a favor?"

"You can ask," Bellamy said, with a sigh. "Just remember, I'm not the hero you are. King Gerard was a cold, ruthless bastard, but at least there was a purpose to most of what he did. King Jarat—he's a monster."

Great, Hal thought. My mother and sister are held prisoner by a monster, and my brother seems determined to join them.

Hal ripped a page from his journal and scribbled a note on it.

Mr. Cordray—
I may have the information you are looking for. I'll be at the
Golden Horn each evening between six and nine.
—A friend

It was a laughably transparent ruse, but it might make Robert curious enough to show up.

303

He handed it to Bellamy. "If you could leave this with the duty officer at the garrison house, I'd appreciate it. I'll cover some of the taverns around here and we'll see if I can lure him out of hiding."

Bellamy nodded, tucking the note away. "I'll do that, Captain. I just want to say—I'm glad you're not dead."

Hal laughed. "Not yet."

"Be careful, all right? I hope we both live to see the day that I can fight under your command again."

"Or I can fight under your command." Hal stood and embraced his friend. "I hope there will come a day that we can quit fighting and share a beer without looking over our shoulders."

TAKING THE BAIT

For the next two nights, Hal had his dinner in the common room of the Golden Horn, watching the comings and goings through the door. He'd chosen that place because it was a busy taproom, the food was good, and it wasn't where he was staying. The only downside was that it did seem to attract a lot of blackbirds, who dined and drank in noisy flocks all evening long. It was hard to sit there nursing a drink when his father was at White Oaks preparing to march on the capital, Alyssa Gray was on her way across the Indio, and who knew how far the enemy had advanced in the north. He couldn't even distract himself by reading because he had to keep his eye out for his quarry.

He was about to call it a night for the second time when

he saw a familiar figure shoulder his way into the tavern, glance around the room, and saunter up to the bar. Robert ordered a cider, sipped it, then scanned the room once more. He leaned in and exchanged a few words with the tapsman, who nodded toward Hal in his corner. Robert slipped him some coin, took a long pull on his cider, flirted with the serving girl, then strolled over to Hal's table.

"Is this seat ta— What are *you* doing here?" he hissed.

"Have a seat," Hal said, shoving the chair out with his foot, "and tell me how you managed to misplace the good sense you were born with."

For a moment, he thought his little brother might refuse, but Robert finally slumped into the chair and banged his tankard down on the table.

"I don't need your help," he growled. "Go on back to White Oaks."

"Oh, I'm going back there tomorrow, and you're going with me. If I can find you, the King's Guard can, too. Every thane on the council has spies and operatives here in town trying to get to the king's hostages. Why do you think you'll succeed when they haven't in three months of trying?"

"Because nobody'd expect me to come looking."

"Right. They wouldn't expect it, because they know you spring from a long line of smart people." Hal leaned toward him. "Look, nobody wants to free our mother and sister more than me, but this is not the right way to do it."

"King Jarat said that if Father's armies lay siege to the city, he'll hang the families from the parapets." Despite his bravado, Robert's voice quivered a little.

That thought, Hal had to admit, was a punch to the gut. It was one more reminder of how impossible it would be to forge an alliance with the north to fight back against the empress.

"Doesn't sound like the new king is much of an improvement over the old one," he said.

"Father won't listen to me. He's going to attack anyway. He says we can't give way to that kind of pressure. And he won't lift a hand to save them."

"Do you think he wants to see Mother and Harper hurt?" Hal waited, and Robert finally shook his head. "Giving in won't help them. Even if the thanes flat-out surrender, Jarat will execute Father and the others, and probably us, too, because he knows we'll come back for revenge. He'll confiscate the estates and fill his treasuries. And he still won't free the hostages."

Robert scowled down at the table. "So, that's it? We give up?"

"No. Matelons never give up. But we don't get drawn into a battle we can't win." As he said this, Hal was a little amazed to hear his father's words coming out of his own mouth. And it seemed a bit hypocritical after his bone-headed moves in Fortress Rocks and Delphi.

Well, he thought, maybe my brother can benefit from

my bad experience. Somebody ought to.

After another minute or two of sulking, Robert nodded. "All right," he said. "I'll come with you. Nobody's responded to my inquiries but you, anyway."

"Fortunately for you."

Robert drew a deep breath, then blew it out. "Isn't there anything we can do?"

"We can hope that King Jarat is smart enough to know that if he takes action against the hostages, there can be no reconciliation, ever. This civil war won't end until he's dead, or we are."

Hal stood. "Now. Where are you staying? We should go get your things and both move somewhere else. We'll leave in the morning. Our luck can't last forever."

Robert drained the rest of his cider and stood, pulling his cloak from the back of his chair. "It's just a few blocks down, close to Citadel Hill."

When they walked out into the spring night, Hal still felt no need for a cloak, though the air was moist, promising rain. You've grown tougher during your time in the north, he thought.

They hadn't gone more than a block down the darkened street when Hal heard the thud of boots on cobblestones and the familiar hiss of swords sliding from their scabbards. Hal and Robert put their backs to a building and drew their own swords, only to find themselves facing a ring of steel.

"Stand down, in the name of the king," one of the swordsmen said, "or we'll gut the pair of you."

Robert broadened his stance, lifting the tip of his blade, and Hal knew he had visions of fighting his way out. His little brother was a devil with a sword, and he'd draw plenty of blood before he went down, but there was no doubt about the outcome. Hal put a hand on his arm. "Lower your blade," he said. "Remember what I said about being drawn into a battle we can't win?"

"That sounds like wise advice, Mister . . . Cordray, is it? I do hope you'll take it." Someone stepped forward, raising a lantern so that it shone down into Hal's face, all but blinding him. The man was tall, slender, dressed in the black of the King's Guard. "Blood of the martyrs," he muttered. "What have we here?" The officer's voice was faintly familiar, but Hal couldn't place it immediately.

He turned to his men. "Disarm them and bind their hands."

The blackbirds complied, collecting the brothers' swords and chaining their wrists.

The officer handed the lantern off to one of the black-birds, so, once Hal's eyes adjusted, he could finally see his face.

It was Lieutenant Destin Karn, the king's spymaster. Son of Hal's nemesis, General Marin Karn.

The situation had rapidly gone from bad to worse.

Hal opened his mouth to speak, but Karn raised a hand

to stop him. "Please," he said. "It's beginning to rain. We'll talk later." He turned to the commander of the blackbirds. "Take them to Newgate. Put them in the Aerie."

"Newgate? But—"

Now Karn's voice turned deadly cold. "Was there something you didn't understand about that order, Sergeant . . . Levesque, is it?" The way he said it, he was taking down names.

"No, sir, it's just that it's unusual to—"

"Did I ask for your opinion?"

Levesque reddened. "No, sir, but—"

"Then why are we still standing here in the rain? Now, go. Set a close guard on them and make sure that they are well provisioned and comfortable. I'll hold you personally responsible if they are not in good condition for interrogation."

"Yes, sir." Levesque turned to his men. "Bring them, and follow me."

Karn turned with a swirl of his cloak and stalked off down the street in the other direction until he was lost in the darkness between the streetlamps.

"Do you know who that was?" Robert said into Hal's ear as they marched down the narrow street.

"That was Destin Karn, the king's spymaster. At least, I assume he still is, under the new king."

"Karn? But that's—"

"This is his son. He was in Delphi for a while. I don't

think you ever met him."

"Oh." A few more steps, and then, "Have you heard of Newgate?" Robert whispered, trying to sound nonchalant.

Hal nodded. "I've heard of it, but I don't know much about it."

What he knew about it was mostly rumors, and mostly discouraging. Newgate was the prison used by the king's intelligence service for prisoners thought to have valuable information that needed extracting. Or political prisoners too valuable to mingle with the general prison population.

He tried to lighten the situation by saying, "Well, you've been trying to get more information about the king's prison. Now we'll see it for ourselves."

"I'm sorry, Hal," Robert said.

"Don't worry," Hal said, though he actually had plenty of worries. How was it that he'd ended up leaving one prison only to end up in another? And he had a feeling that this one would be worse.

CAPTIVES

When Lyss awakened, she was immediately sorry. Everything hurt—her head, her back, her arms and legs. She was one big mass of bruises, and one of her arms seemed to be immobilized, strapped to her side. Worse, she was aware of an unpleasant sensation, as if the world was rocking under her.

I must've taken a really hard blow to the head, she thought, fighting back nausea. The last she remembered, she'd been on the beach near Chalk Cliffs, trying to keep the busker out of the hands of the empress Celestine.

"You're awake," Breon said. His anxious face came into view. "How do you feel, Your Highness?"

She propped up on her elbow. "I feel horrible. Somebody

needs to put me out of my misery."

"There's a lot of rum around, if that's appealing," Breon said.

"No!" Lyss said sharply. She lay back down, waiting for the world to stop spinning. "Where are we?"

"We're aboard the empress's flagship," Breon said. "The *Siren*."

Now that he'd mentioned it, she could hear the wooden hull creaking and complaining all around them.

"Damn," Lyss muttered. "Another bloody, gutter-strumming boat."

"Looks that way."

"I assume we're under way?"

He nodded. "We're a day out."

"So I guess there's no swimming back." Lyss tried to laugh, but it was so painful that tears came to her eyes. More than one rib cracked, probably.

"How about some water?" Breon said.

"Hang on." Lyss took one breath, then another, getting ready. "All right," she said. "I'm going to sit up, and I apologize in advance if I spew all over you."

"Turnabout is fair play, I guess," Breon said.

Happily, she managed to sit up, and there was no spewing.

To her surprise, she was actually lying in a bed, in a fairly plush cabin with a tiny round window that displayed an angry gray ocean.

Breon had shed the filthy clothing he'd worn in their small boat and was dressed plainly but finely in a white linen shirt and loose, drawstring breeches. He'd washed his hair, so that the gold streak stood out. Despite his plain clothing, he resembled a demigod out of stories, one of those beings with one foot in the human world, the other in the divine.

When Lyss looked down at herself, she saw that her blood-mucked uniform was gone, replaced by a white silk gown. She wondered who'd done that, and decided she didn't really want to go further with that investigation.

Breon brought her a cup of water and then perched at the foot of the bed, drawing his knees up and wrapping his arms around them.

"What's going on?" she whispered. "Are we prisoners or what?"

"We are guests," Breon said drily. "The empress is really sorry about losing her temper on the beach." He stopped, cleared his throat, and swallowed hard. "She's eager to make amends." From the expression on Breon's face, he wasn't buying what she was selling.

"Why am I here?" Lyss asked. "Why am I still alive?"

Breon hesitated. "I think she likes you," he said finally. "She likes that you're not afraid to fight back."

"Did you tell her who I am?"

Breon smiled slantwise. "You're Captain Gray," he said, "an officer in the Highlander army."

"Ah," she said. She wished he'd used a less well-known name, but at least he didn't name her the heir to the throne. "I'm sorry about your friend. I wish I could have been of more help."

"At least you had better weapons than me. I had a flute. Music is no kind of match for—for *that*."

"I wasn't all that successful with a bow," Lyss said. "Don't feel bad. Anyway, as long as we're saying sorry, I'm sorry I didn't jump out of the boat when you told us to."

"Me too."

"So, what's this all about? Do you have any idea?"

"It has to do with my magemark," Breon said. "That's all I know."

"So she didn't tell you what it's for or what it means?"

He shook his head. "Maybe there'll be a big reveal when we get where we're going," he said. "I guess the empress put the word out that she was looking for people like me. Aubrey heard there was a reward on offer, and split on me."

"Was Aubrey your sweetheart?" Lyss knew the question was out of line, but found herself asking it anyway.

Breon drooped a little, like a flower in need of water. "I guess 'sweetheart' is too strong for what we had going," he said. "But I thought at least she was my friend."

"From what I heard, she didn't know what the empress's intentions were," Lyss said.

"Obviously she didn't know the empress meant to burn her alive."

"You know what I mean. She didn't know what Celestine wanted with you."

"Maybe," Breon said, "but it's no excuse. It's like when that cove hired me to wait for you on a street corner in Southbridge. I guess I could claim that I didn't know what he intended. He never came out and said it. But, looking back, I had to know he was up to no good. But I did it anyway."

"We've all done things we regret," Lyss said, thinking she had too many to count. "All we can do is try to do better going forward."

"Maybe. I just don't know." He paused, sliding a look at her. "Do you think Talbot and the others will come after you?"

"Sasha will come," Lyss said, without a shred of doubt, remembering the look on the Gray Wolf's face the night of the failed escape. "She will come, if she's still alive."

"I think you're right," Breon said. "She's . . . formidable." He sighed. "Will they even know where to look?"

"I tried to leave a message on the beach," Lyss said. "I hope they can figure it out."

"I hope they hurry," Breon said. "I've got a very bad feeling about this."

"For what it's worth," Lyss said, "I misjudged you, and I'm sorry."

"No," Breon said. "You didn't misjudge me. All those bad things you thought—they were true. I could justify anything, as long as it led to another hit. I lied to everyone— myself most of all."

"Don't be so hard on yourself," Lyss said. It was odd to be in the position of consoling someone who'd led her into an ambush. "If I were picking villains in this, you wouldn't be high on the list."

"I'd be on it, though. You were the one who forced me to get off the leaf. I never could've done it on my own. I don't know how much time I have left, but I'm glad to be clean, and I hope I can make you glad that you saved me."

Lyss felt her cheeks heating. "I'm already glad, Breon. Since we're in this together, I hope we can be friends." She extended her hand, and Breon took it.

IN THE WAKE OF
THE EMPRESS

Cas slowly circled over the city of Chalk Cliffs, losing altitude with each circle he made. The air was still thick with smoke—thick, acrid fumes that burned Jenna's eyes and made her cough.

Bad air, Cas said. *Stinks.*

"I know. At least it might make us harder to see."

Cas and Jenna would be hard to see if we fly to the mountains.

Cas disapproved of Jenna's interest in this broken, fuming city. He was happy that the big guns on shore had quieted, at least.

"That's low enough, I think. Just keep circling a minute."

The ships that had been lying out of sight of land had

come in now, and were unloading soldiers and horses onto the shore. The city was a charred ruin, but the harbor was a hive of activity. The warning they'd delivered had been too little, too late.

Why horse people want to live in burned city?

"I don't think they plan to stay long," Jenna said. Leaning down over Cas's shoulder, she studied the ships anchored in the harbor, looking for the three-masted ship with the siren figurehead.

Jenna's eyesight was sharper by far than that of anyone else of her species, but not nearly as sharp as a dragon's.

"Do you see the ship that chased the ship we burned?"

Cas swept back and forth, twice, then made a larger circle, soaring past the white cliffs with the now-silent guns and out over the ocean beyond the bay.

There.

"Are you sure?"

Cas snorted flame and smoke, vexed that she would ask that question. As they drew closer, Jenna could see that the dragon had called it right.

While the other ships were dropping anchor in the harbor, this one was sailing east under full sail.

"That's interesting," Jenna said. "The armies are staying, but this ship seems to be going back home. Go high, but keep them in sight, all right?"

With a few lazy wingbeats, Cas gained altitude so that the ship below, on the dark water, resembled a tiny toy boat trailing a threadlike white wake.

Jenna debated what to do. It was unlikely that a girl and a dragon could drive an army from Chalk Cliffs, though they could do plenty of damage.

They could fly back west, over the backbone of mountains, and try to find the capital in the north and warn the northerners. But if Jenna lost sight of the ship, she might never find it again. If she meant to make good on her promise to seek vengeance on the empress who had taken so much from her, now would be the time to do it. A ship at sea is highly vulnerable to an aerial assault, particularly a sneak attack.

If only they knew for sure that the empress was aboard, they could reduce it to a smear of ash on the waves.

Yet she and Cas had been training for months so they would be ready to cross the Indio and confront the empress in her lair. As Cas put it: *Burn the nest, kill the hatchlings, claim the hoard.*

Jenna had studied the map she'd stolen from the temple library at Fortress Rocks, tracing a path from shore to shore, past the script that said *Here there be dragons.* There weren't any resting points for a dragon between the Seven Realms and the shoreline of Carthis. It would be a challenge, even though Cas used very little energy when they were soaring.

"What do you think, Cas?" she said. "Are we ready for this? Do you want to follow them home?"

Fish in the ocean?

"Yes," she said, resting her cheek against his hot shoulder. "We can fish in the ocean."

Without replying, the dragon turned northeast and put on speed, following the wake of the empress's flagship across the dark northern sea.

31

GOING FOR BROKE

To Hal's surprise, their quarters in Newgate Prison were reasonably comfortable, at the top of one of the towers of the palace's perimeter wall. Even more surprising, he and Robert were housed together, when common practice was to isolate the subjects of interrogation to make them more pliable and to prevent them from comparing notes and working up a story.

Their guards were a cut above the usual as well, which had its pros and cons. They lacked the random cruelty and greed so often displayed by those in the trade. But they were strict, businesslike, impossible to chat up or bribe. Robert was a born charmer, but he got nowhere with them when he asked if the Matelon ladies were housed in the same building, or if they wanted to put a little money on a game of nicks and bones.

A day passed, and nobody put them to the question, or took them to the gallows or the block. Hal wondered if King Jarat had sent word to his father that he now held two more Matelons, arrested for spying, and invited him to the execution. Perhaps the king hoped that might prompt a bloodless surrender. Maybe he was waiting for an answer before he took further action against them.

Hal knew how his father would answer, and when. He would answer in the time it took his armies to march from Temple Church to Ardenscourt. Hal and Robert wouldn't survive, but neither would the king.

Meanwhile, no doubt the empress was marching.

Look on the bright side, Halston.

Hal couldn't find the bright side of this situation by torchlight.

That same night, just as Hal was deciding whether to lie awake in his bunk or worry upright in a chair, he heard a terse exchange of greetings outside the door, and then the bolts sliding back.

Robert pushed to his feet and stood, hands fisted. Hal closed his book and waited.

The door opened to reveal Destin Karn. He spoke a few quiet words to the guards outside, then entered, closing the door behind him.

He swiveled around to face them, looking them up and

down. He no longer wore the black of the King's Guard; he had changed into rich but subdued court dress, like a snake that had slipped from one skin into another. Whatever colors he wore, he was dangerous.

It was easy to forget that he was a mage, on top of everything else. But then, his hand inside his coat, he walked the perimeter of the room and began murmuring charms.

Hal and Robert looked at each other. Was the spymaster locking them in or soundproofing the room or what? Did he mean to put them to the question right then and there?

Finally, Karn settled onto the broad stone windowsill and extended his long legs in front of him. He crossed his legs at the ankles, the heels of his fine boots resting on the floor.

"Hello, Captain Matelon and Corporal Matelon," he said, sounding amused.

That answered one question—the spymaster knew who they were.

"You're a long way from Delphi. Wait—isn't one of you supposed to be dead?" He rubbed his chin, then pointed at Hal. "You, I think."

Robert said, "My brother has nothing to do with this. He just came to fetch me home. Let him go, and I'll tell you everything I know."

"Corporal, that is a brave thing to say, and exceedingly generous, but it's no way to begin a negotiation, much less a conversation. For one thing, between the two of you, your brother is the more valuable prisoner, being more dangerous to the crown. For another, I have no doubt that if I asked you properly, you would tell me everything you know anyway, and wish that you had more to say."

"You mean to torture us, then?" Robert folded his arms. "I don't care what you do to me, I won't tell you anything."

"You would do well not to issue me a challenge," Karn said, tilting his head back as if he were just a little bored by the situation. "You don't want to arouse my . . . competitive spirit."

"Lieutenant," Hal said, "could I speak with my brother a moment?"

Karn waved his assent, and Hal pulled Robert into the far corner. "Did you mean it when you said you were sorry you got me into this?"

"Of course I am. But—"

"Then could you shut up before you get us into more trouble than we're already in?"

Robert shot a look at Karn, then leaned in close and whispered, "Hal, listen, we can take him, I know we can. And then—"

"He's a mage, Robert. We wouldn't get within ten feet of him. If he questions us, he'll use magic on us. I'd like to think I could resist it somehow, but I have no idea if that's possible. Why don't we find out what he wants? Don't say no before he asks the question. When it comes to answers,

I'll speak for both of us. Is that clear, *Corporal*?"

"Yes, sir." Robert stared straight ahead.

I'm so damned glad I'm not fourteen anymore, Hal thought, looking back from the high ground of seven— no, eighteen. He led the way back and sat on the edge of his bunk, his hands resting on his knees. "What is it you want to know, Lieutenant?" he said.

Karn gazed at Hal a moment, as if he could penetrate all the way to the bone. "You seem to be very hard to kill, Captain," he said. "My father has some skill at killing, and yet he has tried and failed four or five times that I know of, maybe some others that I missed. I'm wondering if you can explain it."

Hal couldn't have said what he'd expected, but it certainly wasn't that. He could feel the pressure of Robert's stare. "Can I explain why he's trying to kill me or why he's failed?"

"My father has never needed much of an excuse to kill people, and I can think of several reasons he'd want to kill you." Karn shook his head. "No, I'm wondering how you've managed to survive this long."

Hal shrugged. "My luck can't hold forever." He gestured, taking in their prison cell. "Obviously."

"That's just it," Karn said. "I think it's more than luck. For instance, any reasonable person would say that your situation now is hopeless. Yet I have no doubt that you will find a way to survive this, too. I think you must be more clever and resilient than I ever gave you credit for."

It was an odd sort of compliment. Should I be thanking him? Hal wondered. Or is he flattering me, suggesting that if I turn traitor, he'll stay the executioner?

When Hal didn't respond, the spymaster sat up and planted his feet firmly on the floor. "You survived the fall of Delphi, when few of your fellow soldiers did. And now you've miraculously escaped and come back to us. Either you are favored by the gods or you have an extraordinary talent. Or is there another explanation?"

Hal was ambushed by a rush of anger. What was he suggesting? That he'd given the city up?

"Is that what this is about? Does the king think I betrayed Delphi to the Fells? Is that the excuse your father is using?" He snorted. "No. I've been fighting under the red hawk since I was eleven years old. I've been nothing but loyal, and this is how I'm repaid—with suicide missions, assassination attempts, and accusations of treason. No, Lieutenant, I'm not proud of surviving, and I'm not proud of losing. I have been a good soldier—the best I could be—and that is all." Hal clenched his fists. "So, you tell me—why is your father, my commanding officer, out to get me?"

By now, Robert was staring at him with a mixture of admiration and alarm.

Hal sat back, breathing hard, thinking, This mage is good at what he does. After lecturing Robert, I've already said more than I'd planned on.

Karn didn't seem at all put off by Hal's heated response. If anything, he seemed amused, almost delighted. "Exactly. I always saw you as more of a hero type than a traitor type." He leaned in close and said, "My father despises heroes. He thinks that honor is a sign of weakness, and treachery is just another tactic. That's where you made your mistake."

Hal and Robert exchanged glances. What was this? Was Karn playing good lieutenant against bad general?

Karn seemed to be waiting for some kind of response. When it didn't come, he said, "I will concede that you are a hero who knows how to survive. And yet, here you are, walking into a trap. So uncharacteristic. It doesn't fit together, and when things don't fit together it makes me curious. This does not come from the king or my father— it comes from me."

Maybe I'm not as smart as you think I am, Hal thought. But as he looked at Karn, at the eagerness in his eyes, at the intensity in his posture, Hal got the impression that the lieutenant was sending a message that he hoped Hal would hear and respond to. That he was looking for something in him.

An ally?

No. People like him don't have allies. They have chess pieces they move on the board.

Still. I've got nothing to lose, he thought. He and Robert

were already prisoners of the crown, subject to execution as traitors and spies. At least he could sieve out some bits of truth that would be harmless to divulge.

"Fair enough," he said. "Here's the truth. I am here because I was taken prisoner when Delphi fell. I was in Delphi when I learned about King Gerard's death. The wolf queen asked me if I thought the death of the king might mean a new relationship between our realms. After twenty-five years of war, that sounded appealing to me." He looked Karn in the eye. "Does that make me a traitor?"

"Not at all," Karn said. "You would find many allies on the Thane Council." He pressed the tips of his fingers together. "You actually spoke to the queen in the north?" Hal noticed that the spymaster did not call her the "witch" or the "demon" or the "harlot," which was a point in his favor. Or a testament to his ability to play both sides.

"Yes."

"What is she like?" He took a breath, then added, "More importantly, what does she want?"

"As you can imagine, she is tired of war. She's suffered many losses. The northerners claim that Arden has been sending assassins into the queendom and murdering people." He looked into Karn's eyes. "Is that true?"

Karn didn't flinch, didn't deny, didn't look surprised. "That's possible," he said, frowning, "though I don't have direct knowledge of it, and by all rights, I should." He paused. "Will she surrender, do you think?"

Hal didn't hesitate. "She will not surrender. Never. She will fight to her last breath."

Karn nodded, as if this didn't surprise him, either. Hal wondered how much of this he already knew through his network of eyes and ears.

"What about King Jarat?" Hal said. "Do you think he would be open to making peace?"

"With the thanes or the queen?"

"Both." Hal was a little amazed to be sitting in a jail cell in Arden, talking politics with the king's chief spy and enforcer.

Karn rubbed his chin. "I must say that the queen in the north has made an odd choice of diplomat."

"I'm not here representing Queen Raisa," Hal said, his temper rising once more. "I came to the capital to try to keep my brother from getting himself killed or captured." He could feel the heat of Robert's glare, and ignored it. "And I came home to make a case for ending the civil war so that we can join with the Fells against a foreign power that threatens both of us."

"Hold on," Karn said, shaking his head. "You've lost me now. What foreign power?"

"After my capture in Delphi, I was moved to more secure quarters in Chalk Cliffs. I was there when the port was attacked by armies fighting for the empress Celestine, known as the empress in the east."

Up to then, Karn had displayed the face of a sharp—distant, detached, and all but unreadable. Now Hal saw a flicker of something in those hazel eyes—something that told him that young Karn had heard of the empress, and that this news shook him to his core.

Hal stiffened, his heart thrumming. What did this spymaster know about the empress? Could Arden have instigated this invasion after all? If so, why would Karn be surprised?

It was only a momentary cracking of the façade, and then Karn had his game face back on. "What makes you think that it was the empress who attacked? Were they flying her banner?"

"I wouldn't recognize her banner if I saw it," Hal said. "I interrogated one of their pickets. He said they sailed for the empress Celestine. Then, after the city fell, I—"

"Hang on—they've taken Chalk Cliffs?" The spymaster's voice was sharp as a blade.

"Aye," Hal said. "They did. The northerners never had a chance. The town is in ruins, everyone in it slain or carried off as slaves, unless some were able to escape to the west."

"And yet *you* got away?"

"During the confusion, I was able to escape by boat through the water gate with some others."

"They didn't have you locked up?" Suspicion glittered in Karn's eyes once again.

"They did, but when it was clear that the city would fall, they let me go. They had no interest in offending a member of the Thane Council. They know they need allies."

Hal waited for Karn to interrupt again, but the spymaster said nothing, only scowled and tapped his fingers on the window ledge.

"So. As I was saying. After the city fell, they began unloading horses and equipment and wagons. Ships were coming and going like buzzards to a corpse. It wasn't a hit-and-run for plunder. It looks like they intend to stay and conquer the Fells—maybe the entire empire."

Now Karn rose and began pacing back and forth. "Why would she attack Chalk Cliffs?" he murmured. "That doesn't make any sense." It seemed as if the spymaster was having a conversation with himself, with Hal and Robert as onlookers.

Hal had expected skepticism, dismissiveness, and doubt. He had not expected this immediate recognition of the danger posed by the invaders from across the Indio.

Well. He is a spymaster, after all. It is his job to know things that others don't.

"Rumor has it that the empress has made an agreement with Arden," Hal said. "Her armies attack in the north, freeing Jarat's armies to subdue the thanes."

Karn shook his head briskly. "Gerard was trying to form

an alliance with the empress, but it fell through. There was no agreement."

"Are you sure?"

Now Karn stopped, and turned, folding his arms. "I am sure," he said flatly. "I would know."

"You missed the attack on Chalk Cliffs," Hal said.

Karn's scowl transitioned to a rueful smile. "I did."

"There was another prisoner who escaped with me," Hal said. "He claimed that the empress attacked the city because she was after him."

"She was after *him*?" Karn went still. "Who was this prisoner? What was his name?"

"He called himself Breon d'Tarvos," Hal said.

"*Tarvos?*" Karn gripped the front of Hal's shirt, pulling him closer so they were eye to eye. "What did he look like?"

Why was the spymaster so agitated?

"He was maybe sixteen or seventeen years old, with red-gold hair. He said he was a street musician. A busker."

"Red-gold hair." Karn released his hold on Hal's shirt. His expression mingled relief and dread, which Hal would have thought was impossible. "Did he explain why he thought the empress was after him?"

Had the busker ever explained? Hal recalled what Talbot had said. *When he saw that ship coming, he was terrified. I'd stake my life on it. When he told us to get out of the boat, he*

333

was trying to save the rest of us. He shook his head. "He never said, but it was clear that he was scared to death."

"Was this busker a mage? Was there anything magical about him?"

Hal shook his head, knowing these questions were springing from some private knowledge that the spymaster had. "Bear in mind that I can't see magic on a person, and I didn't spend much time with him."

The wheels were turning behind those shadowed eyes. "Where is he now, this busker?"

Hal shook his head. "I don't know for sure, but we believe the empress took him aboard her ship and is sailing back home." Hal paused, waiting for more questions, but Karn said nothing, only stared down at his hands, a muscle working in his jaw. Finally, he spoke.

"Can they do it, do you think?"

"Can who do what?"

"Can the empress's forces conquer the empire?"

Hal shrugged. "I've never seen fighters like these—fearless, fast, strong, completely unafraid of death."

Now Karn finally looked up. "Can they do it?" he repeated, an edge to his voice. "I want to know what you think, Captain."

"I suppose it depends on how many more soldiers she can bring to the fight."

"Let's assume that her resources are . . . limitless," Karn said, with a sour smile.

"Then she will almost certainly win, if we remain fractured as we are. For twenty-five years, my father did everything in his power to prevent another civil war. He always said that was a war where everyone loses. Now we're looking at another civil war in Arden, and we're still at war with the Fells. Our coffers are empty and we have sacrificed an entire generation of young men that we sorely need now. We should have spent this time consolidating our hold on the down-realms, building roads and demonstrating to them the advantages of being part of the empire. Instead, we've been pouring treasure into this useless war. The down-realms have been on their own for so long that many of them have forgotten that they answer to us. Who could blame them if they decided to cast their lots with Celestine?"

Hal caught a flicker of movement out of the corner of his eye—Robert shifting from foot to foot, reacting to the longest speech he'd likely ever hear his brother make.

"My opinion?" Hal went on. "If we cannot end this war with the north and join together against the empress, she will come for us, she will win, and we will deserve it."

Karn nodded, and Hal got the impression that the spymaster agreed with his assessment.

"I know you are interrogating me," Hal said, "but I have a question for you."

"You're wondering if King Jarat would be open to making peace with the thanes for the common good."

Karn raised an eyebrow. "Right?"

"Right," Hal said.

Karn studied him, as if deciding whether he should give back a measure of information in return for Hal's. "Our new king is moody and unpredictable, but I think I'm safe in saying that the only way Jarat will make peace with the thanes is on *his* terms. He believes that his hostages will keep him safe—that they are the argument no one can answer."

And, now, thanks to Hal and Robert, the king had two more hostages than he did before.

"He doesn't know my father very well," Hal growled.

"No. He doesn't. And unfortunately, when Jarat hears about Chalk Cliffs, that will reinforce his decision to take a hard line."

"Perhaps if I spoke to King Jarat, I could convince him that—"

"That's not a good idea," Karn said.

"I realize that it's a risk, but—"

"The king doesn't know that you and your brother are here. So. That could be awkward."

Hal glanced at Robert, then back at Karn. "He doesn't know we're here?"

Karn shook his head. "I thought it best not to bother the king with this matter. He has been very busy trying to form a decent council out of the few thanes who have remained loyal." He straightened his sleeves, wrinkling his nose. "The social season has been a disaster. It's a good thing that the marching season isn't far off."

"But, if we're here in custody, doesn't—?"

"This is my prison, and the guards are my people. They have learned not to be curious. Besides, as I said, you're dead. That's an advantage, as you'll find."

While they'd been talking, Robert had grown more and more restless, shifting in his chair, clearing his throat, and so on. Now, apparently, he could not remain silent any longer.

"What if the hostages were freed?" he blurted. "Do you think that would influence King Jarat's willingness to compromise?"

"Possibly," Karn said, his cool gaze brushing over Hal's brother. "Or it might inspire the thanes to attack."

"They are going to attack anyway," Hal said. "Trust me on that."

"I do trust you on that, Captain, which is very odd," Karn said. "Unfortunately, it's highly unlikely that His Majesty will give up what he sees as a winning hand."

"I'm not suggesting that *he'll* free them," Robert said. "I'm saying that *we* should free them."

"Won't that be difficult, locked up in a cell as you are?"

Robert's enthusiasm withered. "Oh. Well. I thought perhaps you could—"

"Free you? Or join with you in freeing the hostages? Are you suggesting that I commit treason, Corporal?" Karn shook his head. "I'm careful about who I partner with. Given your performance so far, I'd be going to the block in no time at all. Have a little patience. In the meantime, are you comfortable? Are you getting enough to eat?"

"Yes," Hal said. "The food is much better than in the prisons in the north."

"That's what everyone says." Karn stood. "Gentlemen. You'll hear from me soon."

After the door closed behind him, Hal heard the bolt sliding shut.

"Do you think he's going to help us?" Robert said, glaring at the closed door.

"I wish I knew," Hal said. Time was passing, and both the empress and the thane armies would soon be on the march. There was no way to know who would arrive in the city first.

WEEPING SISTER

For the first few days of the crossing, the weather was blustery and cold—typical for early spring in the northern oceans. Personally, Breon enjoyed the ride, spending as much time as possible on deck, chatting up the crew and asking questions about the ship, the rigging, and the ports they'd been to. Gathering information that he hoped to use later.

Most were the empress's purple mages, and they were a dour lot, not particularly receptive to his considerable personal charm. Gradually, though, they grew to tolerate him, allowing him to help them in their work and join them on their watches.

The *Siren* was built for speed and maneuverability and not for the tender stomachs of day sailors. Her Highness huddled miserably in her cabin until Breon finally managed to coax her up on deck. Once they were there, he advised her to put her face in the freshening wind and fix her eyes on the horizon. After that, she was less prone to spewing, which made their shared cabin a lot more livable.

Since that day on the beach, when she'd murdered Aubrey, the empress had been sweet, solicitous of their comfort, so kind that butter wouldn't melt in her mouth.

Breon listened hard for Celestine's music, but he heard only the raging storm—the crash of thunder, the creak of the masts and singing of the lines as the sails filled, and the flapping of the sheets when they lost the wind. He watched and waited, looking for a chance to get hold of one of Celestine's belongings that might give him a clue. But she was exceedingly wary of him, as if she knew all his tricks and how to sidestep them.

He meant to make her pay for Aubrey somehow. Now that he was clean, he seemed to have lost his limitless ability to make excuses for himself. He'd done some low-down things in his life. He understood what it was like to have nothing and want something, and know that the only way to get it was to take it. His "manager"—the streetlord Whacks—had taught him that honesty was something only a blueblood could afford. And then he'd come to realize that most bluebloods lie and cheat and steal even if they don't have to. The only difference was that their takings were bigger and they nearly always got away with it.

As they neared their destination in the Northern Islands, the seas rose and the weather worsened. A howling wind drove needles of rain into their faces and made it all but impossible to remain on deck. Visibility was so poor that Breon couldn't see more than an arm's length past the gunwales anyway. He worried that they wouldn't know they'd found land until they broke apart on the rocks.

The seas would rise under them, lifting the *Siren* until she was perched atop a mountain of water. Then she'd begin to slide down the other side, plunging nose first into a trough between the waves so deep that rain and salt water mingled together in Breon's mouth. Eventually, his stomach would rejoin his body and it would happen all over again.

Breon watched as the empress strode up and down the quarterdeck, her hair seething in the wind, barking orders at the helmsman and the first mate, muttering curses at someone named Latham Strangward. It was as if she were in a personal grudge fight against the sea.

She knew what she was doing—that was clear enough. Her crew clung to every order like it was a lifeline that would pull them out of the storm and into the blue.

Her Highness was clinging to the rail, eyes closed as if she could pretend she was somewhere else. Breon leaned close, shouting to be heard over the wind and waves. "If she goes down, let go and jump as far as you can so you don't get pulled under. Then swim like the Breaker's on your tail so you won't get tangled in the lines."

She nodded, so he knew she'd heard him, but said nothing. That was when he remembered that Her Highness couldn't swim.

All right, then.

"Hold my hand," he said, prying one of her hands loose from the rail and gripping it. "Don't let go. When I jump, jump with me."

She gave him that look of hers and said, "Save yourself, busker. I would prefer not to be responsible for your drowning."

"If I drown, nobody will miss me," he said. It was true, now that Aubrey was gone. "In your case, the fate of the realms hangs in the balance."

That wrung a damp smile from her. "If I die here, busker, write me a song. Legends live longer than actual people."

Moments later, they were crushed to the deck as if the air were a lead weight pressing down on them. Just as Breon began to worry that he might suffocate, the pressure was gone. They seemed to pop through an invisible wall, leaving the howl of the wind and the crash of the waves on the other side.

The winds that had been filling the sails and straining the lines to the breaking point died away. The *Siren* glided forward in the sudden silence over a moonlit sea toward an island shrouded in mist and cloud. Overhead, the stars seemed impossibly bright after so many days of gray. Weeping Sister—it must be.

It was not their day to die after all. Maybe. There was a saying Whacks liked to use—"out of the frying pan and into the fire." Breon wondered if it might apply in this case.

The princess opened her eyes. They looked at each other, rendered speechless, which was rare for him, personally.

As they drew closer, Breon saw the source of the mist: multiple waterfalls cascaded from the cliffs, sending up clouds of steam when they hit the cold ocean. Fumes erupted from fissures, and the mountainsides were lit with sullen orange wherever lava leaked through. The Weeping Sister wept scalding tears.

Three tall ships were moored in the harbor, sails rolled and bound to the masts. Warehouses newly built of raw wood squatted in concentric circles around the quay. Surrounding those was what appeared to be a newborn city, devoted to military and marine purposes—barracks and stables and paddocks, a sprinkling of small stone houses in a uniform gray color.

Beyond the warehouses and stretching up the slope were the ruins of a once-great city, built of timber and stone. Now the roofs had rotted through, the walls had caved in, and stone pillars—monuments to the old gods— had toppled and broken.

And, there, overlooking the harbor, extending higher than anything else on the shore, was a marble palace, apparently still under construction. It seemed to glow in the moonlight, as if the walls couldn't contain the light within. The center part looked finished, frosted with elaborate carvings of dragons and sea serpents and sirens. Two wings were like broken-off teeth, still ragged at the top, swarming with workers who resembled insects at that distance. Working through the night.

Breon had an affinity for the music of harbor towns— for the discordant clamor of the flotsam and jetsam that accumulate wherever seafarers come ashore to do business and forget their troubles. They were places where ugly rubbed shoulders with uglier, where utility outranked beauty, where new elbowed forward, embarrassed by the old. It was a place for living and dying and making bad decisions of all kinds.

This looked like no harbor town Breon had ever seen. It was as if it had no soul, no memory, no history, no music at its heart. It told no stories. Breon didn't like it one bit.

On the other hand, Her Highness looked cheerier than

she had in days. She was probably encouraged by the prospect of stepping onto solid ground again. She stood, chin up, shoulders back, drinking in the view, as if storing it away for future use.

The helmsman shouted orders to the rowers as the *Siren* made a graceful turn, coming up alongside the largest of the docks, which was emblazoned with the siren emblem Breon had come to associate with the empress.

The empress descended from the quarterdeck and strode toward them, smiling. "Welcome to Celesgarde," she said. "You'll be housed in the palace as my honored guests." Her purple eyes flicked over them. "I am not surprised that you have an affinity for the sea," she said to Breon. "You have . . . so many gifts." Impulsively, she drew him into her arms, so that his face was pressed into her leathers while her other hand toyed with his hair, raising gooseflesh across his back and shoulders. "I have waited so long for this day," she murmured. "We will be so great together, I promise you."

What did she mean by that? Was she speaking of some sort of . . . relationship?

Breon's heart slammed around in his chest, as if it might break through skin and bone. Fear and revulsion shuddered through him by turns, and his magemark seethed and burned. He steeled himself, focused, reaching out, listening for any whisper of song.

When it came, it was hauntingly familiar, as if it was already embedded in his bones. He couldn't help thinking, *Is it really her song, or my own?*

This is where it all begins.
This is where it all ends.
The shattering,
The rejoining.
Forged in the bleeding earth,
As it has been, it shall be again.
At midsummer,
When the sun pauses in the sky.

It echoed between them, reverberating into a clamor of notes until he pressed his hands over his ears—but there was no way to shut it out.

Finally, blessedly, Celestine released him and turned to Her Highness. "I trust that you are more capable on land than you are on the water." It sounded like some sort of threat or warning.

"I *am* more capable on land," the princess said, with a flash of her usual spirit. The color had returned to her cheeks. She stood, hands on hips, studying the harbor, the ships, the new-built town, the palace—no doubt looking for any vulnerability or advantage in an impossible fight.

Good luck, Your Highness, Breon thought.

This thought was interrupted by shouts from the others

on the quay. They were pointing at the sky, some crouching and covering their heads with their hands. Breon looked up in time to see a dark shape flap across the face of the moon. It circled once, glittering, then beat it toward the mountains, its flight disjointed, erratic, as if it was injured.

They all watched it until it was out of sight. Lyss turned to the empress. "What was that?"

"Sun dragon," the empress said. "The mountains in Carthis are infested with them, but we don't see many of them this far north. Most can't make it through the Boil, but it's good hunting for those who do."

THE BLACK WIDOW

In the days following his visit with the Matelon brothers, Destin wished he could warn Evan that their gambit had failed. But he had no idea where he was. When they'd parted, Evan had mentioned sailing north, which was why, for one heart-stopping moment, Destin had thought that Evan was the prisoner Matelon described, the target of Celestine's attack on Chalk Cliffs. Especially when Matelon said that he was from Tarvos.

But no. This red-haired busker did not match Evan's description. So, who was it? Was it another magemarked target that had brought the empress here?

Be careful, Pirate, he thought. Be smart. Keep moving. In the meantime, he resolved to do whatever he could to keep Celestine from expanding her foothold in the wet-lands. He needed a plan.

These days, though, it seemed events were moving too fast, spiraling out of control. These days, his plans seemed slapdash and reactive. But he had to try.

Destin found Queen Marina on the terrace with the princess Madeleine and a handful of her most trusted ladies—the survivors from among those who had come with her from Tamron when she'd married King Gerard. Whenever Gerard had wanted to punish Marina for some particularly grievous sin, one of her ladies-in-waiting would disappear, to be replaced by a Montaigne loyalist. It was heartbreaking to watch Marina become more and more isolated.

Until Destin was put in charge of the disappearing. He stashed the ladies in a temple in Tamron, and they'd grad-ually returned to their queen since the king's death.

The queen spent much of her time on the terrace, or in the gardens—places where there was less risk of eavesdrop-pers. It was something she'd learned from Gerard. It was a good thing she lived in a warm climate.

When she saw Destin, Marina lit up, rising in a rustle of satin and extending her hand for kissing. "Look, Mad-eleine," she said. "It's Cousin Destin."

Madeleine charged at Destin and threw her arms around him. The princess was nine years old going on twenty-five. It was no wonder—she'd seen too much in her brief life that was unsuitable for children. Or anyone.

When the general had dragged Destin back to Ardens-court, Marina had welcomed him into her small circle of hurt. She would tend his wounds, both physical and emotional, and he did his best to reciprocate, by sharing information and commiseration. By putting as many weapons into her hands as he could.

"Please. Sit," the queen said, waving him to a bench. Destin sat, and Madeleine squeezed in beside him. Marina motioned to two of her ladies, who immediately picked up their basilkas and began to play loudly enough to cover the conversation in case anyone was listening.

The queen was dressed in black and purple, as was her custom these days.

"Mourning suits you, Your Majesty," Destin said. And it did—she looked happier and healthier than he'd ever seen her. The colors she'd chosen set off her raven curls and Tamric complexion.

Marina lifted her skirts and kicked out her feet, exposing bright-red shoes. "I chose these colors in memory of Gerard—to remind me of all the bruises I received at his hands. I don't want to forget that there are worse things than being a young widow."

Destin laughed. "Things can always get worse, but every now and then they get better."

"Maybe," Marina said, her smile fading. "We'll see. I think Gerard should have died sooner, when Jarat was younger and I had more influence over him."

Destin slid a look at the queen. He'd long suspected that Marina knew more about the king's tragic end than she let on. If she did, she had not shared it with him. While they exchanged information, they each had secrets they kept close.

"Speaking of King Jarat," Destin said, "what news of the young hawk?" He and the queen often played at pretty speech when discussing the ugliness at court.

Madeleine leaned toward him. "My brother has been drinking all afternoon with Charles and Georges and Luc." She rolled her eyes. "They're disgusting."

Charles and Georges Barbeau and Luc Granger were members of a group of young lordlings—what the young king called his "privy council." Emphasis on *privy*. Most were in their early twenties, and so a few years older than Jarat (and Destin, for that matter). They were the sons of thane loyalists, and were minor bannermen, with a lot to gain from a relationship with the king. None were tainted by a history with King Gerard, nor were they spoiled by wisdom or experience—or common sense. They were more than happy to take the young king under their tute-lage in the study of drinking, hunting, dicing, wenching, and swordplay.

"I've told you to stay away from them," Marina said. "It's not suitable conversation and company for a young lady."

"How else am I supposed to find out anything?"

Madeleine said. "Jarat was bragging that he's going to marry a northern princess."

It took Destin a moment to process that. "Really? Does he have one picked out?"

Madeleine shrugged. "There's only one left, isn't there? They were talking about all the women they'd had, and would have. Jarat said Father never bedded a wolf, but *he* would, and even a wolf could be tamed with the proper—"

"Madeleine!" Marina scowled at her daughter and thrust out her hand. Madeleine sighed deeply, dug in her tiny purse, pulled out a copper, and dropped it into her mother's hand.

"What's the copper for, Your Highness?" Destin said to Madeleine.

"Mama is trying to teach me dis . . ." She frowned and looked at Marina.

"Discretion, darling," Marina said.

"Whenever I'm . . . indiscreet, I have to pay Mama a copper."

Destin reached behind Madeleine's ear and pretended to pull out a silver. He handed it to her and said, "You were saying?"

Mother and daughter both laughed.

"I think it was just Jarat bragging like he always does," Madeleine said, tucking away the silver.

I hope so, Destin thought, recalling what Matelon had said about the northern queen. "If your brother means to marry a wolf, you should tell him that wolves eat hawks for dinner," he said.

"No," Marina said sharply. "You should *not* tell him that. Now, isn't it time for your dance lesson?"

"She wants me to leave," Madeleine confided in a stage whisper. She kissed Destin on the cheek, curtsied to her mother, and flounced away.

Marina gazed after her. "She will make somebody a clever queen if she lives that long." She turned back to Destin, set out two cups, and poured them both some cider. "What brings you into the garden today?"

It was an odd echo of his garden walks with Gerard, during which he'd receive his marching orders.

Destin nodded toward Madeleine, a bright spot of color disappearing through the gate. "Is there anything to what she said? Is there some kind of plan or negotiation with the north afoot?"

Marina sighed. "Not to my knowledge, Destin, but the king doesn't confide in me much anymore, either. I've been giving him too much counsel that's contrary to his nature. I don't think he trusts me to tell him what he wants to hear. Unfortunately, there are plenty of people at court who will." She fluffed her skirts and offered him a platter of grapes. "But enough about our family squabbles. What do you have for me?"

It was part of their unspoken bargain—to trade information without getting too specific about sources.

Destin sorted through bits of information, setting aside those that were too dangerous to share.

"Do you remember the empress in the east? Who wanted to lend us an army?"

"Of course. That deal fell through, right?"

"Right," Destin said. "But she's brought an army anyway, and invaded the Fells." He watched the queen closely, and she looked absolutely ambushed. The queen had her own sources, but clearly she hadn't known this was coming, either.

She leaned forward. "Does the king know? Is he working with the empress?"

"I was going to ask *you* that question," Destin said. "My sources—on both sides of the Indio—are usually reliable, especially as regards diplomacy with the empire. From what I'm hearing, there has been no communication to or from, which suggests that she is acting on her own." He paused, then continued, knowing that he had to frame this in the right way. "I think I can say with confidence that the king doesn't know it yet, but he soon will. Jarat will think this is good news, that it will free him up to act against the thanes."

Marina raised an eyebrow. "And? You disagree?"

"If King Jarat thinks it's bad having Queen Raisa as a neighbor, wait until he has to contend with Celestine," Destin said. "In just a few years, she has conquered the entire Desert Coast. Her army is larger than ever, and her soldiers are unstoppable. If she invaded the Fells without an agreement with the empire, you can bet that this is just the prelude to her coming south."

Queen Marina studied him, as if she suspected there was more to the story than he was letting on. "Even if what you say is true—which I'm not conceding—why shouldn't we bide our time and build our strength while she is busy in the north?"

"But we aren't building our strength, we're spending men and treasure on a civil war."

"Have you spoken to the thanes about this?"

Matelon tried that, and failed, Destin thought, and he's a much more appealing spokesperson than I am.

"If I walked into White Oaks, I'd never walk out again," he said. "I'm not the best person to reach out to the rebels."

"What is it you want, then?" Marina said, going for the meat of the matter. "What are you hoping will happen?"

"I would like to see both sides come to the table and end the civil war. Then we can send our armies into the north and help them drive off the empress."

"We've been sending our armies into the north for twenty-five years," Marina said, laughing. "They have not been well received."

"One step at a time," Destin said. "First, we end the civil war."

"Done!" Marina said, slapping her hand on the arm of the bench.

Destin released a long breath. "Jarat thinks the thanes won't attack as long as he holds hostages. He's wrong. Arschel Matelon will be marching on the capital any day now."

"And you know this how?"

"No sources, remember," Destin said. "If the rebels reach the city walls, Jarat will begin killing hostages. If he does, there's no way any of us will survive this war."

"You're that sure the thanes will win?"

Destin rocked his hand. "I give them sixty-forty odds—maybe seventy-thirty. Matelon is a seasoned military commander—the best in the empire other than the general. Heresford's no slouch, either. Tourant's an asshole, but he has lots of bannermen to call upon." Destin paused, tilting his head toward the musicians.

Marina gestured, and they retreated a short distance, then resumed playing at full volume.

"I have it on good authority that Matelon's son Halston has returned from the dead to fight alongside them. Everyone who's served under him sings his praises. They say he's a soldier's soldier. He has a huge following in the imperial army."

"He lost two big battles this year," Marina said.

"Yes," Destin said, looking her straight in the eye, "he did. As the general intended."

He waited while Marina connected the dots. She never

needed an extended explanation.

"So. The king's soldiers might desert en masse if they find out that young Captain Matelon is on the other side?" she said.

"It's possible. It doesn't help that Jarat has been slow about paying the troops. At least Gerard was smart enough to keep his armies happy." It was time for the ask. "If we can remove the hostages from the equation, Jarat might see reason and negotiate with the thanes."

Marina considered this. "Is there any way they would accept a truce that would allow him to keep his throne and his head?"

"I don't know," Destin said honestly. "It's early yet, and he hasn't committed any unforgivable sin. There's still time for him to show that he's more reasonable than his father. The thanes really don't want another civil war. They want an end to the war they've been fighting for a quarter century. They want to keep some of their money, for a change."

"So they can fight another war against the empress?" Marina raised an eyebrow.

"Nobody wants that one, either," Destin said. "But in this case we may have no choice. Who knows? A show of strength from us might send the empress back across the Indio, and that would be the best outcome of all."

"But you don't believe that will happen," Marina said.

Destin shook his head. "No, I don't."

"So you want me to help you free the hostages," the queen said.

"Yes," Destin said, meeting her gaze straight on.

"We're talking about women and children," Marina said. "They're being kept in the most secure part of the dungeon. I've been trying to talk Jarat into moving them into better quarters for months. This is not how you treat people you may need on your side later on. If you try to break them out of the pits, there will be casualties, and that will defeat the purpose."

"That's why we have to get them out of the dungeons first. That's where you come in."

"It's been a long time since I've wielded a sword," Marina said, flexing her hand. "We Tomlins are better with stilettos and poison."

Is that how you did for the king?

"I have a plan that will not require swordplay." *I hope.* "Next week, you'll be welcoming nobles and emissaries from all over the empire to celebrate His Majesty's coronation."

Jarat's coronation had been a hurried, secretive affair after the attack on the city and Gerard's death. Now, four months in, he'd decided to host his first major social and diplomatic event, to demonstrate the power and stability of the empire despite the fractious lords. As regent and queen mother, Marina was King Jarat's official hostess, since the king had not yet married.

"I'm not looking forward to that," Marina said, rolling her eyes.

"No?" Destin pretended surprise. "Didn't Jarat promise it would be the party of the year?"

"Compared to what?" Marina nudged a plate of pastries toward him. "Some of the down-realms' representatives will be staying a month with their families. Why not stay and feast at the king's expense? With so many of the estates under control of the rebels, our larders are nearly empty. That means we'll probably be eating beans and barley cakes until the new crops come in. They'll be feasting and dancing alone, because most of the court is either in rebellion or lying low at their country estates. So it will be on me to entertain them." She laughed and poured more wine. "Forgive me. I'm not usually one for whining."

"Could you invite the hostages to the reception? Wouldn't that help fill up the ballroom?"

Marina stared at him. "Have you lost your mind? Why would His Majesty agree to that?"

"The lords of the down-realms will be taking Jarat's measure," Destin said. "Here's a young, untried king whose thanes are in rebellion against him. What better way to demonstrate his power than to have the families of the rebellious thanes bending the knee at his coronation and dancing at his reception?"

"I know some of those ladies," Marina said. "Trust me,

they won't be bending the knee to Jarat. It could get ugly."

"It will be up to me to convince them to be on their best behavior. We also need to make sure that everyone, down to the babes in arms, attends. Nobody gets left behind."

"They'll need clothing—party dresses—and a good scrubbing," Marina said. "It wouldn't do a lot for Jarat's reputation to have them showing up for the reception looking like they've been kept in a dungeon for months."

She's thinking about logistics, Destin thought. That's a good sign. "If you tell me what is needed, I will do my best to procure it."

"You'll need the cooperation of that despicable Luc Granger," Marina said, making a face. In addition to being the king's drinking companion, Granger had been named the king's bailiff. "Unless you kill him," she said, brightening.

Destin raised both hands, palms out. "Eventually. But not now. Right now, I need to know if you're in the game." With that, he put a copper on the table between them.

It was Tamric custom to seal a bargain by putting money on the table. An ante, so to speak.

Marina did not hesitate. She laid her coin beside his.

"Thank you, Your Majesty. I will keep you apprised of my progress."

He rose, bowed, turned to leave, then swung back toward her. "One more thing," he said. "I'm very fond of masquerades."

THE KING'S SPYMASTER

Destin Karn eased his body over the edge of the roof, careful not to send any of the tiles crashing into the castle courtyard below. Anchoring his toes on the stone sill, he poked a foot through the window, verifying that the shutters were open to the breeze. Traveling the high roads of the palace was always easier when the weather was warm.

Gripping the top edge of the window, he swung his lower body through and dropped to the floor, mildly pleased with this accomplishment. These days, he spent less time in operations and more on politics and espionage. It was good to know that he hadn't lost his touch completely.

It was an opulent suite of rooms by any measure,

especially for a bailiff. The king's gaoler generally had quarters in the finest part of the dungeon, which, to be honest, wasn't all that fine.

This apartment offered a lovely view of the river, yet was high enough so that the stench of that open sewer wouldn't reach it, even in midsummer. It was in the same wing as the royal suite, a sign of the king's favor. The furnishings were rich, some of them centuries old, though they'd seen hard use since this tenant moved in.

Destin picked his way through a rubble-field of dissipation—empty wine casks, dirty plates, spilled cups of ale and bingo, random pieces of clothing. The velvet bed curtains had been yanked down and spread before the hearth for a makeshift trysting place. Destin tried not to look too closely, tried not to breathe in the reek of lust and licentiousness.

Not that Destin had a problem with a bit of licentiousness. He did have a problem with the man who lived here.

Luc Granger had begun as an officer in the King's Guard who'd managed to get himself assigned to young Prince Jarat at a time when nobody else wanted the job of babysitting the royal brat. In that role, Granger had spent considerable time wooing the young prince—mostly by enabling Jarat's worst instincts. With Jarat's ascendance to the throne, Granger's star rose rapidly. He'd been named captain of the blackbirds, and then bailiff, giving him responsibility for the Guard, the royal prisons, and the courts. Jarat had recently bestowed on Granger a large holding that belonged to the Matelons. Since Arschel Matelon had been one of the founders of the Thane Rebellion, Jarat felt free to give his estates away. The king had also approved Granger's betrothal to a rich widow, thus ensuring him a title and a fortune to go along with his estate.

That caused some grumbling among the loyal thanes, who disapproved of handing such a fine estate to a commoner. Their outrage was dampened by the fact that the holding was still occupied by Matelon's bannermen, who showed no sign of giving way. Granger seemed to spend much of his time at court trying to persuade King Jarat to send an army to enforce his claim. That and abusing prisoners and tumbling any servant girl he could trap in a back corridor.

Granger resented the spymaster's independence from the Guard hierarchy. A few months ago, the bailiff had thought he could blackmail Destin with some scandal he'd unearthed. Granger found a dead rat in his bed the next night, tagged with his name. And then his fiancée, a fierce and formidable heiress from the down-realms, found one in *her* bed. When she threatened to break off the engagement, Granger reconsidered his choice of a target.

More recently, the young thane had been pressuring Jocelyn Fournier, one of the palace seamstresses, to provide an expanded range of services when he came for a fitting. She was another poor choice of a target, because

Jocelyn was Destin's friend, and one of his most reliable sources.

The next time Granger was on his way to a fitting, he was waylaid by a hooded assailant who beat him soundly and promised to improve the fit of his breeches with a quick bit of surgery if he didn't find another tailor. It was possible that Granger suspected Destin's involvement, but he couldn't prove it, which was what counted, for now.

Destin despised Granger, but he'd learned a long time ago that even the most despicable person could be useful. Especially a despicable person with a secret.

Now Destin settled in to wait. He might have been tempted to sample some of the bailiff's top-shelf wine, but the risk of poison was too great. Granger had made lots of enemies on his way up.

It wasn't long before Destin heard fumbling at the door—somebody who'd been drinking, judging by how long it took for him to manage the latch. The door slammed open and Granger stumbled in. Thankfully, he was alone. He kicked the door shut, which nearly put him down on his back. He stumbled to the garderobe and unbuttoned his breeches, hurrying to unburden himself of excess ale.

When he turned back around, he found himself facing Destin Karn. "What the devil are you doing here, you scummer-sucking, backgammoning molly?" He dragged at his breeches, hurrying to fasten them again.

"I'm not the one with his breeches down," Destin said.

The bailiff blushed hot pink. "This is *my* apartment," he said. "You're the intruder. The king is going to hear about this, I promise you."

"Sit down," Destin said. "I need to talk to you." He shoved a stool toward Granger with his foot.

Granger's gaze slid to the door, then back to Destin. Maybe he decided there was no way he'd reach the door without being intercepted. Maybe he figured he'd have more dirt on Destin to take to the king if he stayed and listened. In any event, he sat and regarded Destin through baleful eyes.

"I suppose by now you've heard that the king intends to invite the families of the rebellious thanes to the inauguration reception," Destin said.

"He—? Right. Of course," Granger said, making a rocky recovery. "I think it is exceedingly gracious of him to allow them to participate. It may even present an opportunity for them to redeem themselves."

"Really? How so?" Destin said, assuming the bailiff wasn't referring to an opportunity to escape.

"Once the rebels are defeated, and their ringleaders executed, His Majesty will need to dispose of the rebels' holdings. One solution would be to allow those of us who have remained loyal to the crown to marry into the old families. To bring them back into the fold, as it were."

"Good idea," Destin said. "It's too bad that you are already betrothed to Lady—"

"A broken engagement is a small price to pay in the cause of unifying the empire," Granger said. "You yourself, Lieutenant, might be in need of an advantageous marriage one day soon."

Destin's patience was rapidly eroding. This was not on any list of topics he wanted to discuss with Luc Granger. "Are you proposing marriage, Granger? This is all so sudden."

Granger flushed. "I am offering you a word of warning," the gaoler snarled. "I have it on good authority that your father's days as general of the armies are coming to an end." He paused, perhaps expecting Destin to leap to the general's defense.

"I'm sure His Majesty will make his decisions based on performance, just as his father did," Destin said calmly.

Looking disappointed, Granger pressed on. "Your father was close to King Gerard, but King Jarat does not share the late king's confidence that the general can deal with a two-front war."

"That's the king's call, of course," Destin said. "Does he have a suitable replacement in mind?"

Granger brushed imaginary lint from his sleeve. "My name has been mentioned."

"Really? Then may I be the first to offer congratulations," Destin said. "Will you be giving up some of your other jobs, or will you keep them all?"

Granger blinked at him.

Clearly this was intended to keep Destin awake at night, worrying. Indeed, it might, since it practically guaranteed victory to the rebels. Granger against Matelon? That was a mismatch of epic proportions.

Ah, Granger, Destin thought. You think you are wielding a big stick, but my stick is so much bigger than yours. Your mistake is that you think I gained power because of my father. The fact is, I gained power in spite of him.

"Then there's the matter of your mother's family," Granger said.

Destin tented his fingertips together. "My mother's family?" Each word was a warning delivered through gritted teeth, but Granger was oblivious.

"She was a Chambord, right?"

"*Is* a Chambord, yes," Destin said. Granger had stumbled on the one topic that might get him killed, despite Destin's best intentions.

"She's still alive? I didn't know that."

"Yes. She is. She prefers to remain at her family's estates in Tamron," Destin said. "She and the general live apart."

"His Majesty has invited Lord Chambord to come to court. Repeatedly."

His Majesty's invitations were more like orders—risky to disobey. But Destin's uncle, his mother's brother, had stayed in Tamron.

"Uncle Charles is devoted to my mother, and she is in delicate health," Destin said. "As I'm sure he told the king when he sent his regrets."

"People are saying that the Chambords are sympathetic to the rebellion," Granger persisted. "And that's why they are not at court."

"Really? What people?" Destin said, his voice a river of ice. "Be specific, now."

"I . . . ah . . . disremember," Granger said, beating a hasty retreat. "So. All I'm saying is that you might be able to safeguard your future with the right marriage to someone willing to . . . overlook your baser proclivities."

Proclivities, Destin thought. An oddly pretentious word for a gaoler. All in all, he was growing impatient with Granger and his volleys of verbal darts. Destin's tolerance of fools went only so far.

"I think we agree that the king's invitation to the families *is* gracious, and generous," he said, forcing the conversation back where it belonged, "but I'm worried that this act of kindness might endanger the *king's* agenda, and possibly his life."

"You are?" Granger leaned forward, all ears. "Why is that? Are you questioning the king's judgment?"

"Not at all," Destin said. "I'm concerned that some of the thanelees might take the opportunity to embarrass King Jarat in front of his down-realm guests."

"That's no problem," Granger said. "I'll handle it. I'll

use the children as leverage."

No, you will not, Destin thought.

"*I* will handle it," Destin said, "but I will need your help. Queen Marina has asked me to accompany her into the—into their quarters. My role is to make the consequences of bad behavior plain. Her role will be to assess what is needed to make them ready for the reception. We believe that is the way to best assure their cooperation."

"The queen?" Granger's bluster faded a bit. "The queen—in the Pit? Absolutely not. That's no place for a lady."

"That's just what I told Her Majesty, and she pointed out that there are at least a dozen ladies down there now—with their children. She is determined to go and invite them personally, then arrange for clothing, bathing, and so on. It would reflect badly on our king if they look as if they've spent months in a dungeon."

The irony of this was, of course, lost on Granger. But the potential blowback from allowing the queen into his domain was not.

"I'll—I'll need a few days," Granger muttered, visibly twitchy.

"We don't have a few days," Destin said. "The reception is a week away. We're coming tomorrow. More importantly, I've received intelligence suggesting that the rebels are planning an attack on the capital while our down-realm visitors are here. They may intend to embarrass King

Jarat—or they may intend to achieve through assassination what they haven't done through force of arms."

By now, Granger was looking a little ill, as if his hard-won role as gaoler and captain of the King's Guard wasn't sitting well. If King Jarat went down, he could expect no mercy from the thanes whose families he'd incarcerated.

Granger cleared his throat. "Isn't it *your* job to prevent that?"

"It's my job to alert the King's Guard when the king may be in danger," Destin said. "That's exactly what I'm doing. It's the job of the King's Guard to protect the royal family. Don't worry, though. If anything happens, we'll both be neck deep in it."

"If we don't know what's going to happen, and when, then how are we supposed to—?"

"As I see it, the biggest point of vulnerability is during the reception, as the ballroom is outside the central keep. It was never meant to be a fortress. So. The king wants to fill out his guest list. The ladies will need someone to dance with. I want a squad of blackbirds in the ballroom. If anything happens, I want them to usher the royal family and the down-realm guests from the ballroom and into the keep. Keep them there until I give the all clear."

"What about the hostages—I mean, the thanes' families?" Granger said.

"In the event of an attack, we'll want to segregate them from the down-realm barons and the royal family," Destin said. "I plan to take them to Newgate and secure them there until the danger is over."

"Ah," Granger said, nodding, avoiding eye contact. "That sounds like a good plan." His expression had shifted from panicked to calculating, and Destin knew he was considering how to turn the situation to his advantage, or find a way to blame Destin if it went wrong. All at once, he seemed eager to bring the interview to a close. "Is that all, Lieutenant? If so—"

"There's one more thing," Destin said, keeping his seat.

"It's late, Lieutenant," Granger said, "and I'll have much to do tomorrow. Perhaps it can—"

"There is a disturbing rumor that pertains directly to you, Captain Granger," Destin said. "I suspect you'll want to hear it."

"To *me*?" Granger said.

"You've told me that you grew up in Southgate," Destin said. "The son of a merchant?"

"Yes," Granger snapped. "What of it?"

"Yet I cannot find anyone who remembers you there," Destin said. "Nor any family. Nor, in the temple, any record of your birth."

"You *dared* to snoop into my background?" Granger stood, as if to walk out, but of course the conversation was taking place in his room. Awkward. He pointed at the door. "This interview is over."

"It is my job to investigate those close to the king, in

order to identify possible threats and conflicts," Destin said.

"If they don't remember me in Southgate, it's because I left there at an early age," Granger said. "Apparently, I didn't make much of an impression."

"I had better luck at Watergate," Destin said.

That landed like a cannonball.

"Really?" Granger said, turning fish-belly pale. "That's surprising. I'm not sure I even know where that is." A sheen of sweat appeared on the bailiff's upper lip. He glanced around, as if the spymaster's minions might be closing in.

"I spoke to your lady mother, who has high hopes that you will come into your rightful inheritance one day," Destin said.

"You spoke to my mother?" The bailiff went from pale to sheet-white. "If you've hurt her, I'll—"

"Tell me, does the king call you Cousin Luc in private?"

With that, Granger drew his sword and lunged at Destin, who dodged aside, stuck out his foot, and sent the bailiff flying so that he landed, hard, on the hearth, his ornate blade clattering onto the stones. Destin sent flash into the sword, heating it to a dull red. After briefly holding its shape, it subsided into a puddle.

"That was my grandfather's sword!" Granger crawled forward, tried to pluck the precious stones out of the mess, then yelped and sat back, sucking his fingers.

"Too fancy a blade for a bailiff, don't you think?" Destin

said. "Pretentious, really. I take it you haven't told the king who you are, which is understandable. Perhaps you find it off-putting that King Jarat's father murdered your grand-father and seized his throne." Destin paused, and when Granger did not respond, continued. "More importantly, do you think His Majesty would find it off-putting that you've been his drinking companion and a member of his privy council all this time, and never saw fit to mention your shared heritage?"

"I am here to serve the king," Granger said sullenly. "That is all."

"I'm sure you are," Destin said. "But King Jarat might be uncomfortable with the notion of having a potential rival for the throne pouring his wine and sitting in on his council, let alone taking charge of his army. He may decide to house you down below, with his many other guests."

Granger sighed and pulled out his purse. "How much will it take to buy your silence? I can offer you a small sum now, and the balance later. Most of my holdings are in land, which would take time to liquidate."

"I am not here looking for a bribe," Destin said. "I am here to offer you some advice—don't cross me. I don't know what kind of games you played in Watergate, but this is not a joust but a battle to the death. Ever since your arrival, you've been blundering about, bullying the help, interfering with your betters, and making the kinds of enemies someone in your precarious position doesn't need."

Scorn replaced the cynicism on Granger's face. "You think you are my better? *You?* I come from a long line of kings. You are the son of a battlefield butcher and a round-heeled Tamric—"

Destin gripped the bailiff by his shirtfront, dragged him to his feet, and hit him, hard, crushing his nose and dislodging a few teeth. Then smashed his head against the mantel.

He heard his mother's voice in his head. *Don't kill him, Destin. Please. Don't kill him. It's not worth it to me to lose you.*

Destin looked into the rubble of Granger's face. "You think you're a deadly, vicious, pitiless bastard, don't you?" he said softly. "You are *nothing*, compared to me. I learned from the master. If the reception wasn't next week, I would kill you now without hesitation. I am offering you the gift of your life, and I suggest you take it, keep your mouth shut, and do as you are told." Destin pulled out a handkerchief and wiped Granger's blood from his own face. "You had better go straightaway to the healing halls and get that repaired before tomorrow. Queen Marina and I will meet you in your office at midday."

When Destin left the palace, he walked along the river, collar up, head down, cursing himself. The meeting with Granger had been going so well, until he'd lost his temper at the end. That was always the way. Just when he thought he had the monster inside him under control, it came roaring to life.

I am not a monster. Evan had made him say it, over and over. Saying it didn't make it true.

Remodeling Granger's face might prove useful, in the short run, if it frightened the bailiff enough to secure his cooperation. In the long run, however, Granger would never forget his humiliation and would eventually seek revenge.

One more task for Destin's mental list: kill Granger. After the reception.

Unlike many at court, who tried to spend as much time in front of the king as they could, Destin valued his privacy. So, in addition to his apartment within the palace, he kept a suite of rooms at the Cup and Comfort Inn on the riverfront. Any kind of pleasure could be had at the Cup and Comfort for a price, but what Destin treasured most was anonymity. This was a place where he could be himself.

So it was with not a little alarm that he unlocked the door to his rooms at the inn to find Lila Barrowhill sleeping in his fireside chair.

He froze in the doorway, but she must have heard him, because she opened her eyes and smiled at him sleepily. "I hope you don't mind that I let myself in. I didn't want to draw attention by sitting outside your door."

Destin stepped inside and shut and locked the door behind him. Then turned to glare at her, his arms folded.

Lila grinned when she saw his expression. "Blood and bones, Karn, I'm so glad you're still alive. It always seems that I'm a lot happier to see you than you are to see me. Well, except for that time you came to Oden's Ford. Then there was that time in King Gerard's garden—"

"How did you find this place?"

"I needed a cup and some comfort, and this place was recommended," she said. She held up a cup she'd no doubt filled down in the taproom. "It's truly amazing. You really can get anything you want here." She winked at him.

"If you're thinking that you can blackmail me, you—"

"Heavens, no!" Lila actually looked offended. "If you think I have any interest in your private life, so sorry, I don't. And I don't want you to have to 'disappear' me. The best thing about being shameless is that I have no interest in shaming anyone else."

Destin couldn't help thinking that she was not quite as shameless as she made herself out to be. But he sighed and slid out of his court coat and hung it up carefully. He then walked around the room, creating wards to frustrate eavesdroppers. Then poked at the fire.

"Karn. You can't have been gone from Delphi that long." She fanned herself. "Do you really need a fire?"

"Did I ask you for your opinion?" With the fire going to his satisfaction, he sat on the edge of the hearth. "How can I help you, Lila? Surely you aren't hurting for business, with a civil war in the offing and the ongoing war with the Fells—"

"And an invasion from the empress in the east." She eyed him, her head cocked. "But you already knew about that." There was a trace of a question mark at the end of that statement. It struck him that she was watching him in the same way he'd watched Queen Marina, trying to ferret out whether he'd been involved.

"Actually, I just heard," Destin said. "What can you tell me about this empress? Did a northern princeling refuse *her* hand in marriage or what?"

"Not all wars are about unrequited love," Lila said.

Destin couldn't help laughing. He'd missed Lila, he had to admit.

"What have you heard?" he said.

Lila gave him a look that said, *You first.* Then relented. "What I know I heard from my relatives on the coast."

"The smugglers?"

"We prefer 'merchants and traders,'" Lila said. "Anyway, they said all the ports on the east coast are in an uproar, trying to fortify against possible attacks by sea, people wondering what the empress's intentions are. They're used to pirates—they know there's always a risk when they put to sea. But this is the first time pirates have come inland, acting like they mean to stay."

"Have they advanced beyond Chalk Cliffs?"

"I don't know," Lila said. "I've been on the road."

"Are you selling magecraft to them?"

She shook her head. "My understanding is that they don't use magecraft. Their soldiers are magelike, but they don't use amulets and they cannot be controlled with collars or defended against with talismans."

"Too bad," Destin said, rubbing his chin. "You think you have a whole new market, and it comes to nothing."

"Exactly. So. How are you getting on with King Jarat?"

"Why?" Destin asked warily.

"This empress is bad for business," Lila said. "I wondered if he would be amenable to helping the northerners boot her out."

Destin stared at her, then burst out laughing.

Now it was Lila's turn to glare at him.

Destin blotted tears from his eyes. It had been so long since he'd had anything to laugh about.

"What's so funny, Karn?"

"I—I'm sure if you explained the damage to your business, King Jarat will get right on it. Maybe you could offer him a split of the profits."

"Well, I wouldn't put it exactly that way, but—"

"I'm serious. He could use the cash. He can use it to buy more ordnance from you." Destin raised his hands, palms up. "Perfect."

"Shut up, Karn," Lila growled.

"Maybe there's something else you can sell the empress,"

Destin said. "I understand that she forces prisoners to drink her blood and turns them into slaves." He lifted Lila's cup and waggled it under her nose. "How about . . . cups? Or maybe a product to get bloodstains out?"

"I'm glad you're enjoying this." Lila grabbed her cup back and drained it.

"Actually," Karn admitted, "I'm not. I know enough about the empress to predict disaster if we're not able to drive her away."

"Then work with me," Lila said.

Spending time with Lila Barrowhill always proved worthwhile, even if it had its price in aggravation. Somehow it was a pleasure to work with a person who never hid behind a façade of respectability.

He rose, opened a secret cabinet, and pulled out a bottle of bingo and two glasses. "Shall we?"

35

THE EMPRESS'S NEW CLOTHES

Lyss and Breon were housed in a luxurious suite of rooms in one of the finished wings of the marble palace. They each had their own bedroom, with a connecting living area. The suite opened onto a terrace overlooking the ocean, but the only way out of the wing was through a locked wrought-iron gate and past a guard post that was staffed with blood mages around the clock.

Servants came and went with food trays and linens, their sandals whispering over the stones. Breon tried to strike up a conversation with some of them, but got nowhere. Lyss finally realized that it was because they were deaf—which is probably the best protection against a spellsinger.

A young woman came in one day with an armload

of nightgowns and silk robes that she then hung in a tall wardrobe. She measured Lyss from top to toe, murmuring her surprise over the battleground of Lyss's body—a maze of old scars and fading bruises.

Lyss tried speaking with her, using the four languages she knew. Clearly the young woman heard, but she didn't understand. Finally, Lyss pointed her thumb into her chest and said, "Lyss." Then she pointed at the girl, who smiled and said, "Lara."

Two days later, Lara brought several bundles of new clothes. There were two sets of garments similar to those that the blood mages had worn—the ones who'd attacked the keep at Chalk Cliffs. Loose-fitting breeches that narrowed just below the knee; a linen overshirt; a long vest, decorated with embroidery and braid; a thick leather belt and leather gauntlets; and a head wrap.

There were also two sets of what looked like a court uniform—fine dress breeches and a long coat complete with braid and glitterbits, the empress's siren insignia on the back. Plus four sets of smallclothes. The boots appeared to have been made to match the boots Lyss was wearing when she was taken captive.

Gesturing, Lara directed her to try the clothes on, to make sure of the fit. They fit perfectly—even the boots fit reasonably well. Lara demonstrated how the head wrap could be worn as a loose cowl or drawn across her face, exposing only her eyes. When Lyss looked in the glass, she saw just another Carthian warrior.

Well, then.

Lyss smiled at Lara. "Perfect," she said, making a turn so the seamstress could see all sides.

Lara smiled back, curtsied, and left.

Lyss sat on the low bed, her mind tumbling from one bad possibility to the next. It seemed that the empress meant to keep her around for a while. That could be good news or bad. She'd heard that the empress somehow turned her captives into mages and forced them to fight for her. Was that what she intended for Lyss?

Lyss could not let that happen, but she couldn't think of how she could avoid it, short of tying strips of sheet together and hanging herself. But she was her mother's sole living heir. Worse, it would mean the end of the Alister line—the line that had survived more than a thousand years against all odds. It was as if she heard her father's voice in her head. *Stay alive.*

No. She would not be the last of the Alisters. She would not.

Lyss walked out onto the terrace and looked down at the ocean below. The marble wall of the palace above and below the terrace was smooth, seamless, impossible to climb. Even if she had a rope, the only place she could possibly go was into the water. The familiar tide of panic rose in her, threatening to drown her before she ever got wet. The empress couldn't have chosen a better barrier to prevent her escape.

She should have spent more time with her father and Cat Tyburn, learning how to get in and out of tight places. But who knew she would end up a princess held captive in a marble tower?

There came a soft knock on the door. "Come!" she said, and Breon sloped in, his face a thundercloud. He wore new clothes, as well—only his were velvet and satin, sparkling with jewels. His narrow breeches and fitted jacket showed off the fact that he was filling in nicely. His hair was the color of rich caramel. It had been cut, but the single gold streak had been left longer than the rest. It was braided, and it glittered in the sunlight that streamed in from the terrace. He would have been beautiful, all on his own, even with a scowl on his face. In this garb, he was dazzling.

They looked at each other—Lyss in her uniform, and Breon in his finery.

"Well," Lyss said, "it looks to me like the empress has very different roles in mind for the two of us. She must be intending to keep us alive a little longer."

"She brought four sets in different colors—each finer than the last one." Breon brushed at the velvet, his fingers leaving little tracks. "This is the plainest of the lot."

Lyss tried to think of something to say. "You look

spectacular, Breon," she said. "Those suit you—you're someone who makes the most of them."

She'd thought she was giving him a compliment, but he didn't take it that way. "I an't a fancy," Breon muttered. He stripped off the jacket, wadded it up, and threw it in the corner. "Everybody keeps trying to make me into something I'm not, just because I'm pretty." He pressed his fingers against his face as if he might somehow rearrange it.

"So . . . you're thinking that the empress means to . . . ?" Lyss swallowed, sorry that she had gotten into the middle of that question without planning how to end it.

"Why else would she give me *these* clothes? *Your* clothes aren't like that. Put a curved blade at your belt and sling a bow over your shoulder, and you'd be a Carthian horselord."

Lyss looked down at her breeches and overshirt. Then looked up at Breon. "Listen," she said, "I have no way of knowing what the empress is thinking. I don't know what she has planned for me. But there are people in this world who wear clothes like yours every single day, and they're not fancies. The nobility, for instance."

"Not where I come from," Breon growled. "This reminds me of the night you and I met—when Whacks gave me some pretty new clothes so I could do something I've been sorry for ever since. I don't want to go down that road again. I'd rather wear rags. If she doesn't mean me to be a fancy, maybe she wants to use me to lure people into trouble."

"My father always told me to try not to worry about things I can't do anything about," Lyss said.

"Easier said than done. Every plan begins with worry."

They came for Breon first. A brace of imperial guards showed up and ordered him to come with them, saying that the empress wanted to see him. He looked fragile next to the bulky guards, his face pale, his eyes wide with fright.

"Wait!" Lyss commanded. To her surprise, they stopped, and turned back toward her. She embraced Breon, murmuring, "See you soon," in his ear.

But she did not see him soon. Hours passed, and dinner came and went, and he did not return. Finally, she crossed through their common area and knocked on his door. No answer. She pushed the door open. "Breon?"

The room was empty. All of his belongings were gone, as if he had never existed.

36

AUDIENCE WITH THE EMPRESS

Lyss slept little that night, wondering and worrying about Breon. So she was in a particularly foul mood the next morning when a handful of the empress's guards came to call. She was feeling reckless, itching for a fight, even one she could not win.

Her visitors included the usual imperial guards, but also a man whose garb resembled her own, the difference being that he was wearing a king's ransom in gold around his neck and at his wrists. His belt was embedded with jewels, the buckle a dragon fashioned in gold.

"Captain Gray, I believe?" he said in accented Common.

"That's right," she said.

The stranger looked her up and down with the kind

of arrogant ownership that, in her present state of mind, might lead to bloodshed. His blood. Alternatively, she might take his gold chains and strangle him with them.

"I'm Captain Samara," he said, jerking his head toward the door. "Let's go. The empress has granted you an audience."

I didn't grant *her* an audience, Lyss wanted to say. But good sense prevailed, and she didn't.

Samara led Lyss out of the rear of the palace and through what once must have been a lovely garden. The leafless skeletons of trees remained, some of them braced against the ocean winds. The beds were empty of flowers, though metal markers still displayed the names of those that had once grown there. Arbors and pergolas were still threaded with the stems of vines, and stone statues and sculptures were everywhere, as if trying to compensate for the lack of vegetation. A leathery-skinned servant swept twigs and debris from the walkways.

"What happened to the garden?" she asked, finally.

"The only way a garden thrives this far north is through magic. When the magic died, so did the garden. The empress has other priorities right now."

Like conquering the Realms? Or hunting down the magemarked?

Speaking of. "Where's Breon?" she said, as they neared the far gate.

"Breon?"

"My friend. We came here together. You took him away yesterday, and he hasn't returned."

"Ah," Samara said, "you are speaking of the empress's brother."

Lyss's stampeding thoughts plunged over a cliff, tumbling until they hit bottom. "Her *brother*?" She gaped at Samara. "Breon is her brother?"

"Of course," Samara said, with the smug assurance of someone on the inside. "Why do you think she has been so eager to find him? Her family has been scattered far and wide, and she is working to bring them all together." He opened the gate and stood aside so that Lyss could pass through. "Now, we must hurry. The empress does not like to be kept waiting."

As they walked, Lyss tried to wrap her mind around what the shiplord had said. Breon was Celestine's brother? That was hard to believe. They were both breathtakingly beautiful, and they both had metallic streaks in their hair— gold for Breon, and red and blue for the empress. There the resemblance ended. Breon was charming, self-deprecating, nonjudgmental, and instinctively kind. Celestine *could* be charming—until she wasn't. Otherwise, she was ruthless, cruel, arrogant, and selfish.

If they were siblings, how had they become separated? And why was it all such a secret? Why didn't Breon know about it himself—unless he'd lied about that, too?

Why wouldn't the empress simply invite her siblings to

a reunion, instead of hunting them across two continents? Of course, there are many reasons a monarch might want to track down siblings. Gerard Montaigne was one example that came to mind—he'd murdered his brothers on his way to the throne.

But why not simply hire an assassin if that was the goal? Celestine had made it plain that she wanted Breon alive and unhurt.

One bit of good news—Breon might be glad to know that he was dressed like a prince because he was one.

The empress was waiting in a small, circular pergola overlooking the sea. She was dressed more simply now, draped in layers of fabric secured by a wide belt, a cowl pulled up over her head. The cowl was the only bit of fancywork—it was elaborately beaded and embroidered. A jeweled, curved blade was jammed into the belt.

Samara bowed to the empress. "Here is Captain Gray, as you commanded, Empress."

Celestine looked her up and down approvingly. "You look like a capable soldier, Captain," she said. "I trust the fit is good?"

"Yes," Lyss said cautiously. "I wondered whether—"

That was when Lyss noticed the chaise parked beside the wall, where its occupant could look out to sea. A familiar mop of hair peeked over the top of it.

"Breon!" Lyss knelt beside him, looking anxiously into his face. He was wrapped in furs, eyes half open but unfocused. He returned a vague smile and absently patted her hand.

"What are you doing out here?"

"He likes to watch the ships," Celestine said, though the only ships in view were moored at the dock.

Lyss stayed focused on Breon's face. "Is that true? I was worried about you. I didn't know what—"

Breon tapped his fingers against his throat and shook his head.

Lyss swung around to face the empress. "What's the matter with him?"

"I've taken his voice for now," Celestine said.

"What do you mean, you've taken his voice?" Lyss's own voice trembled.

"There is a desert plant we call 'secret keeper.' It stills the vocal cords. Unlike cutting out a person's tongue, the effect is temporary."

"Why would you do that to your own brother?"

The empress's eyes narrowed. She looked from Lyss to Samara. "Ah," she said, and sighed. "Captain Samara has been gossiping again."

Samara stood frozen, one hand on the hilt of his curved blade, his face a thundercloud.

"Perhaps he's the one you should be dosing," Lyss said.

The empress nodded. "Perhaps he is. You are dismissed, Captain Samara. The rest of you as well. Go, and take my brother with you."

"But . . . your grace . . . you mustn't risk—"

"Captain Gray is not a mage," Celestine said. "I hardly think it's a risk to speak with her in private, as I intend to do." When he still didn't move, she waved him away impatiently.

Cheeks flaming, Samara bowed. "As you wish, Empress." Motioning to the others, he stalked off toward the palace, his back stiff with rage. His men followed behind, herding Breon along like an errant sheep.

"Captain Samara forgets himself sometimes," Celestine said, when they were out of earshot.

I'll bet he forgets himself a lot of times, Lyss thought. As often as you'll let him.

Celestine gestured at the other chair. "Now. Sit."

Up close, Lyss was surprised at how young Celestine was. If she had to guess, she'd estimate that the empress was not yet twenty. Her coloring was striking, with her purple eyes and tawny skin and silver hair. She was not particularly tall, but she was *plush*, as Lyss's father would say.

Celestine was studying Lyss in turn. "You are quite the legend, Captain Gray," she said. "Are any of the stories I'm hearing true?"

"That depends on what stories you're hearing," Lyss said, wishing that Breon hadn't shared her military name with the empress. "If you're talking about the incident in the taproom of the Thistle and Crown, that was blown way out of proportion."

The empress stared at her, then burst out laughing. "You see?" she said to no one in particular. "That's exactly why I didn't kill you on the beach. It's been so long since I've had anyone around with a modicum of wit. The bloodsworn are so tiresome."

If you're looking for some kind of a court jester or pet, keep looking, Lyss thought.

"I can see that there is magic in you. Is it true that you turn into a wolf in the heat of battle? Are you a . . . shape-shifter?"

Clearly the empress had been doing her homework.

Lyss shook her head. "When I go into battle, I'm in it to win. Maybe that's how that story got started."

"Ah," Celestine said, looking disappointed. "I was so looking forward to seeing that. Most stories have a kernel of truth." She paused, and when Lyss said nothing, continued. "How long have you been fighting for the wetlanders?"

"I took the field when I was twelve," Lyss said, "after my father was killed."

"Your mother allowed that?" Celestine raised an eyebrow.

"She wasn't happy, but she allowed it."

"My mother was very protective of me," Celestine said. "She loved me very much."

What's that about? Lyss thought crossly. My mother loved me more than yours?

"It's hard to send a child to war," Lyss said, thinking of Cam, who'd died defending her in the streets of Southbridge.

"How old are you now?"

"Nearly sixteen." Lyss realized with a start that her birthday—her name day—must be close, if it wasn't already over. Not the way she'd intended to spend it.

"You've moved up quickly, then, if you're already a captain." There was a question hidden in that.

"Unfortunately, every marching season, the war demands a blood price. We often have vacancies that need filling." Lyss paused. "How old are *you*?"

"I am twenty," the empress said.

"You've moved up quickly, then, too."

"I am my mother's firstborn daughter," Celestine said. "So, I rise when my mother falls."

A shiver went through Lyss and the flesh pebbled on her arms as a cloud passed over the sun. Her nurse, Magret, used to say that this meant the wolves were walking over the graves of the queens.

"Are you well, Captain?" The empress was studying her, frowning.

"I am well," Lyss said, fanning herself. "This climate takes some getting used to." More than anything, she wanted to escape this awkward conversation. So she changed the subject.

"Captain Samara said that Breon is your brother," Lyss

393

said. "But—if he's your brother, why didn't he know about it?"

"He once knew, but he doesn't remember," Celestine said vaguely. "I am the eldest of nine children. When I was only thirteen, my brothers and sisters were stolen away by enemies of the empire."

"Enemies?" Lyss hoped the empress would clarify, but that didn't happen.

"My mother would not allow me to go and look for them, because she feared for my safety. After she died, I began the search again, but by then, the trail was cold."

Something wasn't adding up. To Lyss, it sounded rehearsed, like a story the empress told herself and others, but didn't quite believe.

"So . . . enemies of the Nazari stole them, but kept them prisoner? They didn't kill them outright?"

"Clearly not," Celestine said impatiently, "since some of them are still alive."

Something was nagging at Lyss, a familiar scent that came and went. Then she spotted the smoldering pipe on a table next to Breon's seat.

Furious, Lyss scooped it up and flung it over the wall into the sea.

Celestine watched the arc of it until it splashed into the water. "Well, now. That's a waste of some very fine leaf."

"You gave him *leaf*? Why would you do a thing like that?"

"The secret keeper is mixed with it. It soothes the pain of losing his music," Celestine said. "I want him to be happy."

"That won't make him happy," Lyss said, "not in the long run. He'd just managed to get clear of it, and now—"

"Captain Gray, I did not invite you here to lecture me," the empress snapped, flame flickering over her skin. "You are offering opinions on matters you cannot possibly understand. You know nothing about us, nothing about our customs. My brother is charming, and handsome, and no doubt highly capable between the sheets, but you must let go of any hopes of a future with a blooded Nazari prince."

Lyss, speechless, stared at the empress as thoughts tumbled through her head. *She thinks I . . . She thinks we . . .*

"Your Eminence, I—"

"Enough!" The empress's eyes darkened to almost black. "If you cannot do that, this conversation is over and I will find you another role to play."

Lyss's cheeks burned. The threat in those words couldn't be plainer. Unless she wanted to join the bloodsworn, she'd have to remember who held the power. Unless it was already too late.

"I . . . ah . . . yes. I see how impossible that is." Lyss took a deep breath, released it. "I apologize, Empress. I was out of line."

Celestine shook back her silver hair, the fire in her eyes

still burning hot. "You think I am ruthless. I am as ruthless as I need to be to survive in this world. Those who are not of royal blood do not realize what a burden it is to rule, the difficult decisions that must be made."

Hanalea's blood! It seemed that everything the empress said hit too close to home. Maybe Celestine knew the truth about her birthright and was merely toying with her.

"Yes, Your Eminence," Lyss said, eyes downcast, shoulders rounded against sorcery.

"Are you this bold when you speak to your queen?"

"Sometimes," Lyss said. She cleared her throat. "Not usually."

"In the future, I expect you to offer me the same courtesy and respect."

"Yes, Your Eminence," Lyss murmured.

"Good." With that, the storm passed and the sun came out. Celestine gestured for her to sit.

Lyss eased back into her chair, heart still pounding, legs rubbery with relief, as if she'd just experienced a near miss on the battlefield.

Long ago, she'd traded the palace for the army, because on the battlefield the criteria for success were clear. It was all about performance, and that was something she could control. Now she was thrust back into the most dangerous game of all—the game of politics.

Lyss cast about for a safer topic, one that went to tactics. "I am curious about the bloodsworn. I saw them in action at Chalk Cliffs. Are they born or made? What, exactly, are their advantages over line soldiers?"

The empress smiled. "I was hoping you would ask. Come and see for yourself." She stood, and then descended the steps at the edge of the terrace. Lyss followed.

They went down several more flights, until they stood on the lowest level, overlooking a parade ground.

Below, soldiers were drilling—hundreds of infantry, cavalry, both men and women, all dressed like Lyss. They were practicing maneuvers, riding hard, then pivoting, eddying across the barren landscape like some inland sea.

Scummer, Lyss thought, fighting off despair. I thought it was bad when it was just the king of Arden we had to contend with.

"What do you think?" the empress said, nearly into Lyss's ear, making her jump.

"Are these all bloodsworn?"

Celestine nodded. "The bloodsworn are made mages. Their capabilities depend on the strength of the blood mage who creates them. Mine have unmatched physical strength and stamina."

Based on what she'd seen at Chalk Cliffs, Lyss had to agree. But when she looked closer at the troops below, the eddies and whirlpools seemed random, pointless, poorly coordinated. It wasn't clear, exactly, what these exercises were supposed to accomplish. She knew from experience that practicing chaos on the parade ground results in chaos on the battlefield. Then again, the queendom had never had the numbers to take a melee approach to battle strategy. It valued its soldiers too highly.

Is this my future? she thought. Am I going to be marching in the middle of a mob like this, attacking my homeland?

"If I may ask—how do you go about 'making' them?" Lyss tried to keep the revulsion off her face.

"I come from a long line of blood mages with the ability to intervene at the point of death and bring people back as bloodsworn—unfailingly loyal warriors who require little in the way of sustenance. They are fearless, because they feel no pain. The Nazari once dominated the east with their Immortals—the perfect army." She paused. "We have lost strength over the years. Our powers are diluted, and our warriors are not so perfect these days. But they are still damned good. Allow me to demonstrate."

Lyss wanted to say that she'd already seen too much of the bloodsworn, but she stood silently while Celestine called down orders to her officers. They pulled two soldiers from the ranks and lined them up, facing each other, each armed with a curved Carthian sword. Then, apparently, the officers ordered them to go at it.

Lyss was a veteran of the battlefield, and so no stranger to bloodshed, but she'd never seen anything like this. It wasn't a matter of skill—neither was practiced in swordplay. They simply whacked at each other with a dogged determination, oblivious to injury. Blood spattered the ground around them—and, eventually, severed limbs. The fact that they seemed to be fairly evenly matched only prolonged the butchery. Even on the ground, they kept flailing until their officers waded in and beheaded them.

Lyss felt the pressure of the empress's eyes. No doubt this was intended as a test, a promise, and a warning. So Lyss kept her chin up, shoulders back, expression as blank as she could manage.

"Impressive," she said, since Celestine seemed to be expecting a comment. "How many troops do you have to put into this fight?"

"Thousands," the empress said, "and I have the ability to recruit more—as many as needed."

"Success in battle depends on more than numbers, Empress," Lyss said. "It depends on the motivation, strengths, and limitations of your troops and the skill and experience of your commanders. Otherwise, the queendom of the Fells would be part of the Ardenine Empire."

"I agree," the empress said, looking pleased. "I've been impressed with what you have been able to accomplish with so little. It makes me wonder what you could do with unlimited resources."

I guess we'll never know, Lyss thought. It brought to mind the debriefing sessions at the end of every marching season, when everyone agreed that their fighters were the best in the world, and patted themselves on the back—celebrating surviving for another year.

She studied the troops again, trying to pick out the officers. A lot of shouting was going on, but it seemed to have little effect. Wondering if she dared speak her mind, she looked sideways at the empress. "Frankly, they look a little ragged to me."

"I'm finding that the bloodsworn are excellent fighters, when somebody tells them what to do. They are not very creative when it comes to tactics and strategy," Celestine said. "The best strategists are those who are at risk of dying. They have to worry about what will happen if they lose."

Lyss had never considered that. "So the bloodsworn are not good officer material?"

"Not really. Most of my officers are not bloodsworn. Captain Samara, for example. It presents a risk, because, while the bloodsworn are unfailingly loyal, the officers may not be."

Why are you telling me this? Lyss thought.

"You're wondering why I'm telling you this."

Lyss nodded.

"This is a new kind of war for us," the empress said. "We are pirates, Captain. Our experience is in quick raids and quicker retreats."

"You were successful in the attack on Chalk Cliffs," Lyss said.

"That was more like a raid on a port than a major military

operation. We simply stormed in and killed everyone. That isn't difficult. We have some experience with siege warfare, but we are not used to land warfare over distances. Battlefield tactics, troop formations, logistics, and the like are foreign to us. We are also not used to governing once we conquer territory. The Desert Coast of Carthis is one thing—it is a thousand miles long but only about three miles deep before you hit the Dragonback Mountains. So nearly everything is within reach of the sea."

Maybe you should stay home, then, Lyss thought.

She was growing weary of this verbal sparring. It was time to get some answers, even if it was bad news.

"I still don't know why you're telling me all this," she said. "Why did you bring me back to your capital? If you're looking for recruits for your bloodsworn army, it seems you've got plenty of potential soldiers here at home."

Celestine laughed. "I don't want to *add* you to the bloodsworn army," she said. "I want you to lead it."

37

THE TALISMAN

After two more days in Lieutenant Karn's private lockup, Hal was beginning to understand what is meant by "climbing the walls." He was used to working his body hard; in the absence of that, his mind took over. If he tried to read in the light from the window, his mind kept turning to what was happening outside. Where was Captain Gray? Was she still alive? Had the empress turned her into one of her bloodsworn slaves? He imagined the wit and intelligence fading from her brown eyes.

What possible reason could Karn have for keeping his king in the dark about his political prisoners? Were Karn and his father really at odds? Hal worried that the spymaster intended to keep him and Robert imprisoned indefinitely, to prevent them from contributing to the thanes' military efforts.

If Hal felt this way after a few days, it was hard to imagine what it must be like for his mother and sister after months in the dungeon. If they weren't already dead. His little sister, Harper, had a habit of speaking her mind to authority, consequences be damned.

Robert spent most of his time doing push-ups, chin-ups—anything to burn off frustration and useless energy. By the third day, Hal began to join in on Robert's workouts. They were hard at it one morning after breakfast when Hal heard the key in the lock. He levered to his feet and sat on the edge of the bed. Robert mopped his face with his shirt and stood.

Karn strode in, his arms loaded with what looked like clothing. "Good morning, gentlemen," he said, dropping a bundle on each of their beds. "Have you been warm enough? Is the food acceptable?"

"We don't care about the bloody food!" Robert snapped.

Karn raised an eyebrow. "Spoken like a well-fed man."

Hal untied his bundle and unfolded the fabric. He looked up in surprise. "It's a blackbird uniform," he said.

"The actual members call it the King's Guard," Karn said. "Or they are supposed to. Practice saying that."

"You brought us disguises?" Robert said, with a spark of enthusiasm. "But"—he held up a glittery black mask—"don't you think this is kind of obvious?"

"You're invited to a party," Karn said. "Happily, it's a masquerade party. I want you to attend as members of the King's Guard. Now. Try these on and check the fit, sometime when you won't be interrupted. In the meantime, hide them."

"I take it you have a plan," Hal said. He sat motionless, cradling the fabric in his lap, his eyes fixed on Karn.

"I do," Karn said, "but at present it is evolving as we get more information." The spymaster seemed to believe in the maxim that what isn't shared can't reach the wrong ears. "Now, is there anything among your belongings that I could use as a token to your mother and sister? Something meaningful that only the four of you would know about?"

"Are you really going to see them?" Robert took an eager step toward the spymaster, who raised a hand in warning. Robert froze in his tracks.

"Yes," Karn said. "I'm going to see them later today. I need something from you to persuade them to cooperate."

Hal and Robert looked at each other.

"You're not planning to lead them into a trap, are you?" Robert said.

"They are already *in* a trap, Corporal," Karn said, with rising impatience. "I was under the impression that you wanted to try to get them out."

"So you'll help us?"

"It means that I will see what I can do," Karn said. "No promises."

Robert turned to Hal. "Hal," Robert said, "what about Harper's thimble? You had that with you, didn't you?"

Of course, Hal thought. "That's brilliant, Robert," he said. "Nobody would think of that as something important but us."

"Why is it important?" Karn asked.

"Our sister Harper was only six when Hal went to the army," Robert said. "It was really hard for her to see him go, so she gave him her thimble so he wouldn't get pricked."

"I've worn it on a chain around my neck ever since," Hal said, "as a kind of talisman." He lifted the chain over his head and handed it off to Karn, hoping he was doing the right thing. Hal couldn't quiet the voice in his head saying, *This is a trick.*

Karn weighed it in his palm. "Does it work?"

"Well," Hal said, "I'm still alive."

"Ah," Karn said, with a crooked smile. "*That's* your secret." He tucked it away. "I'll only use it if I have to," he said.

"One more thing," Hal said. "If you see my mother, tell her to look on the bright side. That's the advice she's constantly giving me."

"Look on the bright side," Karn repeated. "All right.

There's at least a one-in-a-thousand chance this plan will work."

When he went to turn away, Hal said, "Lieutenant."

Karn turned, waited.

"Why are you doing this?"

The spymaster gazed at him for a long moment, rubbing his chin. "Let's just say that I have a weakness for women and children in peril." Then he was out the door, and Hal heard the click of the lock.

38

VISIT TO THE PIT

It was an odd committee of party planners: Queen Marina, for the carrot; Destin, for the stick; and Lila Barrowhill for logistics. Lila was dressed like a clerk in her scribner blues—all she needed was a pair of spectacles to complete the look. Still, Destin couldn't help wondering who she really was underneath her many disguises.

He wondered if she knew herself.

A subdued Luc Granger met them outside the Great Hall. His face looked nearly normal save for a certain crookedness to his nose. I'll have to get the name of the healer who worked on him, Destin thought. Whoever it is does fine work.

"Your Majesty," Granger said to Queen Marina, "I beg

of you to reconsider this visit. I've not had time to properly prepare for—"

"If the guest quarters are suitable for families of noble birth, I have no doubt I'll survive," Marina said. "His Majesty gave me very little notice that they would be attending this reception, and we must be as efficient as possible."

"In other words, lead the way," Destin said.

To Destin's surprise, Granger did not lead them to the dungeon's main entrance two floors below the Great Hall. Instead, it soon became apparent that they were on their way to the royal wing of the palace—a place frequented only by the royal family, their most trusted servants, and their most servile favorites.

Was Jarat really housing the hostages in the royal apartments? How was that possible, without Destin knowing about it? Without the entire world knowing about it? Not to mention that it would be totally out of character for the brutal young king.

The way in was through the apartment once occupied by King Gerard's mistress, Estelle DeLacroix. DeLacroix was no longer in need of it, since she'd been executed on suspicion of plotting to assassinate the king. At the rear of the poor lady's bedchamber, where the king once found an adder in his bed, was a locked door. Granger unlocked it and motioned them through.

The door opened to a surprisingly large chamber occupied by four blackbird guards, playing cards around a table.

They nodded to Granger like they knew him, and one of them handed him a ring of keys.

"This way," Granger said, opening yet another door to a tiny chamber. From there, a staircase descended into the dark.

It must be a Montaigne family secret, the kind of place you'd keep your brother until you murdered him. Or a traitorous mistress. Or an uncooperative wife.

Or an unscrupulous minion of the king. Destin smiled benignly at Granger.

As they descended the stairs, Granger grew more relaxed, almost chatty. Definitely a bit more daring when it came to taking pokes at Destin. Maybe it was because he was on his own turf. It was disturbing that he'd recovered from yesterday's interview so quickly.

"So, as you'll see, the hostages are safe and sound, right under the king's eye, and totally secure."

They'd finally reached the bottom of the staircase. Granger drew a second ring of keys from his pocket and unlocked the door. After that, it was down another corridor and through another set of doors. Here the air was dank, thick with moisture, and the walls gleamed with sweat. Destin could hear water trickling, and several times they crossed streamlets running across the floor. It was cold, too—a damp cold that penetrated all the way to the bone.

That's when Destin knew: King Jarat *was* stupid enough to keep his hostages in the Pit—only a remote, secret part of it, unconnected to the rest. A place where they would never be found by anyone who didn't know where to look. He sent up a prayer of thanks to whatever god had persuaded him not to bring Matelon along. Even a stoic soul like Matelon couldn't help but react to this.

He glanced at Marina. Her face was smooth, unreadable. She's not surprised, he thought. She knew the Montaignes better than most—at least among those who were still alive.

Finally, they reached another checkpoint staffed with blackbird guards—none of whom were known to Destin. They all seemed to know Granger, though. After some whispered discussion, the group passed through.

Lila had been amazingly silent so far, but now she spoke up. "How many hostages are down here?"

Granger lifted one shoulder in a half-shrug. "Probably thirty. That's not counting the lýtlings."

Marina's head came up. "The *children* are down here?" This revelation had broken through her wall. She'd always had a soft spot for children.

"They'd want to be with their mothers, wouldn't they?" Granger said. "I've asked the guards to gather everyone up for a count."

The next area was better lit, and the air seemed a little more breathable. Destin could see evidence that the families, or their captors, had tried to make their prison more comfortable. Here and there, a rug centered a gathering of random furniture. Families had set up in some of the side chambers, with beds lining the walls, tables and chairs, and draperies hung over the entries to provide a bit more privacy.

"Many of our guests have apartments here in the capital," Granger said, "thus, we were able to bring in their own furniture so that they would feel at home."

"A few months down here, and their furniture will be fit for the midden heap," Destin said.

"Hopefully, peace will be restored before then," Granger said. "It was their choice, of course, whether to bring their belongings in."

"What are they eating down here?" Lila said.

"They are supplied from the kitchens," Granger said. "They do much of their own cooking, since we cannot exactly serve formal meals—that would draw too much attention, all that coming and going. Fortunately, goods keep well down here."

But people don't, Destin thought, pressing his lips together. The families would never forget this, and the thanes would never forgive it. This is not how you treat people that you might want as your allies later on. But maybe Jarat doesn't care. He has Granger, after all, who is probably plotting his overthrow.

Destin could hear voices from farther on. The black-birds had gone on ahead of them, no doubt to begin the "gathering" process.

The families were assembled in a larger chamber in the cave—what seemed to stand in for a great hall. A table— not large enough to accommodate everyone at once, but sizable—stood at one end. Destin smelled woodsmoke, and realized that there must be some sort of kitchen nearby.

They stood in a shabby little group—their faces closed and guarded. He recognized some of them: Lady Matelon and her daughter. Christina Heresford and her four younger children. Her husband, Ross, had been killed in the war with the north. Her eldest, Rafe, was with the rebels at White Oaks. Patrice DeLacroix, mother to the unfortunate Estelle, and wife to Pascal, who had joined the rebels. Danielle Oberon, cousin to DeLacroix. She'd taken full advantage of the family's rise when DeLacroix was Montaigne's favorite.

Several flinched and looked away when they saw Destin. His face was well known at court, his reputation throughout the empire.

Do they think I'm going to torture them? Interrogate them? Murder them?

Well, yes. Why wouldn't they?

Granger came up beside him. "The count is forty-five, Lieutenant. Twenty-eight adults and seventeen children."

Lila wrote that number down, although Destin had noticed that she was taking her own count.

"Lieutenant Karn," Lady Matelon said, fixing on him immediately. "I won't say welcome, because that would be dishonest, and I try to tell the truth as often as I can."

Christina Heresford came up beside her and patted her arm. "Now, now, Marjorie, just because we've fallen on hard times doesn't mean that we should forget our manners." She looked up at Destin. "Can we offer you some gruel, Lieutenant?"

"We're all out of gruel," a voice called from amid the crowd.

"Some bread and water, then?" Heresford arched her brow. "Tell me, Lieutenant, is it true that bread is still wholesome if one cuts the mold off?"

Destin was struck by the iron-spined defiance of these women, kept belowground for months, aware of how tenuous their position was. Strong men do choose strong women, he thought. It's only the weak that are threatened by them.

"Thank you," he said, "but we're actually here for another purpose. Is everyone here? Is anyone missing?"

"There are two babies asleep in the nursery," Heresford said, folding her arms. "Shall we wake them up?"

Destin shook his head. That makes forty-seven, he thought.

He turned to Marina. "Your Majesty?"

"I bring some good news," Marina said. "We're here to invite you to a party."

You could have heard a pin drop in the chamber.

"A party?" Lady Matelon looked at Lady Heresford.

"Who the *hell* is inviting us to a party?" It seemed that her time underground had surfaced the grit in the thanelee.

"His Majesty is entertaining the ambassadors and nobility from the down-realms," Marina said, "and he would like you to be there."

"Why?" DeLacroix said, her body stiff with disapproval. "Is he going to stage an execution for his guests?"

"Let me remind you that King Jarat was not responsible for Lady Estelle's unfortunate death," Marina said.

"Gerard is dead," DeLacroix said. "I expected that, as Jarat's mother, you would exert more influence over—"

"I offer the king counsel," Marina said, a little sharply, "but, like his father, he makes his own decisions. I would argue that *your* influence is limited as long as you are locked up out of sight. This could be an opportunity to forge a new relationship with a new king."

"He can forge a new relationship with us by freeing us and allowing us to rejoin our families," Lady Matelon said.

"That is unlikely to happen anytime soon," Destin said. "But this would afford you a little freedom. It could be a start." Destin knew he should stay out of it. He was no diplomat, and their hatred of him ran deep.

"Why would the king send his spymaster to invite us to a party?" Lady DeLacroix said, tilting her head at Destin. "Are you going to handwrite the invitations, too?"

"The lieutenant is here to protect me from all of you." Marina rolled her eyes, and several of the ladies laughed.

It helped that Marina was popular with the ladies of the court. Despite her limited influence over the king, she was a person who could find a way to get things done behind the scenes. Destin knew for a fact that she had intervened on behalf of many in the room over the years.

"Does he mean to parade us before his guests wearing these clothes?" Heresford swirled her filthy skirts. "Is this really the kind of image he wants to present to his underlords?"

"No, I don't believe he does," Marina said. "I have arranged for you to get some new clothes, if you have nothing suitable. To be honest, I asked for this. I am so damned tired of making conversation with every deadly dull merchant, noble, and official who passes through the city. I could use some help."

Lady Heresford laughed. "You poor thing." They all knew, to varying degrees, what her life had been like with Gerard. Speaking to dull merchants was the least of it.

"When it comes to the rebellion, I don't think it will make a big difference politically. Everybody with a brain in his head will understand why you're there." Marina smiled sadly. "I have missed all of you so much."

Heads were nodding all around, accompanied by a murmur of "We've missed you, too."

"What about the children?" somebody asked. "Are they invited?"

Granger began shaking his head, but Marina said, "Of

course. It would very much please me if every single one of you is there. Every single one of you," she repeated, making eye contact with one, and then another. "Costume parties are so much fun. It should be . . . a night you'll never forget. Jarat is sparing no expense."

"It's a costume party?" This was a child's voice, and the girl sounded excited.

"I'm not coming," somebody said in a loud and carrying voice.

Everyone turned to look and see who had spoken.

"Harper, we'll talk about this later," Lady Matelon said.

"No, Mama, we'll talk about it now." With that, Harper Matelon stepped out front, the Matelon scowl planted on her face. "I am not going to any parties with the swiving king or his swiving court."

"Harper! That language is inappropriate." Lady Matelon tried to pull her daughter back into the safety of the crowd, but she wrenched free.

"Would *despicable* be better?" Harper put her hands on her hips. "You're the one that always tells me to use my words and not my fists."

"Lady Harper," Marina said gently, "I really want to have you at my party. Please come."

Harper wavered, then shook her head. "If it was just your party, Your Majesty, you know I would come. But I refuse to dress up and mince around for *him*. If he wants me at his party, he'll have to drag me there in chains and show his guests how . . . despicable . . . he is."

Granger pushed past the queen. "Listen to me, you ungrateful, traitorous whelpling. If King Jarat invites you to a party, you had better—"

"Shut up, Granger," Destin said. "Let me talk to Harper in private. I think I can persuade her to come." He extended his hand toward her, and all the ladies shrank back as one, looks of horror on their faces.

"She's just a child, Lieutenant," Lady Matelon said, pushing Harper behind her. "Leave her alone. I will talk to her, and you can be sure that she will be there, if that is what the king commands."

"She is not a child, Lady Matelon. If she is old enough to have opinions, and to speak them aloud, she is old enough to defend them."

"Take me instead," Lady Matelon said, chin up, but her voice trembling just a bit.

"You are not the one I'm having an issue with," he said. Then, seeing her stricken face, he relented a little. "You can come with her, if you like. We'll just step into one of these smaller rooms and have a talk."

"Here!" Lila called. She stood at the entrance to one of the cells. "This is clear."

"After you," Destin said. Lady Matelon gripped her daughter's hand and they walked ahead of Destin, backs straight, as if marching to their execution. The room had fallen dead silent behind them.

417

This is why you don't plan parties, Destin thought. Nobody would come. You're never that fun to be around.

The room was set up as sleeping quarters for a family, with pallets on the floor and one actual bed. Thanelee Matelon whispered urgently into Harper's ear while Destin did a quick round of the room, putting up wards against eavesdroppers. Lila stood guard at the door. Always useful, Lila Barrowhill.

Destin returned to where Harper and her mother were standing. As he approached, Lady Matelon drew Harper closer, under the protection of her arm.

"Please don't spell her," Lady Matelon said. "She's promised to cooperate."

"I'm not going to spell her," Destin said. He reached out and tilted the girl's chin up so that he could look into her eyes. "Listen to me, Harper. I really need you to come to this party. I need all of you to come, even the littlest child, and I hope you'll help me by persuading them."

Harper was clenching her teeth, struggling to keep her mouth shut, but he could see the resistance in her eyes.

"Are you the youngest?" Destin said abruptly. "Or are you between your two brothers?"

Her eyes narrowed. "I'm the youngest," she said, "but only by a year. I'm nearly fourteen."

"Which of your brothers are you most like, do you think? Hal or Robert?"

Harper cocked her head, as if trying to work out the

trick, then she glanced at her mother for help.

"Harper is most like Halston, our eldest, who died at Delphi," Lady Matelon said. Then, glaring at her daughter, she added, "Although on days like today, she reminds me of Robert."

"Ah," Destin said, nodding. "Harper, I have something for you." He fished the thimble and chain out of his pocket and held it out to her. "Your brother, Captain Matelon, sent this. He says to tell you that he's been pricked, but he's not dead yet."

Harper's eyes widened in disbelief. "*Captain* Matelon?" She grabbed the thimble and brought it close to her face, examining it. Then looked up at Destin. "How did you know about this? Are there listeners in the walls at White Oaks?"

"Let me see it, Harper," Lady Matelon said.

Harper spun around and displayed it to her mother on her outstretched palm.

Lady Matelon poked at it with her forefinger. Then looked up at Destin, her face hardening. "Are you really the kind of brute who would break the heart of a little girl?"

Destin shook his head. "I'm not in the business of breaking hearts," he said, "though sometimes it can't be avoided. Lady Matelon, Captain Matelon sent another message for you. He said to tell you to 'look on the bright side.'"

"Halston," she whispered, her eyes filling with tears.

"Where is he?" Harper demanded. "Where's my brother? Is he in prison, too?"

"'Where are my brothers?' would be a better question," Destin said. "I can't tell you that, but I can tell you that they really want you to come to King Jarat's party."

"Why are you doing this?" Lady Matelon said, lowering her voice and looking over her shoulder at Lila. "I cannot fathom why you would be working with Halston and Robert."

"Or why they would be working with you," Harper said. "If they even are."

Politics makes for strange bedfellows? Probably best not to go there.

"This enterprise is a risk that I would have preferred not to take." Destin said. "But, as it turns out, Lady Harper, your brothers and I share a common goal. You may question whether I'm telling the truth, but you have to consider the possibility that I am, and weigh whether sticking it to the king is worth it."

The ladies Matelon looked at each other.

"All right," Harper said. "I will come."

"Will you help talk the others into coming?"

She met his gaze. "I will."

"Now. When you speak to the others, you mustn't mention your brothers' involvement, or my involvement, or in any way imply that anything other than a party is in store.

You must simply convey the message that it is critical that they come. Agreed?"

"Agreed."

"Thank you," Destin said, relieved. "Shall we return to the others?"

Harper dangled the thimble in front of Destin. "You should give this back to Hal, to keep him safe." She wore a mask of innocence, but Destin was used to reading faces to see what lay underneath.

She's trying to figure out where he is, whether he's close, whether I'm going to see him, Destin thought. He closed her hand over the thimble. "You can give it back to him yourself when you see him. Now, when we walk back into the other room, it's important that you appear properly chastened, as if I've spent this time schooling you on the consequences of defying the king. I am not the sort of man who delivers hope to political prisoners."

"Maybe you are," Harper said, giving him an appraising look. And then she drew her head in and rounded her shoulders as if she expected a blow to fall at any moment. She fixed her eyes on the floor, her lower lip trembling. The transformation was stunning. She was like a snake shedding one skin and putting on another.

You're not like either of your brothers, Destin thought. You lack their bone-deep instinct for honesty. You might have a future as a spy.

REUNION

Lyss sat her horse and watched her fledgling cavalry go through its maneuvers on the parade ground. It was an exercise in frustration. Her soldiers seemed unable to communicate with their mounts in a meaningful way. Every move the horses made seemed to surprise their riders, with sometimes disastrous results.

"Left TURN!" she shouted. "Now, forward!"

Once again the columns dissolved into chaos, horses rearing and showing their teeth. Several riders ended up on the ground.

"Ghezali!" she shouted to one of the field officers. "I said five paces before the turn."

Ghezali stared at her as if she were speaking a foreign

language. Which she was, in a way. Given that the Carthian army was a mix of nationalities, she used Common as the language of command. She was improving in Carthian—in military vocabulary, at least—but this job was hard enough without hunting for words all day long.

"What is the point of riding back and forth across the field in pretty formations?" Tully Samara nudged his horse closer. "This is a battle, not a dance. Why does it matter how they get to the enemy as long as they get there?"

"Use your eyes," Lyss said, in no mood to indulge the shiplord's constant questions. "The idea is to train the soldier so that, in the heat of battle, he or she can act without thinking."

And if you can't train the man, you train his horse.

"Ghezali!" she shouted. "Go back to the saber-and-lance exercises you practiced yesterday, this time using all gaits," Lyss said, giving up on the complexities of turning. "Make fifty passes across the grounds, and you're done for the day."

Right now, the bloodsworn were as likely to cut up each other as the enemy, which needed fixing. Except the enemy might be her own Highlander army. That was one of many reasons her head was pounding.

Samara knew next to nothing about land-based warfare, and Lyss had no desire to tutor him. Yet he'd ridden out to join her as soon as he spotted her drilling the cavalry. It seemed he was constantly at her side—when he wasn't attending the empress—asking questions and challenging Lyss's answers. He obviously saw her as his rival, given that nearly everyone else on the island was bloodsworn. He resented that Lyss had been given command of the army, and she knew he'd be happy to seize the opportunity to sabotage her efforts or carry tales to the empress. She wished he would go back to sea. And, preferably, drown.

She didn't need the distraction, given the delicate balancing act she was trying to pull off. So she watched the horses sluice back and forth across the parade ground and did her best to ignore him.

She had no intention of grooming an army capable of defeating her Highlanders. What was bad for the Carthian army was good for the Fells. Yet failure had its own risks, especially with Samara taking such an interest in what she was doing. The empress was no fool. Lyss had to make a show of competence, or risk ending up in that mob of bloodsworn, probably under Samara's command. Nearly every night, she'd wake up, sweating, from that nightmare.

Still, it was so damned hard to do less than her best. Lyss had spent years assessing soldiers, making the most of their strengths, and working around their weaknesses. The more she worked with the empress's army, the more she realized that what had worked well in the Fells didn't apply here. She'd always used her soldiers as independent agents, capable of making their own decisions and strategy changes, even in the heat of battle. She had prioritized conserving and protecting her troops, since they were usually outnumbered by the southerners. With the exception of Queen Court and a few other battles, she had avoided confronting the enemy straight on. Her tactic of choice was a series of hit-and-run skirmishes that destroyed enemy morale and wore the enemy down. That had suited the soldiers she led in the terrain they were fighting in. Against overwhelming odds, it had kept Arden out of the north.

These troops had no fear of death, and felt no pain, so they had no need for a personal strategy of survival. They simply charged forward, howling, swinging their curved blades and cudgels, until they rode down the enemy or their horses were cut out from under them.

Lyss found herself constantly playing both sides, considering how to best use the assets she had, and how to best counter them in the field. This would be great preparation for fighting Celestine's forces if she ever got the chance.

In the meantime, her training strategy gradually shifted, until she was no longer training an army that could succeed in the mountains of the Fells. Instead, she was doing her best to train an army that could succeed in the flatlands of Arden.

As she watched, a shadow passed across the parade ground. The horses panicked, rearing and screaming out a warning, dumping several riders to the ground. Lyss looked up, shading her eyes, and saw a winged creature swoop down toward the horses. Its leathery wings all but spanned the parade ground. It glittered in the sun, as if it were covered with blue, purple, and gold armor—or maybe jewels. It seized one of the horses, executed an awkward turn, and then, wings beating hard, it began to climb, heading out to sea again.

Swearing, Samara yanked his bow from his saddle boot and sent an arrow flying. He was a good shot—it pinged against the creature's armor and fell into the water. Lyss watched the beast until it disappeared into the sun.

"Thrice-cursed dreki," Samara spat. "That's twice this week it's gone after the horses."

Turning her attention back to her troops, Lyss saw that one rider had taken a particularly bad spill. He stood, his foot at an impossible angle, and limped toward the barracks.

Lyss shuddered.

"Trust me, General, you feel it more than he does," Tully Samara said. "You must develop a thicker skin."

"If only we had bloodsworn horses," Lyss said, shaking her head sadly, "and bloodsworn ships. We'd be unstoppable."

Samara smiled thinly. "I understand that there are more of your countrymen on the way to join the bloodsworn. That should make you feel at home." Having planted his daily thornbush, Samara heeled his horse and trotted away.

But even a thornbush grows a flower sometimes. And sometimes the loveliest flower has poison at its heart.

That afternoon, Lyss met with the empress on her pavilion by the sea. The empress's current favorite, Tarek, was there, fanning her with a palm leaf and feeding her sugared grapes from a golden bowl. He was very young, extraordinarily handsome, and absolutely terrified.

"You should choose a lover, General," Celestine said, licking sugar from her lips. "You are welcome to Tarek when I am finished with him." She patted his cheek fondly.

Lyss's cheeks heated. "No thank you, Your Eminence."

"Would a girl suit you better?" The empress gestured toward a small group of maidservants sunning themselves on the cliffs nearby. "If none of them suit, we could go farther afield depending—"

"I'm . . . ah . . . really quite busy with . . . other things," Lyss said.

"Too bad," the empress said. "You've been working so hard, and I've been trying to think of a way to reward you."

Lyss cleared her throat. "Your praise is all the reward I need, Empress." *And a promise that I won't have to join your undead army.*

"I think *this* will please you," Celestine said. "You've been saying that you would like to have more officers to work with you in order to manage our numbers. Yet, as we've seen, the bloodsworn do not do well in a command position. So—I have a surprise for you."

She clapped her hands, and her maidservant went into the palace, returning with a small group of battered-looking prisoners, most wearing bits and pieces of Highlander uniforms.

"These men claim that they were officers in your army, Captain," the empress said, gesturing toward them. "Experienced at command of troops in the field. If you can persuade them to serve me without joining my bloodsworn, I will let them live."

Lyss gave the candidates a look-over. Of the six, three were unknown to her. From the looks on their faces, however, she was not unknown to them. The question was, did they know her as Captain Gray or as the heir to the Gray Wolf throne?

The other three, she recognized. Demeter Farrow, a Waterwalker and lieutenant in her salvo; Munroe Graves— son of Lydia Byrne Graves—an artist turned artilleryman; and, finally, like a recurrent bad dream, Quill Bosley.

Bosley. He was definitely the sort to survive when so many other, more worthy soldiers had died. Lyss took a deep breath, then released it. *Just when you think things can't get any worse.*

They'd all seen hard use, from the looks of them, Farrow in particular.

Celestine disentangled herself from Tarek and levered to her feet, "Wetlanders!" she said. "Welcome to Celesgarde. Your lives have been spared because you have been selected to join my army, under the command of General Gray. Do well, and you will be richly rewarded. Disappoint me, and you'll find that there are other ways to serve."

The others stood silently, their eyes shifting from Celestine to Lyss, but swiving Bosley instantly fell to one knee. "Empress," he said, head bowed. "We will not disappoint you."

40

MASQUERADE

"King's Guard black might be your color," Robert said, looking Hal up and down. "You would give any citizen of the empire the shivers."

"If so, it's more the uniform than the man," Hal said, hoping he didn't look as uncomfortable as he felt. He buckled his belt, with its empty scabbard, hoping he'd be given a weapon to fill that scabbard before long. He attached the braid that said he was a private. Privates are a copper a pound—not worthy of notice. At least that was the hope.

That was about as much as he knew of the plan. Hal was the sort that wanted to know from the start what he was getting into and how he was going to get out.

You should've given up on that a long time ago, he thought.

The door banged open, startling the both of them. Hal expected Destin Karn, but instead it was Lila Barrowhill, this time clad in scribner blues. She shut the door behind her, strode over to them, and looked them up and down. "This," she said, stabbing her forefinger into Robert's lapel, "goes on the left side, not the right." He stood there, speechless, while she unpinned a badge and repinned it on the other side.

"Who are you?" Robert managed.

"My name's not important." She turned to look at Hal. "Yours is correct," she said. "Quit gaping."

"Is it just my imagination, or do you work for *every-one*?" Hal said.

"That's me—everybody's girl. Do you have your masks? Good. If there's anything you want to bring with you, get it now, because you won't be back."

That, at least, is good news, Hal thought.

Lila tossed Hal a large cloth sack. "Put all your clothes in here and give them to me. You'll want them later, when you stop being a blackbird. And hurry. It's important that I get you two into position before we get this party started. We can't risk your running into people who might recognize you without your masks."

Hal began stuffing his and Robert's clothes into the bag.

She opened the door and stood aside. "After you," she said.

When they walked out into the corridor, the guards that were usually there were gone.

"Now," their escort said, "glower at everyone and walk like a blackbird until I get you under cover."

"How does a blackbird walk?" Robert whispered.

"Like he's got a burr up his ass," she said.

Hal did his best to comply as they descended to the ground floor of Newgate Prison and out into a light rain. Robert took a deep breath and let it out slowly. Hal knew that they might be going from the pot into the fire, but he felt the same relief to be out of Newgate.

Even though it was a short walk from Newgate to the palace, they were accosted along the way by multiple people—at least their escort was. Everybody seemed to know Lila, from a farrier at the stables to a pantry maid taking a break outside the kitchens to another clerk who called, "Hey, Lila, will you be at the Cold Crow tonight? I've got to win some of my money back."

"No," she said, without missing a step. "I'm working tonight. Maybe at the turn of the week."

They did stop and wait when a velvet-clad merchant drew her aside for a hurried conversation. When she returned, she growled, "Everybody's job is the most important." She put on speed, as if to make up for lost time.

"Is that your name? Lila?" Robert said, hurrying to

keep up as they circled around to the back of the palace.

She shot him a look. "Damn," she said. "I was beginning to like you. Now I have to kill you." She pushed open a door that was hidden behind a clump of shrubbery. "In here."

She led them through what seemed to be a servants' entrance to a pantry and staging area that was no longer in use. Hal could hear the clamor of musicians trying out their tuning in the next room.

"Is that the ballroom?" he said, tipping his head toward the sound. He'd been in there before, for parties during the holidays.

"Yes," Lila said. Opening a cabinet, she pulled out a cloth-wrapped bundle. Inside were two standard-issue blackbird swords and two daggers.

She handed out the weapons. Hal slid the blade home with a satisfactory hiss.

Lila opened another cabinet. It was stuffed with what appeared to be black oilskin cloaks. Again, standard issue for the King's Guard here in the south, where winter was more often rainy than cold.

"Leave the cloaks in here until you need them," she said. "When the party gets under way, ease out and mingle." She opened the door that should have led into the ballroom, but all Hal could see were thick blue draperies. "The hostages will be wearing animal masks covered in sequins—badgers, lions, elyphants, dragons, and so on.

They're all different styles and colors, so the hostages will be harder for the King's Guard to notice when they congregate. Get word to each one of them to drift toward the punch bowl when the temple sounds the quarter hour before ten o'clock. Also—tell them to keep their masks on until they are told to remove them. We don't want anyone picking them out."

"That's a lot of information to deliver," Hal said. "Wouldn't it have been safer to let them know the plan before they come up to the ballroom? What if we miss someone? What if someone notices us making the rounds?"

"Lieutenant Karn wants to make sure nothing leaks beforehand. There are eyes and ears everywhere."

"But—"

"There are twenty-eight adults. See that you get to everyone, and make sure you're not noticed." She paused, and when there was no more protest, she went on. "At ten o'clock, all hell breaks loose, and you will herd them behind the curtain and out through the exit door, handing each one a cloak to put on as they come through. Got it?"

"Where do we go once we get outside?" Robert's eyes were alight with excitement. He was all action, waiting to happen.

"The postern gate will be open, but you won't go there. You'll go back to Newgate."

"*Newgate?*" Hal shook his head. "Why do we go back there?"

"Because it's close, and because nobody will look for you there. Once you're there, you'll get further orders."

"What happens at ten o'clock?" Robert said.

"Like I said. You'll see. Now, I have errands to run." She left through the door they'd come in, leaving Hal and Robert staring after her.

"What just happened?" Robert whispered.

"Damned if I know," Hal said.

Destin Karn descended the now-familiar staircase to King Jarat's secret prison, Luc Granger at his heels, along with a small crew of the king's handpicked blackbirds. There were so many ways this complicated plan could go wrong, with so many untried civilians involved. So he'd have to feed them information just in time for them to put it to use. And he'd have to find a way to do it with Granger shadowing his every step.

The hostages were already assembled, dressed in their party clothes. Lila and Marina had done their work well, with help from Jocelyn, Destin's tailor friend. They wore a combination of clothing fetched from their capital apartments, clothing they'd had with them in the Pit, now carefully cleaned and repaired, and some new acquisitions by Lila for the children.

He took a quick head count. All present and accounted for, including the Matelons. He asked Lady Heresford to hand out the masks. The children, especially, were smitten with the animal masks, arguing over who would get what. He noted that Harper chose a dragon mask, and her mother a badger.

"No pushing," he said, feeling like a stand-in teacher at a grammar school. "There are enough for everyone. Does everyone have a mask? Good. Don't put them on until we get upstairs. I don't want anyone stumbling and cracking their head open, because I'll have to clean up the blood." *I do enough of that as it is.*

The lýtlings seemed to find this hilarious. Their mothers, less so.

Granger seemed unmoored in this sea of women and children, as if they drained all of the swagger out of him, leaving the nastiness behind. "Tell them we'll cut the whelplings' throats if they make a scene," he murmured to Destin.

"Good thinking," Destin murmured back. "That's guaranteed to put them in a party mood."

Taking a step away from Granger, Destin addressed the hostages. "Now, just a word of caution before we go upstairs," he said. "I know you've been put in an awkward situation. This might seem like an opportunity for a show of opposition—some kind of demonstration to embarrass the king in front of his guests. Trust me, it's not. It will accomplish nothing, and it will damage Queen Marina, who stuck her neck out for you. Most importantly, it will put you at risk, since there's no telling how Jarat will react. Does everyone understand?"

There followed a grudging mumble of agreement.

Destin took a deep breath. "Let's go," he said.

WALLFLOWER

It seemed to take forever to get the party started. Hal spent that time going over Lila's orders in his head, worrying about all the things that could go wrong. Who was Barrowhill anyway? She looked like a Southern Islander, and maybe she was, because she swore like a sailor. Was she some minion of Karn's? Had she been spying on the thanes when they'd met at Temple Church?

Karn must have a whole network of people to call upon. But how many of them could be trusted to go along with freeing the hostages?

Finally, the band started up in earnest, and Hal could hear various dignitaries being introduced as they entered the ballroom. When it sounded like the room was sufficiently full of people, he pulled on his mask and motioned to his brother to do the same. "Let's go."

They closed the door gently behind them and found their way to an opening in the drapery. Hal peered out, but flinched back when he saw somebody standing just outside, next to the punch bowl.

The man wore an Ardenine dress uniform and a red hawk mask. He had his back to them, but the general's braid on his shoulders and the shape of him made him easily identifiable as General Marin Karn. He stood, glaring out at the room, arms folded, like a stump rooted to the floor.

Hal raised his hand to stop his brother, who was trying to slide past him. "It's Karn Senior," he hissed.

Robert peered out. "Poor Karn's a wallflower," he whispered.

"Shhh!" Hal knew his brother was trying to dispel the tension, but there was nothing humorous about Marin Karn.

What with the music and the announcements and all, Hal didn't think they could be heard, but he didn't want to take any chances.

King Jarat sat on a raised dais at the far end of the room, his mother and younger sister at his side. One by one, the loyal thanes and their ladies were introduced and walked the length of the room to pay their respects to the king. Botetort, Beauchamp, and Larue, each with his lady on his arm. And then the guests from the far reaches of the empire—the ambassador from Bruinswallow, the Thane of We'enhaven, the Lord Governor of Tamron, and the Lord of the Isles.

The walls were lined with blackbirds—no, King's Guards—sleek in their dress uniforms. Intermingled with them were officers from the regular army. Their assignment tonight would be to dance with any lady in need of a partner. They were armed, though, and from their expressions and posture, they seemed to be expecting trouble.

To Hal's relief, the king summoned Karn Senior to meet the military governor of Watergate, or some such. Once he walked away, Hal and Robert were free to slide out from behind the drapes. They joined the perimeter of social conscripts and waited.

The king really had spared no expense. The ceilings were covered with billows of silk that met in the middle. From that midpoint dangled a huge red hawk made of papier-mâché—the kind that held prizes and candies. Masked servers walked around the room, offering smoked snails, quail eggs, and caviar, along with little biscuits filled with roast meat. Liquor was flowing at several bars. One entire wall was given to desserts.

On any other night, Hal would have taken advantage, given his long period of ascetic living in the north. But tonight his stomach was tied in knots, and he was in no hurry to chance these fancy foods.

It wasn't long before there was a stir in the entryway, signaling new arrivals. There was Destin Karn, gliding across the dance floor to speak to the king, who smiled and nodded. Hal watched with interest as Karn Junior and Senior exchanged stiff nods, their body language as hostile as could be.

They really don't like each other, Hal thought, recalling his conversation with Destin Karn at Newgate. I wonder why.

Karn Junior spoke hurriedly to the band, which played a fanfare, bringing everyone's attention to the dais.

Jarat stood, Queen Marina and Princess Madeleine beside him. "Welcome to the heartbeat of the empire," he said. "Celebrations with good friends and allies are important, even amid the uncertainties of war. We have with us tonight some of the fairest flowers of the realm. Though some in their families have taken up arms against us, we have invited them to join us in the hope that this gesture might be a first step in reaching a permanent peace."

"That's a shitload of scummer," Robert murmured.

"When a king is shoveling it, you listen and you smile," Hal said, clapping along with the other guests.

"Ladies, come forward," King Jarat said.

And they came, straight-backed women ushering their children, walking the length of the room, and curtsying before the royal family. As they did so, the royal crier called out their names. "Lady Patrice DeLacroix and children.

Lady Christina Heresford and children. Lady Danielle Oberon."

"He's not using their titles," Robert muttered.

"It's likely he's given their titles away. From what I hear, he's been handing them out like candy."

"Lady Beatrice Scoville."

"There's Aunt Beatrice," Robert said, frowning. "She looks a lot thinner than before."

Hal scanned the line of waiting families, sure he would recognize Harper and his mother despite the masks. When he didn't see them, sweat began trickling down the back of his neck. Was this just some kind of cruel trick or trap?

Just as he was beginning to panic, the crier called, "Lady Marjorie Scoville Matelon and daughter Harper Scoville Matelon."

Hal's heart twisted as they walked forward, hand in hand, chins up, eyes straight ahead. It was no wonder he hadn't recognized them. For one thing, they were thinner, especially Harper, but that was partly because she was so much taller than the last time he'd seen her. When was that? More than a year ago? She'd pinned her hair up, too, which he wasn't used to.

Hal's breath caught when he saw something glittering at Harper's neckline. It was the thimble.

"Did you see that?" Robert whispered. "It was—"

"I know," Hal said, his voice thick. He still didn't trust Destin Karn, but he'd kept that promise, at least.

Anger nudged aside everything else as the Matelon ladies curtsied before the king and then moved off to the side, where the hostages huddled in a small group, as if unsure what to do next. As if they'd been invited to a party with people they had nothing in common with.

Robert took a step forward, but Hal put out a hand to stop him. "Wait until there's more mingling before we beeline to them. In the meantime, why don't you ask someone to dance?"

His brother gave him an irritated look, then crossed to the gathering of down-realm guests and bowed to an especially lovely young lady wearing a half-mask. Moments later, the band had struck up again, and he was out on the floor with her.

Others among the wall-hangers were moving out into the throng, choosing unescorted ladies, offering their arms. Hal's heart beat faster as he walked toward the gathered hostages, but somebody got there before him.

"Ladies," the masked interloper said, bowing deeply to Harper and his mother. "May I just say that you look absolutely bewitching this evening."

Hal detoured a bit and walked past them, stopping within earshot, pretending to sample sweets from a platter.

"Granger," Hal's mother said, her back stiff with disapproval, her voice icy. She and Harper dipped into the briefest of curtsies.

"Actually, it is Lord Granger now," he said.

"Is it?" his mother said. "Forgive me. It's so difficult to keep up with all of the newly minted lordlings here at court."

Hal struggled not to stare. Usually his mother treated everyone with gracious courtesy, whether she was addressing the king or one of her tenants or a beggar on the street.

Harper, too, was studying Granger, her arms crossed. It reminded Hal of that time he'd found his three-year-old sister standing in the pasture with a stick in her hand. There was a viper in her path, and she couldn't decide whether to go around it or club it to death.

Who the hell was Granger, and what had he done to earn such a chilly reception?

"I am hoping that your lovely daughter will consent to dance with me."

"*Lord* Granger, my lovely daughter is far too young to consider—"

"Let's go," Harper said, shooting a warning look at her mother. She stalked toward the dance floor, with Granger following behind.

Hal's gracious mother glared after him, cursing under her breath. "Harper doesn't know what she is getting into with that unprincipled scoundrel."

Lady Heresford took her arm. "Don't worry, Marjorie, I've sent Helene to keep an eye on them. If anything untoward happens, she'll fetch us right away."

Hal was torn between forcibly cutting in on Lord

Granger's dance and waiting until he had more information. Good sense prevailed, and he found himself bowing to his mother. Up close, he could see that, despite her fine clothes, months in a dungeon hadn't done her any good at all.

"Thanelee Matelon," he said, swallowing hard. "May I . . . may I have the pleasure of this dance?"

He could tell that she was about to come back with a snappish reply, but then she froze, staring at him as if she could see through the mask to the man underneath.

"Thank the Maker," she whispered, her voice husky with tears. "It's really you. I wasn't sure whether to believe it or not."

Hal offered his arm, and she accepted, and he led her out onto the dance floor. He tried hard to remember the steps she'd taught him so painstakingly. Tears were spilling down her cheeks, but she didn't miss a step.

"Don't cry, Mother," he whispered. "They'll think I'm stepping on your toes."

That brought a smile.

"Now," he said, "Robert is here, too. Don't look," he hastened to add. "I'll tell you what I know about the plan, and then you tell me about Granger."

When he'd finished, he said, "Can you remember that? Any questions?"

"I'll remember."

"Good. Now I need to get the same message to one

adult in each and every one of the families. Can you help me with that? I think if you and Harper do it, it will be less obvious."

"Of course," his lady mother said. "I will make sure that everyone knows."

"Now tell me about Granger."

"He came out of nowhere, moved up in the King's Guard, and now he's serving as bailiff," she said, with brisk brevity. "He's taught King Jarat everything he knows about debauchery, and also handles a lot of his dirty work. Jarat has rewarded him by giving him Whitehall."

"Whitehall?" Now Hal understood his mother's barely concealed anger. Whitehall had been held by the Scovilles for centuries, since just after the Breaking. His mother had brought it to the marriage as her dowry. It was close to White Oaks, and they'd often stayed there as children. "He couldn't have taken possession of it, surely. I was just at White Oaks. The armies are massed, and the thanes are preparing to march."

"How *is* your father, dear?" his mother said, smiling at Lady DeLacroix as she swept by. "He takes things so much to heart, and he's not as young as he used to be."

"Father's furious, as you'd expect, and determined to win. Now about Whitehall."

"Granger hasn't taken possession—and he never will, if your father and I have anything to say about it. I think he's trying to hedge his bets. He's already betrothed, mind you, to an heiress in the down-realms who is considerably older than he is. But now he's thinking that if he marries Harper, that will damp down resistance to his claiming Whitehall, even if the thanes prevail. If they don't, he could make a case for claiming White Oaks, too. After all, they go so well together."

"He won't if I kill him first," Hal muttered.

"Don't scowl like that, dear, it will give you frown lines one day, mark my words. No. I will kill him myself."

Hal stared at his mother. "What?"

"Better me than you. You're young and you have your whole life ahead of you. Now that I have you back, I won't have you throwing it away. I'm old, I've had my children, enjoyed the love of my life, and what's important is my legacy."

"Mother, do you really think—?"

"Danielle!" she said, waving at Lady Oberon like she was having the best time ever. "That dress is so becoming." And then, hardly missing a beat, said, "I almost cut the bastard's throat the other day, when he came to see us in the Pit. He was sniffing around Harper, and I'd had enough, but then I heard about this party and couldn't resist finding out what it was all about."

Hal all but stopped dancing. "He's keeping you in the *Pit*? Women and children in the *Pit*?"

"Don't raise your voice, dear. It's His Majesty's private little prison. It wasn't so bad, once we evicted most of the vermin."

Except for the human vermin, Hal thought. "No killing will be necessary, because we're getting you out tonight. Now I'd better move on, or people will gossip about Thanelee Matelon, endlessly dancing with someone young enough to be her son." He stepped back and bowed. She curtsied, and he watched her walk away, cloaked in her usual dignity.

If we survive this, I won't make the mistake of underestimating her, ever again, he thought.

42

MOTLEY CREW

The rooftop garden at Fellsmarch Castle had been one of Ash's favorite boyhood haunts. It was planted deep with memories of time spent with his mother in sociable silence, planting, weeding, pruning, and harvesting, in tune with the rhythms of nature. Here he could bask in sunlight all year round, above the politics and drama of life in the capital.

Here he'd read, and dreamed, and grown the herbs and medicinals important to the healing trade.

Now he was back in the garden, planning the impossible with an improbable crew.

They sat in a circle in the garden temple, in the light

from the waxing moon. Adrian sul'Han, runaway prince. Evan Strangward, Carthian pirate and weather mage. Sasha Talbot, a member of the queen's Gray Wolf guard. Finn sul'Mander, wizard and healer. Hadley DeVilliers, wizard and commander of the Fellsian navy. Julianna Barrett, queen's councillor for intelligence and diplomacy.

He'd hoped to include Rogan Shadow Dancer as well, representing the clans, but he'd left on some mission or other to the upland camps or the coast. That might be just as well. Shadow was a bit of a loose cannon.

They'd all been sworn to secrecy. They all looked at him with a mixture of curiosity and wariness.

It was no wonder they're wary, Ash thought. They don't know you. He'd been closest to Finn, and even he had become a stranger since they were boyhood friends.

It was his job to win them, and he'd never practiced being charming.

"Thank you for coming," Ash said. "Once I explain what this is about, each of you is welcome to opt in or opt out, no questions, no hard feelings. I just ask that none of this be shared outside of this circle. Agreed?"

When everyone nodded, he continued. "As you know, my sister Alyssa was taken captive by the empress Celestine of Carthis in an attack on the port of Chalk Cliffs. We assume she's being held prisoner somewhere in the east. I plan to rescue her."

Talbot flinched, then pointed at Strangward. "Why is

he here?" she said, in her blunt fashion.

"Strangward is a weather mage and a skilled pilot with an intimate knowledge of the Desert Coast. We'll need him."

"Huh," Talbot said. She shifted on the hard temple floor, wrapped her arms around her knees, and fixed the pirate with a suspicious gaze. "What's in it for you? Why would you risk your life to save our princess?"

"I am here to stop the empress, free my homeland, and save my own skin," Strangward said. "It seems to me that the best way to do that is to join in on a rescue of the wolf princess."

"Before we get into the weeds on this, are we sure Lyss isn't being held in the keep at Chalk Cliffs?" DeVilliers said.

"Corporal Talbot saw her being taken aboard the empress's flagship just off Chalk Cliffs," Ash said.

Talbot nodded. "Plus, she left a message on the beach," she said.

Finn's head came up. "She did? Before she was carried off, she had time to write a note?"

Talbot reached into her uniform tunic and pulled out a piece of paper that had been folded and refolded many times. Carefully flattening it, she held it up for everyone to see.

AG + BdT

Finn squinted at it. "What does that even mean?" he said.

"Alyssa Gray plus Breon d'Tarvos," Talbot said.

DeVilliers raised an eyebrow. "The busker?"

Talbot nodded. "Plus, there was an arrow pointing out to sea. That means they were carried off by ship."

"How do you get that?" Finn said. "That looks more like a lover's inscription. Saying they ran away together."

"Well, she didn't have time to write a whole story," Talbot said, scowling, folding the paper up again.

"Even if we assume she was alive on the beach, and carried away aboard ship, how do we know that she is still alive?" Julianna said.

"She is," Talbot said, without hesitation. Then added quickly, "Captain Byrne says so. He says that he would know if the line was broken."

"Can he tell where she is?" DeVilliers said. "That would help a lot."

Talbot shook her head. "He says that her bound captain might, if she had one. His primary connection is to Queen Raisa, and now—" She paused, took a breath, and looked down at her hands. "It would help if Lyss had a bound captain of her own."

The mysterious connection between queens and the captains of the Gray Wolf guard had existed for more than a thousand years. After the magical disaster known as the

Breaking, Queen Hanalea the Warrior was the first to take a bound captain, who happened to be a Byrne. Ever since, it had always been a Byrne.

Bound captains were magically compelled to defend the Gray Wolf line at all costs. They had the ability to anticipate threats and counter them, and to track their queens, even over long distances. When Ash's sister Hana was killed in the borderlands, her bound captain, Simon Byrne, died fighting at her side.

The ritual that bound captain to queen was a closely held secret, known only to the captains, their queens, and the presiding speakers.

"In order to do that, we'd have to involve Captain Byrne," Ash said. "I can't imagine that he would approve."

"He might," Talbot said. "I've been reading up on it in some old texts. The captain's first allegiance is to the Line, not to an individual queen. In order to save the Line, he might give the go-ahead. Anything we can do to improve our odds, we should do." Talbot raised her chin, meeting Ash's eyes unflinchingly.

Hmm, Ash thought. Obviously, she already has a plan. I'm going to have to find out more about this.

Julianna shifted her weight and glanced at Finn, then back at Ash. "Speaking of the queen, has she approved this idea of a rescue mission?"

"No," Ash said. "I haven't asked her." He raked his hand

through his hair. "I know it's unforgivable—to leave again after being gone for so long, especially since she's so worried about Lyss. It's a terrible thing to do to my mother. But it's the right thing to do for the realm. The only way to succeed with this is to launch a quick, surgical strike— in and out before we're noticed. I'll understand, though, if that's a deal-breaker for anyone."

"How'd you choose us?" DeVilliers said.

"I'm trying to keep this operation secret. Most people in the realm still think I'm dead—nobody will miss me. That's why I'm not inviting the High Wizard, the captain of the Queen's Guard, or the general of the army. If they disappear, people will notice, and wonder what they are up to—not to mention the effect their absence would have on the war effort."

"So we were chosen because we're unimportant?" DeVilliers said, tilting her head back and looking at him down her nose.

"Unfortunately, some of you are *very* important," Ash said, "but you all have skills that we need for success. For instance, you are the best ship's master this side of the Indio, and Talbot, you're a member of Lyss's personal guard, and you know Lyss better than anyone. Finn, you are an academy-trained wizard and apprentice healer, and we'll need all the firepower we can get against these blood-sworn warriors. If you're willing to take time away from your new calling."

"Of course," Finn said. "I *will* need to ask permission from Lord Vega, but—"

"We need to ask forgiveness, not permission," Ash said. "If my mother forbids us to go, then it's treason to disobey. Plus, if word leaks out to the empress's spies, it will put all of our lives at risk, Lyss's most of all." As he said that, he was ambushed by a memory of the day of the attack at Oden's Ford, when he'd wanted to tell his mentor, Joniah Balthus, that he was leaving, and Lila talked him out of it. It seemed like a lifetime ago.

"What about me?" Julianna said. "I want to help, but I'm not sure my skills fit this kind of mission."

"Besides," Finn said, taking her hand, "your absence *will* be noticed."

"Hang on," DeVilliers said, "let's hear the plan, and then we can figure out what kind of crew we need."

The "plan" was embarrassingly sketchy, given that they had little information about what they would find on the other side of the Indio. DeVilliers and Strangward were the only ones among them that had been anywhere near the Desert Coast. Strangward had no memory of being to the Northern Islands, but he had studied the history of the Nazari Empire and knew the Desert Coast as well or better than anyone.

"Let's look at the map," Ash said.

Strangward spread a map over the mosaic floor of the temple and they all leaned in.

"It is rumored that Celestine is rebuilding her capital amid the ruins of the old capital," he said, pointing. "Here."

"Her bloodsworn mentioned taking prisoners to a place called Celesgarde," Talbot said.

Strangward looked up at her in surprise. "Right," he said. "Celesgarde."

"How well-protected is the harbor?" DeVilliers ran her finger over the spits of land enclosing the port. "Are there cannon on the heights?"

Strangward shook his head. "I don't know. What I do know is that the islands are protected by a barrier of storms."

"Really," DeVilliers said, raising a skeptical eyebrow. "Storms that just . . . stay there. All the time."

"It's magery," the pirate said. "A boundary created by the empress's enemies. It's kept her contained until recently." He seemed to be picking his way carefully. "All I know is what I heard when I was young. The trick will be to get through it without sustaining so much damage that we can't get out again."

"You're a weather mage, right?" Julianna said. "Can't you do something about that?"

"I can't count on it," Strangward said. "These storms were created by a powerful stormlord. I've never tried to counter that kind of magic."

"Any idea how many bloodsworn she has stationed there?" Talbot said.

Strangward shook his head.

"Well," Julianna said, "we could fill a briefing book with everything we don't know."

"Maybe it's better that we don't know," DeVilliers said, rolling her eyes. "We'd stay home."

"I recommend that we make a stop in Tarvos," Strangward said. "If there's any ship that can get through to Celesgarde, it's *Sun Spirit*. Plus, we could add to our numbers with my Stormborn crew."

"I'll match my *Sea Wolf* and my crew against any of yours," Hadley said, lifting her chin and glaring at him.

"We're not on-boarding anyone's crew," Ash said. The last thing he wanted was to set sail outnumbered by a crew blood-bound to Evan Strangward. "We're going to have to get along with what we have."

Now Strangward and DeVilliers were new-made allies. They both looked around the room, shaking their heads, as if unimpressed.

"No offense, but Strangward and I are the only sailors among us," DeVilliers said. "We can't sail with a crew of two, unless you intend to cross the Indio in a jolly boat."

"Isn't it likely that Celestine's crew will recognize *Sun Spirit* and *Sea Wolf* both?" Julianna said. "You've each been sailing these waters for years. As soon as you're spotted, she'll know she's under attack."

"That can't happen," Ash said. "If it comes to a fight, it's over."

"I have another ship that might serve," Evan said. "It was my first ship, in fact, a small ketch. I've sailed it in coastal waters with a crew of two, though five would be a better number for blue-water sailing. It is not well known on either coast. I used it early in my . . . career, before I acquired larger, faster ships. I don't believe Celestine would recognize it, especially if we modified the rigging."

"I'm guessing that ship is in Tarvos," DeVilliers said.

Strangward nodded. "Again, I suggest we sail *Sea Wolf* from here to Tarvos with a mixed crew—yours and mine. Then a small number of us will take the ketch to Celesgarde. We'll need to come up with a story."

"It still ends with us in Tarvos," Ash said. "Your stronghold. With all due respect, that doesn't sit well with me."

"The crossing will give us a chance to get to know each other better," Evan said. "Possibly you'll change your mind when—" He stopped, listening. "Someone's coming."

Now Ash heard the thud of boots on cobblestones, and the door to the temple was flung open. It was the queen's guard Ruby Greenholt, all out of breath, cheeks flushed. "Prince Adrian! It's the queen. She's fallen ill. Please hurry."

43

TWO-STEP LILY

They'd laid her out next to the hearth in her sitting room. Amon Byrne knelt beside the queen, his face taut and pale, Magret Gray on her other side.

A ring of bluejackets kept the area around them clear. Behind the blue line stood Aunt Mellony, Micah Bayar, and an array of other faces.

Ash didn't remember how he made his way to his mother's side. All at once, he was there, pressing his fingers into her cold skin, feeling her life draining away under his hands.

His mother's eyelids were blue, and her lips were tinged with it as well.

"Tell me what happened," he said to Byrne, as he continued his physical examination. "Tell me everything."

"We came here after dinner," Byrne said. "That's not unusual. We were all drinking wine, talking, when she collapsed."

Ash flinched. He'd found the poison; he could trace its icy passage through her body. The sensation was oddly familiar.

"Bring the cup," he snapped. Ash slid his arms under the queen, lifting her from the rug and carrying her into her bedchamber, where he laid her on the bed.

Moments later, Talbot set the cup on the bedside table. It was a jeweled cordial cup, one of the few heirlooms his mother used on a regular basis. It had belonged to her mother, his grandmother, whom he'd never met.

Ash was afraid to lift his hands, afraid his mother would slip away in the interval. "Have a look, and tell me what's in there," he said, tipping his head toward it.

"There's no more wine," Talbot said, tilting the cup to catch the light.

"Can you see anything in the bottom, on the sides, any residue?"

She held it up to the lamp on the mantel. "No, nothing I can see."

"Let me sniff it."

She held the cup under his nose and he took a cautious breath. The scent struck a chord of memory in him.

When had he smelled that before?

Something his mother had said came back to him. *Scent is the seat of memory. It is how wolves recognize family, friends, and enemies.*

"Where did the wine come from?"

Byrne thrust a carafe in front of his face. "There's still some left. We were all drinking from it, and nobody else seems to be affected." He peered into the carafe. "There's something sludgy, here, in the bottom."

He started to shake it out onto his palm, but Ash said, "No! Don't touch it. It may be toxic through skin." Even as he said it, he thought, *that doesn't make sense. They all drank from the carafe. My mother is the only one down.*

Still, Byrne dumped the residue onto a plate and held it out for Ash's inspection. It appeared to be plant material, leaves, maybe. Ash sniffed at it cautiously. Also familiar, but different from what he'd scented in the cup.

"Talbot," he said. "Go to Strangward's quarters and bring back some of those leaves they use to brew tea."

She took off at a run.

"We've called for Lord Vega," Captain Byrne said. "But—is there anything I can get for you, anything you need?" He swallowed hard. "Anything at all?" he whispered, as if hoping the gods were listening.

Ash shook his head, wishing there was something he could ask for, an antidote he knew would help.

Unbidden, Taliesin's words came back to him, like a

curse she'd laid on him long ago. *The time will come when you will wish that you were a better healer.*

He turned back to his mother, pressed his hands into her shoulders, sent up a prayer that he could last long enough to do some good, and called the poison to him.

It was like a body blow that brought tears to his eyes and formed a bitter film on his tongue. His head swam, and his skin prickled and crawled.

Again. Oddly familiar.

Taking a deep breath, he called the poison again. Black spots swam before his eyes, and it took everything he had to keep from fainting.

Scent is the seat of memory. He was drowning in memories—of that morning in the market, of his father saying, *No. Wait for help. You're not strong enough.* Of the scent of death. His amulet buzzed against his chest, as if trying to get his attention.

He was startled when somebody touched his arm. Talbot was back with a cloth bag filled with the herb the pirates called tay. "Put a bit on the plate, next to the other, and wet it down," Ash said.

Talbot complied. They looked virtually identical. Ash sniffed at them again. They both had the same fragrant, toasty scent.

"We're still searching the quarters the Carthians occupied," Byrne said. "We'll bring you anything else we find." He leaned closer. "Is it the same?"

Ash hesitated, then nodded. "It's the same," he said. "But it's not what poisoned the queen."

Byrne gazed at him, understanding kindling in his eyes. "Somebody's trying to blame them, then. To distract us from the real poison."

Ash nodded. Despair bubbled up inside him. Who knew there were so many poisons in the world—poisons that he'd never seen, never studied, didn't know how to treat?

"Call Speaker Jemson," he said, hoping the speaker could call on a higher power.

And then, like a miracle, his childhood friend, the healer Titus Gryphon, was there, looking across the bed at him. "How can I help?" he said simply.

After that, it was the two of them, trading off, supporting the queen's breathing, her heartbeat, keeping her blood flowing, sharing the burden of the poison but not making much headway otherwise. Magret Gray helped, too, fetching and carrying, cooling her mistress's brow, nursing the Gray Wolf queen as she had since Raisa was little.

Adrian couldn't help worrying that he was just pushing the poison into every part of her body. Sweat rolled down his face and dripped onto the coverlet. He blotted at his forehead with his sleeve. His amulet grew warmer and warmer as the battle for his mother's life continued.

Captain Byrne stood by, his hand on his Lady sword, his face pale and haggard. Standing guard as always. Micah

Bayar lurked in the corner of the room, like a mourner waiting for a funeral to begin.

Others packed the doorway—Aunt Mellony, chewing her lower lip, fingering her pearls. Julianna beside her, face pinched with worry.

Then the human blockade parted and Harriman Vega swept in, with Finn a pale shadow on his heels. "Make way," he said. "We are here to attend the queen." He dropped his kit bag on the floor at the foot of the bed with a thump.

"Thank the Maker," Mellony whispered, giving Julianna a reassuring squeeze.

Ash and Titus looked at each other across the queen's bed, sharing a question silently between them. Ash could tell that Ty didn't want to let go of their patient, either. Behind him, Magret muttered, "We're doing as well as anyone can. We don't need him."

And, yet—he had to give way. Vega had years of experience in the healing halls that Ash couldn't match. It would be wrong to refuse his help because he was a pompous ass. Ash had too much blood on his hands already. He didn't want to preside over his mother's death as well.

He nodded at Titus, took a deep breath, and let go of his mother.

Vega took hold of his amulet, bowed his head, and murmured a charm that sounded more like a prayer. He rested his hand on the queen's forehead, murmuring another charm. She flinched under his hand, the first she'd moved since she collapsed. Her eyes flew open, staring into the wizard's face. Then closed again.

Ash's amulet seethed and burned, all but blistering the skin of his chest beneath.

Vega looked up and shook his head. "She's gone," he said. "I'm sorry."

Captain Byrne appeared to fold, bringing his fist to his chest as if to prevent his heart from ripping free. Aunt Mellony began to cry in deep, heaving sobs.

Adrian reflexively wrapped his hands around his amulet and heard his father's voice, as clear as the day he died. *Ash. Take me to her. Take me to Raisa. There's not much time.*

Ash stared down at the amulet his father had put into his hands that day in Ragmarket. Then dropped to his knees beside his mother's bed. She still lay cold and silent. He set the amulet on her breast and brought her hands up, doing his best to wrap her fingers around it. The amulet brightened under her touch, brightened so that it illuminated the entire room. Then he closed his hands over hers, to keep them in place. He could feel the heat of the flashcraft through her skin.

It was as if his mother was lit from within, her skin like time-darkened parchment with a candle behind it. And gradually, though it might have been a trick of the light, it seemed that the color was returning to her cheeks.

"Prince Adrian." It was Vega's voice behind him, a

clamor in his ears. "I did everything I could. Please. You must let her go."

"Go to hell," Ash said.

The healer leaned in beside him, reaching for the serpent amulet. Flame exploded from under their fingers. Vega pitched himself backward, landing on his ass with a metallic clatter.

Familiar. But he couldn't focus, with his head still clouded from the poison.

"Ash," Finn said. "Please. Don't blame Lord Vega. It's not his fault. He was too late, is all."

He's always too late, Ash thought.

"Leave him be, Finn." It was Bayar, of all people. He leaned down and whispered something in Finn's ear, and Finn and Vega withdrew.

Help me, Ash. He could feel his father's presence, his embrace.

Ash braced himself. *Take whatever you need. Take whatever is left.*

Power flowed from the amulet, a river of magic that joined the three of them together. The queen took a breath, released it, took another breath. Ash could see her eyes moving under the lids, as if she were dreaming. Her fingers tightened on the amulet, and she smiled. Ash pressed his fingers into her wrist, and her pulse thrummed strongly under the skin.

And, then, his father's voice again. *I sent her back to you.*

You are spent, and I need to go. Come see me in Aediion. You and your mother and sister have enemies at court. Enemies on the Council. Don't give your trust easily.

And his father was gone.

Eventually, he felt Ty's presence beside him. "Can I help?"

"Yes," Ash said softly, without taking his eyes off his mother. "Get everyone out of the room except for you, Magret, Jemson, Talbot, and Byrne. Now."

Ty nodded and slipped away. Dimly, Ash heard people protesting, demanding answers as they were ushered from the room.

"But . . . can't we help?" Julianna said. "Isn't there anything I can do for Aunt Raisa? If we can figure out what kind of poison was used, perhaps my eyes and ears—"

"At least let me sit vigil with my sister's body," Aunt Mellony argued.

Once the door was closed, it was blessedly quiet.

The queen opened her eyes, looked around wildly, then seemed to relax as she focused in on Ash's face. "Adrian," she said, smiling. "I saw him. I spoke to your father. It was—it was miraculous." Tears leaked from her eyes. "He's been with us—with all of us—all along. But he couldn't find a channel, a way to connect." She looked down at their joined hands, the light from the amulet leaking out between their fingers. "We were together at last. I have missed him, so very much. I wanted to stay."

"But you didn't," Ash said, unsure exactly what she meant.

She shook her head. "No," she said. "There is work still to do, and there are battles yet to be fought. Han will help us. He says to come to him—that you'll know how." Then, looking past Ash, she spoke, a little impatiently, to someone he couldn't see. "Go, sisters. I will stay awhile longer in this world." She seemed to listen for a moment, then said, "Just because it's never been done does not mean it cannot be done. Now. Go and speak with my daughter. She needs to know."

Captain Byrne fell to his knees beside the bed, his weathered face wet with tears. "Rai," he said, in a low, husky voice. "I don't understand. My connection to you—to the Line—is broken. I—I thought— How can I protect you if there's no longer a bond between us?"

"Shhh," she said, ruffling his hair, then smoothing it down again. "I will explain. Han gave me a message for you, too. When one door is closed, another opens. We have much to talk about. But right now, I am so very sleepy." With that, she closed her eyes, still smiling, and slept.

They all stood speechless, until Speaker Jemson knelt next to Byrne. "Let us give thanks to the Maker for this miracle that we've all witnessed. Shall we pray?"

And they did.

When the speaker had finished, Ash returned to his examination of the cup. Though it was apparently empty, it still carried that faint, familiar scent, like old stone and rot. When he carried it to the window, in the daylight he could see a pinprick of light passing through to the inside. There seemed to be a tiny hole under one of the jewels on the outside. Using his belt blade, he pried at the stone, an amethyst, finally working it loose.

Underneath, he found a tiny wad of plant material. He scraped it out of the hole and onto a glass plate. This time, the scent surfaced a different memory.

He was back in Taliesin's cottage at Oden's Ford. They'd been going through her little book of poisons, studying each one from a healer's perspective. Since she grew many of the plant sources in her garden, they were able to move from plant to processing to final product to treatment.

There was one poison that she didn't grow in her garden. She kept it sealed in a glass jar, buried under a stone in the garden, unearthing it only for teaching purposes.

"Don't touch it!" she'd snapped when he unstoppered the jar. "Be careful about breathing it in."

"What is it?" he'd said, startled by the urgency of the warning. When they worked with poisons, the Voyageur usually relied on him not to be stupid.

"It's called 'two-step lily,' because victims rarely manage two steps before they go down."

Ash eyed it with new respect. "How do I treat it?"

"Pray," his teacher had said. "I've never known anyone to survive it."

When he'd sniffed at it, it smelled of death and decay. Even then, it was hauntingly familiar, but he couldn't remember why.

Now he remembered.

Head swimming, stomach churning, he set the cup aside and washed his hands thoroughly.

"I suppose you have a good reason for damaging your grandmother's cordial cup." Ash looked up, and met Magret's eyes.

He nodded. "The poison was embedded in the cup, under one of the jewels," he said. "When wine was poured into the cup, the poison diffused into the wine. So it wouldn't help to have a taster. Everyone drank from the same carafe, but she was the only one poisoned. Depending on who examined her after death, the fact that it was poison might have been overlooked. If it was suspected, we would blame the Carthians."

"Do you know what kind of poison it was?" Talbot asked.

"We'll take a closer look at it in the dispensary," Ash said. "It's too risky to try to analyze it with so many people around. I'm pretty sure it's two-step lily."

"Two-step lily?" Titus spoke up from his seat at the queen's bedside.

Ash nodded. "It's most potent when it's injected under the skin—for instance, if it's daubed on an arrow or a blade. It takes longer when ingested orally, but as far as I know, it's invariably fatal. Until today, I guess." He paused. "I can't be sure, but I believe that it was what was used by the assassins who murdered my father."

"I've never heard of it," Titus said, "and I always considered myself well schooled in poisons."

"That was probably the idea—to use something that nobody here in the north would identify. It grows in only one or two places, high in the Heartfangs. The only reason I know about it is because of Taliesin. The Voyageurs came from the Heartfangs originally." He released a long breath. "Whoever did this had a good knowledge of poisons and how to handle them."

"Do you think Taliesin had anything to do with this?" Byrne said. "As supplier to agents from Arden, or—?"

Ash shook his head. "Anything's possible, but it seems unlikely. When we met up in Delphi, Taliesin saved my life. She could have finished me off at any time in Oden's Ford. Instead, she tipped you off as to where I was."

"Who had access to the cup?" Byrne asked Magret.

Magret snorted. "Everyone. I mean, everyone in Her Majesty's inner circle, her council, her ladies-in-waiting, servants, and so on. She was the only one who drank out of that cup, and everyone who paid attention knew it. It's not like a person would have to time it just right. Once you treated the cup, it would sit there like a land mine, waiting to be set off." Magret's cheeks were pinked up, always a sign of danger for the unwary.

"When was the last time she drank from the cup?" Ash said. "Before tonight, I mean."

"Probably within the week," Magret said. "It's always kept here, in her rooms. She never takes it to the dining room."

"All right," Ash said. "I asked you all to stay because you are the people here at court that I trust with my mother's life. There is at least one assassin in the palace, and there may be more. Captain Byrne, if there is anyone else among the Wolves that you trust without reservation, they can be added to the watch. We're going to say that the queen is quite ill, at death's door, in fact, and can have no visitors."

"What about the princess Mellony and your cousin Julianna?" Magret said. "I know they are worried sick."

"No other visitors," Ash repeated. "If need be, tell them that you are worried that the poison has contaminated the room, and you don't want anyone else exposed to it. I want my mother's meals fetched directly from the main kitchens by one of you. Use the tunnels so you're not seen. Ty, I'm putting you and Magret in charge of the queen's care."

Ty eyed him suspiciously. "Why do I get the impression that you're not going to be here?"

"Because I won't be."

"Prince Adrian." It was Talbot, her back straight, her expression a mixture of nerves and resolve. "Would it be possible to speak with you and Captain Byrne privately?"

DREAMS TO NIGHTMARES

Lyss knew that Celestine would be watching her and her new officers for signs of collusion, conspiracy, or betrayal. Meanwhile, her Highlanders probably wondered what the hell was going on—how their Captain Gray had ended up commanding the empress's army.

It was urgent that they get their stories aligned, but it was also a risk. Though none of them had the blank, blunted expressions she'd seen on the bloodsworn, it was still possible that one or more of them were spying on her on behalf of the empress.

Hopefully they would be patient, keep their mouths shut, and wait for her to make the first move. In the meantime, she installed them in the new barracks Celestine had built for her swelling army, and scheduled a meeting with them for the next day.

At the appointed time, Tully Samara swaggered in, introduced himself as the commander of the empress's navy, and said that the empress had asked him to sit in so that he could learn more about wetland tactics.

That might have been true, or he might have been there to spy for the empress, or to spy for himself. Whatever his motive, Lyss didn't want to fight that battle at this particular time. So she proceeded with the briefing, reviewing the command structure and assets of the empress's forces while the expressions on her new officers' faces shifted from wariness to alarm.

She knew what they were thinking—how could the queendom possibly prevail against this? Which was fine. She wanted them to know what they were up against. They kept looking at one another, as if hoping someone else would ask a question.

Finally, Graves spoke up, asking what he probably thought was a safe question. "Captain Gray," he said, "what should we know about these bloodsworn soldiers in order to . . . make the best use of them?"

"Having fought against them, you know that the bloodsworn are strong, fearless, and difficult to kill. They are also unflinchingly loyal to Her Grace, the empress." She paused a moment, making sure the message hit home. "In other words, you can rely on them to stay loyal to their mistress, no matter what the incentive."

Graves nodded, glancing at Samara, and then at his comrades. "Thank you, ma'am."

Farrow cleared his throat. "Ma'am. Captain. It would help to know what our mission will be. That will help us better focus our training."

The Waterwalker was missing an eye, and one side of his face had been badly burned. That made it hard to look at him straight on, but Lyss did. "The empress has not shared her plans with me, but I imagine that we will be deployed back to the Realms. No doubt that is why the empress has recruited officers who have experience fighting in that environment. Most of her forces are accustomed to naval battles and coastal raids."

"So." Graves again. "So we may be sent to fight against the Highlanders? The clans?"

"We will go wherever the empress sends us, which is the role of a soldier, after all," Lyss said, conscious of Samara's gaze. "It is not the job of soldiers to get into questions of policy. It is evidence of the empress's mercy and confidence in us that we remain free men and women. The best guarantee of our future is to succeed in our mission, whatever it is."

"Yes, ma'am," Graves said, exchanging unhappy glances with the others.

"I never said that it would be easy," Lyss said softly. She glanced at Samara, who was watching through narrowed eyes, and thought, There's no way I can pull this off—outsmart Celestine under so many pairs of hostile eyes. She had never felt more alone.

I have to. I have got to find a way to survive, and get home. The line does not die here.

Every night after dinner, Lyss had taken to running up the slope from the waterside, both to keep her body in fighting condition and to wear off the anger and tension and dread that built up during the day. Beyond the area of the harbor, the land sloped steeply upward, evidence of the island's volcanic origin. She would run and run and run, straight up the mountain, often with a full pack on her back, until her lungs were exploding and her knees trembled, threatening to give way.

She leapt over steaming fissures, granite boulders, and lava pools. She kept running until she was clear of the fuming sulfur scent that seemed to permeate everything at sea level, and she could breathe the clean cold air that reminded her of home.

Even at this height, the weather barrier that surrounded the island persisted, but she could see the stars overhead, and somehow that was enough. She'd lie on her back, her body steaming in the cold, looking for the Crown and Sword, the Wolf Pack, the Tears of the Queens, and the other constellations she'd known since childhood. Somehow, it made her feel closer to home.

She would pull out the rose locket her father had given her and study the tiny portraits of her mother, her brother, her sister. *This is what you're fighting for. This.*

She often thought of Halston Matelon, wondering if he still lived. She hoped he did, and was looking up at the same stars. She wished she had a keepsake of some kind—something of his to wear against her skin. Soldiers always carried keepsakes—not so much as a promise from one person to another, but more as a promise to themselves that they would survive, and that there would be a future worth living in.

All that time she'd spent with the flatlander, and she couldn't help thinking she should have looked harder, and closer, and memorized every tiny detail. Some, she could recall vividly—those eyes the color of the gray-green ferns on the north side of the mountain. The stick-straight black hair that flopped down over his forehead when he'd been in the field too long. Broad shoulders, narrow hips, a muscled ass that made even uniform breeches look good.

But his nose—what did that look like? She had totally neglected his nose. Did he have any tattoos? She'd never had a thorough look.

She loved the way he moved. He was at home in his body, and it showed. He covered ground like somebody who knew where he was going and would find a way to get there without leaving anyone behind. His lovemaking (what she'd known of it) was much the same.

It never took her long to move from those fine physical assets to *who* he was. The way he took care of his men in the field, leading by example, playing the hand he was given without complaint. Fierce, determined, *there*.

He had much to learn about northern women. Still, even when they disagreed, he was teachable, weighing her arguments before he countered.

That was what took this beyond a wartime crush. She might be building a house around a single brick, but this brick was all she had.

It was evidence of how deeply into daydreaming she was that the first she knew she had company was when somebody said, "So this is where you go every night," practically in her ear.

She scrambled to her feet, her sword in her hand, her body acting before her mind returned to earth.

It was Bosley, dressed in his desert warrior garb, his curved blade at his side, an arrogant smile on his face. It didn't look good on him.

Dreams to nightmares.

"What are you doing here?" she demanded.

"You first," Bosley said.

"I came up here to be alone," Lyss said, returning her sword to its scabbard. "Obviously, you didn't, if you followed me up here."

"I was actually asking a . . . broader question," Bosley

said. "Why is the heir to the Gray Wolf throne serving the empress in the east?"

"I'm here for the same reason you are," Lyss said, ignoring the title, doing her best to control her temper. "I am a prisoner of war who has been ganged into the Carthian army. Given the alternative, I agreed."

"But you're not just another prisoner, are you." Bosley took a step toward her.

"Lieutenant Bosley." Emphasis on *Lieutenant*. "I am here as a captain in the Highlander army and a prisoner of war. Although we are prisoners, it is in our best interest to maintain discipline and the chain of command. If we play our cards right, we may survive this."

"But you are training the enemy," Bosley said. "Some would call that treason."

Why, oh why didn't I throw you off a cliff when I had the chance?

"I am also learning more about the bloodsworn every day."

"So." Bosley took another step toward her. "Then you are *actually* working against the empress?"

"I am *actually* trying to survive, and protect my officers if I can," Lyss said, unwilling to hand Bosley any kind of weapon. "Now. As I said. I came here to be alone. I did not come here to discuss strategy with a subordinate. You are dismissed."

"You can't have it both ways," Bosley said. "If we are both soldiers, as you say, is that any way to treat a comrade? I would have expected a warmer welcome."

Lyss's always-brittle temper snapped. "What don't you understand about *go away?*"

The arrogant expression dissolved into anger. "Let me make myself clear, *Princess,*" Bosley snarled. "You may be valuable to the empress as a capable commander, but you are even more valuable as the heir to the throne of the Fells—the only surviving heir, I might add. You are in no position to look down your nose at me. I would suggest that you think before you speak."

"Is that a threat?" Lyss said, her voice a low growl. "Because *that* would be treason."

"There need be no unpleasantness if you do as I say," Bosley said. "In fact, you may come to enjoy collaborating with me."

Bosley made *collaborating* sound like a filthy word. Lyss, speechless, stared at him.

Taking her silence as assent, Bosley moved in closer. "Don't worry. We will maintain appearances in front of the others. In public, I will be as subordinate as any other soldier. But in private, *I'll* be giving the orders. With any luck, I'll plant a baby in your belly before we return to the Realms. *Consort to the queen.* I like the sound of that."

Lyss couldn't help herself. Despite her vow to play it

smart and survive, the whole idea was so revolting that she burst out laughing. "Lieutenant, I'd rather be eaten alive by wolves," she said.

Never underestimate the fury of an asshole when he's crossed. Bosley barreled into her, pitching her to the ground. Her head struck a rock, the impact rendering her temporarily senseless. When she came to, Bosley was ripping at her clothing, muttering curses. Her sword was gone. She groped for her belt dagger, but that was gone, too.

She kneed him, hard, in the privates, causing him to howl and loosen his grip. She flipped him over her head and rolled to her feet, scanning the ground for her blades. Spotting the glitter of metal in the moonlight, she scrambled toward it and scooped up her dagger. Just in time, because Bosley was somehow up again and wrapping his arms around her from behind, pinning her arms to her sides so that she couldn't reach anything vital.

"If this is the way you want it, I will drag you back to the empress and turn you in. No doubt she'll reward me handsomely."

"I doubt it," Lyss said. "She'll lose a capable commander and gain a scummery bumfiddle." With that, she went limp, which threw Bosley off balance so that she fell forward with him on top. Squirming, she twisted enough to slash at him with her blade. It ripped open his shoulder, but that wasn't enough. All it did was send him into a murderous rage.

Wrenching the knife from her hand, he pinned her to the ground, raised the blade, and spat, "You never know when you're beaten, do you?"

It was one of those moments when time slows to a crawl. The knife seemed to pause at the top of its arc, Bosley's twisted face hovering over her like a demonic death mask.

A shadow fell across the two of them as something massive came between them and the bright shield of the moon. She heard a harsh cry, like that of a raptor on the hunt, and a sudden wind ripped at her clothing and tore her hair from its braid. Bosley was just turning his head to look when something smashed into them, driving all of the air from her lungs.

Bosley screamed, his eyes widening in terror and pain. When Lyss looked past him, all she could see was a silhouette blotting out the stars. She smelled charred flesh, felt a searing heat, heard the rattle of claws on rock, and then Bosley's weight was gone.

She propped up on her elbows in time to see Bosley rising into the night sky, silhouetted against the flaming beast that had him in its claws. The lieutenant's arms and legs waved frantically so that he resembled a crawfish in the talons of an osprey. Her knife pinged onto the ledge next to her.

It was the dragon that had spooked the horses on the parade ground—or one very like it. As if called by her thoughts, it extended its head toward her on a long, sinuous neck. Flame and smoke boiled from between its massive teeth, searing her skin from several feet away until she thought it would blister and peel. It studied her with golden, reptilian eyes.

Abruptly, it turned away, the force of its wings scouring the ledge. It seemed to be having trouble gaining altitude with the weight of Bosley added to its own. Finally, it soared off the side of the mountain, circled out over the abyss, and dropped the lieutenant into space.

If it was possible to be relieved, grateful, and terrified at the same time, Lyss was there. Grabbing up her knife, she scrabbled crablike across the ledge, scooped up her sword, and made a run for the downhill trail. Before she'd gone more than a few paces, the dragon was ahead of her, driving her back with torrents of flame.

Lyss threw her knife, aiming for the creature's eyes, but it glanced off its armored head. She dove to the side, rolling into a small ravine, where she hoped the underbrush would hide her from view. But the dragon's breath set the foliage aflame, flushing her from her hiding place. Hugging the cliff face, she launched herself downhill, hoping to put enough distance between them that she could find another hiding place.

But it was foolish to think that a human on foot could escape a dragon in the air. It landed in the trail ahead of her, spreading its wings to block the way.

When it was clear she wasn't going anywhere, Lyss put her back to a rock face and waited, sword in hand, for death.

45

A NEW ALLIANCE

The drama unfolded below them on the ledge—first a loud, hand-waving argument, then a clinch.

They are mating, Cas suggested. *That's how it begins—with fighting. Let them finish.*

"Mating doesn't begin with fighting," Jenna said. "Anyway, when did you get to be an expert on mating?"

Not human. Have instinct.

"Humans have instinct, too."

Maybe. Too much thinking, gets in way.

Right, Jenna thought. Too much thinking.

After months of communicating only with each other, they were beginning to share vocabulary, and Jenna was adopting Cas's thrifty speech.

"Can we go lower? Without hitting the mountain, I mean?"

With an irritated snort, Cas circled lower, losing altitude gradually.

Ordinarily, that maneuver would have been child's play for the young dragon, but the flight through the stormwall had badly damaged one of his wings, making straight flight difficult, fine aerobatics all but impossible. Gradually, he was growing stronger. Jenna hoped that by the time they came up with a plan, they would be able to execute it.

In order to make a plan, they needed more information. Hence their current mission—looking for one of the empress's soldiers they could question.

As they closed in on the couple, Jenna could make out more of the conversation. The male wanted to mate. The female most definitely did not. Jenna caught the words *princess* and *empress* and *treason*.

Were there princesses on the Desert Coast as well as empresses?

The female didn't look like a princess, from Jenna's limited experience. Both parties were dressed in the garb of the empress's soldiers, though neither had the smudgy glow she'd seen before.

All at once, the male charged at the female, knocking her backward. Pinning her to the ground, he began tearing at her clothing.

See? Mating.

"No," Jenna said. "This is not how humans mate. This is wrong."

The female sent the male flying and scooped up her knife. She managed to draw blood before the male had her down again. Then he had something in his hand—something that glittered in the moonlight. Her knife.

"Cas. Stop them. Hurry."

The dragon folded his wings and plummeted earthward. Jenna knew from experience how that looked from below. They'd been flying so high, they were all but invisible to human eyes, especially at night. Now they descended so fast that they would be on their prey before the male and female knew what hit them.

Jenna scented blood as the dragon's claws sank into the male's back. He screeched, kicked, and flailed while Cas struggled to lift him into the air. Jenna could feel the dragon's heart pounding against her chest, feel his blazing heat beneath the scales.

The female stared up at them, eyes wide, blood spattered across her face.

Jenna?

"Kill the male. Catch the female."

With one final effort, Cas swooped off the mountain and let his cargo go. With that weight gone, they rocketed skyward.

By now, the female had retrieved her sword and was making a run for it. Cas circled around and drove her back with torrents of flame. She threw her knife, dove, rolled, scrambled, then, finally, made her stand like a warrior, feet slightly apart, sword at the ready.

Cas landed heavily on the ledge a short distance away, folding his wings as best he could. He swung his head toward the female—the *girl*—breathing in her scent. She raised her sword in warning.

Jenna slid to the ground, into the shelter of Cas's wing. Then stepped out from behind it so that she could get a better look at their captive.

The empress's warrior stared at Jenna as if she'd emerged from the dragon's bunghole. The girl's hair was the color of winter-seared wheat. It had been braided, but now was mostly hanging free around her battered face. She was tall, muscular, and fierce. Her curved blade was the kind carried by the empress's bloodsworn.

"Drop the sword," Jenna said in Common.

The soldier flinched, as if she hadn't expected human speech. She swiped blood from her face with her sleeve, glanced to either side as if looking for options, then finally let her sword fall to the ground at her feet. Chin up and defiant, she met Jenna's eyes.

There was something familiar about her that raised gooseflesh on the back of Jenna's neck. A fist of memory squeezed her heart and drove the air from her lungs.

Wolf, Cas said, before Jenna could put it into words.

Yes. This girl had the same wolfish aspect as the healer Adam Wolf. While the healer had smoldered, this wolf burned hot. She was wilder, more savage.

Cornered wolf. And then, nudging her back into the shelter of his wing, added, *Wolf pack.*

Out of the darkness they came, silent as smoke, with their thick gray fur and brilliant, intelligent eyes. Their hot breath froze on their muzzles and ruffs and their massive paws barely dented the earth.

With her attention focused on Cas, the warrior did not seem to notice the wolves all around her.

The wolves gazed at Jenna and Cas for what seemed to be a long time, then turned as one and melted into the darkness. Jenna, awestruck, stared after them.

By now, the warrior was growing restless. "This is your meeting," she snapped, in Common. "What do you want?"

"Who are you?" Jenna said, the words awkward in her mouth after the ease of communicating mind-to-mind with Cas.

"I'm Alyssa Gray," the soldier said. "Captain." She spoke in a clipped fashion, like a prisoner of war identifying herself.

"Who was that?" Jenna pointed toward the canyon with her chin.

"Quill Bosley. Lieutenant."

"You both fight for the empress?"

With a flicker of hesitation, Gray said, "Yes. I am—was—his commanding officer."

"Why was he attacking you, then?"

"Because he does not understand the chain of command," the wolf girl said.

"What?"

Gray rolled her eyes. "Because he has the talent of a turd floating in an ego the size of the ocean."

Jenna laughed, which took her by surprise. Stop it, she thought. This is the enemy. You must interrogate her, and then you must kill her, so that she doesn't give you away.

Meanwhile, Gray had been studying Jenna with equal interest. "So—you were *riding* the . . . uh . . . dragon?" she said, as if choosing her words carefully.

Tell her my name is Cas.

"She doesn't need to know that," Jenna said, in their silent speech.

"Yes," she said aloud.

"I didn't know that the empress had . . . a flying army," Gray said, clearly fishing for information. "How many dragons do you have?"

Tell her people don't "have" dragons.

"Let me handle this."

Gray was looking from one of them to the other as if she suspected that she was being left out of something.

"I am more of a scout," Jenna said.

"Who are you scouting for?"

It was striking how quickly Gray turned the conversation, as if she were used to questioning prisoners, issuing orders and having them obeyed.

"I ask the questions, you answer," Jenna said. "Isn't that how it works in an interrogation?"

"Is that what this is?"

"Where are you from?" Jenna said. "You're not from around here."

Neither are you.

Jenna lost patience. "Cas."

Cas straightened his neck, bringing his head to within a few feet of Gray, so that his fuming breath swirled around her. The captain skipped back a step as Jenna caught the scent of scorched wool.

"It seems . . . very well trained," Gray said, then leapt back again to avoid a gout of flame.

Trained? Cas's scales rattled as he bristled.

"We're partners," Jenna said. "Cas is sensitive about what you call the 'chain of command.' Now, where are you from?"

"I'm . . . from the wetlands," Gray said. "That's what they call it here. From the mountains in the north."

"The north?" Jenna's heart accelerated. The healer was a wolf from the north, too. "What are you doing here?"

"I was captured in the fall of Chalk Cliffs," Gray said.

"The empress brought me back here and drafted me into her army."

"You don't shine like the others."

Gray licked her lips. "No. I don't shine like the others."

"How many of you are there?"

"Prisoners, officers, or troops?" She spoke with precision, like a soldier.

"How many troops?"

"Tens of thousands," Gray said. "More every day."

"What does the empress intend to do with these troops?" Jenna said. "What is the plan?"

Gray cocked her head, clearly puzzled that the empress's scout was asking a soldier about the empress's plans. "The empress hasn't shared that with me," she said.

"If you had to take a guess," Jenna persisted. "What do you think she is planning?"

"If I had to take a guess," Gray said, "I would say that she plans to conquer the Seven Realms."

"When?"

"Soon."

Jenna pulled a scroll from her carry bag. "Sit," she said, gesturing toward a flat spot on the ledge.

Warily, Gray sat cross-legged. Jenna sat across from her and unrolled the scroll on the stone between them, anchoring the corners with pebbles.

Cas extended his body into a semicircle around them and promptly went to sleep. He still tired easily when forced to fly for long periods or when carrying extra weight.

Gray kept peering nervously at the dragon coiled around them. Jenna touched her shoulder and pointed to the map she'd drawn.

It was an aerial view of Celesgarde. It was all there—the wharves, the buildings, the marble stump that was the beginnings of a palace. The rows of tents represented with little triangles.

Gray stared down at it, then raised her eyes to Jenna. "This is fine work," she said, as if surprised. "Did you draw this?"

"Yes." Truth be told, Jenna was rather proud of it.

No. Don't be taking a liking to this girl. She is the enemy.

"I need to know where the empress stays," Jenna said, running her fingers over the harbor front. "Is she in the marble palace yet, or is she sleeping somewhere else?"

Gray straightened, understanding dawning on her face. "You don't work for the empress at all, do you? Who do you work for?"

"I work for myself," Jenna said.

"You're planning to attack the capital," Gray said, unable to hide her excitement.

"I am planning to attack the empress," Jenna said. "If she is in the capital, then I will attack the capital."

"Why?" Gray said, leaning forward, her hands on her knees. "Why are you doing this on your own?"

"I'm not on my own," Jenna said. "I'm with Cas. And

I have my reasons. Now," she said, meaning to put an end to the counterinterrogation, "tell me, Captain: Why do I see a wolf in you?"

It was a tactic that had worked well on the healer, and it did not disappoint now. Gray folded a bit, as if she'd taken a hard punch to the gut, and her face turned the color of ashes. She took two hard breaths, clenched her fists, then looked up at Jenna.

Once again, the wolf was cornered.

"What—what do you mean?" Gray said.

"I fly with dragons," Jenna said. "You run with the wolves."

Gray was doing her best to look baffled, but it came off as slightly nauseous.

"You see, I've met a wolf like you before. We met in Ardenscourt, but he was from the north."

Gray's head came up. "What do you mean, someone like me?" she said. "Do you mean that he looked like me?"

Jenna studied her critically. "No, not really. He was a red-haired healer, a lone wolf with wounded eyes. He wore a snake pendant—"

Gray came up on her knees and gripped Jenna's shoulders, her face a battleground between heartbreak and hope. "A healer? A red-haired healer?" she all but shouted, so that Cas raised his head in alarm. "What was his name?"

Gray was asking questions again, but Jenna didn't care.

"He had many names," Jenna said. "He called himself

Adam Freeman. I called him Adam Wolf. Neither was his real name. He had strong, gentle hands, and he talked to horses." She forced her mind back to the images that had poured in when they joined hands. "He saw his father die in a snowy street, his blood spattering the cobblestones."

"Ash!" It was more a primitive cry than a word. "You saw him in Ardenscourt? When?"

Jenna's heart leapt. This fierce wolf warrior knew the healer, under yet another name. She'd be able to tell her where he came from and where he was now. She could fly to him, and they could—but no. Her excitement abated a little as she realized that couldn't happen anytime soon. Cas would have to be completely recovered before they launched an attack on the empress or tried to batter their way through the stormwall again.

"When did you see him?" Gray repeated, louder than before.

"First, you tell me. What is the healer's real name, and what is the connection between you?"

For a long moment, they sat, knee to knee, and all but nose to nose, staring at each other, each holding on to her secrets and trying to decide whether to trust the other.

"His real name is Adrian," Gray said finally. "And he was—or is—my brother."

46

PARTY OF THE YEAR

Destin Karn leaned against the wall, nursing his drink, watching and waiting. The Matelons were working the room, chatting with each of the guests at one time or another. They exceeded Destin's rather low expectations, though he guessed that nobody survived at the Ardenine court for long without learning some knack for connivery. The captain and the corporal flirted gamely and danced awkwardly, which fit in with the role they were playing. They really needed to work on their blackbird swagger.

Even Destin danced a little, choosing his targets carefully. For instance, he cut in when Granger seemed determined to monopolize the young Lady Harper all night long. He was afraid that if he didn't intervene, one of the Matelon brothers would. Or the lady herself would punch Granger out.

After two circuits around the dance floor, she spoke. "You're a good dancer," she said, cheeks flaming. "That loathsome Bailiff Granger needs to learn some better manners."

"That's why I cut in, Lady Matelon," Destin said. "I was tired of watching you fend him off. What did you two talk about?"

"Mostly he talked about himself, about his horses and hounds, and how he wants to tear down Whitehall and build a bigger house, and how a marriage between us made a lot of sense."

"Did he mention that he's already engaged?"

She scowled. "That didn't come up."

"What did *you* say?"

"Very little."

"Good thinking," Destin said. "The other piece of advice I have for you is to keep lots of people around the two of you at all times. If anything happens that you don't like, scream bloody murder. Oh, and under no circumstances should you let him fetch you a drink, not even a cup of cider. And, here—" Destin slid a dagger from one of his many hidden sheaths and handed it across. "Hide this well. Don't use it unless you have no choice. If you have no choice, the best entry point is here." He demonstrated the proper placement by tapping just above his own collarbone. "Aim the blade downward and keep pushing until it won't go any farther."

She stared down at the dagger, then up at Destin. "You're saying I should *kill* him?" Clearly she thought it must be some kind of a trick or trap.

"If you have to."

"I can't take this," she protested, running her fingers over the fancywork. "It looks like some kind of heirloom."

"Oh, it is," Destin said, closing her hands around the hilt. "I think it will find a good home with you."

Harper looked around for witnesses, then slid the blade into her bodice, settling it between her breasts so that the hilt was hidden. Then gazed up at him, her head tilted, eyes narrowed.

"What is it?" he said.

"I appreciate your looking out for me, Lieutenant. What I don't understand is why."

Destin looked over her shoulder, to where his father was hugging the other wall. "When I was a little older than you, I failed to protect someone close to me, and I've regretted it ever since. I should have acted sooner and with more . . . precision."

"I'm sorry for your loss," she said.

He half-smiled. "I'm a lot better at killing, these days."

The song came to a close and he bowed to her. "It's getting close to ten o'clock," he said. "Keep your mask on, Lady Matelon." He walked away, toward the punch bowl, feeling the pressure of her gaze on his back.

By twos and threes the others followed, some lost in conversation and seeming to wander closer by accident, others apparently there to quench a sudden thirst. Several young children raced to that end of the room, their mothers chasing after.

Granger returned to his quarry as soon as Destin left her side. But then the elder Lady Matelon intervened, giving him a sound scolding and sending him on his way with a thunderous look on his face.

If tonight's operation isn't successful, I suppose I'll have to kill him, Destin thought.

Maybe even if it is.

Hal flinched when the clock in the temple tower finally struck ten. The sound was still reverberating through the ballroom when the entire building shuddered. It sounded like an explosion coming from the direction of the temple. Then another, from the barracks. Then a blast from the direction of the armory. Moments later, another thunderous explosion, which must have been the munitions going up.

All hell will break loose, Lieutenant Karn had said. Another promise kept.

The party guests screamed and milled about, covering their ears, unsure which way to run. General Karn bolted from the hall, probably heading for the garrison house.

The King's Guard and soldiers came to life, herding the king and his down-realm guests through a doorway and out of the ballroom, toward the central bailey, the most robust fortification in the palace. All except . . .

"Mother!" King Jarat cried, turning back and scanning the room. "Where's Queen Marina? Where's Princess Madeleine?"

"Your Majesty, please come quickly," one of the blackbirds said, hustling Jarat toward the door. "No doubt the queen and your sister are already in the bailey."

Jarat hesitated, still searching the ballroom with his eyes, until a brace of guards half-carried him through the doorway.

Hal was so distracted by all of this that he nearly drew his sword when Destin Karn gripped his arm. "Go!" Karn said. "Get them out now! I can't be seen with you."

Hal and Robert herded the bewildered families back behind the fountain, through the draperies, and into the hidden pantry. When all were through, they crowded elbow to nose in the serving area. Robert stationed himself just inside the exit door to hand out cloaks. Hal pulled on his own cloak and slipped out into the courtyard to see if the area was clear.

It was still raining, and harder now, which was a good excuse for them all to be wearing cloaks, plus likely to discourage gawkers from being out in the streets. Did Karn arrange for that, too? Hal wondered. Now he could see that the temple was on fire, the armory was burning, and smoke was billowing up from the barracks. Civilians were running past him, away from the armory, while black-birds and soldiers were running toward it. This meant that nobody was looking in on the ballroom or noticing people emerging from the servants' entrance.

Hal poked his head back into the pantry. "It's clear," he said. "Send them out, and when I have half of them, I'll take them to Newgate. You bring the other half. Pretend you're running to safety."

Hal waited by the door, and as the families poured through, like a cloud of black wraiths in their cloaks, he instructed them to take their masks off and hide them underneath. One of them didn't bother to remove her mask, but flung her arms around Hal and buried her face in his shoulder.

Harper.

"Everyone said you were dead," she whispered, her voice thick with tears.

Hal patted her back, his own cheeks suspiciously wet, but maybe that was just the rain. "Not yet," he said.

When he'd counted twenty-five, he called in to Robert, "I have twenty-five, including Mother and Harper, which means you should have twenty-two, including babies and children. Count them carefully, and when you have every-one, follow me to Newgate."

Hal set out for Karn's private prison with his charges.

He found that it was more like a cat-herding expedition than a forced march. The children broke away and stomped through puddles. They threw their heads back, catching raindrops on their tongues. Mothers and older sisters chased them down, edging them back onto the proper path. As he watched, Harper scooped up a four-year, parking him on her hip and walking him back to the others.

They haven't been outside for three months, Hal thought, his anger rising. Harper's been looking out for these little ones all this time.

When they passed the postern gate, it was clotted with blackbirds, armed to the teeth, questioning and searching everyone who passed through. The explosions had been a good distraction, drawing soldiers and guards away, but now getting out was going to be a problem.

When they reached Newgate, Lila Barrowhill was there at the gate, directing them into the small courtyard just inside. As they passed through, Hal counted, and then he counted Robert's lot when they arrived. They seemed to have one extra person.

Someone tapped him on the shoulder. He swung around and saw that it was Queen Marina and her daughter, the princess Madeleine, cloaked up like the others.

"Young Matelon," she said. "I thought that was you. I'm so glad to see that rumors of your death were exaggerated."

"Your Majesty," Hal said, totally ambushed. "I didn't— what are you doing here?"

"I planned this party, remember," the queen said. "Jarat is more like his father every day—looking for someone to blame for his failures. I'd rather he blame me for the hostages' escape than Destin. And I really need to get Madeleine away from Ardenscourt before her brother matches her with some monster."

But now that the queen and her daughter had joined them, there should be forty-nine in all. There were only forty-eight.

Following them through the gate, he counted again. Someone was missing.

His mother grabbed his arm, her face pale and strained. "Have you seen Harper? She was with us, and—I don't know what happened to her. Do you think she wandered off?"

They both knew better. Harper had too much common sense to wander off—not now.

"I'll look for her," Hal said, turning back toward the gate, to find someone standing in the gap. Two someones.

It was Luc Granger, with a knife to Harper's throat.

47

DOUBLE-CROSS

"Well, now," Granger said. "How does it happen that, in the confusion after the explosions, the families of the rebellious thanes end up here—at the entrance to Lieutenant Karn's private prison? Before you passed through the gate, I was able to intercept young Lady Matelon. When I attempted to question her, the little minx pulled a knife on me." He scanned the crowd. "Now. Where is Lieutenant Karn? He has some explaining to do."

Harper had her narrow-eyed, scheming face on. Please, Harper, Hal thought. Don't make any sudden moves.

"She's just a child," his mother said. "You cannot blame her for trying to defend herself when she is attacked in the streets."

"Where she shouldn't have been in the first place," Granger said. "An attack on a member of the nobility is a serious offense. It's a shame, because I'd hoped that— well, so very disappointing." His smug expression belied his words.

"Let her go, Granger," Queen Marina said, taking a step toward them.

"Your Majesty!" Granger said. "And little Princess Madeleine. Curiouser and curiouser." He didn't look curi- ous, though. He looked delighted.

"My lord," Hal said. "I think you are misunderstand- ing what you see. My corporal directed us to escort these women and children here to Newgate where they could be safely held until we have identified and neutralized the threat." The tactical language, at least, came easily to Hal.

"Is that your story?" Granger's confidence dwindled a bit, but only just. "Well, we'll see. Guillaume should be back at any moment with the King's Guard."

"In the meantime, Lord Granger, why not allow them to go inside, out of the rain," Hal said. "If any of them fall ill, my corporal will have my ass."

Granger licked his lips. "Everybody stays here," he said, "until we sort this out." He looked around again. "Where the hell is Karn?"

"Ow!" Harper cried. "You cut me!"

It all happened in a split second. The startled Granger dropped his blade hand away enough that Harper was able to twist in his one-armed grip, seize his hand with both of hers, and plunge the blade into his neck, leaning in so it penetrated all the way to the hilt.

Robert, who'd been edging closer the entire time, barreled into Granger, knocking the thaneling onto his back on the cobblestones, where he lay, both hands scrabbling at the knife, blood bubbling from his mouth.

Hal leapt to help his brother, but there was no need. Granger was gone.

"*Now* he looks disappointed," Robert growled, "the greedy, gutter-swiving, ass-licking—"

"Language, Robert," Lady Matelon said. She stood over them, one arm around Harper, who was pale as parchment, shaking so that her teeth rattled together.

"Are you all right, Harper?" Hal sat back on his heels, looking up at her. "Did he cut you?"

"I'm fine." Harper's voice trembled, just a little. When several of the lýtlings began to cry, she forced a smile and said, "Don't worry. The bad man won't hurt us."

They shouldn't be here, Hal thought. Children should never have to witness a scene like this.

"Speaking of surviving the night, we've got to go." It was Karn's friend Lila. "Everyone! Into the building. Now, before the bad man's friends show up!"

Hal and Robert exchanged glances. It seemed very strange to be rushing back into prison when they had gone to so much trouble to get out. Was this just some kind of new trap or power play by Destin Karn, who'd been notably absent since the explosion? Was he trying to gain custody of the hostages for his own murky purposes?

They had no choice, really. Leaving Granger lying in the street, they entered the prison, crossing the threshold, into which was carved: The Truth Shall Make You Free. They descended several staircases, each level danker, the air thicker and more oppressive. Harper gripped Hal's arm, leaned close, and murmured, "Don't tell me we're going back to the Pit?"

"We'd better not be," Hal said, with a dark look at Lila.

Eventually, they seemed to hit bottom, and then struck out horizontally into what now seemed to be a natural cave, only lightly shaped by the hand of man. At one turning, Lila pulled a large crate from an alcove in the wall, unlocked it, and handed a dozen torches to those in the lead. They were flashcraft, and began to glow as soon as they were lifted from the crate.

Some of the lýtlings began to fuss. Their mothers pressed on grimly, carrying their children if necessary. Hal and Robert ended up carrying two of Lady Heresford's four children. Hal had long since accepted the fact that they were so far in, there was no going back. With the distance they'd traveled, at least it was unlikely they were still anywhere near Citadel Hill.

Finally the tunnel sloped upward, in some places growing so steep that steps had been carved into the cave floor.

The air freshened and became noticeably cooler and drier.

Finally, Queen Marina came up beside Hal. "Lady DeLacroix really cannot go much farther, and your mother is struggling, too. If we collapse, then it's going to slow us down considerably. We need to say something. If we still have miles to go, we're going to need to stop for a rest."

Hal nodded, though at this point he wasn't exactly sure who was in charge of this enterprise—he or Barrowhill or the queen.

He was threading his way forward toward Lila when he noticed that the oppressive darkness was thinning, the walls to either side becoming visible, even beyond the reach of the torchlight. They were obviously nearing an opening to the outside. It wasn't bright—likely the sun hadn't yet risen.

As the others began to notice, some of them put on speed, children tugging at their mothers' hands, stumbling over rocks in their eagerness for the long, scary journey through the dark to end. Up ahead, Lila stopped, turned, and waited for them to catch up.

When the entire group was gathered, Lila said, "This is where we surface. We should be outside the city, beyond whatever perimeter the King's Guard has put up. I need everyone to wait here while I check and make sure our transportation is ready to go."

"I'm thirsty," a little boy whined.

"Don't worry," Lila said, ruffling the boy's hair. "They'll

have food and drink for you." She disappeared through the cave entrance.

She wasn't gone long, but by the time she returned, some of the lýtlings had curled up on the floor or on their mothers' laps and gone fast asleep.

"All right," Lila said. "The wagons are just outside. Each one holds about ten people. There's room for everyone. I want families to stay together and board the same wagon. We need to be well on our way before the sun comes up."

As the families began trickling toward the door, Hal took hold of Lila's elbow. "Well on our way where? Where are we going?"

Lila cocked her head. "Didn't you talk to Lieutenant Karn about that?"

"He's been tight-lipped," Hal said. "He's told us just enough to get this far."

Lila shrugged. "You'll have to ask him. I'm just the hired help." She rubbed her thumb and fingers together, signifying payment.

Hal's temper was fraying. "I would *like* to ask him, but I haven't seen him since the blasts went off." He followed Lila out of the cave to find himself in a pitch-dark copse of trees at the bottom of a ravine. He could hear water running somewhere nearby, and the soft nickering of horses.

Where were they? It was hard to judge how far they'd traveled in the dark.

Lila pointed them down the ravine to where it opened up into an abandoned farmyard. The house had long since been burned. The barn and outbuildings were still standing, though, and four wagons were lined up, each with a team of four sturdy mountain ponies.

The wagons were enclosed, so as to keep passengers out of the weather and out of sight of prying eyes. They resembled the wagons used by clan traders to transport their goods—something rarely seen in the empire these days.

The first family was climbing into the first wagon. The driver was muffled in a scarf and coat that seemed too heavy for the weather. He'd placed a step next to the wagon to make it easier to climb in. As each one passed, he handed him or her a wrapped bundle and a deerskin flask—the promised water.

As each wagon filled, it pulled away, rolling down the farm lane and disappearing into the trees.

"This doesn't look familiar," Hal said, touching Robert's arm. "Do you know where we are?"

Robert shrugged. "We should be on our way to Temple Church to join Father and the others. So I'm guessing we're somewhere north of the city."

"Maybe," Hal said. "But I've been up and down the North Road between Ardenscourt and Delphi way too many times. I don't remember seeing a stretch this remote." He squinted up at the sky, but between the sodden clouds and the canopy of trees he couldn't get a fix on their location. The rain seemed to muffle sounds, the mist lending an air of risk and mystery.

"Well," Robert said. "We wouldn't want to come up too close to the road, would we? It's probably just that—"

Hal put his hand up. "Hang on. Isn't that the last of the wagons?"

Robert stared as the wagon rounded the curve and disappeared. "Hey!" he said, running a few steps after it until he must have realized it was no use.

Hal turned to find Barrowhill striding toward them. "That's the last of them," she said. "The queen and the princess are with them. Let's hope they don't run into any trouble along the way."

"We were supposed to go with them," Hal said. "Isn't that what we agreed on?"

"My agreement is with Lieutenant Karn," Barrowhill said, brow furrowed. "I thought he'd have filled you in."

"No," Hal said through gritted teeth. "He did *not* fill us in."

"You mean you got into this without really knowing the plan?" Barrowhill shook her head. "That's never a good idea."

Automatically, Hal thrust out an arm to prevent Robert from leaping forward and throttling her. "What is the plan?" he said.

"Well." Barrowhill looked from Hal to Robert. "It's not really my place to— Look! Here he is now."

Destin Karn materialized from among the trees like a black-clad wraith.

DOUBLE
DOUBLE-CROSS

In his blackbird cloak, Karn looked sharp and deadly as an obsidian blade. Hal was feeling fairly deadly himself.

"I met the wagons on the road, so I'm glad to see that our guests are on their way," the spymaster said. "A good night's work, and the only casualty was poor Granger. I was so impressed by young Lady Harper. If she ever expresses an interest in—"

"Where have you been?" Hal demanded. "Where are my mother and sister and the rest of the families? Robert and I were supposed to escort them to White Oaks."

"They're not going directly to White Oaks," Karn said. "But, don't worry, they will be safe and comfortable—and out of the king's hands. That will free everyone to negotiate in good faith."

"If you meant to double-cross us, why not just leave us to rot in Newgate?" Robert said, his hand on the hilt of his sword.

At that particular moment, mage or no mage, Hal was ready to draw his own sword and make the spymaster bleed, to the Breaker with the consequences.

"How have I double-crossed you?" Karn said, with a puzzled frown. "We had a common goal—to take the hostages out of the hands of Jarat Montaigne, and we have done that. No doubt he'll be more amenable to striking a deal with the thanes with his bargaining power diminished."

"It seems to *me* that your goal was to take the hostages out of the king's hands and take custody of them yourself," Hal said. "For what purpose, I don't know, but I intend to find out."

"That's easy enough," Karn said. "I'll tell you. But first, let me ask you a question. What is likely to happen if the hostage families are returned to the thanes?"

We'll all live happily ever after? Hal thought. *I can take an army north?*

"Will your father and his allies be more likely to come to the table?" Karn persisted.

Hal wanted to say yes, but he knew in his bones that wasn't true. He shook his head. "Freed of worry about the hostages, the thanes will march on Ardenscourt and depose the king sooner rather than later."

"Won't that be nice? Maybe your father will be crowned king. King Arschel," Karn said, as if savoring the phrase. "You and Robert can be princes. Though Matelon had better watch his back. I happen to know that the DeLacroix family is moving behind the scenes to make sure that it's King Pascal. In fact, an attack on the capital could be the starting point for a new civil war. Meanwhile, the empress is marching. As things stand, I suspect whoever wins will have a very short reign."

Hal thought of the harbor at Chalk Cliffs, full of the empress's ships, of the beaches teeming with horse soldiers, and he had to agree.

"I know your father has a policy against giving in to the demands of hostage-takers," Karn said. "He won't accept an unsatisfactory deal on account of them. And Jarat would never offer a reasonable deal as long as he held the hostages. It will be my job to convince Jarat to offer terms that the thanes can accept. The fact that his mother and sister are with the hostages might help that case. It will be your job to persuade the thanes to sign on."

"I'm a soldier," Hal protested, "not a diplomat."

"Who better to convince an old warrior like your father?" Karn said.

"That's not going to happen," Hal said. "It doesn't matter who's holding the hostages. It just means that he'll be even more determined to hold you accountable."

"Perhaps some of the other thanes will be more receptive," Karn said. "To be honest, I am not close to the young king. As spymaster for the kingdom, it will be my fault that the hostages escaped. By the time Jarat realizes that he needs me—or, at least someone smarter than Granger— I'll have taken my bow on Executioner's Hill."

"Do you really think so?" Hal said skeptically. "Surely General Karn would intervene to—"

Karn laughed. "You *have* been away from court a while, haven't you? My father will do everything in his power to pin it on me. If he intervenes, it will be to put the noose around my neck."

"If the thanes take the city before then—"

"Then they will be fighting each other for the honor of executing me," Karn said. "You see? No matter what happens, I will need leverage to protect myself and those who are important to me."

Hal was mystified. Who was the spymaster trying to protect—other than himself?

"If what you're saying is true, the thanes are smelling blood in the water," Hal said. "Even if King Jarat offers improved terms, they will not be in the mood for negotiation."

"I realize that this is a desperate plan, but such are the kind made by desperate men. I will do everything in my power to prevent the empress from claiming the west as well as the east."

Hal and Robert exchanged glances. Hal had his own reasons for wanting to march against the empress, but what drove Karn? He seemed the type that would land on his feet no matter what. It brought to Hal's mind his own conversation with Lyssa Gray, when he assured her that her life wouldn't change much under Arden's rule.

This spymaster has secrets, too, he thought. Hal needed to buy time, to consider what move to make next.

"All right," he said, as if giving in. "The thanes will want to know who's holding our families now. What am I supposed to tell them?"

Karn frowned, thinking.

"The queen in the north?" Barrowhill suggested, leaning against a tree and using the blade of a dagger to strip dirt from under her nails.

"If I tell them it's the queen in the north, I know exactly what will happen," Hal said. "My lord father already thinks I've been bewitched by the wolf queen. If I told him I helped put our families into the enemy's hands, he would know it for sure. He'd clap me in irons and send in the priests."

"Oh!" Barrowhill said, looking up from her work. "Damn, that's too bad."

Something in the way she said it caused them all to turn and look at her.

"What do you mean?" Karn said.

"I mean that I'm serious," Barrowhill said. "They *are* on

their way to the queen in the north."

"You sent Harper and Mother to the witch in the north?" Robert practically shouted.

Hal put his hand on his brother's arm and shook his head.

Karn's hand crept to his amulet. "Explain yourself," he said in a flat, deadly voice.

"There's this other part of the plan that I didn't go over yet," the smuggler said. "While the thanes and your spoiled boy king dither over who gets what manor house and title, the empress is on the march. I need things to move a little faster."

"Go on," Karn said, a muscle working in his jaw.

"You see, I have family in every port on the east coast," said Barrowhill. "The empress has already taken Chalk Cliffs, and Spiritgate will be under attack before long. If you think she'll stay north of the border, I have some genuine clan-made goods to sell you. My family depends on the sea for a living."

"So," Karn said. "You betrayed us. And probably collected a pretty price from the queen for doing it."

"*Betrayed* is such a negative word," Barrowhill said. "I think we're all agreed on the final goal. I just want to move things along a little faster."

"I see," Karn said. "And what's this final goal? Barrowhill makes a fortune? I don't remember signing on to that."

Barrowhill shook her head, looking a little hurt. "We

all want to send the empress Celestine back east. That's what we agree on. When word reaches King Jarat that Spiritgate is under attack, he'll wake up to the danger. But if the thanes have their way, he'll be dead by then."

Karn took a step toward her. "Tell me where they are, or you'll wish you had."

Barrowhill's dagger came up so quickly that he took a step back again.

"You haven't even heard my plan yet," Barrowhill said. "I promise, it's a good one. Kill me, and you'll never hear it. Anyway, they've already set sail by now."

"Southgate, then," Karn said, with a brisk nod. "That's the only port close enough. It might be that we can—"

Hal began to laugh, which seemed totally wrong, but once he started, he couldn't stop. They all looked at him as if he'd gone mad.

"Forgive me," he said, swiping at his eyes. "It's just so refreshing to see Lieutenant Karn swigging the same bitter medicine he dishes out."

"Captain Matelon," Barrowhill said. "I know you have no reason to trust me, and many reasons not to, but I hope you'll believe me when I say that the families will be perfectly safe—from the northerners, anyway. I've heard from my sources that you've been a guest in the north. Were you well treated?"

"Yes," Hal said cautiously, wondering why a smuggler would know that.

"And you also had some experience with the empress? You were in Chalk Cliffs when it was attacked?"

"Yes."

"As soon as you came home, you tried to convince your father to let you take an army north to aid them against the empress."

"Who told you that?"

Barrowhill pulled out an apple and took a bite. "I talk to everyone," she said, chewing. "I have a plan that will give you an army sooner rather than later. But you might not like some parts of it."

"I cannot wait to hear it," Karn said, rolling his eyes.

Barrowhill went down on one knee, spreading her arms wide. "Matelon," she said. "How would you like to be king?"

TIES THAT BIND

Leaving his mother under the care of Ty Gryphon and Magret Gray, Ash met with Sasha Talbot and Captain Byrne in the sitting room of the queen's chambers.

Talbot was visibly nervous, but determined and seemingly well prepared.

"Hear me out," she said. "As you know, Captain Byrne, I've been researching queens and their bound captains in the temple library. I've asked you some questions, too. From what I've seen and read and heard, having a bound captain now would make Lyss safer, and I'm for anything that would do that."

She stopped, as if waiting for questions or arguments, but Byrne only nodded. "Go on," he said.

Once started, it turned into a landslide of words. "I may be getting above myself, but I've spent the last three years of my life by Lyss's side, and I—I don't think there's anyone more devoted to her. I know her as well as anyone, and if I could trade my life for hers right now I would do it.

"I know the captain of the Gray Wolves has always been a Byrne, at least for a thousand years, and you might think I shouldn't be angling for the job, but I have to speak my mind. Simon's gone, and I'm here.

"Long story short, I'm asking to be named Princess Alyssa's bound captain. Now, rather than later." She stood there, then, her fist on her heart, back straight, jaw clenched, as if waiting to be turned down.

Byrne didn't turn her down. He'd gazed at her, his eyes narrowed, rubbing his chin. Then he glanced at Ash and simply said, "Let's talk about it in private, Corporal Talbot. I want you to know what you'd be signing on for."

They must have come to an understanding, because, just two days later, Ash was called to participate in a binding ceremony.

The ceremony took place in the small temple within the queen's rooftop garden, accessible by secret stairs from the queen's bedchamber, and by others from the family wing of the palace.

When moonlight flooded through the glass, the handful of celebrants cast long shadows on the stone floor. But Hanalea breathed, as the saying went. The wind from the Spirit Mountains rattled the walls and drove shards of cloud across the night sky, obscuring, and then revealing, the eagle moon.

Ash wore his father's robes, the Waterlow ravens over top. Sasha Talbot was barefoot, dressed in a loose, rough-spun dedicate's robe. She shifted from foot to foot, as if eager to see it done and over with. The naval commander Hadley DeVilliers wore a dress—something Ash had seen her do maybe once or twice in his life.

It was the first time Queen Raisa had left her rooms since the day she was poisoned. Magret Gray and Titus Gryphon had carried her in on a litter and set her down in a chair. She was wrapped in upland furs, covered in clan-made blankets, her pale face wearing a fierce expression that said, *Still a wolf.*

Participants could be distinguished from witnesses by their degree of nervousness. Hadley was as fearless as anyone Ash knew, but she stood, hands clenched, mumbling words under her breath, practicing. Speaker Jemson and Captain Byrne stood to either side of a small table bearing the regalia, which included a stone basin, a knife, a crystal bottle, and a silver goblet.

Ash shivered. Lately, it seemed that his life was one blood ritual after another.

"Welcome," Speaker Jemson said, hauling Ash back to the present. "I apologize for the hour, but it was important that we do this without alerting any enemies of the Line.

Tonight, we will celebrate not one but two milestones. Hopefully that will make it worth disturbing your sleep." He paused, but nobody laughed; so he went on.

"We will begin with the binding ritual, a ceremony that is at least a thousand years old. It has occurred on a battlefield, at a roadside inn, inside a prison, and aboard ship. Believe it or not, this is the largest group ever assembled for the purpose. The essentials are a willing soldier, the blood of the line, soil from the mountain home, and a speaker of the Old Church. Up to now, the ceremony has been held in secret—even from the royal family—and the willing soldier has always been a Byrne."

Talbot licked her lips, as if worried that she might be declared unworthy at the last minute.

Jemson smiled at her. "But times change, secrets are revealed, and traditions deserve examination. Perilous times require a certain . . . flexibility of practice and an agility of mind and spirit. We began descending this slippery slope, as some would say, with Captain Amon Byrne, who was bound to the princess heir Raisa ana'Marianna before she was crowned queen, and before his father, Edon Byrne, had passed away. This was done because then-princess Raisa was in danger. We continued this practice with Princess Hanalea, when Simon Byrne was bound to her."

Jemson looked to Captain Byrne, who said, "Now Hana is dead, and Simon is dead, the Line is in grave danger, and there is a need for a new guardian. This time, it seems that the best candidate to perform this service to the line is not a Byrne, but Corporal Sasha Talbot."

Talbot's cheeks pinked up, but she kept her eyes on the floor.

"We have brought you all together to serve as witnesses. Going forward, you will hold the memory of what we do here, and be ready to testify to it if need be." He looked around the circle. "Are you willing to be the memory of the realm?"

"We are," the chorus came back.

"Corporal Talbot," Jemson said, "are you willing to be bound forever to the line of Gray Wolf queens that began with Hanalea?"

"Yes, sir," Talbot said, bringing her fist to her heart.

"Bare your arm, Corporal," Jemson said, picking up the knife.

Talbot did, scraping back her sleeve. Jemson ran the tip of the blade down her forearm so that the blood welled up and dripped into the stone basin.

Now the speaker held up the stoppered bottle. "Behold the blood of the line," he said. He didn't specify whose.

Do they keep Lyss's blood on hand, just in case? Ash thought. Is it our mother's blood? Or does it go all the way back to Hanalea? He couldn't seem to shut down his scientist mind.

Jemson spoke more words over the bottle, pulled the stopper, and tipped a small amount into the bowl. Lifting it, he swirled the contents together.

As the ceremony continued, Ash thought of all the bound captains since Hanalea, all the secret ceremonies held with one purpose—to protect the Line and assure that it continued into the future.

I'm bound to the Line by blood, too, he thought. I will not see it end while I live and breathe.

Ash's amulet warmed against his skin. More and more, he was hearing his father's voice again, though he'd not yet achieved the kind of meeting his father'd had with Alger Waterlow, their ancestor. He hoped, with practice, he would be able to see his father again in Aediion—that meeting place between worlds. Again, he heard his father's voice.

You don't get what you don't go after.

Jemson poured the contents of the bowl into the silver cup, then held the cup out to Talbot. Talbot wrapped both hands around it, knuckles white, as if afraid she might spill it on the way to her mouth.

"Sasha Talbot, we ask of you this thing, that you be bound to the Gray Wolf line of queens, and, specifically, to the blood and issue of Alyssa ana'Raisa, Princess Heir of the Fells. You will swear that her blood is your blood, that you will protect her and her line until death takes you. Will you?"

"I will," Talbot said, her voice strong and forceful, despite her jitters.

"Then drink to signify."

Tilting her head back, Talbot drained the cup, then staggered backward, all but toppling over. Captain Byrne seemed ready for that. He grabbed her arm to steady her, deftly plucking the cup from her grip before it fell. She put her hands over her ears, her eyes wide and panicked, an array of emotions tracking across her face.

"You'll learn to shut it out," Byrne said, "and filter it, so you only take in what's useful." He glanced around, as if self-conscious at having these long-held secrets exposed in front of an audience.

Gradually, Talbot seemed to find her footing, resuming her ready stance.

The ceremony continued, as more blood was mingled with the earth in the garden to signify the connection between the queen, the bound captain, and the mountain home.

"Now," Jemson said, "we have one more milestone to celebrate. Most of you know that today is the princess Alyssa's sixteenth birthday. It is our tradition here in the north that the sixteenth birthday is the day of Naeming, when young people choose their vocation, and when the heir to the Gray Wolf throne is named the Princess Heir. We had hoped to celebrate this day along with her, and with the queendom at large. At present, Princess Alyssa is too far away to celebrate with us, and so we have chosen a proxy, who will bring the good news to her." He turned to Hadley. "Captain DeVilliers, are you willing to serve as proxy for the princess heir in this celebration?"

"I am," Hadley said.

Jemson went on to describe Lyss's accomplishments, mostly on the field of battle, and the virtues and talents she would bring to the throne. This ceremony, at least, was familiar, since Ash had been present at his sister Hana's name day ceremony. His mother participated in this one, her voice ringing out strongly as she asked Hadley the Three Questions. Clearly Hadley had been studying, because she delivered the Three Answers flawlessly.

Ash had never heard of this option for the naming ceremony—that of having a proxy—but Jemson said it had been done in the past, in times of war, or to solemnize a marriage between two people separated by distance.

Finally, Hadley knelt beside the queen's chair and bowed her head. Queen Raisa leaned toward her and set the tiara of office on Hadley's head. "Rise, Princess Alyssa ana'Raisa, named heir to the Gray Wolf throne." She paused, then whispered, "Rise, Gray Wolf."

Ash found himself joining a chorus of voices. "Rise, Gray Wolf."

On the other side of the eastern ocean, in the city of Celesgarde, Alyssa ana'Raisa stood on her terrace, looking to the west, where the sun must be setting beyond the boundary of wind and water known as the Boil.

As on so many nights before, she'd awakened in the midst of a vivid dream of home. This time, she'd been in her mother's rooftop garden. Talbot knelt before her, her sword resting across her outstretched hands, offering her blade like a knight in a story.

I'm coming.

After that, Lyss couldn't sleep. Her mind seethed with plots and plans and schemes, each examined, tested, and discarded.

The meeting with Jenna Bandelow had kindled a spark of hope that still smoldered at Lyss's core. Hope that her brother might be alive. Hope that she'd found an ally. Hope that she could use that connection to turn disaster into triumph.

Lyss and the dragon-rider were both keeping secrets, still treading carefully, doling out information bit by bit. For instance, Lyss had shared Ash's real name, but hadn't mentioned that she was the heir to the Gray Wolf throne. Jenna hadn't disclosed the reason for her campaign against the empress, or shared the story of how she'd met Ash, or explained her kinship with the dragon she called Cas.

They'd agreed to meet regularly, in the same place, to discuss strategy. Jenna was a predator at heart—she wanted to separate her target from the herd and go in for the kill. Lyss worried that a poorly planned attack would only alert the empress to Jenna's presence and send Celestine's armies into the mountains to hunt for them.

She had a little time, at least until the dragon healed.

The shutters rattled under the assault of the wind. The weather was bad, and getting worse, even for a place where wicked weather was the norm.

Lyss threw the doors open and walked out onto the terrace, facing the ocean and the storm head-on.

The wind teased her hair out of its braid and frothed the Indio into gray peaks and valleys that smashed against the seawall below her feet. Waves like packs of gray wolves, leaping higher and higher, scrambling for a purchase on the wet stone. The hairs on the back of Lyss's neck prickled, and she shivered.

I need to get home, she thought, even if the only way to get there is at the head of a Carthian army.

She saw Breon only at a distance, and always in the presence of the empress. He was like a bird in a gilded cage, dressed in his court finery, attended by serving girls seemingly chosen for their beauty.

I am going to save him, too, somehow, Lyss thought. She was, after all, in the habit of making impossible promises and dreaming impossible dreams.

Spray needled her face, startling her. She thought it was rain, until she tasted the salt water on her tongue. That couldn't be happening—she was too high above the water. But when she leaned forward, she could see that now the waves were crashing just below the top of the wall. The leading edge of the Boil had rolled closer, so that she could have reached out a hand and touched it.

The ocean was coming to her. The wind continued to howl, although now it sounded more like . . .

No, she thought. That's impossible.

As she backed away from the edge, she breathed in the familiar scent of lodgepole pine and wet fur. When she turned, meaning to flee back into the safety of her room, she all but ran into a massive silver wolf with gray eyes. The wolf's fur was matted with the wet, and she dripped seawater onto the stones. As Lyss stood frozen, the wolf shook, spattering the entire terrace with droplets.

"You are a long way from our mountain home, Granddaughter," the wolf said.

Lyss began to tremble, until she was shaking uncontrollably. Her mother often told stories of visits from their ancestors, the Gray Wolf queens, in wolf form. They usually came in times of trouble, bringing wisdom and warnings when the Line was at risk, or change was coming.

The wolves had been the unseen guardians of her childhood. The wolves had walked when Hana died, when their father died, when the assassins had come for Lyss in Fellsmarch. When the wolves walked, her mother kept her close. In Lyss's experience, the wolves always brought bad news, though she'd never seen them herself. Maybe it was because she was never meant to be part of the Line. Maybe it was because she'd not yet been crowned princess heir, though her mother had seen them several times in the year before her coronation.

Lyss took one step back, then another. As she did so, she felt rather than heard the sound of paws hitting stone as more wolves arrived. Soon the terrace was packed with them. She was surrounded by a sea of silver fur and glittering eyes.

"Who are you?" Lyss whispered, her teeth all but rattling together.

"I am Hanalea ana'Maria, your many-greats grandmother," the gray-eyed wolf said. Another wolf stepped out from behind her, this one with green eyes. "And this is Althea ana'Isabella, also my granddaughter. We bring greetings from your ancestors, the Gray Wolf queens."

"All right," Lyss said, a stone of dread in her middle. "Why are you here?"

"We are here because the Line of Queens is broken, and you must pick up the pieces," Hanalea said.

"What do you mean? Are you saying that my mother— that my mother is *dead*?" Lyss's voice rose until that last word came out in a kind of shriek. Regret sluiced over her like a rogue wave, nearly knocking her off her feet. She'd refused to go home and mourn with her mother, and that had led to a cascade of misfortunes, ending in this.

But Althea and Hanalea were shaking their heads. "Not exactly," Hanalea said. "It's . . . complicated."

"What do you mean, it's *complicated*?" Lyss shouted. "A person is dead, or she isn't."

But that wasn't exactly true, was it? Case in point—the bloodsworn, who seemed to be somewhere between. Were they saying that her mother had—had—

"*Complicated* is what happens when people don't honor boundaries," Althea said, curling her lips away from her teeth and looking down her nose at Hanalea. A murmur rose from the gathered queens, mingled agreement and dissent.

"That's what we *do*, Thea," Hanalea said. "We cross boundaries. How else could we offer counsel to the living queens?"

"*That's* been tradition for more than a thousand years," Althea said. "But this thing with Alger Waterlow—and now Raisa—it sets a bad precedent."

Alger Waterlow? He'd been the founder, with Hanalea, of the New Line of Gray Wolf queens. But that was a thousand years ago.

"I chose love," Hanalea said. "This New Line of queens was founded on love, and breaking the rules, and I stand by that choice. And that was the counsel I gave to Raisa."

"*That's* turned out well," Althea said.

"The end of this story isn't written yet," Hanalea said. "The journey through it is important."

Lyss felt like a mortal in one of the old stories watching the gods squabble over her future.

"Hey!" she said.

The two wolves turned to look at her, ears pricked

forward. The other wolves shifted and murmured.

"Since you've come all this way, I would like to be included in the conversation," Lyss said. "You've said that the Gray Wolf line is broken, but my mother isn't dead— well, not exactly—but I still don't know why you're here, or what happened to my mother."

"Raisa ana'Marianna was poisoned," Hanalea said gently.

"Poisoned?" Lyss's knees buckled, and she would have fallen, but the wolves pressed in around her, supporting her, keeping her upright. "When? And how? And by whom?"

"Three days ago," Hanalea said. "We don't know the answers to your other questions."

Three days ago. Lyss had awakened from a sound sleep, in a panic. She'd had that dream again, the one that had haunted her ever since the summer Hana was killed. Everyone was dead, and she stood on Hanalea Peak, alone with the wolves.

Althea sat, wrapping her tail around her feet. "Raisa crossed over and joined us, thereby breaking her connection to the living Line. Then, what did she do, but she turned right around and went back."

"She went . . . back?" Lyss clutched handfuls of fur to either side, but the queens didn't seem to mind.

"Your *father* interfered," Althea said.

"My—father?" Lyss whispered. "He was there?"

"It must be that troublemaking Waterlow blood,"

Althea said. "First he arranged these trysts between Hana and Alger, and then he—"

"*You* have Waterlow blood, dear," Hanalea pointed out drily.

"Highly diluted," Althea said.

"Anyway, he healed your mother and persuaded her to go back and rejoin the living," Hanalea said. "But now we have a problem."

"My mother is alive!" Lyss said, her emotions in a whiplash of confusion. "How is that a problem?"

"The Line was broken," Althea said. "And that means that, technically—"

"Not just technically," Hanalea said. She looked into Lyss's eyes. "That means that you—Alyssa ana'Raisa—you are now the Gray Wolf queen."

Turn the page for a preview of the fourth and final book
in the SHATTERED REALMS series:

DEATHCASTER

SHIP OF FOOLS

Adrian sul'Han shivered, drawing the collar of his clan-made storm coat up to his chin. Spring might have come to the realms he'd left behind, but sea ice and icebergs still cluttered the surface of Invader's Bay. He could hear Captain Hadley DeVilliers shouting orders from the quarterdeck to their mingled Carthian/Fellsian crew as the *Sea Wolf* threaded her way through the ice toward the open sea.

Sailing toward Lyss, if there was any justice in this shattered world. A debatable point.

It had been Hadley's idea to launch their mission from the Frozen Sea north of Wizard Head. For one thing, the Empress Celestine now controlled the queendom's only deepwater port at Chalk Cliffs. For another, the success of this mission depended on absolute secrecy. It was unlikely they'd meet any other ships this far north at this time of year. After all, nobody in his right mind would *choose* to be here.

Nobody who wasn't desperate for a win in the wake of so many losses—Hana, Jenna, his father. Ash did not want to live on as the survivor of another failure. He would save his sister and save the Line or die in the attempt.

Not a trade I'd make. Stay alive.

Ash flinched. He looked around, but nobody was near enough to have been heard over the howl of the wind. He gripped the serpent amulet more tightly, his knuckles white, as if he could squeeze a response from the metal and stone.

"Da?"

Nothing.

Ash's breath hissed through his teeth. It had been this way since the night he and his father had partnered to bring his mother back from the dead. He'd hear a whisper in his ear, or feel a presence like the brush of a feather or the tendrils of a dream, or hear his father calling his name amid the shriek of the wind and the crash of the waves.

But it was all one way. No matter how hard Ash tried, he couldn't seem to enter the borderlands between life and death.

Come see me in Aediion, his father had said. *You and your mother and sister have enemies at court. Enemies on the Council. Don't give your trust easily.*

"A little help here, Healer?" The voice was edged with impatience.

Ash looked up. High above, the magemarked pirate Evan Strangward clung to the rigging like a spider, shining like a ship's lantern in the night. He'd been up there for hours, facing the brunt of the weather without complaint, manipulating wind and waves to open a path through the ice for the *Sea Wolf*. At the same time, he kept her sails filled, driving them forward as fast as they could safely go. Maybe faster.

"Sorry," Ash said, moving back into position in the bow of the ship, receiving the blessing of freezing spray and stinging sleet. It was his job to clean up after the weather mage—to clear away the obstacles the pirate missed, blasting icebergs into bits, softening the slabs of ice that floated into their path so the ship's hull could penetrate them without damage.

Watching Strangward at work was like visual poetry, his amulet flaring under his fingers as he gathered power, then both arms sweeping forward, shaping, coaxing, cajoling, commanding, like a temple maester, a conductor of wind, ice, and water. He was agile as a cat, maneuvering over the spars to get the right angle, swinging from mast to mast as if unaware that he was more than a hundred feet above the decks. He seemed impervious to bad weather.

He'd left his storm coat on the deck below, saying it only got in his way.

Maybe he hadn't the range of magic enjoyed by wizards in the Realms, courtesy of their ability to work charms, but there were clear advantages to being a specialist. Ash had seen limited weather-wizardry from his parents' friend Fire Dancer. As a clan-born wizard, Dancer had combined the uplander's easy connection with the natural world with the raw magic of wizardry. But Dancer's weather magic was a whisper next to Strangward's roar.

Evan's roar. The pirate had asked them to call him Evan, but, given the history between them, that wasn't easy to do.

"If you'd have told me I'd be sailing under that blood-sucking pirate, I'd have laughed in your face."

Ash spun around. Two of Hadley's crew huddled next to the foremast shrouds, their eyes fixed on the pirate, their faces clouded with resentment.

"My cousin's ship went down off Baston Bay, and it was the swiving Stormcaster that done it." The sailor shuddered and spat on the deck.

"Every time a ship is lost, they blame it on him," the other one said, jerking his head toward the pirate. "He can't have done for all of 'em. Anyway, we an't sailing under him. DeVilliers is captain, long as we're at sea."

"Mind the telltales," Strangward called down, causing the two of them to jump. "Trim the jib sheets—*now*."

"Tell *him* that," the first one said, hurrying to adjust the sheets. "Maybe Captain DeVilliers is the master on paper, but she'll go to the bottom with the rest of us if he decides to founder us."

Ash sighed. Though the pirate seemed painfully eager to win the rest of them over by proving his value to the mission, his efforts seemed to have the opposite effect. The Stormcaster was hated and feared all along the coast. Sailors were superstitious by nature. Plus they were so often at the mercy of weather that the Stormcaster's command of it was intimidating and unsettling, even for those who'd been raised with wizardry.

"Impressive, isn't he? Almost scary."

Ash jumped and turned to find Finn standing next to him, his eyes fixed on the pirate.

"If you like a show-off," Ash said, stuffing his hands into his pockets.

That should have drawn a laugh from the Finn he remembered. Instead, his friend drew in a breath, then let it out slowly. "Do you think we can pull this off?"

Ash swiped water from his face with his sopping sleeve. "Pull what off?"

"Get in and out of Celesgarde? Rescue your sister?"

"I wouldn't be here if I didn't hope for that," Ash said. "Why? Are you having second thoughts?"

"Not really," Finn said. "I'm just trying to estimate the odds of success."

"Maybe it's better not to look at the odds at all," Ash said, rolling his eyes. "I was a little surprised that you agreed to come, since you had to postpone the wedding and all."

"Duty trumps desire," Finn said. "Julianna understands that we all must be willing to sacrifice for the greater good."

That sounded stuffy, even for bookish Finn. It was the kind of thing people say to you when *you're* the one who's going to be doing the sacrificing.

"I'm not sacrificing anyone if I can help it," Ash said. "I've already lost my father and my sister. My mother still hasn't recovered. Too many of my friends have died in this war, or been gravely wounded, you included. I think we've done our bit."

"It's never enough," Finn said, pain flickering across his face. He rubbed his forehead with the heel of his hand. Though he was bare-headed, his hair plastered down by the wet, he didn't seem to feel the cold.

"Are you all right?" Ash said, putting a hand on Finn's shoulder.

"It's just . . . I've been having these headaches, ever since I was wounded," Finn said. "They're getting worse instead of better. And sometimes—it's like I have these spells when I miss things. I just blank out." He shook his head. "I think I'm losing my mind."

Worry quivered through Ash. Once again, he was

reminded that while he'd pursued a career as an assassin in the south, Finn had waged a war on a different battlefield—one in which he saw his friends slaughtered, and probably blamed himself for surviving. Both of them were marked by what they'd seen and done—things they would prefer to forget.

"Listen," Ash said. "Sometimes that's how the mind works. When we're under stress, it protects us by giving us an out when we need one."

"Well," Finn said, with a bitter laugh. "Stress is an appropriate response to stressful times."

I should have asked more questions, Ash thought. I should have made sure Finn had recovered enough to deal with this.

What kind of a healer are you?

Unable to help himself, Ash sent a tendril of soothing magic through his fingers into Finn's shoulder. He yanked back his hand, fingers stinging, as Finn twisted away.

His friend stood, his back to the rail, one hand on his amulet. "Do not presume to heal me, Adrian," Finn said, between ragged breaths. "I am not broken."

"I'm sorry," Ash said, mortified. "I was only trying to—"

"I know what you were trying to do," Finn said. "Don't." He turned away and disappeared down the forward ladder.

Ash sucked his blistered fingers.

The time will come when you will wish you were a better healer.

It seemed that Taliesin's curse would be with him his entire life.

They'd been at it for hours, but now—finally—they were escaping into the open sea. Once out of the bay, the seas roughened and the winds intensified, but at least the minefield of ice thinned, suggesting that their watch was nearly over.

"Stand down, Your Highness," Hadley called from the quarterdeck. "You too, Strangward. You've done a yeoman's job. Now, go aft and get warm."

"I'll be down in a little while," Evan said, gripping the spar with his knees and leaning down toward her. He looked soaked through and half-frozen, the watch-cap he always wore on deck was sodden, and yet, he seemed illuminated, as if energized by his connection to the elements. "I'd better make sure we're well out of the shallows and possible coastal traffic before I leave off."

Ash was close enough to Hadley's position at the rail to see the storm brewing in her expression. She opened her mouth, as if to respond. Then, spotting Ash, she shut it again, turned on her heel and stalked back to the helm.

They were just a few days out, but friction was already growing between Strangward and his stormborn and Hadley and her veterans.

Evan was used to giving orders, not receiving them.

Though they'd all agreed that Hadley would serve as ship's master during the seafaring portion of their journey, he seemed to view Hadley's commands as the beginning of a conversation and not the last word. When he ordered Hadley's crew around, they resented it.

For their part, the Carthian crew was unflaggingly loyal to the pirate, always looking to Evan to verify Hadley's orders before following them. Ash could tell that it was getting under her skin.

Ash knew he needed to do something, but wasn't sure what. This is why Lyss is the officer and you're not, he thought.

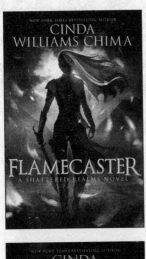

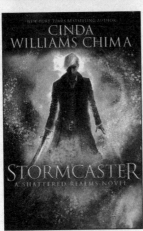

Muhlenberg County Public Libraries
117 South Main Street
Greenville, KY 42345